The Deadly Life of Diana Penn

The Cheviot Hills Time Travel Series - A Middle Falls Universe Novel

Shawn Inmon

Kirsten McKenzie

SSP

Also by Kirsten McKenzie

The Ithaca Time Travel Trilogy
ITHACA BOUND
ITHACA LOST
ITHACA FOUND

The Old Curiosity Shop Time Travel Trilogy
FIFTEEN POSTCARDS
THE LAST LETTER
TELEGRAM HOME

The Cheviot Hills Time Travel Series
THE DEADLY LIFE OF DIANA PENN

Standalone Paranormal Thrillers
PAINTED
DOCTOR PERRY
THE FORGER AND THE THIEF
THE VAMPIRES OF YORK TOWER

Short Story Anthologies
LANDMARKS
NOIR FROM THE BAR
REMAINS TO BE TOLD

Also by Shawn Inmon

Middle Falls Time Travel Series

The Unusual Second Life of Thomas Weaver

The Redemption of Michael Hollister

The Death and Life of Dominick Davidner

The Final Life of Nathaniel Moon

The Emancipation of Veronica McAllister

The Changing Lives of Joe Hart

The Vigilante Life of Scott McKenzie

The Reset Life of Cassandra Collins

The Tribulations of Ned Summers

The Empathetic Life of Rebecca Wright

The Successful Life of Jack Rybicki

The Many Short Lives of Charles Waters

The Stubborn Lives of Hart Tanner

The Alternative Lives of Aiden Anderson

The Encore Lives of Effie Edenson

The Regretful Life of Richard Bell

The Anxious Lives of Edwin Miller

The Tumultuous Lives of Karl Strong

The Ambitious Lives of Evan Sanderson

The Topsy-Turvy Lives of Hattie Kildare

The Unrepentant Lives of Reggie Blackwell

The Indomitable Lives of Tuesday West

The Collected Lives of Chuck Burke (releases December 16, 2025)

Middle Falls Related Stories

The Heartfelt Life of Max Hartfield: A Middle Falls Time Travel Short Story

A Mutt in Time: A Middle Falls Mushu Tale

Tethered: A Middle Falls Ghost Story

The Final Christmas of Robert Burke: A Middle Falls Short Story

Middle Falls Holidays: A Middle Falls Short Story Collection

The Cheviot Hills Time Travel Series (Middle Falls Universe)

Alex Hawk Time Travel Adventure Series (Kragdon-ah)

A Door Into Time

Lost in Kragdon-ah

Return from Kragdon-ah

Warrior of Kragdon-ah

Prince of Kragdon-ah

Mists of Kragdon-ah

Tribes of Kragdon-ah

Armies of Kragdon-ah

Battle for Kragdon-ah

Lost Eden: A Portal Fiction Adventure

Stranded

Marooned

Exiled

The Chronicles of Altor

The Precipice

All Fall Down

Ashes, Ashes

Arkana Sword and Sorcery Adventure

Kradak the Champion

Kradak the Unbeatable

An Arden Flux Space Adventure

Fire and Prey (releases October 10, 2025)

Both Sides Now (True Love Story)

Feels Like the First Time

Both Sides Now

A Lap Around Series

A Lap Around America

A Lap Around Alaska

Standalone and Other Works

Rock 'n Roll Heaven

Death by Podcast

Life is Short: The Collected Short Fiction of Shawn Inmon

Chad Stinson Goes for a Walk: A Short Tale of Obsession and Possession

This edition published August 2025 by Squabbling Sparrows Press

ISBN 978 1 991331 55 7 (paperback)

Cover design: Linda Boulanger

Chapter One

The telephone on Diana Penn's spindly hallway table rang with the insistence of the past demanding attention. Its black surface, polished by decades of hands now long still, reflected the weak December light. She let it ring. Eight decades had taught her that unexpected calls rarely brought welcome news, and forty-plus years in MI6 had honed that wariness into an art form.

From her position by the bay window, Diana watched as the council workers demolished the old playground in Pickering Park, the excavator's mechanical arm tearing through rusted swing sets with methodical efficiency. They'd been at it for days now, clearing the site for the modern playground the council had promised for years.

Her fingers, swollen with arthritis, curled around her Spode teacup. The matching blue-and-white saucer had been lost in the war, never to be replaced. Like neckties, she mused, saucers were remnants of a more formal age. Decorative but obsolete. Rather like herself.

The cottage itself was a study in careful anonymity, each object selected to suggest nothing more remarkable than a retired widow's refuge. Neighbours would see only the neat garden, the lace curtains, the precisely arranged Victorian whatnot shelf in the front window.

They probably wouldn't notice the lack of family photos or the antique elephant foot umbrella stand stuffed full of an assortment of walking sticks and ancient umbrellas strategically placed next to the front door.

Her computer gathered dust in the corner, unopened since a well-meaning colleague had insisted she needed some sort of social media account. She liked to imagine her virtual garden was still growing somewhere in the digital ether, spreading like ivy through the internet's back alleys.

The screen reflected her image: silver hair swept back in a neat chignon, supermarket glasses, and a cardigan chosen for warmth rather than style. The lines around her eyes spoke of squinting into foreign suns, her frown line deepened by years of working with imbeciles. Years of watching and waiting and wondering if this time the intelligence would prove true.

The phone fell silent. In its wake, she heard the rumble of machinery against frozen soil and the murmur of workers' voices. The excavator had stopped, its bucket poised mid-air as several workers gathered around something in the freshly turned earth. Perhaps they'd found a body? That would give Nancy Robbins another reason to gossip at church this weekend. Such an evil harridan. The thought surfaced with the regularity of an old pocket watch, reliable and unwelcome. She and Nancy had maintained their frosty relationship for over sixty years, and a thaw wasn't anywhere in sight.

A mother stood outside her postage stamp of a front garden, bouncing an excited toddler on her hip as they watched the commotion. The authorities should have closed off the street while the diggers tore up the ground. But the council, in its infinite wisdom, had deemed it "low risk", and they'd only put up flimsy barriers around the immediate worksite.

Diana took another sip of tea, her eyes drawn to the peculiar way the workers were now backing away from whatever they'd found. Her intelligence training kicked in, evaluating the workers' body language. Something wasn't right.

She leaned forward, squinting through the bay window. The excavator had unearthed what appeared to be metal canisters caked in soil and corroded with age.

Even from this distance, Diana's experienced eye recognised them instantly. Live ordnance, unexploded bombs that had likely been there since the war.

Diana's teacup froze halfway to her lips. The excavator operator was gesturing towards the canisters, appearing ready to scoop them up. He didn't realise the danger. None of them did.

Diana's hands shook, slopping tea onto her cardigan. Those weren't training rounds. They were live bombs. And from the deteriorated condition, dangerously unstable.

She needed to move. Now.

Her teacup slipped from her hand and clattered to the floor, the porcelain shattering on impact. Tea spread in a dark stain across the carpet, but Diana hardly noticed.

Her body protested as she pushed herself up from her chair, joints crackling like kindling. The young mother was still there, watching, her child now waving at the workers with enthusiastic squeals.

"Get back!" Diana shouted through the glass, but her voice emerged as a croak. Stumbling towards the front door, she fumbled for her walking stick, knocking it against the umbrella stand. The elephant foot teetered, then crashed to the floor. By the time she'd steadied herself, the digger's bucket was already heading south towards the bombs.

Her fingers found the door latch, and struggled with the safety chain. The cold hit her face as she pulled it open. "Watch out, those are—" The rest of her warning died in her throat as an apocalyptic roar boomed through the winter air. A sound she hadn't heard since Hitler's doodlebugs had struck London during the war. Some sounds you never forgot, no matter how many decades had passed.

Time stretched like old elastic. She saw the mother's smile fade, and the child's hands reaching towards the sky, and saw frost glinting on the uncut grass as the workers' eyes widened in dawning recognition.

Well, Nancy Robbins, Diana thought as the world turned white, *I suppose you'll have something to talk about in church this week after all.*

Chapter Two

Diana Penn opened her eyes.

Blinking, she shifted, trying to move the scratchy wool blanket away from her cheek. Somewhere in the distance, a rooster crowed. The faint smell of wood smoke tainted the air. Her body felt light, unburdened. The arthritis that had been her constant companion for decades was absent.

A voice called from somewhere below. "Diana! You'll be late for your shift if you don't get a move on!"

Her eyes snapped open. That voice. A memory she'd buried decades ago.

Diana pushed herself upright, and the movement came with such unexpected ease that she tumbled from the narrow bed. Her hands flew out to steady herself, and she froze, staring at them. Gone were the swollen knuckles and liver spots. These hands were young—smooth, strong, and capable. Hands that hadn't yet held a gun, coded a message, or erased a name from a ledger under orders.

"What in God's name?" she whispered, her voice higher, clearer than it had been in half a century.

Weak winter light seeped around the edges of a small window covered by heavy curtains, barely illuminating the room's corners.

Diana recognised this room—the sloped ceiling with its flaking white paint, the worn rag rug, the wooden dressing table and matching chair. A tiled washbasin perched in the corner, with a bevelled mirror hanging above it. An austere bar of carbolic soap sat in a floral porcelain dish—the sharp, medicinal smell of it reaching her even from across the room. This was her bedroom at Willow Farm, where she'd been billeted with the Women's Land Army during the war.

How could this be?

Her mind scrambled for logic, but along with being impossible, the room was undeniable. The familiar roughness of the sheets beneath her fingers, the scent of damp wool from her old jumper draped over the chair —it was all too vivid to be memory alone. Orwell once warned that if your eyes tell you something is real, you'd be a fool to trust anything else. But this? This couldn't be real.

Could it?

Diana stood, marvelling at how easily her body responded. No creaking joints, no sharp pain in her hip, no stiffness in her lower back. Just the supple strength of youth. As she stretched, her flannel nightgown fell to her ankles, ready to tangle her first unsteady steps. It was funny how quickly she'd remembered hating that nightgown. It would take another decade before she discovered the unparalleled comfort of men's pyjamas. Once she'd moved into her own flat, with no one to cast judgement, she'd worn nothing else to bed—crisp cotton PJs in summer and cosy brushed cotton ones in winter.

The chilly morning forced her to dress quickly in the Land Army uniform hanging on the door. Her body remembered the routine while her mind reeled. The green jumper was scratchy against her skin, the brown breeches stiff with yesterday's mud.

The small mirror above the washbasin confirmed what she suspected. Diana Penn, twenty years old, stared back at her. Round-cheeked, clear-eyed, with thick chestnut hair falling past her shoulders. She traced the smooth contours of her face with trembling fingers.

"I'm dead," she murmured. "The bomb in Pickering Park killed me. Or is it irreparable brain damage?" Or perhaps this was heaven's idea of a joke —sending her back to relive the most tedious period of her life.

The endless milking, the back-breaking fieldwork, the provincial gossip and petty squabbles of village life. Years of rural monotony before she'd escaped to London and begun her real life in intelligence.

And yet, this didn't feel like death or heaven. It felt like... a reset. A second chance. A phrase from her MI6 training surfaced in her mind: When all else fails, adapt to the new parameters of the mission.

"Diana!" that voice came again, more insistent this time. "The cows won't milk themselves, girl!"

Ah, Mrs Whitaker.

Diana remembered her now—a stout, ruddy-faced woman with greying hair perpetually escaping its pins, and a face roughened by decades of farm work and grief. She had been more than just a landlady, more than a supervisor—she had been a mother when Diana had none. After losing her own mother in the Blitz, Diana had thrown herself into the Land Army, hoping that exhaustion would stamp down her grief. But it was Enid Whitaker's quiet, steady presence that had truly saved her.

It hadn't been in grand gestures or spoken words. It was in the way Mrs Whitaker pushed an extra slice of bread onto Diana's plate at supper, even when rationing made every crumb precious. The way she left a stone hot water bottle at the foot of Diana's bed on bitter winter nights. The way she had smoothed Diana's hair one evening, thinking the girl was asleep, after a rare nightmare had left her trembling.

Diana also remembered the lack of gratitude she'd shown the older woman. She'd been so caught up in her own grief, her own importance, that she'd taken the quiet acts of service Mrs Whitaker had shown her as a given.

Diana's stomach twisted as she then remembered that she'd been at Willow Farm when Mrs Whitaker received news that her son Trevor had been killed in action. She couldn't recall when the news had arrived. Which part of her stay here had she woken up in? Had their lives already been marked by that awful, black-edged telegram? Or was it still looming just beyond the horizon?

Even with the wisdom of her advanced years, she still had no words to soften the woman's grief. She'd had no words back then. And had carried on with her life. But now she wished, more than anything, that she had at least tried.

Diana's hands moved automatically to braid her hair, muscle memory from a lifetime ago guiding her once-again nimble fingers. Her mind raced, sorting through possibilities and impossibilities with the efficiency of the intelligence analyst she'd been—would be?—for four decades.

And now she was back, at the beginning of it all.

Diana finished fixing her hair and reached for the drawer where she kept the hairpins. She paused seeing that they were exactly where they should have been. Which was impossible, unless this wasn't a dream or a dying hallucination? Had she been catapulted back through time? How?

"Whatever this is, it's real," she whispered. "Or real enough that the distinction doesn't matter?"

Diana glanced at the small calendar tacked to the wall. December, 1944. The war was far from over, but the tide had turned. If she remembered correctly, this was just after the failed German counteroffensive in the Ardennes. The Battle of the Bulge, as it would eventually come to be known.

She slipped her feet into the heavy work boots by the door, feeling the worn leather conform to her feet as though she'd never stopped wearing them. Before descending the narrow staircase to face Mrs Whitaker and the day ahead, Diana pressed her palm against the rough plaster wall, grounding herself in this new reality.

"Well, then," she murmured, "let's see what this is all about, before the nurse wakes me up to tell me I lost both my legs in the bomb blast."

The stairs creaked under her weight, each sound a memory resurrected. In the kitchen, Mrs Whitaker stood at the stove, her broad back to the door. The familiar scene hit Diana like a sledgehammer. The tea kettle whistling on the stove, the wireless playing in the background, the wooden table scrubbed to pale perfection, the smell of porridge and yesterday's supper. All so very real. Her heart skipped a beat as she faltered in the doorway.

"There you are, finally!" Mrs Whitaker turned, wooden spoon in hand. "I was thinking you'd gone and died in your sleep."

Diana's laugh caught in her throat. "No," she said. "Quite the opposite, I think."

"What's that? You'll be glad of the hot breakfast today—it's freezing out there."

Diana sat at the scarred kitchen table, the same table she'd last sat at nearly sixty years ago, and accepted the bowl of steaming porridge pushed towards her. As she ate, she listened to the woman's familiar morning chatter about rationing and the vicar's sermon and how the butcher's son had been called up now that he was of age.

If this was death, it was disappointingly mundane.

The normality of it was overwhelming. Diana had lived an entire lifetime since last eating at Mrs Whitaker's table. She had decades of service, first to the King, then to the Queen. And now, somehow, she still couldn't determine if this was heaven or purgatory.

"You're quiet this morning," Mrs Whitaker observed, peering at her over half-moon spectacles. "Not coming down with something, are you? We can't have you ill for the Christmas dance. I know you said you weren't going. But all the young women are going to be there. It would be a wonderful opportunity for you to make some... well, for you to mingle with the others."

The Christmas dance. Diana immediately conjured up a scene of the village hall decorated with paper chains and real boughs of holly, the band playing Glenn Miller songs, the punch spiked with something stronger than fruit juice. Wearing a skirt and blouse borrowed from her host, she'd spent a miserable evening pressed against the wall, watching others dance while nursing a grudge against the world for sending her there. Not much had changed here then.

"No, I'm quite well," Diana assured Mrs Whitaker. "Just thinking about what needs doing today."

"There's the milking, and Mr Hayes wants help with the last of the winter vegetables. And don't forget, you promised to take those mending patterns to Mrs Robbins this afternoon."

Mrs Robbins, the mother of Nancy, high-and-mighty Robbins. Hearing the name sent a jolt through Diana. Nancy Robbins, the woman who would become her nemesis, but had once been her friend. How long until their feud began? Diana embarrassed herself by not remembering. Had it already started?

Diana finished her porridge and washed her bowl in the waiting basin of tepid water. Her mind was already mapping out possibilities, cataloging resources, identifying potential allies and threats.

Just as she'd been trained to do, just as she'd done in capitals across the world during her long career.

"I'd best get to those cows," she said, reaching for her coat on the peg by the door. The heavy wool settled around her shoulders like armour.

Mrs Whitaker nodded. "Oh, and there was a message for you yesterday. The American girl from the Hollister place—Ellen, is it? She wanted to know if you'd meet her at the Twice Brewed tonight. Something about a book you'd promised to lend her. She also left her gloves here when she called. Fine leather things—not the sort you want to lose. I've put them on the hall table."

Diana paused with her hand on the door latch. Ellen Wilson. Another name from the far edge of her memory. Ellen Wilson, with her dark auburn hair, and a smile full of American confidence and too many perfect teeth.

Ellen, who'd disappeared one night in February 1945, never to be seen again.

"Yes," Diana said slowly. "Of course." She'd return the gloves and see what book Ellen had in mind, although lending books seemed unlikely for her. Still, she could well use this chance to prevent whatever fate had befallen the girl. That at least was something she could focus on.

As she stepped out into the brittle morning, frost crunching beneath her boots, Diana Penn—both young and old, novice and expert—grimaced at the thought of enduring this charade. It definitely seemed that the God she didn't believe in was having the last laugh. And if she truly was trapped in this second chance at life, she would navigate it with the same detached efficiency that had served her for decades. No point in forming attachments to people who would fade into irrelevance once she found her way back to her real life.

Chapter Three

Diana's breath hung in clouds before her as she set off down the lane. The cold bit at her cheeks, sharper than she remembered. Or perhaps it was that her arthritic bones had made her too scared to venture out on a proper winter's morning for the past decade.

Memory was a curious thing. She knew with certainty that the farm lay to the west, beyond the village green and past the Norman church with its weathered tombstones. But the precise route eluded her. Decades of maps and safe houses and foreign countries and just-in-case escape routes had overwritten this simple path from her billet to the fields where Mr Hayes would be waiting.

Time and the pallid December light rendered the once familiar landmarks strangers. At the end of the lane, the red painted telephone box stood out as a bright spot on the landscape. The fingerpost that should have marked the crossroads had disappeared years ago—an early precaution against German paratroopers who might use such signage to navigate. Diana smiled at the thought of Hitler's troops trying to navigate streets such as Fanny Street, Pudding Chare, Giggle Alley and Squeeze Belly Alley, Ha-Ha Road, and her personal favourite, Whip-Ma-Whop-Ma-Gate.

She hesitated at the junction, calling upon the geographical memory that had once allowed her to navigate Prague blindfolded. Left or right?

She closed her eyes, letting muscle memory guide her. Her feet turned right without conscious thought.

"Good morning, Miss Penn!"

Diana startled, her hand reaching for a weapon that wasn't there and wouldn't be there for years yet. A tweed-clad figure on a bicycle wobbled past, his satchel bulging with what had to be the morning post.

"Mr Fleming," she responded, the name surfacing from some buried recess of her mind. The postman. She almost lifted her hand to wave, but he was already pedalling towards his next delivery.

Diana tugged her coat tighter. The fabric felt rough, but warm. Made from real wool, not like the synthetic blend of the cardigan she'd been wearing when she'd what? Died? She'd forgotten how clothing used to feel. Clothing that was built to last a lifetime instead of just a season.

Stuffing her hands into the gloves she'd found in the pockets of her coat, the silence struck her most profoundly. There was no drone of distant traffic. No planes overhead every few minutes. Just the crunch of frost beneath her boots, and the call of a blackbird from a nearby hedgerow. The faint bleating of sheep echoed from somewhere beyond the next hill. The air tasted clean, with loamy undertones from the surrounding fields.

A rabbit darted across the lane ahead of her, followed by another and then a third. Wildlife had reclaimed spaces in the wake of human withdrawal. With so many men at the front, and so much land left fallow because of shortages of labour and machinery, nature was slipping back into the gaps. The woody winter architecture of the hedgerows wilder than they would become in the post-war years of efficient farming, when everything that wasn't immediately profitable was dug up and paved over.

The church spire appeared over the next rise, the familiar silhouette of St Michael's a beacon of constancy. As Diana drew closer, she noticed the iron gates that graced the churchyard entrance in the modern day were missing. Of course, the war effort melted down the original gates for munitions like so many railings, park benches, and decorative ironwork across Britain. Only the stone pillars remained. She wanted to whisper to the pillars that one day soon replacement gates would arrive.

She paused to catch her breath, another novelty of youth. In her eighties, every incline was a challenge to be conquered in stages.

Now her lungs drew in the crisp air without protest, her heart beating steady and strong beneath her jumper.

From this vantage point, Diana could make out the patchwork of fields extending all the way to the horizon. Some still bore the remnants of autumn harvests, others lay fallow under frost. A narrow lane wound between them, leading to Hayes Farm. To her job.

The countryside had a stripped-back quality in December—trees standing bare against the sky, fields shorn of crops. Everything essential, nothing extraneous. Rather like wartime Britain itself.

She spotted movement—a young woman atop an ancient tractor, its engine puttering reluctantly as she manoeuvred it towards the implement shed, black smoke belching in the cold air. A precious bit of rationed fuel being used for essential work. The young woman raised an arm in greeting, a cheery wave that Diana returned. Her stomach somersaulted at the extraordinariness of her situation. How on earth could she be standing on the side of a country road waving to a girl on a tractor? It made absolutely no sense.

Still grappling with the absurdity of the situation, Diana couldn't help her mind drifting back to the realities of wartime England. Fuel was in short supply, and anything non-essential had to wait for spring, meaning that the tractor would soon be put away for most of the winter.

Funny, the things that stuck. She could still walk the streets of Istanbul in her mind and picture half a dozen dead drops hidden behind postboxes and crumbling walls. But she'd basically blanked out her memories of her wartime service in the heart of the Northumberland countryside. And the girl on the tractor? Diana doubted she could remember her name—even with the KGB holding a gun to her head.

Diana continued along the lane, her internal compass gradually reorienting itself. She passed a cottage with windows crisscrossed in tape to prevent shattering from bomb blasts. A faded poster was visible through the glass: "Dig for Victory!" The garden was a riot of neat rows of leeks, Brussels sprouts, and kale, all holding firm against the frost.

A dry stone wall marked the boundary of Hayes Farm. Diana traced her gloved fingers along the rough stone as she followed it to the gate. The familiar sensation triggered a cascade of memories: the weight of milk pails on summer mornings, the smell of hay being turned in July, the sweet rot of apples in the orchard come autumn.

"Now then," she murmured to herself as she pushed open the wooden gate to the farmyard. "Let's see if I remember how to milk a bloody cow."

The farmyard opened before her, precisely as it existed in her memory, yet somehow more vivid. Chickens scratched at the frozen earth, seeking invisible treasures. Smoke curled from the chimney of the farmhouse. A collie bounded towards her, barking in welcome or warning, she couldn't tell which.

"Jess!" The name came to her lips unbidden. "Good girl."

The dog skidded to a halt, head cocked in suspicion at this person who knew her name yet smelled wrong. Diana remained still, letting the animal approach at her own pace. After a moment's consideration, Jess sniffed at her outstretched hand, then allowed Diana to scratch behind her ears.

"She'd have you doing that all day if she could."

Diana looked up to see Mr Hayes emerging from the barn, pitchfork in hand. Short, stocky, and with the same weathered face and watchful gaze.

"Good morning, Mr Hayes," Diana said, straightening. "Mrs Whitaker said you needed help with the winter vegetables?"

He nodded towards the stone outbuilding beyond the farmhouse. "Need to check the root cellar stores before Christmas. Some of the parsnips we brought in last month are showing rot, and we can't afford to lose any more. The carrots need sorting too. See that you separate the good from the questionable." He paused, studying her face. "You look peaky, girl. Weather getting to you?"

Diana almost laughed. If only he knew. "I didn't sleep too well," she said, which wasn't a lie. Death wasn't known for restful slumber.

"Well, there's a pot of tea in the kitchen to warm you up before you start." He turned back. "One more thing, I need you to pop into Blyde's to pick up a few things later. The ration book and my list is on the mantlepiece in the kitchen," he said, before disappearing into the barn.

Diana stood motionless in the yard. Was she experiencing a trauma-induced hallucination? Was oxygen deprivation causing vivid memory recall? Or perhaps she was in a coma, her brain trying to make sense of hospital sounds by incorporating them into a dream narrative?

Jess nudged at her hand with her warm, wet nose, jolting Diana back to her surroundings.

With a deep breath that crystallised before her, she headed to the kitchen and the promised cup of tea. Whatever game was afoot, she'd need her wits about her.

Diana entered the farmhouse kitchen, grateful for the warmth but already planning how to minimise interactions with these phantoms from her past. She would play along for now, observing, gathering data. But she would not—could not—allow herself to care. Not about Mr Hayes, not about Ellen Wilson, not about any of them.

After all, she hadn't survived forty years in intelligence by rushing in unprepared. Even if, technically, those forty years hadn't happened yet.

Chapter Four

Fortified by a strong cup of tea, Diana made her way to the dairy, which was just as she remembered—cold, damp, and smelling of milk and animal warmth. Only four of the six stalls were occupied, the Ayrshires standing patiently, their breath visible in the light that filtered through the grimy windows. The other stalls stood empty—a reminder of the seasonal rhythm of dairy farming. Winter always meant less milk, with some cows being dried off until spring calving. The familiar routine beckoned: fetch the milking stool from its hook, grab the zinc pail, check that everything was clean.

But where was the bloody stool?

Diana stood in the centre of the dairy, turning slowly. Right now, decades of being told to observe before taking action warred with the urgency of the unmilked cows and Mr Hayes's imminent inspection.

"Looking for something?"

Diana jumped. Jenny Jenkins—that was the name she couldn't recall earlier—stood in the doorway, a coil of rope slung over one arm.

"The milking stool," Diana admitted. "I could have sworn it hung there." She gestured to an empty hook by the door.

Jenny laughed. "Mr Hayes moved everything around last week, remember? Said it was more efficient."

She pointed to a corner where several stools now leaned against the wall. "Though if you ask me, he's finding things to do whilst he waits to hear about Arthur."

Arthur? How did he fit into the picture? His son? Brother? Husband? No, not a husband. Diana trawled through her memory as she collected the sturdy wooden milking stool. The ghost of her future self knew how important detailed records were, so she should be able to remember.

Settling beside the first cow—Mabel, if memory served—Diana positioned the pail and reached for the udder. Her hands hesitated. *Arthur Hayes, his son.* Killed in action somewhere in Europe. Her throat clogged with the memory. She was hazy on the specifics, but she remembered the man's all-encompassing grief, and what he did next.

Was she allowed to change history? What would happen if she hid the rifle Arthur's devastated father would use to end his heartbreak?

Mabel uttered a low, painful moan, bringing Diana's thoughts back to the present. Mabel's yield would be meagre today. The winter diet of hay and limited feed meant each cow gave barely half what they'd produce in summer.

"Come on, then," she muttered to herself. "You've dismantled bombs in Budapest. You can milk a cow."

Her first attempts were clumsy, drawing an irritated swish of Mabel's tail. Diana adjusted her grip, letting her hands remember their old work. Just as the rhythm began returning—squeeze, pull, release—a flash of memory struck her.

Good Lord, this isn't Mabel.

It came back to her in a sickening rush. This wasn't gentle Mabel at all, but Bertha—the temperamental Ayrshire with the distinctive dark patch over her left eye that Diana had somehow missed in her distraction. Bertha, who was notorious for her vicious kicks and foul temper. Bertha, whom even Mr Hayes approached with caution, and whom Diana had been expressly forbidden to milk during her first months on the farm.

"Bloody hell—" she said, already pushing backward.

Too late.

The cow's leg tensed, and Diana caught the movement from the corner of her eye a fraction of a second before the hoof connected with her temple. The blow sent her sprawling across the dairy floor, her head striking the corner of a metal milk churn with a sickening crack.

Pain exploded through her skull, then rapidly dulled to a curious numbness. Diana found herself staring up at the dairy ceiling, aware of the cold seeping into her back from the flagstone floor and the distant sound of Jenny's scream. Dark spots bloomed across her vision like spilled ink.

"Diana! Oh my God, Diana!"

Jenny's face appeared above her, pale with horror, then seemed to fade away into a gathering grey mist.

How absurd, Diana thought distantly. *Killed by a cow after surviving Prague and Berlin and Istanbul.*

Then the grey mist swallowed her completely.

Chapter Five

Diana Penn opened her eyes.

She sat up with a jolt, hands flying to her temple where Bertha's hoof had connected. Nothing—no pain, no wound, not even the ghost of a headache. She looked down at her hands. Young, smooth, capable. The same hands that had failed to recognise which cow was which.

"Diana! You'll be late for your shift if you don't get a move on!"

Mrs Whitaker's voice drifted up from downstairs, exactly as it had the morning after the bomb in Pickering Park. Diana swung her legs over the side of the narrow bed, steadying herself against a wave of disorientation.

She'd died. Again.

The weak winter light filtered through the small window, casting the same patterns on the floor she'd seen yesterday. Or was it yesterday? The sloped ceiling with its flaking white paint, the worn rag rug, the wooden desk. All exactly as before.

Diana crossed to the small calendar tacked to the wall. December 1944. With exactly the same days crossed out in pencil as when she'd first awakened.

She'd reset. Again.

Diana ran her fingers through her thick hair, trying to process this new development.

Being sent back through time after her death in Pickering Park had been strange enough, but this was something else entirely. She'd died in 1944 and, instead of moving on to whatever awaited beyond death, she'd been returned to the same morning. As if someone had turned back the pages of a book to start the chapter again. The North Americans would call this Groundhog Day.

"Diana! The cows won't milk themselves, girl!"

A bubble of hysterical laughter rose in Diana's throat.

"Coming!" she called back, her voice steadier than she felt.

As she dressed quickly in her uniform, Diana's mind raced. Nothing had happened as she'd expected. Not the bomb in Pickering Park that had sent her back through time, and certainly not the cow that had sent her... where, exactly? Round in a circle, it seemed.

Was this her punishment? To die again and again, reliving the same days in an endless loop? Or was it a chance to try different paths until she found the right one?

Ellen Wilson is still going to disappear in February, Diana reminded herself. *Mr Hayes is still going to receive that telegram at Christmas. And someone is going to bury live bombs in Pickering Park.*

She paused with her hand on the doorknob. If dying simply reset her to this same morning, then perhaps she had more freedom than she'd first thought. She could try different approaches, take risks, use the knowledge gained in one life to inform her choices in the next.

But first, she would have to avoid being kicked to death by Bertha the cow.

Diana squared her shoulders and headed downstairs. The same smell of porridge greeted her, the same sight of Mrs Whitaker at the stove. Everything identical to yesterday. The first yesterday.

"There you are, finally!" Mrs Whitaker turned, wooden spoon in hand. "I was thinking you'd gone and died in your sleep."

Diana's laugh caught in her throat, emerging as a strangled cough. "No," she said. "Not in my sleep. More's the pity."

"What was that, dear?"

"Nothing."

Mrs Whitaker pushed a bowl of steaming porridge across to her. "You'll be glad of the hot breakfast today. It's freezing out there."

Diana spooned sugar into her porridge.

The same precious spoonful Mrs Whitaker had allotted her yesterday —or rather, today. The paradox of her situation made her head spin more than Bertha's kick had.

As she ate, she listened to Mrs Whitaker's morning chatter about rationing and the vicar's sermon and how the butcher's son had been called up now that he was of age. Word for word, it was identical to their previous conversation.

This time, however, Diana paid closer attention to Mrs Whitaker herself. The woman was only in her mid-forties, but worry had etched permanent lines around her eyes and mouth. Worry for her missing son, Trevor. Worry that had been all too justified, as Diana recalled the telegram that would confirm his death.

Could she prevent that? It seemed like an almost impossible task.

"You're quiet this morning," Mrs Whitaker observed, exactly as she had before.

Diana swallowed a spoonful of porridge. "Just thinking about the day ahead," she replied, varying her response slightly.

Mrs Whitaker nodded. "Don't forget, you promised to take those mending patterns to Mrs Robbins."

The patterns. Diana had completely forgotten about them yesterday. Or rather, Bertha's kick had derailed those plans.

"I'll deliver them straight after my shift at Hayes Farm," Diana promised. "And thank you for breakfast. I don't know if I've said how much I appreciate everything you do for me?"

For someone expertly trained in spycraft, Diana almost missed the slight rising of Mrs Whitaker's eyebrows as she almost inhaled the hot porridge.

After finishing her breakfast and washing her bowl in the waiting basin of tepid water, Diana's mind turned to the day ahead. Was this how the afterlife worked? You just repeated your life?

"I'd best get to those cows," she said, stifling a yawn as she reached for her coat on the peg by the door.

"That's the spirit," Mrs Whitaker nodded.

The walk to Hayes Farm was exactly the same. First, she crossed the Whitakers' back field before clambering over the wooden stile into the lane marked by the cherry red telephone box.

Mr Fleming, the postman, cycled past, right on cue.

"Good morning, Miss Penn!" he called.

"Good morning, Mr Fleming," she responded with more confidence this time, before adding, "Lovely morning."

"If you like freezing your toes off!" he called back over his shoulder, already pedalling off to his next delivery.

Diana pulled her coat tighter and continued walking, her mind cataloguing every detail to compare against her first experience. The rabbits darting across the lane. The distant bleating of sheep. The church spire appearing over the next rise. All precisely as before.

When she reached Hayes Farm, the familiar scene unfolded once more. Chickens scratched at the frozen earth, smoke curled from the farmhouse chimney, and Jess the collie bounded towards her, barking in welcome or warning.

"Jess! Good girl," Diana said, crouching to let the dog approach at her own pace.

After an identical moment's consideration, Jess sniffed at her outstretched hand, then allowed Diana to scratch behind her ears, just as she had done yesterday.

"She'd have you doing that all day if she could."

Mr Hayes emerged from the barn, pitchfork in hand, right on schedule. Short, stocky, and with the same weathered face and watchful gaze. A man who would lose his son and then himself in a matter of days—unless Diana could prevent it.

"Good morning, Mr Hayes," Diana said, straightening. "Jess deserves all the scratches. Such a good girl. What do you need me to do today?"

He gave her the same instructions as the last time—checking the root cellar stores, sorting parsnips and carrots, separating the good from the questionable, and to make time to drop into Blyde's. But this time, when he paused to study her face and said, "You look peaky, girl. Weather getting to you?" Diana was prepared for the question.

"Just thinking about my plans for Christmas Day," she said.

Hayes grunted, clearly uninterested in such feminine concerns. "There's a pot of tea in the kitchen to warm you up before you start."

"Thank you," Diana said. Then, before he could turn away, she added, "Has there been any news from Arthur?"

Why had she just asked about him? The boy was no concern of hers. Not really. He was doing his duty.

Hayes stiffened at the mention of his son. "Nothing since last month. Post is slow from the front, that's all."

As Hayes disappeared into the barn, Diana stood in the yard, gathering her thoughts. The day was unfolding exactly as before, but this time she wouldn't let herself be killed by Bertha the cow. What a stupid way to die.

After a decently strong cup of tea, Diana headed towards the dairy, which was exactly as she remembered it from her last fatal visit: cold, damp, and smelling of milk and animal warmth.

Six Ayrshire cows stood in their stalls, their breath visible in the light that filtered through the grimy windows. But this time, Diana approached cautiously, already scanning for the wooden stool in the corner where Mr Hayes had relocated it during his reorganisation. As she collected it, she carefully studied each cow, noting their distinctive markings with the attention to detail that had once kept her alive in Budapest and Prague.

"Looking for something?" Jenny Jenkins stood in the doorway, a coil of rope slung over one arm, just as she had before.

"Just getting my bearings," Diana replied smoothly. "Some mornings I need to remind myself which cow is which."

Jenny laughed. "Mr Hayes would have your guts for garters if you mixed them up. Especially with Bertha." She nodded towards the third stall, where the temperamental Ayrshire with the distinctive dark patch over her left eye regarded them both with undisguised malice. "Remember how she nearly took my hand off last week?"

And my head yesterday, Diana thought grimly. "Trust me, I'm steering well clear. I still can't believe that Bertha made the winter milking cut," Diana remarked, eyeing the notoriously ill-tempered cow.

Jenny nodded grimly. "Best producer we've got, more's the pity. Mr Hayes couldn't afford to dry her off, not with the milk quotas so hard to meet in winter. The man from the Ministry was round last week, giving Hayes an earful about production numbers."

Diana moved deliberately towards the gentle Mabel in the first stall.

"Bertha is all yours," she promised, positioning the stool with care, now placing it slightly farther from the cow's hind legs than she had before. "I value my life too much to tangle with her."

One brush with death by bovine was quite enough.

Settling beside Mabel—the real Mabel this time, with her calm demeanour and white-tipped tail, Diana reached for the udder with newfound respect. Her hands moved confidently now, the rhythm coming naturally: squeeze, pull, release. Squeeze, pull, release. The satisfying sound of milk hitting the metal pail brought a smile to her face.

"You're in fine form today," Jenny called from the workbench. "Usually takes you half the morning to get into the swing of things."

Diana shrugged, continuing her work. "Must be the promise of Christmas. It's put a spring in my step."

As she milked, her mind turned to Ellen and her impending disappearance in February. Whatever lay ahead in this strange, repeated day, Diana was determined to gather as much information as possible. Perhaps there were clues she had missed the first time?

At midday, Mr Hayes sent her into the village with his ration book and a short list. "Need to collect the weekly allowance from Blyde's," he'd said.

Diana used the farm's bicycle for the short ride into Cheviot Hills, the cold air stinging her cheeks as she pedalled down the narrow lane. The village high street stretched before her, a modest collection of stone-fronted shops that appeared almost unchanged in the intervening sixty-odd years. Blyde's Grocery occupied a narrow building squeezed between the red-brick facade of Barclays Bank and the post office. Further along, she could see the butcher's shop with its empty display window, and then the small haberdashery, which would become one of half a dozen charity shops filling Cheviot Hills' high street in the distant future.

At Blyde's Grocery, Diana overheard a familiar voice and turned to see Mrs Patterson—the same Land Girl coordinator who'd assigned her to Willow Farm—tearfully telling the shopkeeper about her nephew, reported missing after a bombing raid over Germany. The woman's hands shook as she counted out her ration coupons, clearly struggling to focus.

Diana felt a flicker of irritation. Emotional displays made her uncomfortable, and Mrs Patterson's distress was slowing down the queue. When Mrs Blyde gently suggested Mrs Patterson sit down for a moment, Diana couldn't suppress a sigh at the further delay.

The sigh earned herself a pointedly terse look from the shopkeeper, but Diana had her own shopping to complete and didn't see how public grieving helped anyone. The boy had been doing his duty to the country. Sad, but a fact of life during war. Hadn't she carried on after the death of her own mother?

Back at the farm, Diana resumed her work beside Jenny, her mind still processing the scene at the shop with clinical detachment. *The boy had been doing his duty.*

"Did you hear about the plane that went down near Wooler?" Jenny interrupted, her voice echoing in the cavernous shed.

Diana looked up. She didn't remember this from her first life, but then again she barely remembered talking with Jenny then. "No, what happened?"

Jenny leaned forward conspiratorially. "RAF training flight, they say. But Mrs Robbins swears she heard German voices in the field on her way home from the pub."

"German voices?" Diana echoed, genuinely surprised. "What would German soldiers be doing in Northumberland?"

"Well, you know Mrs Robbins," Jenny said, with a dismissive wave. "A few too many sherries, if you ask me. Besides, the RAF was crawling all over the place within hours. Very hush-hush." She grinned wickedly. "I wouldn't mind meeting a Jerry or two in the dark, though. Would make a delightful change from farm boys who can't even grow a decent moustache yet."

"Jenny!" Diana scolded, genuinely shocked by the girl's recklessness. "You don't mean that?"

"I'm only joking." Jenny laughed. "And I also heard that Thomas Hawk is going around saying that he swears he saw figures moving through the bracken up on Yeavering Bell last night. Said they looked like smugglers. 'Course, his wife thinks he was seeing things after staying up all night with the searchlights. Smugglers. In Cheviot Hills? It's probably Mrs Robbins' Germans."

Before Diana could answer, the distinctive drone of aircraft engines cut through the morning quiet. Both women tilted their heads towards the sound. Diana counting them by habit—one, two, three heavy bombers, flying high, their engines a deep, throbbing hum that seemed to vibrate in the air itself.

RAF, she was almost certain, from the familiar pitch and rhythm of their engines. The sound was something she could never forget. It transported her instantly to nights spent in London during the Blitz, where the air was heavy with smoke as they waited for the next wave. She could still remember the frantic rush down to the tube stations, the echo of footsteps and the nervous chatter of strangers, all trying to find shelter while the German bombs rained down overhead. The bombers above now —no longer the enemy's—brought with them the same tightness in her chest, a reminder of the nights she'd spent with her hands clenched, praying for the sound of the all-clear.

The shadows at the dairy door shifted, and Diana looked up to see a man's silhouette. Tall, broad-shouldered, wearing an RAF uniform.

"Morning, ladies," he called, his accent crisp and educated.

"Morning." Jenny giggled.

Diana studied the newcomer with interest. His uniform fit a little oddly on his frame, and there was something about his bearing that triggered her intelligence agent's instincts. This man was not what he seemed.

"Flight Lieutenant James Crawford," he introduced himself, stepping into the dairy. "But please, call me Jim. I was hoping to find someone who might point me in the direction of Cheviot Hills."

As he moved into the light, Diana felt an odd doubling of memory— like two photographs laid one over the other, slightly out of alignment. She knew this man. Or she would know him. But the memory stayed just out of reach, like a word on the tip of her tongue.

"Diana Penn," she heard herself say. "Pleasure to meet you, Flight Lieutenant. You're a long way from your base."

He smiled, and something in Diana's chest tightened. "The pleasure, Miss Penn, is entirely mine. Sadly, I had a spot of engine trouble," he explained smoothly. "Had to set down in a field about two miles back. Lost my bearings somewhat once I was down on the ground. You know how it is."

A lie, Diana was certain. Though whether it was a harmless one or something more sinister remained to be seen. "The village is just over the next rise," she said, pointing vaguely. "You can't miss the church spire."

"Very kind of you, Miss Penn." His eyes lingered on her face a moment too long. "Perhaps I'll see you again?"

"Perhaps," Diana replied noncommittally.

Something about the man didn't sit right with her, and her decades of intelligence work had taught her to trust such instincts.

Jenny shot her a puzzled look, clearly baffled by Diana's lack of enthusiasm for the handsome officer. "I'll show you the way, Flight Lieutenant," she offered eagerly. "I'm headed that direction myself."

Crawford tipped his cap to Diana. "Until we meet again, then."

Jenny was already halfway out the door. "You'll be okay to finish the rest of the cows, won't you? Including Bertha!"

But Jenny had shot out the door before Diana could answer, already chattering away with the mysterious airman as they disappeared into the weak morning light, leaving Diana alone with the Ayrshires. As she continued milking Mabel, she pondered the appearance of the officer. His eyes sparked a memory she couldn't quite grasp. Had she met him during her future career as an MI6 agent? Or was it something else entirely?

Once she finished with Mabel, Diana moved cautiously to the next cow, giving Bertha's stall a wide berth. Whatever game was afoot in Cheviot Hills, Diana wouldn't let a temperamental cow cut short her life again.

Chapter Six

By late afternoon, Diana's arms ached with a burn she hadn't felt in decades. The physical demands of farm work were a stark reminder that while her mind held decades of experience, her body was still adjusting to its renewed youth. Jenny hadn't returned from her impromptu tour guide duties, leaving Diana to manage the afternoon chores alone.

"Bloody Jenny," she muttered, hefting another burlap sack of stored root vegetables. The musty scent of earth still clung to the misshapen carrots as she sorted through them, discarding those showing signs of black rot and carefully repacking the sound ones. "Bloody war." Her voice echoed in the cold store room, startling a chicken that had wandered in, seeking shelter from the frost.

The pilot's face haunted her thoughts like a poorly developed photograph—present but frustratingly unclear. Each time she tried to focus on his features, they slipped away like smoke. She knew him. Or would know him. The certainty gnawed at her with the same persistence as the December wind whistling through the barn's wooden slats.

The physical labour left her too exhausted to maintain her usual analytical distance. Emotions she thought long buried surfaced with each strain of muscle.

Anger at Jenny's careless flirtation with the mysterious pilot, frustration at her own memory, and a deep, burning resentment towards whatever cosmic force had dropped her into this moment in time.

As she worked, Diana's mind drifted to a more pleasant memory—the Café Landtmann in Vienna, where she'd spent countless evenings in the 1960s. The café had been her sanctuary during those tense years of the Cold War. Elegant enough to justify regular visits, busy enough to avoid suspicion. The coffee had been excellent, the pastries divine, and the clientele deliciously dubious. Soviet agents had discussed operations over Sachertorte, dissidents passed messages in folded newspapers, and she'd once witnessed a choreographed dance of East German and American operatives pretending not to notice each other while sipping a Melange.

Those had been her golden years, when Vienna straddled the divide between East and West. Where every conversation had carried weight, and every glance had meaning. The thrill of it had made her feel more alive than she'd ever felt before or since. Was this God's idea of cosmic justice? Sending her back to sort misshapen carrots in the dead of winter instead of letting her relive her finest moments?

She watched the hens cluck and bustle around her feet. "You lot are easier to manage than half the agents I worked with," she muttered. "And far less likely to double-cross me, come to think of it."

"Talking to the chickens now, are we?"

Diana whirled around, dropping the sack of carrots. Fred Hayes stood in the doorway, his face crinkled with obvious amusement.

"Just thinking aloud," Diana said, rescuing the stray carrots before any of the chickens could skewer one with their razor-sharp beaks.

"About that pilot fellow, no doubt." His tone was gruff, but there was worry beneath it. "What was he doing wandering around here?"

Diana's attention sharpened. So she wasn't the only one who'd noticed. But before she could probe further, Hayes shook his head.

"Best finish up here. Storm's coming in from the hills. You'll want to be back at Mrs Whitaker's before it hits."

The wind was picking up, rattling the barn doors. Somewhere in the gathering darkness, Jenny was probably still batting her eyelashes at Flight Lieutenant Crawford or flashing her knickers. The girl was a walking, breathing man magnet. But in these times, love was often fleeting, so she took whatever opportunities presented themselves, regardless of risk.

"You're as slow as a carthorse today," Hayes observed as she gathered her things. "Not ailing with something, are you?"

Diana shook her head. "Just tired. And…" she hesitated, then decided truth, or a version of it, might serve best. "I keep feeling like I've forgotten something important."

Hayes grunted. "At your age? Wait until you're my age, lass. Then you'll know what forgetting feels like."

If only you knew, Diana thought, pulling her coat tighter against the rising wind. *If only you knew.*

Diana was halfway to the gate when she remembered Mrs Whitaker mentioning something about lending Ellen a book. How could she possibly remember what volume she was supposed to have offered to lend?

"Mr Hayes," she called, turning back towards the farmhouse, "I don't suppose I could borrow a book?" She'd remembered this was how she'd spent most of her time in her first life, ensconced in her bedroom, reading books borrowed from either the library or from Mr Hayes. Escaping from reality.

"Take your pick, but mind you bring it back," he said, pipe in hand.

The well-stocked study was Hayes's sanctuary. Lined with overflowing bookcases, Diana was reminded that Hayes collected books the way other men collected hunting trophies or fishing flies. Her eye caught the familiar spine of a Collins Crime Club edition, its distinctive red-and-gold lettering still crisp despite the worn edges. Agatha Christie's *The Body in the Library*. Perfect. She'd read it the first time around, but couldn't recall the ending now. Too many plots, and too many lives lived.

"Found what you need?" Hayes asked as she emerged, book in hand.

"Yes, thank you."

Hayes nodded, tamping down his pipe tobacco. "Best take care on your way back. That weather's coming in fast, and there's more than a squall or two brewing tonight."

Diana tucked the book into her coat pocket. "What makes you say that?"

"Just a feeling." He struck a match, the flame illuminating his weathered features. "Like the air before a thunderstorm. You can taste it coming."

Yes, Diana thought as she stepped out into the gathering dark. *That's exactly what it feels like.*

Ellen had told Mrs Whitaker that she'd be at the Twice Brewed Inn, and to Diana, the walk there seemed longer than she remembered. The wind had picked up, carrying with it the bitter promise of rain. Pale moonlight slipped through breaks in the racing clouds, just enough to illuminate the once familiar path. Though "familiar" was perhaps the wrong word—she hadn't walked this route in decades, yet her feet seemed to remember every dip and turn, even if she didn't.

The Twice Brewed loomed dark against the night sky, its windows carefully screened with the heavy blackout curtains required by law. Only the thinnest sliver of light escaped beneath the door. Diana felt for the iron door handle and stepped into the sudden warmth. She shrugged her coat off in the small entrance vestibule before pushing through the inner door to the public bar. The room was lit by carefully shielded lamps and the glow from the fireplace, whose flames were fortunately much higher than the regulations allowed. With the bar half-full, muted conversation competed with the occasional crack of logs in the grate. The air was thick with pipe smoke and the smell of meat pies, bitter ale, and decades of gathered comfort, all of it seeming more intense in the enforced dimness.

Diana stood just inside the door, letting the sensations wash over her. And then a memory hit, so vivid that it stole her breath. A similar room, but at a different time. And a man sitting opposite her in one of the wooden snugs, his face in shadow. The rich taste of steak and a surprisingly excellent claret. His hand reaching across the table to touch hers, and...

The memory dissolved like sugar in tea, leaving only the ghost of wine on her tongue and questions she couldn't answer. When had that been? Who had he been? The harder she tried to grasp the details, the faster they slithered away.

Diana scanned the room. The usual suspects were there—farmers warming themselves after a day in the fields, a pair of uniformed Home Guard members nursing their pints, with a rotund bulldog asleep under the table, the local gossips clustered near the fire. But there was no sign of Ellen Wilson with her mouthful of American teeth in a too-wide smile and her sophisticated laugh cutting through the provincial murmur.

How strange to search for someone she hadn't seen since the 1940s.

In fact, someone who would soon disappear, leaving behind hundreds of questions and the faint scent of Tangee lipstick. Diana touched the buttery softness of the leather gloves in her pocket. Was she supposed to stop Ellen from vanishing? Was that why she was here? Did she even have the power to make that change?

The door to the vestibule rattled, letting in a gust of bitter wind and Ellen Wilson appeared, looking impossibly elegant despite her mud-splattered Land Army uniform, flushed cheeks and hair escaping its regulation tie in artful wisps.

"Diana!" Ellen's voice carried across the pub with that distinctly American ability to fill a space. Before Diana could react, Ellen enveloped her in a bear hug that smelled of fresh air, horses, and perfume.

Diana stiffened at the girl's touch. Hugs and overt affection were not something she normally experienced.

"You're frozen solid," Ellen declared, already steering Diana to the bar. "Charlie! Two port and lemons, be a dear." She flashed the barman a smile that could have melted steel. "And look, a booth just opened up. Providence, wouldn't you say?"

Diana found herself swept along in Ellen's wake, settling into the wooden bench of the empty snug whilst Ellen bustled off to collect their drinks. Left alone for a moment, Diana pulled her scarf off, taking her time to fold it neatly whilst she caught her breath. The American's enthusiasm was exactly as Diana remembered it, and so un-English-like that it made her squirm.

Ellen returned with their drinks, sliding the port and lemons onto the table with a satisfied smile.

"Cheers!" Ellen said, clanking her glass against Diana's.

Diana swallowed down a wince at the frivolity of it all.

As they sipped their drinks, a young woman at the neighbouring table began sobbing into her beer. Diana vaguely recognised her as one of the other Land Army girls, but couldn't have named her if a gun had been held to her head. She was clearly distressed, which caught Ellen's attention.

"Should we..." Ellen began, half-rising from her chair.

"Leave her be," Diana interjected. "She's probably had some bad news. Best not to interfere." The words came out more coldly than she'd intended, but Diana found herself resistant to the idea of becoming involved with someone else's emotional crisis.

She had a job to do, and she just had to get through this minor blip in time before she could return to her work, to her duty to King and country.

Ellen frowned. "But she looks so lonely. Maybe she needs—"

"She needs privacy to process whatever's happened," Diana cut her off. "Not strangers poking their noses in." She turned her back on the crying girl, ending the discussion but still caught Ellen's eyes watching the girl with obvious worry. Diana felt a tiny twist in her gut at her own callousness, but dampened it down. She had more pressing concerns in her life.

Desperate to change the subject and cover her discomfort, Diana reached for Mr Hayes's copy of Agatha Christie's newest release. "I brought the latest Christie." She pulled out the Collins Crime Club edition.

"Oh, I thought you were bringing a copy of *Forever Amber*. You promised." Ellen's eyes had flattened with disappointment. "I've heard it's absolutely scandalous. Margaret—you know, the WAAF officer at Acklington—says Boston banned it. Can you imagine?"

Diana's heart sank. *Forever Amber* by Kathleen Winsor. The scandalous book everyone was whispering about at the time. She glanced down at the borrowed Christie novel and cursed her memory.

"I'm so sorry, I forgot."

"Oh well, never mind. I'm sure it's just as good." Ellen took a sip of her drink, leaving a perfect lipstick mark on the glass. "Actually, I'm glad you brought something else. Imagine if my host family found that hidden under my pillow! I mean, things are bad enough with them as it is."

Diana frowned, memories surfacing of Ellen's frequent complaints about the Hollisters. How they expected her to work from dawn until well after dusk, treating her more like a Victorian scullery maid than the agricultural volunteer she was. There had been the endless mucking out of stables, the backbreaking toil in the fields, the scrubbing and polishing of the house—all on top of her official Land Army duties. It had never sat right with Diana.

And then there was Mr Hollister's legendary roving eye.

Diana's stomach twisted as she recalled the way Ellen had spoken about him—not in the usual, exasperated way they talked about lecherous old men at the pub, but with real unease. The lingering looks, the way his hand would brush against her waist when squeezing past.

And the way Mrs Hollister ignored it, always finding some reason to send Ellen into his orbit.

It came flooding back to her.

Had the police ever questioned that man after Ellen disappeared? She couldn't remember. What she could remember was the indifference. No one in Cheviot Hills seemed worried about one young woman vanishing.

"Probably got herself in the family way," had been the consensus, shrugged off between pints at the pub, over gossip exchanged at the grocer's.

Diana had never believed it. Not for a second. Ellen wasn't that way inclined. Sure, she talked a big game, flirted and giggled over dog-eared romance novels, but when had any of them really had opportunities for mucking around? They were exhausted at the end of each day, covered in dirt and sweat, their hands raw from the cold.

Diana swallowed hard, her fingers tightening around the stem of her glass. Ellen wouldn't have just left. Something had happened to her.

Diana just hadn't figured out what. Yet.

Interlude One
UNIVERSAL LIFE CENTRE

Marta drummed her fingers against her desk in the vast Temporal Room that seemed to stretch on forever, her eyes fixed on the milky white cylinder before her. The pyxis pulsed and glowed with an inner power. It showed both a realistic scene as it occurred and the subject's emotions—confusion, determination, and something deeper that made the instrument glow with an intensity Marta hadn't seen in decades.

Around her, countless other watchers sat at identical desks, each with their own pyxis that glowed with the collected emotions of their charges. Bertellia had taught her well—emotion was energy, and energy fed The Machine. But Marta had found that watching this person had always been different. The woman's life had been a masterclass in contained passion, measured responses, and calculated risks.

Until now.

Marta had watched the scene with the buried bombs with an odd detachment. To the Watchers of the Universal Life Centre, death was simply part of the cycle of lives. A movement from one situation to the next.

She adjusted the pyxis, moving it slightly counterclockwise. The cylinder's surface rippled, showing her the young woman and another woman at a pub.

Marta could see what lay ahead on the timeline of both women—the truth of the other woman's disappearance gleamed like a dark thread in the tapestry of time. But that woman wasn't her charge and she was forbidden to interfere.

"Focus on your own assignments," Bertellia had once said, tapping Marta's pyxis with one elegant finger. "The Machine requires balance. We observe, we collect, we feed. We rarely interfere."

The woman's timeline had shifted. Her original path—the quiet retirement, the gradual fade into obscurity—had been obliterated by that single moment in Pickering Park. Now the possibilities sprawled before Marta like branches of lightning, each one crackling with potential.

She adjusted the temporal focus again, watching the young woman's fingers trace the spine of a novel. Wrong book, wrong time, right instinct. The pyxis thrummed. The girl was clever, but now she had the benefit of decades of experience wrapped in youth's vigour.

"You're going to try to save your friend, aren't you?" Marta asked the image in her pyxis. "Even though you have no idea what happens to her."

The cylinder pulsed in response.

Marta glanced around the vast room, but the other watchers remained focused on their own pyxis, collecting the everyday emotions that kept The Machine running. Love, hate, joy, sorrow. The infinite spectrum of human feeling.

Marta had watched the woman for too long to underestimate her. She'd observed the subject's entire career in intelligence. She'd seen her make impossible choices, witnessed her sacrifice personal happiness for duty time and time again. Perhaps this was her reward? Or her punishment? Sometimes it was hard to tell the difference.

The pyxis dimmed slightly as Marta watched the subject step out into the night. Even now, having found herself in such an unusual and untenable situation, decades of training controlled the girl's emotions. But underneath that discipline, Marta could see the burning determination.

Marta settled back in her chair.

"Show me," she whispered to the pyxis. "Show me what happens next."

Chapter Seven

The evening at the Twice Brewed had been unexpectedly pleasant, filled with Ellen's animated chatter about archaeology and village gossip, until the American had insisted on cycling Diana home through the worsening weather rather than let her walk alone in the cold. In her first life, Diana had stayed for one drink, returned the gloves, and walked home alone. She'd recognised that Ellen had tried to be her friend, but Diana had had no real interest. Still, she remembered how hard it had been to deny the American girl, who was so oblivious to Diana's attempts to rebuff her.

The bicycle wobbled beneath them as Ellen pedalled them both down the lane, with Diana perched precariously on the carrier rack. The night air nipped at her exposed skin, but the port and lemon warmed her from within, dulling the bite of December's chill.

Ellen skidded to a stop outside Willow Farm, and Diana swung her leg over, hopping unsteadily off the bike.

"Promise you'll come to the Christmas dance on Saturday," Ellen called over her shoulder as she straightened the handlebars, her American accent cutting through the darkness. "And save me a dance! If I have to spend another night dancing with ancient widowers and Mr Hollister, I'll probably shoot myself."

Diana promised.

She watched Ellen cycle away, her silhouette fading into the gathering darkness. The girl's distinctive scent of Tangee lipstick and that expensive French perfume she drowned herself in despite rationing, lingered in the air long after she'd disappeared down the narrow lane.

What on earth was she doing promising to go to the Christmas dance?

Mrs Whitaker was ladling stew into sturdy earthenware bowls when Diana entered the kitchen, the steam carrying the homely aroma of root vegetables and the faintest hint of rabbit. Diana's mouth watered. Her ancient self had subsisted on tinned soup and toast, her arthritic hands making proper cooking too painful to bother with. Food straight from the farm was a luxury she'd forgotten.

"The American girl brought you back, then?" Mrs Whitaker stated, setting a bowl before Diana. "She'll break her neck one of these nights."

Diana wanted to wolf down the stew, but she forced herself to savour each spoonful. The carrots and turnips from Hayes Farm, the herbs from Mrs Whitaker's kitchen garden, even the meagre portion of meat took on new significance with every bite reconnecting her to this place, and this time.

After supper, Mrs Whitaker switched on the wireless, its familiar brown Bakelite casing glowing softly as the valves warmed up. The BBC Home Service filled the kitchen with a string quartet playing something soothing and patriotic. Diana sipped her milky tea, watching as Mrs Whitaker settled into her usual spot in her armchair, her knitting needles at the ready.

The woman's hands moved ceaselessly, creating order from chaos, turning wool into comfort for distant soldiers. If the war could be won by knitting alone, Mrs Whitaker would have defeated Hitler single-handedly years ago.

Diana watched Mrs Whitaker. Not through the eyes of a twenty-year-old, who'd only ever seen an older woman worn down by life, but with the perspective of someone who'd lived her own lifetime.

Mrs Whitaker's greying hair and the lines around her mouth spoke of worry, not age. At most, she was in her mid-forties, perhaps a few years younger than Diana had been when she'd recruited her first agent in Berlin.

"Why did you never remarry?" The question slipped out before Diana could stop it.

Enid Whitaker's needles faltered mid-stitch. "I beg your pardon?"

Diana flushed, but persisted. "After Mr Whitaker passed. You were still young. *Are* still young."

The knitting resumed, the click-click-click filling the silence. "Young?" Mrs Whitaker gave a humourless laugh. "I haven't felt young since Mr Whitaker returned home from France. The gas took almost twenty years to kill him, but he was as good as dead the day he stepped off that hospital ship." She counted stitches under her breath before continuing. "When you've watched someone you love die inch by inch, marriage loses its charm."

Diana thought of her own life. She'd never married. Always too busy fighting other people's wars. She'd never loved, either.

"I'm sorry," Diana said. "That was rude of me."

Mrs Whitaker's expression softened. "You're allowed to ask such questions at your age, dear. It's expected." She held up the half-formed sock. "Besides, who'd have time for a husband with all this knitting to do?"

Diana watched her resume her knitting, her eyes focused on her craft, her ears attuned to the dulcet tones of the *BBC's Nine O'Clock News*. The final report contained grim updates from the Ardennes, warnings of fuel shortages, with the usual clipped voices reminding them to "make do and mend" and that "loose lips sink ships." Diana stretched out her legs, letting the warmth from the small coal fire seep into her bones. She debated with herself whether she should tell Mrs Whitaker that the war was nearly over. That within six months they'd be drowning under garlands of bunting and celebrating in the streets.

"Well, that was cheerful," Mrs Whitaker said. "But we've had worse," she added matter-of-factly. She reached over, twisting the dial. "Time for something lighter."

The jaunty melody of *Much-Binding-in-the-Marsh* filled the room, and Diana leaned back, smiling as the voices of Kenneth Horne and Richard Murdoch launched into their usual banter about the hapless airmen at the fictional RAF station. In her own time, they were long gone —voices from a past preserved only in old recordings. But here, in this moment, they were alive, their quick wit and easy charm cutting through the evening's worries, making both women momentarily set aside their worries.

Mrs Whitaker chuckled. Then, as the wireless carried on with the next gag, she set down her knitting. "Speaking of airmen..."

Diana turned to her.

"Mr Fleming came by this morning, *Not* with bad news, thank the Lord," Mrs Whitaker announced, the familiar flicker of apprehension tainting her voice. Every visit from the postman still made her breath catch. She exhaled. "Says there was a training crash up near Wooler last night. Some sort of accident in the hills. He says the place was awash with airmen clearing away the debris. That's all he knows. He reckons they don't want anyone poking about."

Diana leaned forward. "Did he say what kind of plane?"

Mrs Whitaker shook her head. "Just that they were in a hurry to get it cleared away. Makes you wonder, doesn't it? How many more of our lads have to die before Hitler does?"

Diana curled up on the couch with her tea and let the comedy wash over her as she pondered the news. "Training crash," Diana repeated, the wheels of her mind turning. "Did Mr Fleming mention anything about the symbols on the wreckage?"

Mrs Whitaker looked puzzled. "Symbols? You mean like the RAF roundel?"

Diana nodded. "My brother was mad about planes. He could identify them from the tiniest details." The lie came smoothly, one of thousands she'd told over the decades. Or thousands she would tell.

"I didn't know you had a brother," Mrs Whitaker said, her blue eyes round above her glasses.

"I don't like to talk about him," Diana lied again. When had she first started lying? Had she always been a liar? Did it matter?

After what felt like an interminable appraisal from the older woman, Mrs Whitaker returned to her knitting and Diana finished her tea in silence. After the show finished and they listened to the weather forecast ("continuing cold with frost in most areas"), Diana bid Mrs Whitaker goodnight. The narrow staircase creaked beneath her feet as she climbed to her small bedroom.

She lit the bedside lamp, and the small flame flickered unsteadily for a moment before settling into a steady glow. The house had electricity, but out here in the countryside, the supply was temperamental at best.

Power cuts were common, and Mrs Whitaker, ever practical, insisted on keeping the old oil lamps and candles handy, just in case.

Diana sat on the bed and flexed her toes, snug inside their woollen socks. She hadn't realised how much she'd taken for granted the simple miracle of a body that moved without protest. By the time she was sixty-three, she'd been in almost constant pain somewhere or other in her body. The creeping aches had started so subtly she'd dismissed them at first: blaming the cold for her stiff fingers, an uncomfortable bed for the dull pull in her lower back, and an awkward slip down a low step for a dicky hip. By the time she admitted it might be more than age or weather, the arthritis had settled in like an unwelcome guest. She'd been relegated to swallowing chalky painkillers and applying all-but-useless hot compresses. If this really was a second chance, she'd decided, she would damn well look after her body this time. And enjoy it.

Diana quickly shed her clothes, swapping them for the long flannel nightgown, before moving to the washstand. The water in the porcelain jug was ice cold against her skin as she performed her ablutions, scrubbing her face with the harsh carbolic soap. She missed the fragrance-free, sensitive-skin toiletries she used to rely on. Products with names that promised youth in a bottle, which wouldn't be available for another three or four decades. In the mirror, her youthful face stared back at her. No wrinkles, no age spots, no tissue-thin skin prone to bruising and bleeding at the slightest touch. Just unblemished skin, bright eyes, and an honest beauty that she hadn't realised she'd once possessed. She paused, her fingertips lingering on her cheek. Maybe the carbolic, for all its austerity, was actually better for her skin?

Diana climbed into bed, extinguished the lamp and pulled the patchwork quilt and scratchy blankets up to her chin. The sheets were cold and damp despite the stone hot water bottle Mrs Whitaker had placed at the foot of the bed earlier. As she lay in the darkness, she tried to make sense of it all. Was this heaven? Purgatory? Some cosmic joke? Or had that bomb in the park triggered something impossible—a genuine second chance?

If this was real—truly real—then Ellen Wilson would disappear in less than two months. But perhaps, with her decades of training and experience, Diana could prevent it from happening again?

She'd failed the first time around. She'd been too young and too naïve to recognise the danger until it was too late.

Then her mind drifted to the pilot, Flight Lieutenant Crawford. Perhaps she'd been imagining things, but there was something wrong about him. Nothing she could name, but he seemed like an unprepared understudy stepping up to play the lead in a theatre production.

And then there were the bombs in Pickering Park. Someone put them there, and they must have known that they weren't dummy bombs. Surely the future risk should have been enough to stop anyone in their tracks? Someone must have engineered the situation, Diana was certain. But why?

She turned onto her side, the bedsprings protesting beneath her. Outside, an owl hooted, the sound carrying in the winter night. And in the distance, she heard the drone of an aircraft.

"One day at a time," she murmured into her pillow. "First Mr Hayes, then Ellen. Then... then everything else."

Sleep claimed her, dragging her down into its depths with the same relentless power that had pulled her back through time. Her last conscious thought before surrendering was that, whatever else happened, she would not waste this second chance.

Chapter Eight

The morning frost crunched beneath Diana's boots as she made her way across the village green towards the assembled crowd. Saturday morning drill exercises with the Home Guard were compulsory for all members of the WLA. Another patriotic duty to add to the endless list of wartime obligations. Diana clutched her gas mask box tighter, its canvas strap already chafing against her shoulder despite the thick wool of her jumper. She'd rather be mucking out pig pens. At least pigs were honest about their intentions.

The other land girls had already gathered near the war memorial, their breath forming small clouds in the December air. Diana had remembered some of them. There was Jenny Jenkins, obviously, who worked with her at the farm. Nancy Robbins (there was no way on God's green earth that she could forget her) standing perfectly poised despite the early hour, and several others whose faces she couldn't quite remember and whose names had faded with the passage of time. The girls chatted amongst themselves with the easy camaraderie that Diana envied but couldn't seem to access. Every time she'd approached such groups in her first life, conversation had withered like flowers in frost.

"Diana!" Jenny spotted her across the park and glanced at the other girls before waving her over with characteristic enthusiasm.

Diana approached the group, trying to recall their names.

The sturdy girl with calloused hands and dirt permanently embedded beneath her fingernails would be Susan, she thought. And the tall one with the careful posture must be Kathy Morrison from the Hawks' place.

"Hello, Diana," Susan said with a brief nod before turning back to regale the others with tales of her ongoing battle with a particularly obstinate sow.

"Knocked me flat on my backside, she did." Susan laughed. "Right into the muck. Took three of us to get her back in her pen, and I swear she was smirking the whole time."

The others erupted in sympathetic laughter, sharing their own stories of agricultural misadventures. Diana listened, picking up conversational clues. Yes, definitely Kathy Morrison, and the third girl was Margaret something-or-other from beyond the village.

"That sounds dreadful," Diana found herself saying. "I sometimes think that pigs are cleverer than we give them credit for."

She caught Jenny's surprised expression and the quick smile crossing her face. Jenny clearly hadn't expected her to contribute. Diana realised how accustomed they'd all become to her keeping herself apart from these sorts of conversations. Or any conversation.

"Exactly!" Susan agreed enthusiastically. "Evil clever, that one is."

Diana noticed how easily Susan had replied to her comment, as if her participation was perfectly natural, even though Diana had spent years keeping her distance from their easy camaraderie. She hadn't seen the point of getting to know them. These girls would form their own tight bonds, marry local lads after the war, and settle into comfortable domestic lives. She was just passing through.

A sharp whistle pierced the morning air, and PC Aldridge emerged from the church hall like a bantam cock surveying his domain. A lean man in his fifties whose uniform barely showed any wear. As the local constable, PC Aldridge also served with the Home Guard, drilling with farmers and shopkeepers to prepare for threats that seemed increasingly distant. He'd dressed for today's occasion in his Home Guard uniform, complete with webbing that looked suspiciously pristine compared to the other men's battle-worn gear. His brass buttons caught the weak sunlight, polished to a mirror shine that spoke of vanity rather than military preparedness.

"Right then, ladies and gentlemen!"

Aldridge's voice carried across the green with the authority of a man convinced of his own importance. "Today's exercise will simulate a German parachute landing in the village. The WLA girls will serve as civilian evacuees, whilst the Home Guard demonstrates proper defensive procedures."

Diana suppressed a snort. She doubted PC Aldridge's little theatrical performance would bear any resemblance to reality.

The Home Guard unit assembled behind their self-appointed commander consisted mainly of farmers and shopkeepers too old or unfit for regular military service. Mr Hayes stood amongst them, his face betraying mild embarrassment at the proceedings. Beside him, old Mr O'Hara from the chemist's fumbled with his rifle, whilst the baker, Mr Cromwell, looked as though he'd rather be kneading dough than playing soldiers. Ed Fries, the town's only watchmaker, seemed more interested in patting his bulldog than listening to the instructions.

"The scenario," Aldridge continued, consulting a clipboard with theatrical importance, "is as follows: German advance scouts have landed in Hartwell Wood. Their objective is to secure the village communications and supply lines before the main invasion force arrives." He gestured grandly towards the small telephone exchange housed in Mrs Campbell's front parlour.

Ellen Wilson materialised at Diana's elbow with that peculiar ability to appear suddenly without seeming to have walked from anywhere.

"He's taking this rather seriously, isn't he?" Ellen murmured.

Diana glanced at her sideways. In her first life, she'd felt intimidated by Ellen's easy casualness and confidence. The American had a sophistication that Diana knew she'd never attain. In any lifetime.

"Some men need their little wars," Diana whispered.

Aldridge had produced a battered megaphone from somewhere and was now addressing his assembled forces with the fervour of Napoleon at Austerlitz.

"Remember, lads, the enemy is cunning, ruthless, and highly trained. They won't hesitate to use women and children as human shields. That's why we must remain vigilant, disciplined, and ready to take decisive action at a moment's notice."

The girls exchanged glances.

Susan rolled her eyes so dramatically that even Aldridge might have noticed if he hadn't been so enamoured with his own performance.

"Now then," Aldridge continued, "Miss Robbins and Miss Jenkins will position themselves near the post office, representing terrified villagers seeking protection. Miss Wilson and Miss Penn will attempt to reach the railway station. That's your evacuation point. You must try to avoid capture by enemy forces."

Nancy stepped forward with a smile that suggested she'd been anticipating this moment. "PC Aldridge, shouldn't we be given some indication of what routes might be safe? In a real situation, surely the local constabulary would have intelligence about enemy movements?"

Aldridge puffed up like a courting pigeon. "Excellent question, Miss Robbins. In actual combat conditions, information would indeed be limited and potentially unreliable. That's precisely what makes this exercise so valuable."

Ellen leaned closer to Diana. "Translation: he hasn't thought this through properly."

Diana had to swallow her laughter.

The "exercise" that followed was a masterclass in military incompetence disguised as patriotic enthusiasm. Aldridge had positioned his men with no apparent strategy beyond ensuring maximum visibility for his own leadership. Mr Hayes crouched behind the war memorial looking deeply uncomfortable, whilst the baker had managed to get himself tangled in a length of rope that was supposed to represent communication wire.

The girls were instructed to make their way across the village green whilst avoiding "capture" by the Home Guard. What this meant in practical terms was unclear, as Aldridge had failed to establish any actual rules of engagement beyond shouting "Bang! You're dead!" whenever he spotted movement.

Diana and Ellen found themselves belly-crawling across the frost-hard ground, their overalls collecting mud and twigs. Ellen's hair was escaping its pins, and her usual composure was showing signs of strain.

"This is absolutely ridiculous," Ellen muttered as they paused behind the base of a moss-covered Roman mile marker, or what was left of it. "I swear I'll lose my mind if Aldridge keeps this nonsense up much longer."

"Aldridge is playing at being a soldier. Actual warfare bears no resemblance to this theatrical nonsense."

They watched as Nancy and Jenny performed their roles as "terrified villagers" with varying degrees of theatrical commitment. Nancy had embraced the drama wholeheartedly, clutching at Mr Cromwell's sleeve whilst pleading for protection in tones that would have done justice to an Italian opera. Jenny, meanwhile, appeared to be fighting back laughter as the baker attempted to demonstrate proper rifle handling and nearly shot himself in the foot.

"How are we supposed to reach the station without being seen?" Ellen asked, gesturing towards the open ground they'd need to cross. "Aldridge has positioned himself right in our path, with a clear view of the entire approach."

"The drainage ditch runs parallel to the lane," Diana observed. "If we stay low and time our movement with when that train pulls out of the station, then the noise would mask any sound we make—"

She stopped herself. These people weren't her responsibility, and their amateur theatrics weren't her concern.

"Or we could just walk across and let him capture us," Diana continued with deliberate indifference. "It's not as though any of this matters."

Ellen stared at her with her head cocked and her eyebrows raised.

Diana shrugged. "I read adventure novels."

Before Ellen could respond, a tremendous crash echoed across the village green. Aldridge, in his enthusiasm to demonstrate proper combat movement, had tried using the old Victorian bandstand as a vantage point. The ornate structure showed obvious signs where decorative ironwork had been removed for the war effort, leaving only the wooden framework and railings. Already weakened by years of woodworm infestation and winter neglect, the rotted timber couldn't support his weight. The remaining wooden railing gave way with a splintering crack, sending Aldridge tumbling through in a cascade of splinters and woodworm-riddled debris.

Mrs Campbell, who had been observing the proceedings from her front window, emerged with the sort of controlled fury that only a woman of a certain age could properly muster.

"Aldridge!" Her voice carried across the green with crystalline clarity. "What have you done to our bandstand?"

Aldridge scrambled to his feet, his uniform now decorated with rust stains and splinters of wood, and his face aflame.

"Mrs Campbell, I apologise, but this is an essential military exercise."

"Essential?" Mrs Campbell's tone could have frozen the Thames. "Where the Nazis have so far failed to destroy our beloved heritage, you managed to do it in one morning, all in the name of playing toy soldiers."

The other Home Guard members drifted closer, the exercise clearly over. Mr Hayes helped Aldridge to his feet with a hefty pull, whilst failing to fully hide his smile.

"Perhaps we might consider the exercise concluded," Mr Hayes suggested diplomatically. "The lads have had a good morning's training, and no real harm done."

But Mrs Campbell was far from finished. As the chairwoman of the Women's Voluntary Service, as well as being a long time Women's Institute committee member, she wielded considerable influence in village affairs. More importantly, she was the exact sort of woman who'd built the Empire through untold hours of volunteering and mucking in, and would undoubtedly survive its decline.

"This is precisely the sort of nonsense that gives you lot a bad name," she declared, surveying the wreckage of the bandstand with the air of a general inspecting a battlefield. "Playing soldiers whilst real soldiers fight and die in foreign fields."

Aldridge's flush deepened. "With respect, Mrs Campbell, civilian defence preparations are absolutely vital to—"

"Civilian defence?" Mrs Campbell's eyebrows rose to impressive heights. "Constable, when did you last complete a proper patrol of the district? When did you last check that everyone was obeying the blackout regulations? When did you last do anything more useful than polish your uniform buttons?"

Diana watched this exchange with genuine interest. She was enjoying the sight of Aldridge being dismantled by a woman half his size and twice his age. His authority, such as it was, dissolved like sugar in rain under Mrs Campbell's withering assessment.

"I carry out my duties in full accordance with regulations," Aldridge blustered.

Mrs Campbell smiled with the sort of sweetness that preceded an execution by firing squad.

"Do you indeed? Then perhaps you could explain why some people in Cheviot Hills seem to swan about with unlimited gasoline, or why certain individuals seem able to obtain rationed goods that the rest of us can only dream of?" she said.

The watching crowd fell silent, and Diana noticed several meaningful glances between the villagers. Looks that suggested Mrs Campbell's accusations weren't random.

"I'm sure I don't know what you're suggesting."

"I'm not suggesting anything, Constable." Mrs Campbell's voice carried across the green. "This village has been fortunate to avoid serious enemy action thus far. But if that changes, and I pray to God it doesn't, we'll need real leadership, not make-believe posturing."

Ellen nudged Diana's elbow. "Remind me never to cross that woman," she murmured.

Diana couldn't hold her laugh this time.

The exercise devolved into embarrassed mutterings and hasty equipment gathering. Aldridge attempted to restore some dignity by barking orders about proper kit maintenance and next week's training schedule, but his audience was already dispersing. Mrs Campbell fussed about the ruined side of the bandstand with the same efficiency she brought to organising charity bazaars, co-opting the slower Home Guard members to help her.

As Diana walked home alone down lanes devoid of any signage, she reflected on the morning. Looking at it without any bias, she could tell the other girls were trying to befriend her. But part of her kept telling herself that they weren't, that they simply didn't like her—that they found her awkward and standoffish, too serious, too different from their easy camaraderie. She'd always believed they merely tolerated her presence because they had to work alongside her, that their invitations were out of politeness rather than genuine warmth. Apart from Ellen, that is. She'd done the right thing in maintaining her distance. It was better that way. There was no way she was staying in this town, just like the first time round when she'd returned to London as soon as possible after the end of the war. There was no one here she needed to ever see again. With the exception of maybe Ellen. Maybe.

Chapter Nine

Diana woke with a gasp, her heart racing. For one disorienting moment, she thought she was back in her cottage on Burn Lane, dreaming about ferociously attacking Germans in Pickering Park with her walking stick, the Land Army girls at her side. A completely bonkers dream. Then the spartan decor of the room came into focus, and the bone-deep chill that no central heating system would ever permit settled around her shoulders like a familiar weight.

This was real. She was here. 1944.

She shivered and pulled the blankets tighter, reluctant to leave their meagre warmth. The hot water bottle had long since cooled and was now a dead weight against her feet. From downstairs came the homely sounds of breakfast preparation and the wireless, with Mrs Whitaker humming along.

A week had passed since the Home Guard training exercise, and Diana found herself settling into an unexpected rhythm. Jenny had definitely warmed to her since Diana had begun contributing to their conversations, even going so far as to encourage her to attend the Christmas dance—an invitation Diana had surprised herself by accepting.

Diana sat up, wincing as her bare feet touched the icy floorboards. The contrast between her youthful body's resilience and her elderly self's limitations remained startling.

The small bedroom revealed itself in the grey half-light of early morning that managed to seep around the edges of the heavy blackout curtains. Diana examined her surroundings, to remind herself who she'd once been when the world was her oyster.

The room was spartan but not without personality. A small bookshelf held a modest collection—Jane Austen, the Brontës, a dog-eared copy of *The Thirty-Nine Steps*. No sign of *Forever Amber*, the book she'd promised Ellen. A simple wooden cross hung on the wall above the bed, and a plain ceramic water jug and basin sat on the narrow dressing table. An old wooden glory box stood at the foot of the bed, its lid scarred with age and use. A colourful rag rug covered part of the wooden floor, adding a touch of warmth to the room.

"Diana! Your breakfast's getting cold!" Mrs Whitaker's voice carried up the stairs, interrupting her exploration.

"Coming!" she called back, hastily pulling on her clothes.

Downstairs, light filled the kitchen, with the blackout curtains pulled back to admit every possible ray of winter sunshine. Mrs Whitaker stood at the stove, stirring a pot of porridge.

"I was worried you might have frozen solid up there," she said by way of greeting. "I'd wager that was the coldest night we've had this winter."

"Sorry," Diana said, taking her seat at the table. "I was just worrying about what on earth I'm going to wear to the Christmas dance now that both Jenny and Ellen have invited me."

Mrs Whitaker ladled porridge into a bowl, smiling like the Cheshire Cat. "I'd heard a rumour that you'd decided to go." She set the bowl in front of Diana. "Oh, and please don't forget to deliver those patterns to Mrs Robbins. I can't bear the thought of that woman having another reason to criticise me."

Diana froze with her spoon halfway to her mouth. *Mrs Robbins? Nancy Robbins' mother?*

"The dress patterns," Mrs Whitaker continued, as if reading her mind. "Now, speaking of dresses..." She wiped her hands on her apron and disappeared into the sitting room, returning a moment later with something draped over her arm. "Mrs Hawk mentioned you might need something suitable for tomorrow night's dance."

She shook out the garment with slightly awkward movements.

It was a dress in deep forest green, the fabric good quality but clearly pre-war, with a fitted bodice and modest neckline.

"It belongs to Mrs Hawk's daughter. Well, it did before she married," Mrs Whitaker explained, her words coming in a rush. "She's expecting again, so she hasn't worn it in forever. Mrs Hawk thought it might suit you, though I'm afraid it's not very... well, it's not the latest fashion." She held it up uncertainly. "It will complement your colouring, at least."

Diana examined the dress. Whilst dated, it was the sort of dress a respectable young woman might wear to a church dance. Not elegant, but appropriate. And still better than the tweed skirt and mustard yellow blouse she'd borrowed from Mrs Whitaker's wardrobe last time.

"That's very kind of Mrs Hawk, and you," she said, accepting the dress, trying not to wrinkle her nose at the faint whiff of mothballs. "Thank you for thinking of me."

"I could take it in a bit if you like? It might be a bit loose on you," Mrs Whitaker said, staring at Diana's waist.

"I'm sure it will be fine as it is," Diana replied, trying to dampen down the growing regret for her initial enthusiasm about attending the dance.

"Of course, dear. I'm sure you'll... well, I hope you enjoy yourself."

Diana paused, studying Mrs Whitaker's wistful expression. "You're coming to the dance too, aren't you?"

Mrs Whitaker's hands stilled. "Oh no. These things are for young people. I'll be quite content here with my knitting and the wireless."

"But surely you'd enjoy the music? And seeing everyone?" Diana pressed, surprised by her own concern. In her previous life, she remembered being relieved to attend alone, free from the obligation of making conversation with her landlady. But only after the older woman had forced her into agreeing to attend.

"I haven't been to a dance in years," Mrs Whitaker said with a self-deprecating laugh. "Wouldn't know what to do with myself."

Diana stepped closer, genuine warmth creeping into her voice. "You could keep me company. I'd feel much more comfortable with a friendly face nearby."

Mrs Whitaker looked up, eyebrows raised. "You'd want me there?"

"Very much," Diana replied. The thought of Mrs Whitaker spending the evening alone whilst the village celebrated suddenly seemed unbearable.

"Besides, someone needs to make sure I don't disgrace myself," Diana said.

A slow smile spread across Mrs Whitaker's face. "Well, when you put it like that... I suppose I could dust off my dancing shoes. For your sake."

"Of course," Diana agreed, feeling an unexpected lightness in her chest. "Thank you. I'll be careful with the dress, and you can make sure I behave myself."

"See that you do," Mrs Whitaker replied, her eyes sparkling as she turned back towards the stove. "Now eat your porridge before it gets cold. And you'd best head over to Mrs Robbins straightaway with those patterns. She's been waiting all week, and you know how she gets."

Diana remembered. The memory surfaced of Nancy Robbins's mother—a formidable woman with sharp eyes and a sharper tongue, who ran the local Women's Institute with military precision and judged everyone against standards that would have made the King himself fall short.

"I'll go right after breakfast," Diana promised, dreading the encounter even as she spooned up her porridge. Nancy Robbins had been her friend once, before whatever had caused their decades-long feud. Perhaps this second chance would allow her to avoid that pitfall as well. But first, she had to face Nancy's mother and explain why she'd forgotten to deliver the patterns. From memory, she'd rather face Hitler himself.

Mrs Whitaker folded back the newspaper with a sharp snap as she scanned the morning's headlines over her cup of tea. She began reading aloud, as was her custom with anything she found particularly noteworthy.

"Listen to this," she said. "It's from the Secretary of State for War himself—'All Home Guard units are hereby required to return issued weapons and equipment to designated collection points. This includes rifles, ammunition, and any training ordnance still in unit possession.'" She looked up over her spectacles. "About time too, if you ask me. Old men playing at soldiers. Sometimes, I think half the men in our Home Guard are happy that we're at war."

Diana nodded in agreement as she finished her breakfast. Through the years, she'd known a number of men who thrived on the drama of conflict, even when their part in it was largely imaginary.

"Can't see PC Aldridge handing over his toys," Mrs Whitaker added with a knowing look. "He rather enjoys his personal arsenal."

Later, as Diana shrugged into her coat, her hand brushed against her pocket, and she felt the smooth leather of Ellen's gloves. She'd completely forgotten to return them. Diana withdrew the gloves, examining them in the morning light.

Exquisite soft kid leather, a deep burgundy colour, with tiny pearl buttons. Silk lined and embroidered on the inner cuff in gold thread were the initials "E.W." These weren't just expensive; they were the kind of luxury item that had all but vanished from Britain during wartime.

Diana had remembered more about Ellen now, the fragments of her history coming together like pieces of a jigsaw puzzle. Unlike most Americans who'd fled Europe when war broke out, Ellen had been studying archaeology at Cambridge when Hitler invaded Poland. Most unusually, she'd elected not to return home, wanting to finish her degree before volunteering for the Land Army when the university scaled back operations for the war effort.

Being an American, they'd billeted her with the Hollisters, with Mr Hollister being American himself, although his wife was English.

Diana slipped the gloves back into her pocket. She would return them today, along with an apology for being unable to find her copy of *Forever Amber*. Where on earth had she left it? She couldn't remember ever reading it at any stage during her life, let alone during the war.

"Might I borrow your bicycle, Mrs Whitaker?" Diana asked, lifting the satchel of patterns from the polished brass hook by the door. "I'll deliver these before I head to the farm. I'd rather not delay Mrs Robbins any longer than I already have."

Mrs Whitaker nodded. "A wise decision. Mind the front brake though. Remember it catches if you pull too hard."

The bicycle was an old Raleigh roadster, its once-black paint worn to a dull, weathered grey. The leather saddle, cracked and stiff from years of rain and sun, creaked as Diana pressed a tentative hand against it. Strips of cloth were wrapped around the handlebars in place of the original rubber grips, which had long since perished.

At least the tyres held air.

A small miracle in these days of rubber shortages—and when she spun the pedals, the chain moved with a reassuring smoothness.

Christ! How long had it been since she'd last ridden a bicycle?

Diana wheeled the bike out of the shed and mounted it with trepidation. Fortunately, her body remembered the action, even if her mind had forgotten. The breeze bit at her cheeks as she pedalled down the lane, but the exercise soon warmed her. Diana enjoyed the simple physical pleasure of cycling—the rhythm of her legs, the rush of air, the sense of freedom that came with speed. Her older self had given up cycling decades ago, after a nasty fall in Prague had left her with a fractured wrist and three broken ribs.

The Robbins house stood on Church Lane, a substantial Victorian villa that had been the local doctor's residence. Its bay windows and ornate gables had once impressed her. Now, with the perspective of having lived in a dozen countries and seen everything from Arabian palaces to Swiss chalets, she found it merely handsome in a solid, country seat sort of way.

Diana leaned the bicycle against the low garden wall and straightened her coat before approaching the front door. She took a deep breath, steeling herself for what was to come. Her hand had barely touched the brass knocker when the door swung open.

"Diana Penn! You certainly took your time getting here."

Mrs Robbins stood in the doorway, a vision in tweed and pearls despite the early hour. Her silver hair was arranged in perfect waves, and her face, though lined, was carefully powdered. Even in the midst of war, with rationing and shortages affecting everyone, Agatha Robbins maintained standards.

"I'm so sorry, Mrs Robbins," Diana began, extracting the patterns from her pocket. "I was meant to bring these yesterday, but—"

"The entire Christmas programme may be delayed because of your carelessness," Mrs Robbins cut in, taking the patterns with a disapproving sniff. "Nancy's in the drawing room."

Diana followed Mrs Robbins through the hallway, noting how the house still smelled of beeswax polish and lavender. Some things remained constant despite the war. A coal fire that burned more generously than any Diana had seen since her return heated the drawing room.

The Robbins family had connections to a local coal merchant—another detail that surfaced from the depths of her memory.

Nancy sat at the piano, her fingers dancing over the keys as she practiced what sounded like a Christmas carol. She looked up as they entered, her face breaking into a smile that Diana found startlingly genuine. This wasn't the Nancy Robbins who crossed the street to avoid speaking to her. This was a girl of eighteen, pretty, with fair hair curled into fashionable victory rolls and blue eyes that hadn't yet learned to narrow with suspicion whenever Diana approached.

"Finally!" Nancy stood, smoothing down her skirt. "Mother's been beside herself. We need those patterns for the Sunday school children's costumes."

"I'm sorry," Diana said, watching as Mrs Robbins handed the patterns to her daughter. "It slipped my mind."

Nancy's expression softened. "Well, you're here now. That's what matters." She glanced at her mother. "Mother, may I show Diana what we've done for the Christmas programme? Perhaps she could help with the angel costumes."

Mrs Robbins pursed her lips. "I suppose so. But don't dawdle. Those patterns need to be cut today if we're to have everything ready by Christmas Eve."

Once her mother had left the room, Nancy's formal posture relaxed. "Ignore Mother. She's been impossible since they announced more sugar rationing." She perched on the piano stool, gesturing for Diana to take the armchair nearby. "So I hear you are going to the dance tomorrow? Ellen says you're saving her a dance."

Diana nodded, speechless at the casual friendliness of this Nancy. She was so different from the woman who would one day become her nemesis. What had happened between them? She couldn't recall the specifics, only the aftermath: decades of cold shoulders, snide remarks, and cultivated animosity.

"Mrs Whitaker lent me a dress," Diana said, settling into the armchair. "It belongs to Mrs Hawk's daughter."

Nancy blinked, her eyes wide. "I'm sure it's nice."

And there it was. A flicker of the woman Diana remembered. On the surface, Nancy's words were perfectly polite.

But Diana could feel the judgement simmering underneath. She shook her head, trying to concentrate on the 1944 version of Nancy Robbins in front of her.

"I'm wearing a new dress my aunt sent from London," Nancy added, smoothing her hair with careful pride. "She has friends in the West End who know how to find things, even with the rationing." She then leaned in slightly, lowering her voice. "Did you hear about the plane crash near Wooler? Father says it wasn't one of ours."

Diana leaned forward, alert. "What do you mean, not one of ours?"

"He says the RAF is being very hush-hush about it all." Nancy's eyes gleamed with the excitement of sharing forbidden knowledge. "And there's a new squadron at the airfield—not regular RAF, Father thinks. Special operations of some kind. One of them came into the shop yesterday, wanting some ink."

The shop. Nancy's father ran the village's only stationers and booksellers. Another piece of the puzzle clicked into place.

"Did you catch his name?" Diana asked, keeping her voice casual. "The airman, I mean."

Nancy smiled, her eyes a million miles away. "He was ever so handsome. Dark hair, quite tall. Crawford, I think his name was. Though Mother doesn't approve of us girls getting too friendly with the airmen," Nancy added quickly, her cheeks flushing. "She says they're here today, gone tomorrow. And that most of them only want one thing. 'Why buy the cow when you can get the milk for free?'" The words came out in a rush, as if rehearsed. Diana noted the defensive tone. Was Nancy secretly stepping out with someone her mother wouldn't approve of? Flight Lieutenant Jim Crawford?

"Nancy! The patterns!" Mrs Robbins's voice carried from somewhere else in the house.

Nancy sighed dramatically. "Coming, Mother!" She stood, gathering the patterns. "Are you staying? You could help us cut the fabric."

Diana shook her head, also rising. "I can't today. I'm expected at the farm."

Nancy looked disappointed. "Well, I'll see you at the dance, then," she said, smoothing her skirt. "Mother's bringing her elderflower cordial and a bottle of her ginger wine. It won first prize at the Women's Institute competition last summer."

Chapter Ten

Diana woke to the sound of a robin singing outside her window, its cheerful notes a stark contrast to the leaden sky that promised snow before nightfall. Saturday, the 23rd of December. The day of the Christmas dance, and two days before Mr Hayes would receive the telegram that would shatter his world.

She lay still for a moment, savouring the unexpected luxury of a morning without farm work. Mrs Whitaker had insisted she take the day off to prepare for the dance—"You'll want to wash your hair, and it'll never dry in time if you're outside all day." Diana suspected it had more to do with Mrs Whitaker wanting help with the jam tarts she'd volunteered to bake for the refreshment table, but she wasn't about to argue.

The floorboards were icy beneath her feet as she rose and dressed quickly in her everyday clothes. Woollen stockings, a heavy skirt, and a jumper darned at the elbows. Later would be time enough for the sensible green dress hanging on the back of her door.

Downstairs, Mrs Whitaker was already elbow-deep in pastry dough, her normally neat kitchen a battlefield of flour, sticky smears of jam, and the faint, sugary scent of warmed syrup.

"There you are," she said, not looking up from her work. "The range needs stoking, and we're nearly out of kindling. There's a pile of wood behind the shed that needs chopping."

Diana nodded, taking up the poker to stir the dying embers in the kitchen range before adding more coal. The familiar domestic routine felt strangely comforting and so different from her solitary existence in the cottage on Burn Lane, where she'd spent her days watching the world through her bay window, drinking too much tea and rereading old case files she'd smuggled out of the archives.

With the fire blazing, she stepped outside to deal with the kindling. The air was sharp with frost, carrying the clean scent of pine from the hills and the distant smoke of coal fires. Diana found the axe where it always rested, its handle smooth with age and use. Her muscles remembered the motion—feet planted, back straight, the satisfying thwack as the blade bit into wood. Soon she had a respectable pile of kindling, enough to see them through Christmas at least.

As Diana worked, her mind catalogued the events to come. The dance tonight, where virtually everyone in Cheviot Hills would gather at the village hall. The RAF men from the local airfield would be there in force, possibly also the mysterious Flight Lieutenant Crawford. Ellen would be wearing something elegant from home, no doubt. As well as Nancy Robbins and her mother, Mr Hayes, Jenny Jenkins. Faces from a past that was now, impossibly, her present.

"You'll catch your death out here without a proper coat," Mrs Whitaker called from the kitchen door, breaking into Diana's thoughts. "Come in and have some tea before you turn into an icicle."

Diana gathered an armful of kindling and followed Mrs Whitaker inside, grateful for the warmth of the kitchen. A pot of tea was already brewing on the table, and the sweet, comforting scent of jam and pastry filled the air.

"You've been quiet since yesterday," Mrs Whitaker observed, pouring tea into two chipped cups. "Something on your mind?"

Diana hesitated. How could she possibly explain what was truly occupying her thoughts? That she was living a second life, armed with knowledge of events yet to unfold? That she was trying to prevent a disappearance, a suicide, perhaps even uncover a spy in their midst?

"Just thinking about the dance," she said instead.

Mrs Whitaker nodded, adding a generous spoonful of sugar to her tea from her secret stash, hoarded for special occasions.

"It's the first dance for a while for you, isn't it? Not much appetite for frivolity after losing your mother?"

Diana nodded, surprised that Mrs Whitaker had recognised the significance. She had indeed avoided dances and celebrations after her mother's death, finding the contrast between others' joy and her own grief too stark to bear. Until now, she hadn't realised that Mrs Whitaker had noticed, had understood.

"You're allowed to enjoy yourself, you know," Mrs Whitaker continued, rolling out more pastry with firm, economical strokes. "Living doesn't dishonour the dead."

Diana swallowed against the tightness in her throat. "I know."

"Good." Mrs Whitaker cut neat circles from the pastry. "Now, once you've finished your tea, I need these tins greased, and then you can start on the syrup tart. The village hall needs to see that the Willow Farm women know their business."

The morning passed in a haze of domestic industry. Diana greased tins, spooned jam, rolled scraps of pastry, and pressed crimped edges under Mrs Whitaker's expert direction. By midday, the kitchen table was covered with cooling tarts and syrupy treats, their golden crusts promising sweetness despite wartime shortages.

After a simple lunch of bread and cheese, Diana filled the copper bath with water heated on the range—another luxury saved for special occasions. She washed her hair with the precious sliver of lavender soap Mrs Whitaker had been saving, then sat by the fire to let it dry, reading a copy of Ngaio Marsh's *Death and the Dancing Footman* while Mrs Whitaker continued her seemingly endless knitting.

"I'm thinking of baking a spiced apple cake," Mrs Whitaker said suddenly, her needles never pausing. "For tomorrow."

Diana looked up from her book. Most people had been saving ingredients for weeks, if not months, to make anything remotely special for Christmas. A homemade cake, simple but rich with spice, spoke of an optimism that caught her by surprise.

"Would you like some help?" she offered.

Mrs Whitaker nodded, a smile filling her face. "I would. Been setting things aside for months—a spoonful of sugar here, a handful of dried apple there." She paused, then added quietly, "Just in case Trevor makes it home..."

The hope in her voice was almost unbearable. Diana knew Mrs Whitaker's son wouldn't return—not this Christmas, not ever. But she couldn't bring herself to extinguish that fragile hope. Perhaps some foreknowledge was better left unshared.

"I'm sure he'd love that," Diana said instead, her voice gentle.

As the afternoon faded into early evening, Diana retreated upstairs to prepare for the dance. She laid out her undergarments—the plain white cotton that was all that was available these days—then carefully removed Mrs Hawk's daughter's dress from its hanger.

The forest green fabric was in good condition despite its age, the colour rich and deep in the lamplight. Diana slipped it over her head, adjusting the fitted bodice and modest neckline. The dress was slightly loose on her frame, as Mrs Whitaker had predicted, but it hung well enough. While it wasn't the height of fashion, the green did complement her colouring, bringing out the warmth in her eyes and lending her pale skin a healthy glow.

She smoothed the skirt, noting how the fabric fell in gentle folds rather than the dramatic swirl of more fashionable cuts. It was exactly the sort of dress a respectable young woman would wear to a church dance— appropriate, modest, and entirely unremarkable. Which, Diana reflected as she pinned her hair into a simple arrangement, was probably for the best given what she was experiencing.

Her hair, dried into soft waves, was pinned back on one side with a tortoiseshell clip lent by Mrs Whitaker. A touch of lipstick, and she was ready.

Mrs Whitaker was waiting at the foot of the stairs, already dressed in her best blue suit with a cameo brooch at her throat. She stopped mid-sentence when Diana appeared, her eyes widening.

"The colour does suit you beautifully. Mrs Hawk was quite right about that."

Diana felt a flush rise to her cheeks.

"You look perfectly lovely," Mrs Whitaker continued. "And it fits you well enough, despite being a touch loose. Mrs Hawk will be pleased to know it's being put to good use," she said, bustling about, collecting her handbag and gloves. "Mr Richards is coming round with his cart to take us to the hall. Says he'll pick up the pies as well, save us carrying them in this cold."

The wait for Mr Richards gave Diana time to examine her reflection in the small mirror by the door. The young woman who looked back at her was bright-eyed, clear-skinned, and hopeful in a way that decades of intelligence work had stripped from her. Would anyone at the dance recognise the woman she would become? Or was that Diana gone forever, replaced by this new version with a chance to rewrite her history?

The rattle of wheels on the lane announced Mr Richards' arrival. Soon they were settled in the back of his cart alongside the carefully packed pies, a horse blanket spread across their knees against the biting cold. The journey to the village hall was short but bone-chilling, the winter air sharp enough to steal breath.

After opening the door, the hall revealed itself in a blaze of light. Bunting hung from the rafters, and sprigs of holly decorated every available surface. A small band was setting up at one end, and tables laden with refreshments lined the other.

Inside, the crush of bodies and the buzz of conversation hit Diana like a physical force. The hall was filled to capacity, a sea of familiar faces that she simultaneously knew and didn't know. Men from the Home Guard stood in groups. The land girls clustered near the punch bowl, their everyday uniforms replaced with whatever finery they could muster. And there, by the band, a contingent of RAF men in their blue uniforms, drawing admiring glances from every young woman in the room.

Diana scanned the crowd, trying to place each face, to remember who they were now and who they would become. That might be Mr Peterson—she had a vague memory of him dying young, maybe of a heart attack. The woman in the floral headscarf looked familiar too, mostly because Diana remembered that her son was the only boy from Cheviot Hills held in a Japanese POW camp. And the good-looking lad with the straggly moustache was Billy Thomas. Funny that his name came back to her straight away. She'd never known him personally, but he'd gone on to be the MP for the area, and she'd seen him on the news in later years—still with the same limp moustache.

So many lives, so many stories, all intersecting in this one moment in time. Diana felt dizzy with the weight of it all.

"Diana!" Ellen's voice cut through the noise.

And suddenly the American was there, resplendent in a deep red dress that complemented her auburn hair. "You look absolutely stunning! That colour is perfect for you."

"So do you," Diana said, meaning it. Ellen was beautiful tonight, her vitality drawing eyes from across the room.

"I've been dying to introduce you properly to someone," Ellen said, taking Diana's arm. "Jim—Flight Lieutenant Crawford. Jenny said you already met him at Hayes Farm? He's absolutely fascinating. Did you know he speaks four languages? And he's been all over Europe before the war. Just wait until you talk with him properly."

Diana allowed herself to be pulled through the crowd, her heart pounding. This was her chance to get closer to the mysterious airman.

Crawford turned as they approached, and Diana felt a jolt of recognition so strong it nearly stopped her in her tracks.

"Flight Lieutenant Crawford," Ellen said, her American accent more pronounced in her excitement, "you remember my dear friend Diana Penn, don't you? Diana, Jim tells me you two had a brief encounter at the farm."

Crawford smiled, extending his hand. "Miss Penn, it's a pleasure to see you again. And in more salubrious circumstances!"

As Diana took his hand, a fragment of memory surfaced—a café in Vienna, 1962, a man across the table raising a glass of wine in a silent toast. Same eyes, and the same measured smile. Impossible. And yet, here he was.

"I have to admit that I feel rather more at home in the cow shed than here," Diana said, studying his face. "I feel as though we've met somewhere before, Flight Lieutenant. Perhaps in London?"

His smile didn't falter, but something flickered in those familiar eyes before he answered.

"I have one of those faces, Miss Penn. Very plain and highly ordinary. You'd be amazed at how many people think they've met me before. Now, please, you must call me Jim."

Chapter Eleven

Diana climbed the narrow staircase at Willow Farm, her feet aching gloriously with every step. The familiar creak of the third tread seemed to scold her for returning well past midnight, though Mrs Whitaker, still flushed with punch and Christmas spirit, had uttered not a word of reproach.

In her small bedroom, Diana eased off her shoes and sank onto the edge of her bed. The green satin dress whispered against her skin as she reached back to unfasten it, fabric cool to the touch, despite the hours of warmth from her body and the crowded village hall.

A peculiar giggle escaped her lips, so girlish and unfamiliar that it startled her. When had Diana Penn ever giggled? Certainly not during the Cold War years in Berlin, nor during tense exchanges in Cairo back in '73. Perhaps not since her mother had died in the Blitz—or perhaps not since this very night, the first time around?

The dress slid from her shoulders, and she hung it on the back of the door before pulling on her flannel nightgown. Sixty years of careful habits made her fold her stockings precisely, despite the lateness of the hour and the pleasant fog of fatigue clouding her thoughts.

Diana slipped between the sheets and burrowed beneath the patchwork quilt, savouring the memory of the evening as it played behind her closed eyelids.

Mrs Whitaker had surprised everyone by agreeing to a foxtrot with Mr Richards, her face transformed by a smile that erased years of worry. For those precious minutes, she wasn't the woman anxiously awaiting news of her missing son; she was simply Enid, enjoying a Christmas dance.

Ellen had turned heads all evening in her crimson dress, her American confidence drawing attention from every officer in the room. Yet whenever Diana caught her eye, Ellen would wink conspiratorially, as if they shared some delicious secret. Several times, she'd darted over to whisper amusing observations about the various dancers—mostly unflattering, occasionally scandalous.

"Did you see Mrs Robbins's face when Reverend Taylor asked her to dance?" Ellen had whispered behind her punch cup. "Like she'd bitten into a lemon whilst trying to smile for a photograph!"

Jenny had been in her element, flitting from one RAF officer to another with inexhaustible energy. Her laugh, bright and uncomplicated, had rung out above the music as she dragged reluctant partners onto the floor or charmed extra servings of punch from the watchful Mrs Robbins.

And then there was Flight Lieutenant Crawford—Jim—with his perfect dance-floor manners and his eyes that seemed to see straight through her careful facade.

"You're not quite what you seem, Miss Penn," he'd said as they waltzed to a slightly uneven rendition of *The Blue Danube*.

"Neither are you, Flight Lieutenant," she'd countered, surprised by her own boldness.

His smile had deepened, revealing a dimple in his left cheek. "Perhaps that's why we get along so well?"

Diana hugged her knees to her chest beneath the blankets, trying to reconcile the contradictions of the evening. She'd intended to remain in the shadows, a wallflower by choice, as she had so often been during her first life. A habit that had served her well throughout her intelligence career. Instead, she'd found herself more on the dance floor than off it, drawn into the celebration by some combination of Jenny's infectious joy and Jim's enigmatic presence.

The Royal Doulton stoneware hot water bottle shifted as she stretched her legs, reminding her of the winter chill beyond her cocoon of blankets. Diana rolled onto her side, her mind drifting back to Crawford. There was something about the way he held himself.

Something about the precise intonation of his vowels, the careful way he scanned a room—that triggered her professional instincts. If she'd met him during her MI6 days, she would have marked him as someone of interest: too composed, too observant. Not to mention the unsettling sense that she could have sworn she'd met him in Vienna during one of the countless intelligence operations that had consumed her adult life.

But how could that be possible? Unless—

Diana sat bolt upright in bed.

Unless he was like her? Unless he, too, was living a second chance at life? She knew she'd never met him in Cheviot Hills in her first life. His appearance here was entirely new.

The thought was preposterous. And yet, hadn't her very presence here defied all rational explanation? If she could find herself transported through time at the moment of her death, why couldn't someone else?

"Don't be ridiculous," she whispered to the darkened room. "You've no evidence for such a theory."

Even so, she couldn't dismiss the possibility entirely. The way Crawford had looked at her when she'd mentioned the feeling they'd met before suggested more than coincidence.

Diana lay back down, pulling the blankets to her chin. Tomorrow would bring Christmas Eve, and with it, the telegram that would shatter Mr Hayes's world. She had to focus on what she could change, on the tragedies she might prevent. Ellen's disappearance in February, Mr Hayes's suicide. These were concrete events she could influence.

Flight Lieutenant Jim Crawford and his secrets would have to wait.

As she drifted off to sleep, snow tapping against her window, Diana wondered about the version of this night from her first life. Had she danced then? Laughed? Had she felt, even briefly, that the war and its sorrows might someday end?

She couldn't remember. That Diana—the young woman untouched by decades of secrecy and service—felt increasingly like a stranger, a ghost whose footsteps she felt obliged to follow. Would it be wrong to forge an alternative path?

Her last conscious thought before sleep claimed her was that perhaps both versions of herself deserved a night of dancing, of forgetting the weight of knowledge and responsibility, even if just for a few precious hours.

In her dreams, Diana danced through a snow-covered Vienna, her partners changing with each turn, until finally she found herself dancing with Flight Lieutenant Crawford, whose eyes never left hers and whose embrace spoke of a connection she'd never experienced.

Diana woke to Mrs Whitaker's humming drifting up from the kitchen below. The melody was unusually buoyant this morning, almost celebratory, which made Diana wonder what had put her landlady in such particularly high spirits.

Her legs ached pleasantly as she swung them over the side of the bed—a souvenir from countless dances. Dressing quickly against the morning chill, she made her way downstairs, following the enticing aroma of toast and tea.

Mrs Whitaker stood at the stove, her back to the door, still humming as she stirred something in a small pot. Without the usual weight of worry on her shoulders, she looked years younger.

"You're in fine spirits this morning," Diana said, settling at the kitchen table.

Mrs Whitaker turned, a smile lighting her face in a way Diana couldn't remember seeing before. "Why shouldn't I be? It's nearly Christmas, the snow's cleared, and for once I haven't had to listen to Mrs Robbins boasting about her collection of pre-war stockings." She set a steaming cup of tea in front of Diana. "We showed them all how Willow Farm women can dance, didn't we?"

Diana smiled, wrapping her hands around the warm cup. "I wasn't sure Mr Richards would ever let you go. He seemed quite smitten."

A faint blush coloured Mrs Whitaker's cheeks. "Don't be daft. Harold Richards is just lonely since his Margaret passed, that's all." She busied herself with the porridge. "Though I will say I haven't enjoyed myself so much in years. I'm glad you persuaded me to go."

Diana faltered, her teacup halfway to her lips. "Persuaded you?"

"Of course." Mrs Whitaker spooned porridge into bowls. "I wasn't going to attend, not with Trevor still missing. It felt wrong celebrating when he..." She trailed off, the shadow of worry briefly returning before she squared her shoulders. "But you were right. Life must go on."

"And Trevor wouldn't want me sitting alone in the dark. Besides, I need to have something to talk with him about when he gets back. Something other than carrots and cows."

Diana stared into her tea, a peculiar hollowness opening in her chest. In her first life, Mrs Whitaker hadn't attended the dance. She'd stayed home alone with her knitting and her worries, while Diana had gone with Ellen and spent the evening standing awkwardly against the wall, watching others celebrate. How had she missed the sadness in the older woman's eyes? How had her younger, more self-absorbed self not thought to invite Mrs Whitaker along?

"I'm glad you came," Diana said, meaning it more than she could express.

Mrs Whitaker nodded, her expression softening. "Well, someone had to keep an eye on you girls. The way that Flight Lieutenant was looking at you. Like he wanted to eat you up." She shook her head, but her eyes twinkled. "Handsome fellow, though. I'll give him that."

After breakfast, Diana bundled up against the December chill and set off for Hayes Farm. The muddy lanes glistened with melting frost, and her boots left clear impressions in the soft earth. As she walked, she considered the ripples of her changed actions. A simple invitation to Mrs Whitaker had altered the woman's Christmas experience entirely. What else might she change, simply by being a bit more aware, a bit more considerate than she'd been the first time around?

The farmyard was unusually quiet as Diana approached. No chickens scratching in the yard, no Jess bounding up to greet her. The stillness made her uneasy until she heard laughter coming from the kitchen—a sound so rare at Hayes Farm it stopped her in her tracks.

She followed the sound, knocking on the kitchen door before entering. The warmth hit her, along with the smell of strong tea and wood smoke. Jenny sat at the scrubbed wooden table, her cheeks still flushed with memories of the previous night's excitement. Around her, coils of rope lay in organised piles, her nimble fingers splicing and braiding frayed sections.

Mr Hayes stood by the stove, stoking the fire, his usually stern face softened with what might almost have been a smile.

"There she is!" Jenny exclaimed. "Our belle of the ball! I was just telling Mr Hayes how you had every officer in the place asking for a dance."

Diana hung her coat on the hook, embarrassed by the attention. "Hardly. That was you, as I recall. I couldn't keep track of your partners."

Jenny laughed, her fingers never pausing in their work with the rope. "Oh, I made the rounds, all right. But you and that Flight Lieutenant—very cosy, that looked."

Mr Hayes grunted, though without his usual disapproval. "Tea's hot," he said by way of greeting, gesturing to the pot on the table.

Diana poured herself a cup, grateful for its warmth. "What's all this?" she asked, nodding to the piles of rope.

"Winter work," Mr Hayes explained. "Can't do much in the fields now, so might as well get the gear ready for spring." He picked up a length of frayed rope. "Jenny here's got a knack for splicing. Better than some sailors I've known."

Jenny preened at the rare compliment. "My dad taught me. He was on the fishing boats before the war." She leaned towards Diana. "But enough about rope. Did you see Ellen's dress last night? Where on earth did she get something like that in wartime?"

"American," Mr Hayes muttered, as if that explained everything.

"It was more elegant than even what Mrs Campbell was wearing," Jenny continued, "and everyone knows the mayor's wife has a closet full of clothes from Paris from before the war."

"So they say," Diana agreed, remembering the woman's carefully preserved finery. In 1944, clothes that had been fashionable pre war, were now precious treasures, maintained and altered to last through years of clothing rationing.

"And she had the nerve to look down her nose at Ellen's dress!" Jenny shook her head, her hands twisting a complicated knot into the rope. "As if it wasn't the most beautiful thing in the room. Pure jealousy, that's what Mrs Robbins said."

Diana sipped her tea, enjoying the simple camaraderie of the kitchen. This, too, differed from her first life. She'd spent the morning after the dance nursing her irrational jealousy of the attention Ellen and Jenny had garnered from the officers. She'd stewed alone in her room, counting the dances no one asked her to join, tallying compliments she hadn't received. Now, somehow, she found herself included in this domestic scene, sharing gossip and warmth instead of bitter envy.

"The Americans have everything, don't they?" Jenny said.

Oblivious to Diana's thoughts, she continued, "Ellen says at home they hardly notice the rationing. Can you imagine? Stockings whenever you want them, and chocolate, and lipstick!" She sighed. "Makes you wonder why she stayed here at all, with the Hollisters treating her so poorly."

Mr Hayes frowned. "What's that about the Hollisters?"

Jenny's eyes widened as she realised she'd spoken too freely. "Oh, nothing really. Just that Mrs Hollister works her rather hard, and Mr Hollister..." She trailed off, suddenly finding the rope interesting.

"Mr Hollister, what?" Mr Hayes pressed, his voice sharpening.

Diana intervened, recognising the dangerous territory. "Mr Hollister can be rather demanding, I believe. Farm work isn't exactly an archaeological dig at Cambridge."

Mr Hayes's frown deepened, but he let the subject drop, turning back to the stove. "Best get that rope finished before lunch, Jenny. Got some different work for you both this afternoon."

Jenny rolled her eyes at Diana when Mr Hayes turned around, but her fingers flew faster over the rope. Years from now, such skills would be replaced by mass-produced synthetic cordage that rarely needed repair.

Despite the pleasant conversation, Diana couldn't help glancing anxiously out the window every few minutes, watching for any sign of Mr Fleming's bicycle. Was today the day? She tried to recall the precise timing—was it Christmas Eve or Christmas Day itself when the telegram about Arthur Hayes arrived? The details blurred after so many decades, but the dread was crystal clear.

As she finished her tea, she caught Mr Hayes looking at a small framed photograph on the shelf—his son Arthur in uniform, smiling with the innocent confidence of youth. How could she possibly prepare this man for what was coming?

Flight Lieutenant Crawford and his mysteries would need to wait. Right now, there was only this kitchen, this moment, and the crushing knowledge of grief that hung suspended in time, waiting to descend like the blade of a guillotine.

Chapter Twelve

Christmas Eve day stretched before them with deceptive tranquillity. Frost glittered on the bare branches of the apple trees that dotted Hayes Farm, and a thin mist hung over the distant hills, slowly burning away as the weak winter sun climbed higher.

After leaving the warmth of the kitchen, Diana picked her way across the frozen farmyard, a wooden bucket swinging from her gloved hand. Inside was a steaming mixture of kitchen scraps, vegetable peelings, and yesterday's porridge—a precious offering for the pigs that made up the entire Hayes Farm Pig Club's current holdings. The club, a modest affair with only five members from neighbouring farms, and fully registered with the Small Pig Keeper's Council, allowed them to keep swine legally despite rationing restrictions. Every Friday, Diana dutifully collected food scraps from the village for the pigs to turn into valuable protein.

Mr Hayes maintained meticulous records of the pigs' weight gain in a ledger kept on the kitchen shelf, ready for inspection by the Ministry of Food. The ledger, however, only reported three of their five pigs. The other two—including the massive sow currently eyeing her from the pen— were their insurance against the hunger that gnawed at the edges of the wartime winter. A small act of rebellion against a system that demanded half of everything they produced.

"Muck the pen while you're at it," Mr Hayes called from where he stood by the barn, his breath forming clouds in the frigid air. He'd also left the cosy kitchen to repair the broken handle of a hay rake, his weathered hands working gloveless despite the cold, binding the splintered wood with twine and strips of leather.

Diana's gaze drifted towards the lane. The pigs' enclosure lay behind the henhouse, a ramshackle affair of wooden slats and corrugated iron, deliberately positioned to be invisible from the main road. Inside, the swine—massive creatures with surprisingly intelligent eyes—shuffled eagerly at her approach, their snuffling growing more insistent as they smelt the bucket's contents.

"Patience," Diana murmured, stepping carefully through the gate. The ground beneath her boots was a churned mixture of mud, straw, and manure, frozen into treacherous ridges that threatened to upend her with every step.

She tipped the bucket into their feeding trough, watching as they shouldered one another aside, snorting and jostling for position. There was something comforting in their single-minded focus, their complete immersion in the present moment with no thought for what came before or after. Did pigs ever get the chance of reincarnation? She laughed at the bizarre thought.

As she turned to fetch the shovel propped against the fence, Diana caught the familiar sound of bicycle wheels on gravel. The steady click-click-click of the postman's approach fixed her in place, her fingers tightening on the bucket handle, willing time to stand still.

Mr Fleming appeared at the end of the lane, his bicycle wobbling as he navigated the rutted path, his leather satchel bulging with Christmas cards and letters. But it was his face that sent ice through Diana's veins, and the grave set of his mouth as he scanned the farmyard for Mr Hayes.

She knew that look. Had seen it countless times during her career. The bearer of bad news, searching for his target.

Time seemed to slow as Mr Fleming dismounted, propping his bicycle against the stone wall. He reached into his satchel and withdrew not a letter, but the distinctive buff-coloured paper of an official telegram that had brought dread to countless homes throughout the war.

Diana abandoned the bucket, her feet carrying her across the yard without conscious thought.

Mr Hayes had noticed the postman now. He straightened from his work, the broken rake forgotten in his hands. For a heartbeat, he resembled a statue—a man carved from granite, immovable and eternal.

Then Mr Fleming removed his cap, holding it against his chest as he approached.

Diana saw understanding dawn in Mr Hayes's eyes. She saw the moment when hope collapsed into certainty, when the last fragile threads of "missing" shattered against the reality of "killed in action."

The rake handle clattered to the ground, with Mr Hayes following, his knees giving way as if some essential part of him had simply ceased to function.

"No," he said, the word more breath than sound. "No."

Diana reached him just as Mr Fleming extended the telegram, his own face a picture of solemn pity.

"I'm sorry, Mr Hayes," Fleming said, his voice pitched low. "Truly sorry."

Diana crouched beside the farmer, her hand on his shoulder. She felt him trembling beneath the worn tweed of his jacket. Fine shudders that had nothing to do with the December chill.

Mr Hayes stared at the envelope, making no move to take it. His face had aged a decade in seconds, with new lines appearing around his mouth and across his forehead. "Arthur," he whispered, his son's name a prayer and a plea in equal measure.

Diana took the telegram from Mr Fleming's outstretched hand. "Thank you," she whispered. "I'll see to it."

The postman nodded, relief flashing across his features. No one envied his duty as the bearer of such tidings. He retreated to his bicycle, wheels clicking more softly now, as if they too understood the need for solemnity.

Somewhere in the distance, a crow called, its harsh cry cutting through the silence. The pigs continued their contented snuffling, oblivious to the human drama unfolding beyond their pen. And inside the farmhouse, the clock ticked steadily onward, marking time as it always had and as it always would.

But for Mr Hayes, Diana knew, time had just shattered into before and after. Everything that came next would be measured against this defining moment.

She didn't open the telegram. There was no need. The contents would be the same as they had been in her first life—couched in formal language that did nothing to soften the blow, full of phrases like "regret to inform" and "killed in action" and "service to King and country."

Instead, she stayed beside Mr Hayes, her hand steady on his shoulder as his breathing became ragged, then caught on a sound that might have been the beginning of a sob.

"I knew," he said, so quietly that Diana almost missed it. "When I woke up this morning, I knew."

A father's intuition? Or the resigned expectation that had shadowed so many families throughout this endless war?

"I'm so sorry," Diana said, the words painfully inadequate.

Mr Hayes looked up at her, his eyes red-rimmed but dry. "Why him?"

The question caught her off guard. Diana could have lied, could have offered up some empty words about the futility of war. But looking into his ravaged face, she had no words.

She sighed. "I don't know."

Mr Hayes nodded once, as if her honesty were the only comfort he could bear. With trembling fingers, he took the envelope from her hand, tucking it into his jacket pocket without opening it.

"I should..." he began, then faltered

"You should come inside," Diana replied. "I'll make some tea."

She helped him to his feet, supporting more of his weight than his pride would have allowed under normal circumstances. As they moved towards the farmhouse, her eyes drifted back to the abandoned bucket by the pig pen and the splintered rake handle lying on the frozen earth — bleak reminders of how war left nothing untouched.

Tomorrow was Christmas Day. And across the country, families would gather around tables, open modest gifts, celebrate as best they could amid rationing and blackouts and absent loved ones. But here at Hayes Farm, there would be only grief and the terrible, yawning emptiness where Arthur should have been.

Diana tightened her grip on Mr Hayes's arm, guiding him through the kitchen door. She had failed to prevent this pain. Perhaps it had been inevitable? Written in time long before her return. But she would not leave him to face it alone, not this time.

In her first life, she had avoided the farm after the telegram arrived, uncomfortable with the raw emotion, unsure what to say or do. She had left Mr Hayes to his solitary grief, only to discover his suicide on Boxing Day.

But not this time, she vowed. *Not this time.*

Chapter Thirteen

Diana sat at the kitchen table in Hayes Farm, a cup of cooling tea between her palms, watching Mr Hayes with careful glances. The day stretched before them, the weight of grief hanging heavy in the air.

Mr Hayes had barely moved from his chair since receiving the telegram. The envelope remained in his breast pocket, directly over his heart, as if he couldn't bear to let the physical evidence of his son's death stray far from him.

Jenny had kept herself busy, stoking the fire, preparing food that no one wanted to eat, her usual chatter silenced by the solemnity of the occasion. Now she hovered by the stove, uncertain, casting worried glances towards Mr Hayes.

Diana's mind searched for the memory of what happened next—or rather, what would happen if she did nothing. In her first life, she'd retreated to Willow Farm that evening, taking Christmas Day off as Mrs Whitaker had insisted. She'd abandoned Mr Hayes with his grief, only to find him on Boxing Day morning in the back paddock, the rifle close to his cold, dead hand. The image struck her with such force that she flinched.

Funny how her mind had blocked that memory, although the experience had hardened her.

Surely he must have known that it would be her or Jenny who found him? She had to remind herself how much he was hurting before she could find a way to forgive him for what he'd done.

She couldn't let that happen again. Not when she had the chance to change it.

"I should go into the village," Diana suggested, breaking the silence. "To tell the Reverend about... this."

Mr Hayes looked up, his eyes hollow. "Why?"

"Because—" Diana hesitated, searching for the right words. "Because he's known Arthur since he was a boy. And because no one should go through grief alone."

Mr Hayes stared at her for a long moment before giving a slight nod, neither agreement nor refusal, but acknowledgment of her words.

Jenny moved closer, relief clear in her face at the prospect of action. "I'll go," she offered. "I'm faster on the bicycle."

Diana shook her head. "No, I'd like you to stay here with Mr Hayes. Perhaps make some sandwiches? Neither of you has eaten since breakfast. I'll take the van."

Jenny nodded.

"I'll be back soon," Diana promised, rising from her chair. "We'll get through this, Mr Hayes. Together."

Mr Hayes grunted something non-committal and turned towards the door. Diana jerked her head at the farmer, and Jenny nodded. Diana hoped that Jenny's nod meant that she understood that she should keep Mr Hayes occupied and prevent him from wandering off alone with only his dark thoughts for company.

Outside, Mr Hayes's old Bedford lorry sat like a patient beast, its forest green paint chipped and weathered. Diana ran a hand along its bonnet, remembering. The cab smelled of hay and tobacco when she climbed in, the leather seat cracked but still comfortable. The key slid into the ignition with a familiar resistance.

"Come on, old girl," Diana murmured, pumping the accelerator twice before turning the key. The engine coughed, protested, then rumbled to life. The steering wheel felt enormous as she guided the lorry through the farmyard and onto the narrow lane that led towards Cheviot Hills.

She passed the Twice Brewed Inn, smoke curling from the chimney, promising warmth and comfort within.

What she wouldn't give to be inside now with a port and lemon, or even a glass of wine. Anything to dull the edge of anxiety that had lodged itself beneath her ribs.

The road wound ahead, frost-touched hedgerows guiding her path. Her hands gripped the wheel with unnecessary force, knuckles whitening. Her mind wasn't on the task at hand, but back at Hayes Farm.

The lorry rounded a bend, the road narrowing as it cut through a small copse of winter-bare trees. Diana eased off the accelerator, wary of the slick patches where frost still lingered in shadowed spots.

She didn't see the American jeep until it was too late.

It came hurtling around the corner ahead, engine roaring, firmly on the wrong side of the road. Diana had a split-second impression of wide eyes behind a windscreen, a mouth open in surprise or warning, before she wrenched the steering wheel hard to the right, trying to avoid the collision.

The impact, when it came, was deafening. Metal tore into metal with a sound like the world ending. Diana felt herself flung forward, weightless for an impossible moment, before the windscreen shattered against her face. Pain bloomed, bright and terrible, then immediately receded as darkness crowded the edges of her vision.

As her consciousness ebbed, her thoughts weren't of herself or the stupid, reckless American driver, but of Mr Hayes. She had failed him. Again.

Her last coherent thought was wondering if she might meet Arthur Hayes in whatever waited beyond this life. Would he understand what she had tried to do for his father?

The darkness claimed her.

Chapter Fourteen

Diana Penn opened her eyes.

"Diana! You'll be late for your shift if you don't get a move on!" Mrs Whitaker's voice drifted up the stairs, as familiar now as the ceiling above Diana's head.

Diana sat up, touching her face, searching for any residual injuries from the crash that she'd surely just experienced? But whatever had occurred had been wiped away by the glitch in time, which now seemed to govern her life.

She swung her legs over the side of the narrow bed, frustration building. Another attempt, another failure. How many lives would she cycle through before she found the right path?

"Coming!" she called, pushing herself upright.

This time would be different. This time, she would save Ellen Wilson, Mr Hayes, and herself.

And she would be damned more careful about how she went about it.

Chapter Fifteen

On the day of the Christmas Dance, Diana stood in front of her small mirror, adjusting the forest green dress that belonged to a woman she'd never met. The dance was mere hours away, but her mind was far from the festivities. She could only think of tomorrow. Christmas Eve morning, and the telegram that would arrive at Hayes Farm.

There was no way she could possibly save Arthur Hayes from dying in the war. That she knew. But she could save his father from the grief-stricken decision he would make. She just needed a better approach than fetching the Reverend *after* the telegram arrived.

"You look like you're planning a military campaign rather than attending a dance," Mrs Whitaker observed from the doorway.

Diana started, caught off guard by the older woman's perception. "Just thinking about the war."

"Christmas is a time for joy, not for worrying," Mrs Whitaker chided, though her own eyes held the familiar shadow of concern for her son. "At least for tonight. Now, come help me with my hair. I'll not attend a dance looking like I've just been for a roll in the hay. The Willow Farm women will not be undone by a recalcitrant bobby pin!"

Diana could only laugh.

Since inviting Mrs Whitaker to come with her to the dance, the older woman had been like a dizzy school girl mooning over her first crush.

Upon entering the village hall, she was struck with by how warm and welcoming the space was. Evergreen boughs and paper chains transforming the utilitarian wooden hall into something almost magical. Diana moved through the crowd, nodding to familiar faces but keeping her attention fixed on one particular target.

Reverend Taylor stood near the refreshment table, a cup of punch in his hand, his dog collar barely visible beneath the woollen scarf he still wore against the December chill. Tall, thin, with a full head of chaotic grey hair and kind eyes behind wire-rimmed spectacles, he looked exactly as Diana remembered him.

She waited until the band struck up a waltz before approaching him.

"Reverend Taylor," she greeted him with a theatrical curtsy. *Where had that come from? She didn't do theatrical anything!* "I don't suppose you'd honour me with a dance?"

Surprise flickered across his face before warming into pleasure. "Miss Penn, how lovely. I'd be delighted, though I must warn you I'm rather out of practice."

As they moved onto the dance floor, Diana panicked slightly as the music began. Dance lessons at secondary school were so long ago that they were almost a Jurassic memory. She apologised to the reverend more than once for her clumsy footwork, as she struggled to remember the steps.

"I'm glad to see you here tonight," the reverend said after one such apology. "Mrs Whitaker mentioned how hard you've been working, barely taking any time for yourself."

"I have," Diana agreed, seizing the opening. "Mr Hayes has been very kind, considering my inexperience when I first arrived. I was honestly hard pressed to know which end of the cow was which!"

The reverend nodded encouragingly, guiding her through a gentle turn. "Fred Hayes is a good man. Carrying a heavy burden with his son at the front. Same with Enid and her boy Trevor."

Diana drew a careful breath. "That's something I wanted to discuss with you. Would it be possible for you to visit Hayes Farm tomorrow?"

"For morning tea, perhaps?" She hesitated, then added, "I think Mr Hayes could use some spiritual comfort during the Christmas season."

Reverend Taylor answered without hesitation. "Christmas Eve morning would be fine. I have preparations to make for the evening service, but I could come around ten?"

Relief flooded through Diana. "That would be perfect. Thank you."

The rest of the evening passed in a blur of music and conversation. Diana danced with Jim Crawford, watching his eyes for any sign that he, too, might be living a repeated timeline. She laughed with Ellen, storing away the sound of her friend's voice against the knowledge of what might lie ahead. She even managed a dance with Mr Hayes himself, who moved with surprising grace for a man more accustomed to farm work than festivities. And Mrs Whitaker proved to be quite the dark horse on the dance floor. Dancing with Mr Fleming, Mr Hayes, the reverend, and even Cheviot Hills' future MP, although his lack of skill on the dance floor led to a number of good-natured grimaces from Mrs Whitaker.

And although she wasn't superstitious by any stretch of the imagination, Diana crossed her fingers on more than one occasion and found herself touching the wooden benches. If there'd been a cellar of salt on the table, instead of a bowl of punch and platters of sandwiches, she would have thrown some of that over her shoulder too. She did not want to die again. This resurrection thing was getting out of hand. No wonder Jesus only did it once.

Christmas Eve morning dawned clear and cold, frost etching delicate patterns on the window panes and crunching beneath Diana's boots as she made her way to Hayes Farm. The world seemed to hold its breath, waiting.

Diana joined them in the kitchen. Jenny was already braiding the rope, while Mr Hayes bent over his books at the table. The wireless filled the room with tinny music until the pips of the *BBC's Nine O'Clock News* stopped their chatter, but there was nothing new in the broadcast. Sadly, the one death every Englishman prayed for wouldn't take place for several months, in a German bunker, and not at the hands of a brave Allied soldier.

Diana fixed her attention on the clock. Nearly an hour before Reverend Taylor was due to arrive, an hour and a half before Mr Fleming would arrive with his telegram.

That hour stretched endlessly as they completed their chores. Diana checked the lane every few minutes, straining for the sound of the Reverend's bicycle, or the postman's.

At ten minutes past ten, wheels crunched on the gravel. Diana fully expected to see Reverend Taylor's familiar figure dismounting from his bicycle, but instead, it was Mr Fleming. His breath clouded around his face as he stamped his feet against the cold.

Diana's heart sank as she abandoned the pig bucket, already knowing what Mr Fleming carried in his leather satchel. She watched him scan the farmyard, his eyes settling on Mr Hayes by the barn, still attempting to repair the broken handle of a hay rake. The postman's grave expression confirmed what she already knew—the telegram had arrived before the reverend.

The scene played out as before—Mr Fleming dismounting, the buff-coloured telegram, Mr Hayes collapsing as understanding dawned. When the postman was on his way, leaving them alone with their grief, Diana helped Mr Hayes back to the farmhouse. Jenny's shocked face met them at the kitchen door, and together the girls guided him into the kitchen. No words were needed. Almost every family in every city and town in England knew this feeling.

The trio's tense moment was broken by the sound of a bicycle bell and a hearty hello from the barnyard. Diana exhaled with relief. The cavalry had arrived.

Reverend Taylor appeared on the threshold, his normally neat appearance dishevelled, a smudge of dirt on his cheek and his spectacles askew. "So sorry I'm late," he began, stepping into the warmth of the kitchen. "You wouldn't believe what happened on the lane just past the Twice Brewed. An American jeep came tearing around the corner, driving on the wrong side of the road! Nearly ran me into the ditch. If I'd been going any faster, it would have been a head-on collision."

He paused, taking in the solemn tableau before him—Mr Hayes, rigid with grief, Diana, pale-faced, and Jenny, wringing her hands by the stove.

"Obviously driven by a foolish Yank," the Reverend added softly.

His eyes moved from face to face. "But I see there's something more pressing than my near-miss."

Diana stepped forward, touching his arm. "Arthur Hayes," she said quietly. "The telegram just arrived."

Understanding transformed the Reverend's face. "Fred," Reverend Taylor said simply, crossing the kitchen to take the farmer's hands in his own. "I am so very sorry."

Something in Mr Hayes cracked at those words—as if the reverend's acknowledgment of his grief made it both more real and more bearable. His shoulders slumped, and when he spoke, his voice was rough with emotion.

"He was a good boy," he whispered. "Better than I deserved."

"He was," the reverend agreed, pulling up a chair to sit beside him. "And he knew how proud you were of him."

As Reverend Taylor began speaking in low, comforting tones, Diana caught Jenny's eye—her look suggesting that this moment belonged to Mr Hayes and his grief. They would give him the privacy he needed, while ensuring he wasn't alone.

Out in the barn, Jenny busied herself with the milking, while Diana checked on the livestock, ensuring everything was secure for the night. The routine tasks gave them both purpose, a way to be useful when words seemed hollow.

"Do you think he'll be all right?" Jenny asked as they finished, her face pinched with concern.

Diana considered the question, remembering the parallel timeline where Mr Hayes had not survived his grief. "Not today," she said honestly. "Not tomorrow. But eventually, yes. With help."

Perhaps this time she'd found the right way forward? But would she now have to repeat the next sixty-odd years? And if she did, did she want to follow that same path?

Chapter Sixteen

Diana woke on Christmas morning to the smell of cinnamon and nutmeg drifting up from Mrs Whitaker's kitchen. For a blissful moment, she existed in the warm cocoon of her bed, before memory rushed in like the winter draught beneath her door. Mr Hayes and his telegram. Arthur. The grief that would consume a father if she didn't intervene.

She dressed in her Sunday-best blouse and smoothed the skirt she'd pressed the night before. Her reflection in the mirror showed the worry already etched into her features.

Downstairs, Mrs Whitaker moved about the kitchen without her usual melodic humming, her face drawn. The wireless sat silently in the corner, its Christmas cheer unwelcome this morning.

"Merry Christmas," Diana said, hovering in the doorway.

Mrs Whitaker turned, flour dusting her apron and a sad smile creasing her face. "And to you, dear. I've made gingerbread. Trevor's favourite. Used the last of my sugar ration, but Christmas demands something special, doesn't it?"

Diana nodded, her throat tight. The hope, and fear, in Mrs Whitaker's eyes was unbearable. She still believed her son might come home, while Diana carried the knowledge that the telegram would arrive in January, bringing news that Trevor had died fighting in Europe.

"Mrs Whitaker," Diana began, accepting the cup of tea the older woman pressed into her hands. "I was wondering if we might invite Mr Hayes to join us after church today? He shouldn't be alone, not with the news about Arthur."

"Poor Fred," Mrs Whitaker breathed, pressing a flour-covered hand to her chest. "He must come here. No one should be alone on Christmas Day." Her eyes clouded, perhaps imagining herself receiving similar news about Trevor.

"I'll ask him at church," Diana promised, sipping her tea.

Mrs Whitaker nodded, turning back to her baking with renewed purpose. "I'll make extra for dinner. We can stretch the ham, and there are potatoes enough. It won't be a feast, but it will be something."

"Thank you," Diana said.

Together, they finished their preparations for church, and Mrs Whitaker wrapped her precious gingerbread in a tea towel. Neither spoke much, each lost in her own thoughts as they donned their coats and set out for the village.

The winter morning was clear and cold, their breath fogging before them as they walked the familiar path to St Michael's Church. Frost glittered on the hedgerows, and the distant hills stood sharp against the pale blue sky. Other villagers joined them as they neared the church, exchanging Christmas greetings.

St Michael's stood as it had for centuries, its Norman tower rising solid and reassuring against the winter sky. Local rumour held that in 1145, the church's defiant minister refused to halt a Christmas service when Baron Eadric of Harthwaite's men rode through the village, demanding supplies for the king's campaign. The baron, enraged, ordered the doors barred and the church set alight — but a sudden downpour saved the building, and the baron's horse threw him from the saddle as he watched, breaking his neck.

The bell tolled now, calling the faithful to worship, its tone cutting through the crisp air. Diana's eyes scanned the churchyard, searching for Mr Hayes among the arriving parishioners, but saw no sign of him. She found herself wishing for some divine intervention of her own. Just enough to bring Mr Hayes safely to church.

Inside, evergreen boughs and holly decorated the ancient stone pillars, their scent mingling with beeswax and incense.

The church was nearly full, the worn pews crowded with villagers in their Christmas best. At the back, a sea of blue uniforms marked where the airmen stood, both British and American, squeezed in so tightly they resembled sardines in a tin.

Diana followed Mrs Whitaker to their usual pew, still watching the door for Mr Hayes. The organ wheezed into life, leading the congregation in 'O Come, All Ye Faithful,' but Diana found herself unable to join in. Her eyes fixed on the empty space where Mr Hayes usually sat.

As the service progressed, with Reverend Taylor's sermon touching on hope in dark times, Diana's anxiety mounted. The church was stifling despite the December chill, the press of bodies and the weight of her knowledge making it hard to breathe.

When the final carol began, she could bear it no longer. Murmuring an apology to Mrs Whitaker, Diana slipped from the pew and made her way down the side aisle, avoiding the curious glances of her fellow parishioners as she pushed through the heavy oak door into the blessed cool of the churchyard.

Outside, Diana paced between the ancient gravestones. She and Mrs Whitaker had walked to church from Willow Farm. Mr Hayes's farm lay in the opposite direction, a good four miles away. Even if she left now, it would take her nearly an hour to reach him on foot—time she feared he might not have.

"Damn," she whispered, an oath that would have scandalised her younger self, but which felt entirely adequate given the circumstances. Why hadn't she thought to check on Mr Hayes before church?

The church door opened behind her, releasing a wave of organ music. Diana turned, half-expecting to see Mrs Whitaker, but instead found Jim Crawford, his head cocked to one side.

"Miss Penn," he said, approaching with measured steps. "I didn't think you were the type to walk out on God mid-chorus," he said, lighting a cigarette. "Bit bold for Christmas morning, don't you think?"

Diana studied him, this man who triggered memories she couldn't quite grasp. In his RAF uniform, he looked every inch the officer, yet something in his bearing spoke of a different kind of training altogether.

"I'm not in the mood for witty remarks," she said evenly. "Mr Hayes received word yesterday that his son died in action. He's not at the service, and I'm worried something's happened to him."

Jim's expression sobered. "I see. And you need to reach him quickly."

It wasn't a question. Diana nodded, surprised by his understanding.

"Let me help," he said, nodding towards a haphazard cluster of military jeeps parked in the lane. "I'll drive you there."

Diana hesitated for a moment, and briefly wondered if it had been Jim driving the jeep which had killed her. Although whatever suspicions she harboured about Jim Crawford paled compared to the urgent need to reach Mr Hayes.

"Thank you," she said. "But remember to drive on the left."

Jim looked at her as though she'd just suggested that he drive blindfolded before he led her to a mud-splattered jeep. He opened the passenger door with old-fashioned courtesy before circling back to the driver's side and clambering in. The engine started with an obscenely loud roar in the peaceful village.

Jim handled the jeep with the easy confidence of someone accustomed to far more demanding driving conditions than quiet Northumberland lanes. Despite her urgency, Diana studied his profile, searching for clues to the recognition that nagged at her.

"You're very kind to help a stranger on Christmas Day," she observed as they passed the Twice Brewed, its windows steamed from within, promising warmth and festivity to those less burdened by knowledge of what might come.

Jim's hands tightened on the steering wheel. "You're hardly a stranger, Miss Penn. We've met before."

The statement hung between them, loaded with implications. Diana's pulse quickened. Could he possibly mean...?

"At the dance," she tried, testing the waters.

His lips quirked in what might have been amusement. "There as well."

Before Diana could press him further, the jeep rounded a bend, and Hayes Farm came into view. The familiar buildings looked bleak against the winter landscape. And with no smoke rising from the chimney in the bitter cold, Diana's stomach clenched with dread.

Jim brought the jeep to a halt and turned to her, his expression grave. "Shall I accompany you?"

Diana considered the offer. Having another person present might complicate matters, yet something in Jim's manner suggested he was no stranger to difficult situations. And if Mr Hayes had his rifle...

"Okay," she decided. "But let me deal with him when we find him."

They approached the farmhouse on foot, the frozen ground crunching beneath their shoes. The door stood ajar, and Diana pushed it open, the familiar smell of the Hayes kitchen greeting her: wood smoke, tobacco, and the lingering scent of yesterday's cooking.

"Mr Hayes?" she called, stepping inside. "It's Diana."

No answer. The kitchen stood empty, with the range cold, and the unwashed supper dishes from the day before still piled in the basin. Diana moved further into the house, aware of Jim following close behind.

The sitting room was similarly deserted, although a half-empty glass of whisky on the side table suggested Mr Hayes had been there. Diana's eyes flew to the wall above the fireplace, where she knew he kept his shotgun mounted on display.

It was gone.

She spun around, nearly colliding with Jim. "The gun," she whispered, pointing to the empty brackets. "It's missing."

Jim's expression hardened, a transformation so sudden and complete that Diana revised her assessment of him yet again.

"The barn," she said, already moving towards the door. "Or the paddock behind. That's where he'd go."

They hurried across the yard, the winter sun offering little warmth. Diana called Mr Hayes's name, hoping for an answer even as she braced herself for what they might find.

No response came, but as they approached the barn, Diana caught the distinctive smell of pipe tobacco—Mr Hayes's one luxury amid the austerity of wartime farming. Relief surged through her like a physical force.

"Let me," Jim said quietly, stepping ahead of her. He reached for the door, easing it open with deliberate caution.

"Mr Hayes?" Jim called, his voice low but steady as he leaned forward, peering around the corner before stepping back to let Diana through.

The farmer sat on an upturned crate, pipe in hand, staring at something on the ground before him. The shotgun lay across his knees, broken open, and unloaded. As Diana entered, he looked up, his weathered face a mask of grief that made him appear decades older than his fifty-odd years.

"Diana," he acknowledged, his voice rough from tears or silence or both. "Shouldn't you be at church?"

"I was worried," she replied, moving closer. Her eyes stayed fixed on the shotgun, although its harmless state eased the knot of fear in her chest.

"Cleaning it," Mr Hayes said, following her gaze. "Nothing more." He gestured with his pipe towards the barn floor, where a cloth and bottle of gun oil lay beside several shotgun shells. "Habit. Always clean my gun on Christmas morning, ready for the Boxing Day shoot."

Diana crouched beside him, close enough to offer comfort but maintaining enough distance to respect his privacy. Behind her, Jim remained near the door, a silent, watchful presence.

"Mrs Whitaker and I hoped you might join us for Christmas," she said gently. "No one should be alone on Christmas Day."

Mr Hayes stared at the barn wall, his eyes unfocused. "Told Reverend Taylor I'd be fine," he muttered. "I meant it, too. Not the first Christmas I've spent alone."

"But the first since—" Diana stopped, uncertain how to proceed.

"Since Arthur died," Mr Hayes finished for her. He drew on his pipe, the ember glowing bright in the dim barn. "Aye. First of many, it seems."

Diana reached out, covering his hand with her own. "Please come with us. Not for your sake, if you don't wish it, but for Mrs Whitaker's. She's made extra food, and it would be a kindness to her. She's still waiting for news of Trevor, you know."

At the mention of Mrs Whitaker's missing son, something shifted in Mr Hayes's expression. The shared burden of uncertain grief, perhaps, or the recognition that his pain was not unique in this war-torn world.

"I'm not fit for company," he warned, but his tone had softened.

"None of us are," Diana replied. "But we manage."

Mr Hayes finally seemed to notice Jim standing by the door. "Who's this, then? Not one of ours." The last was said with a vague gesture that encompassed the village and its inhabitants, marking Jim as an outsider.

"Flight Lieutenant Jim Crawford," Jim introduced himself, stepping forward with a respectful nod. "I offered Miss Penn a lift when she was concerned about your welfare."

"RAF, eh?" Mr Hayes studied him with the shrewd assessment of a farmer accustomed to judging livestock at a glance. "You'll have seen things, I expect."

"Yes, sir," Jim agreed. "More than I care to recall, most days."

Mr Hayes nodded and began reassembling his shotgun with practiced movements.

"Best I put this away, then," he said, rising stiffly from the crate. "There'll be time enough tomorrow morning before the shoot starts."

Relief washed over Diana as she followed Mr Hayes back to the farmhouse, watching as he returned the shotgun to its place above the fireplace. Jim waited outside in the jeep, as Mr Hayes gathered a few items —a bottle of homemade sloe gin wrapped carefully in newspaper, and a string bag filled with vegetables.

As they emerged into the yard, Mr Hayes paused, looking back at the silent farmhouse. For a moment, Diana thought he might change his mind, and retreat into the grief that had claimed him in her previous timeline. Instead, he squared his shoulders and turned towards the waiting jeep. "Well, then," he grunted. "Can't keep Mrs Whitaker waiting, can we?"

With Diana seated between the two men in the jeep, the warmth of their bodies a shield against the December chill, she allowed herself to savour this small victory. Mr Hayes alive. A real tragedy averted.

It was, she decided, the perfect Christmas Day gift.

Chapter Seventeen

When Jim pulled into the yard at Willow Farm with a sombre Fred Hayes slumped in the passenger side of his jeep, Diana watched Mrs Whitaker quickly take the measure of the atmosphere as she hurried everyone inside. Despite Jim's protests that he was more than happy returning to base to partake of their Christmas meal, Mrs Whitaker insisted that he stay to celebrate with them, admonishing the man that she would brook no argument and there would be no changing of her mind.

Diana helped Mrs Whitaker add another place setting to the dining table. Like many farmhouses built for large families, the room was designed to accommodate holiday gatherings and harvest celebrations, but Mrs Whitaker normally kept it closed up—a practical measure to conserve heat and reduce cleaning.

Today, however, she'd unbolted the doors and had drawn back the heavy velvet curtains to admit the winter sunlight. Mrs Whitaker had instructed Jim to coax a fire to life in the blackened hearth, which now crackled pleasantly, dispelling the chill and musty scent of disuse.

Mrs Whitaker's good wedding china had been brought out for the occasion, the delicate blue pastoral scenes on the dinner plates elegant against the heavy Irish linen tablecloth.

"My mother gave this set to us as a wedding present. Royal Doulton's

'Watteau' pattern. I think of my parents every time I use it," Mrs Whitaker murmured as she positioned a cup so its handle turned to the right.

Diana thought back to the one remaining thing she had of her mother's —a single cup and saucer from her parents' own wedding china, salvaged from the bombed site of her home. She'd never had her own wedding set. Not being married tended to put a stop to that sort of thing.

Still, despite her sad memories, Diana handled the porcelain with reverence, noting the slight crazing in the glaze that spoke of being well used. Each piece decorated with cobalt blue pastoral scenes of figures reclining under flowering trees. Scenes that whispered of more peaceful times. Several pieces bore almost imperceptible chips. Diana thought them more like battle scars from Christmases past.

"Put Lieutenant Crawford at the head of the table," Mrs Whitaker instructed, adjusting a dinner plate with meticulous care. "And Mr Hayes at the other end."

Diana placed the fourth plate accordingly, admiring how the firelight caught the gilt edging. The room was warming nicely thanks to Jim's efforts with the fire. He now stood by the hearth, stoking the flames with a brass poker, his uniform jacket draped over the back of a nearby chair.

"Reminds me of my grandmother's house," Jim remarked, glancing at the farmyard paintings on the walls and the heavy oak furniture, which was almost gothic in its style.

Mr Hayes busied himself at the sideboard, pouring his homemade sloe gin into small glasses. His hands were steady despite his grief, the familiar ritual of hospitality giving him purpose. He seemed smaller somehow, diminished by his loss, yet holding himself together through sheer force of will.

"A small tipple before lunch," he said, passing the glasses around. "Berries from the hedgerow behind the farm. Elizabeth's recipe." He spoke his late wife's name with the same careful reverence with which he handled the crystal glassware.

"Lunch will be served in twenty minutes," Mrs Whitaker announced, appearing in the doorway with a tea towel over her shoulder. "Diana, be a dear and help me with the vegetables. The potatoes are nearly done, but I need someone to watch the sprouts while I finish the gravy."

Diana followed Mrs Whitaker back to the kitchen, where the range radiated heat, its surface crowded with steaming pots. The smell of roasting potatoes and meat filled the air, mingling with the sharp scent of Brussels sprouts. The kitchen was the heart of the home, even on this special day when they were using the dining room.

Jim joined them in the kitchen, rolling up his shirtsleeves. "How can I help?" he offered. "My mother insisted all her children learn basic cooking. Said no son of hers would starve if left to his own devices."

"Sensible woman," Mrs Whitaker approved, turning her attention to a small joint of ham simmering in a pot of water. It wasn't much—perhaps two pounds at most—saved from her precious monthly meat ration and augmented by Mr Hayes's contribution of two rabbits he'd snared the previous week.

The kitchen filled with the homely bustle of Christmas preparations. Diana watched the others with fascination—the way Mrs Whitaker moved between range and dining room with economical grace, how Mr Hayes roused himself to carve the meat, the ease with which Jim adapted to the conditions of the farmhouse kitchen. These were rituals she'd forgotten, swept away by the tide of years and the isolation of her latter days.

"The table's set, the food's nearly ready, but I've forgotten the Christmas pudding!" Mrs Whitaker exclaimed, pressing a flour-dusted hand to her forehead.

"I'll fetch it," Diana offered.

The pudding waited in the larder, wrapped in cheesecloth and suspended from a hook to keep it safe from mice, and Diana carried it reverently to the kitchen, where Mrs Whitaker plunged it into a pan of boiling water to reheat. "It should have had brandy," she sighed, "but we'll make do with what we have."

What they had proved to be a feast by wartime standards. The ham was more than enough with the addition of the roast rabbit. Potatoes roasted in the drippings, their skins crisp and golden. Carrots and parsnips from Hayes Farm, glazed with a precious teaspoon of honey. Brussels sprouts from Mrs Whitaker's garden, harvested that morning from beneath a crust of frost. Bread sauce made with stale crusts soaked in milk and flavoured with an onion studded with cloves. And crowning it all, a gravy boat filled with thin brown gravy made from bones and vegetable water, lovingly stirred to coax maximum flavour from minimal ingredients.

Diana helped transfer the dishes to the dining room, where they found space among the plates and glasses.

The room had transformed during her absence—Jim had lit the candles in the silver candelabra that stood in the centre of the table, and the firelight danced on the polished wood and gleaming china. For a moment, it was possible to forget the war, to imagine this was Christmas in a world at peace.

Mrs Whitaker untied her apron, smoothed her best blouse, and gestured for everyone to sit. "It's not what we'd have had before," she apologised, "but it's better than many will have today."

"It looks wonderful," Jim said with genuine appreciation.

Mr Hayes nodded agreement, his eyes lingering on the empty chairs. No one commented on them, just as no one mentioned the shadow that had crossed Mrs Whitaker's face when she'd unconsciously set out five plates before catching herself.

"Let us say grace," she suggested, composing herself.

They bowed their heads as she spoke the simple blessing, asking not just for gratitude for the food before them but for protection for those who couldn't be with them—Trevor, somewhere in Europe if he still lived; and Arthur, now beyond the reach of earthly prayers.

The meal proceeded with the careful restraint typical of English gatherings—polite murmurs of appreciation, passing dishes, conversations that skirted the edge of deeper feelings. But, as the food warmed them and Mr Hayes's sloe gin loosened tongues, the atmosphere softened.

Mrs Whitaker shared stories of pre-war Christmases, when the larder had groaned with good things and the farmhouse had echoed with Trevor's childish excitement. Mr Hayes recalled how Arthur had once fashioned a toboggan from barrel staves and spent Christmas afternoon careening down the hill behind the farm, returning home soaked to the skin but triumphant.

Even Jim contributed, describing festive traditions from his own childhood—though Diana noted he avoided mentioning any specifics.

As they finished the main course, Diana gathered the plates, stacking them to take back to the kitchen. Mrs Whitaker produced the Christmas pudding with a flourish, setting it on the table.

"It should have had a sprig of holly on top," she fretted, "but the birds stripped the bush bare this year."

"It's perfect as it is," Diana assured her, spooning out portions onto the delicate dessert plates.

The pudding was dense and moist, rich with the flavour of spices and dried fruit. Mrs Whitaker had sacrificed her entire monthly sugar ration to make it, supplemented with grated carrots for sweetness and a precious jar of blackberry jam from the previous summer's foraging.

"This reminds me of my grandmother's pudding," Jim remarked, closing his eyes as he savoured a spoonful. "She insisted on stirring sixpences into the mixture. Broke my cousin's tooth one year."

Mrs Whitaker smiled at the compliment. "No sixpence in this one. Your teeth are safe. Although in better times, I'd have had proper brandy butter to go with it."

After pudding came a small cheese board—a wedge of crumbly Wensleydale, accompanied by Bath Oliver biscuits that Mr Hayes had somehow produced. They lingered at the table, sipping the rest of the sloe gin and watching the winter light fade outside the window.

"Right then, time for gifts," Mrs Whitaker said, clearing the cheese board and setting it back on the sideboard.

Diana rose to help, but Mrs Whitaker shooed her back to the table. "Leave it. Christmas comes but once a year, and the dishes will wait."

With a rustle of tissue paper, she retrieved a small parcel from behind the couch. "Here you go, Diana," she said, her voice softening for just a moment. "Something I thought you might like."

Diana's fingers traced the edges of the delicate paper, peeling it back to reveal a cosy knitted shawl, the soft wool a rich shade of evergreen. "A little something to keep you warm, and glamorous," Mrs Whitaker added, her eyes twinkling.

Mr Hayes cleared his throat, looking uncomfortable. "I've got something too. For you both." He reached into his jacket pocket and withdrew two small items, placing them on the table — unwrapped, but carefully handled.

"You shouldn't have," Mrs Whitaker protested, though her eyes brightened at the unexpected offering.

"Go on," Mr Hayes insisted, pushing them closer. "It's not much, but with Arthur gone..." He faltered, then steadied himself. "Well, seemed right that the people closest to me should have these."

Diana and Mrs Whitaker exchanged glances before picking up the items. Mrs Whitaker's was a small, faded jewellery box, still elegant despite the worn edges.

"Oh, Fred," Mrs Whitaker breathed, opening it to reveal a Victorian gold pin fashioned as a spray of flowers, tiny amethysts glittering amid seed pearls. "This is too much."

"Belonged to my Elizabeth," Mr Hayes said. "She always said it should go to Arthur's wife someday. But now..." He shrugged, the simple gesture conveying a world of grief. "No sense in it gathering dust in a drawer, is there? She'd have wanted it worn."

Diana took her gift — a delicate gold bangle engraved with a pattern of oak leaves and acorns. "It's beautiful," she whispered, struggling to find words adequate for the moment. "Thank you."

Mr Hayes nodded, clearly uncomfortable with their emotion. "Elizabeth had small wrists like yours," he said, addressing Diana. "Always complained she couldn't find bracelets to fit. A jeweller in Newcastle made that one specially for our anniversary."

Diana slipped the bangle over her hand, feeling it settle perfectly around her wrist. She caught Jim watching her, his expression unreadable.

"I have something for you too, Mr Hayes," Mrs Whitaker said, rising from the table. She disappeared for a few minutes before returning with a brown paper package. "Not as valuable as your generous gifts, but it should keep you warm on your morning rounds."

Mr Hayes unwrapped the parcel, revealing a hand-knitted scarf in dark blue wool. "You've always been an expert on the needles," he said as his fingers traced the careful stitches with evident appreciation. "Every year my Elizabeth would predict you'd win the WI knitting prize, and every year she was right."

"Thank you," Mrs Whitaker said, her eyes suspiciously bright. "Elizabeth was a good friend whose apple pie could never be matched."

Diana swallowed hard. She knew Mrs Whitaker had knitted that particular scarf for her son. Did she suspect that he wasn't coming home? She blinked away the tears as she rose to fetch her own humble offerings— a jar of lavender hand cream for Mrs Whitaker, made with oils and flowers she had saved from the garden. She hesitated, guilt twisting in her stomach as she glanced at Mr Hayes. How had she not thought of him? Had she been so self-absorbed that she'd invited him to Christmas lunch and never considered a gift?

Her voice was low, tinged with regret. "I'm sorry, I should have thought to have something for you."

Mr Hayes waved a hand dismissively. "At my age, I don't need gifts. Being here's enough."

Jim cleared his throat. "Well, Christmas is for gifts." And he magically produced a small packet of pipe tobacco. The label crumpled but still intact. "It's not much, but Merry Christmas, Mr Hayes."

The older man blinked in surprise, then nodded, his voice rough. "Thank you, lad. Elizabeth always said a good smoke made the world seem a little kinder. And call me Fred."

Jim grinned.

"Now this is a proper Christmas," Mrs Whitaker declared, dabbing at her eyes with a handkerchief. "First one that's felt real since the war began."

Jim tapped his spoon against his glass. "Thank you for having me, but I feel rather awkward," he admitted. "Finding myself included in your celebration with nothing to offer in return." He hesitated, then reached inside his shirt to withdraw two flat objects wrapped in plain brown paper. "Except perhaps these. Not much compared to the spectacular meal and company I've enjoyed."

He placed one before Mrs Whitaker and the other by Diana's plate, a huge smile on his face.

"Goodness, you needn't have brought anything," Mrs Whitaker said, as her fingers were already working at the wrapping.

"You didn't know you were staying," Diana said, her eyes boring into his.

The brown paper fell away to reveal a bar of Cadbury's Ration Chocolate—a precious wartime treat that was almost impossible to obtain through ordinary channels. The plain wrapper bore the familiar Cadbury's name, but Diana knew this chocolate would be different from peacetime varieties—made with dried milk powder and less sugar due to rationing restrictions, yet still a luxury beyond the reach of most.

Mrs Whitaker gasped. "Chocolate! How?"

"American connections," Jim said with a grin. "They're rather more generous with their rations."

"The Yanks get everything," Mr Hayes grumbled, but without real rancour.

Diana unwrapped her own chocolate bar. Such a simple thing, yet in 1944 Britain, as precious as the gold bangle now circling her wrist.

"I'm afraid it doesn't compare to handmade gifts," Jim apologised.

"Don't be daft," Mrs Whitaker said, already dividing her bar into precise squares. "I haven't tasted chocolate in forever. It's a wonderful gift."

"Indeed," Diana agreed, meeting Jim's eyes across the table. "Though I suspect there's more to your American connections than you're letting on."

A shadow of something crossed his face before he smiled. "Perhaps," he conceded. "But Christmas isn't a day for interrogations, is it?"

Diana conceded the point with a nod. Jim Crawford continued to intrigue her. Was he, like her, a traveller out of time? How had he come to have gifts for them all in his pockets when he hadn't known he'd be invited to stay for Christmas lunch?

Mrs Whitaker, oblivious to Diana's speculation, passed around her chocolate with the air of a queen bestowing royal favours. "Just a small piece each," she insisted. "We'll save the rest for later."

The afternoon stretched into early evening, the short winter day already fading to dusk. Jim glanced at his watch, then reluctantly stood. "I should get back," he said. "They'll be missing me at the base."

"And I should see to my livestock," Mr Hayes added, also rising. "Bertha doesn't know that it's Christmas."

Diana laughed at the thought of the evil Bertha celebrating the birth of Jesus.

Mrs Whitaker began wrapping leftover food in waxed paper. "Take some with you," she insisted, pressing a package into Mr Hayes's hands. "It'll save you cooking for yourself tonight."

As the men prepared to leave, Diana followed Jim onto the front step, drawn by questions she couldn't articulate.

"Thank you," she whispered. "For driving me to the farm this morning." She paused, her cheeks flushing as she looked at him. "I'm sorry I have nothing for you. I didn't think..." She trailed off, feeling the weight of her unspoken words.

Jim buttoned his uniform jacket against the gathering dusk. "I'm glad we found him when we did," he replied, his breath visible in the cold. "And spending Christmas Day with you is gift enough."

Diana hesitated, trying to decipher his meaning, before pushing on. "You said we'd met before. Before the dance, I mean."

His eyes met. "We have," he confirmed. "Though perhaps not in the way you're thinking."

Before she could press him further, Mr Hayes emerged, his new scarf wound tight around his neck and his parcel of food clutched in one hand. "Ready, Flight Lieutenant?" he asked. "I'd be grateful for that lift home if the offer still stands."

"Of course," Jim replied, touching his cap to Diana in a gesture that belonged to another era. "Until another day, Miss Penn."

She watched them drive away, the jeep's outline growing indistinct in the gathering darkness. The gold bangle felt oddly comforting against her skin. She hadn't expected gifts today, hadn't expected any of this warmth and kindness. She'd spent so long without either, that she'd forgotten what it felt like.

Mrs Whitaker appeared beside her, her own new brooch pinned to her blouse. "He's an interesting young man, your Flight Lieutenant Crawford," she observed. "Not quite what he seems, I shouldn't wonder."

Diana glanced at her, surprised by the perception. "What makes you say that?"

Mrs Whitaker shrugged, her eyes still following the distant jeep. "You don't reach my age without learning to read people. That young man has old eyes." She turned back towards the warmth of the house. "Come along, as much as I'd like to leave it till later, there's washing up to do. And I want to hear more about your young man."

As Diana followed her inside, she wondered about Mrs Whitaker's words. *Her young man.* Had she ever had a young man? No. She'd been a lone wolf all her life. But that didn't need to be her life this time around. Did it?

Perhaps that was why Jim Crawford intrigued her so. Because when their eyes met, she recognised something of herself—someone out of place, out of time, carrying secrets no one else could comprehend.

The gold bangle caught the light as she rolled up her sleeves for the washing up, its engraved pattern a reminder of how everything was connected in ways she didn't understand. Tomorrow, she promised herself as she plunged her hands into the warm dishwater, submerging the bangle, she would try unravelling those connections. But for tonight, it was enough to have shared this Christmas Day—to have created a moment of peace in a world still at war.

Chapter Eighteen

The days after Christmas passed in a blur of winter fog and brief daylight. Diana trudged through her duties at Hayes Farm, keeping a watchful eye on Mr Hayes. Sometimes she'd catch him staring at nothing, before he'd shake himself and return to work with grim determination.

If the situation with Mr Hayes wasn't bad enough, there'd also been an unsettling moment in town. Diana had just stepped outside Blyde's when she nearly collided with Ellen emerging from the post office with a bundle of mail in her hands.

"Diana!" Ellen beamed, her smile lighting up her face.

Before Diana could respond, Mr. Hollister's voice cut across the square, sharp and commanding. "Ellen! There you are." He strode towards them, face thunderous. "I told you to collect the post and return immediately. Mrs. Hollister is expecting us for lunch."

Ellen's face had drained of colour.

"Wasting time gossiping when there's work to be done," he snapped, ignoring Diana entirely. For a moment, his mask of civility slipped, revealing something colder beneath.

The harshness in his voice made Diana's skin crawl—but it was Ellen's reaction that truly struck her. The way she shrank in on herself, shoulders tight, head down. This wasn't the first time.

"Of course, Mr. Hollister," Ellen murmured. Her usual confidence gone.

His expression quickly smoothed into polite neutrality as he noticed Diana still watching. "Miss Penn," he said with a nod, before turning back to Ellen. "Come along. We've wasted enough time."

Diana watched them walk away, noting how his hand gripped Ellen's elbow just a shade too firmly.

At least today she didn't have to think about Mr Hayes, or Mr Hollister. Today was New Year's Eve, and Mrs. Whitaker had declared it a holiday, insisting that young people ought to celebrate the promise of 1945, even with the war grinding on. So Diana and her friends had gathered—along with every other young person—in the warmth of the Twice Brewed.

"The Romans thought the new year began in March, you know," Ellen informed them as they huddled around their cottage pies at the Twice Brewed that evening. "Much more sensible, if you ask me. Starting fresh when things are growing, and not in the dead of winter."

Diana smiled into her drink. "I imagine the Romans regretted ever setting foot this far north. Poor sods probably never felt warm again after being posted to Northumberland."

"I regret being born this far north. I hate to think what those poor Italian boys thought of our dire weather," Nancy Robbins added with a tight smile that didn't quite reach her eyes. Diana noticed how Nancy's gaze kept darting between her and the door, as though waiting for someone.

Diana sipped her port and lemon, thinking back to a long-ago visit to the British Museum, where she'd seen letters excavated at Vindolanda Roman Fort in the 1970s. Actual letters from Roman soldiers, scrawled on slivers of wood, begging to be sent anywhere else. One poor fellow had written home asking for "more socks," moaning about the "wretched weather."

"To the poor Roman centurions and their cold feet. May they rest in peace," Ellen said, raising her glass in a mock toast.

"Speaking of weather," Nancy continued, her voice brightening, "have you heard about the New Year's cinema showing? They've got *The Way Ahead* with David Niven. Father says it's marvellous."

Diana vaguely recalled the wartime propaganda film. But it had been decades since she'd last seen it. "I've heard it's quite good."

"Mr Hargreaves at the Regal Palace Cinema has arranged a special New Year's Day matinee," Nancy explained, smoothing her hair with practiced precision. "Father spoke with him yesterday to confirm."

Ellen clapped her hands together with un-English enthusiasm. "Oh, we must go! A proper cinema outing—just the thing to start 1945!"

"I've already asked Flight Lieutenant Crawford," Nancy added, a triumphant gleam in her eye as she glanced at Diana. "He said he'd be delighted to escort us."

Diana felt a twist in her stomach that had nothing to do with the pie she'd just eaten. "Did he indeed?" She kept her tone neutral, despite the sudden flutter in her chest.

"Don't pretend you're not pleased," Ellen teased, oblivious to the shift in Nancy's expression. "He hardly took his eyes off you at the Christmas dance." She lowered her voice to a stage whisper. "And Mrs Whitaker told me all about your Christmas dinner and how gallant he was."

Nancy's knuckles whitened around her glass. "You had dinner with him? On Christmas Day?"

"Mrs Whitaker should keep her observations to herself," Diana muttered, though without real irritation. The older woman had indeed waxed lyrical about Jim's manners and his thoughtful nature at every opportunity since Christmas Day.

"It wasn't planned," Diana added, noticing the strain around Nancy's mouth. "Mr Hayes needed company, and Jim—Flight Lieutenant Crawford —offered his help." That was putting it mildly, given the circumstances, but Nancy didn't need to know about Mr Hayes's near-suicide.

"I think it's lovely," Ellen declared, missing the tension crackling between her friends. "There are far too few good men left, what with... well, you know. One must seize opportunities when they present themselves."

Nancy's smile had turned brittle. "Yes, some of us seem particularly adept at seizing opportunities, don't we?"

Diana swirled the remains of her drink, wondering how she'd missed this dynamic the first time around. Or was this new animosity a ripple effect of Diana's changed actions?

Relationships were security risks, after all—or at least, that's what she'd told herself through half a century of solitary service.

But here, with the pub's warmth wrapping around her and 1945 just hours away, Diana wondered if she'd missed something vital in her first life. And whether this strange second chance might allow her to grasp it.

"The cinema would be a pleasant diversion," she conceded, trying to ignore both Ellen's triumphant grin and Nancy's darkening scowl.

The pub door opened, admitting a blast of frigid air and several RAF officers, their uniforms a splash of colour against the inn's dark wood panelling. Diana's gaze found Jim immediately—taller than the others, his expression brightening as he spotted their table.

"Ladies," he greeted them, removing his cap as he approached. "May I join you?"

Ellen practically pushed Nancy along the bench to make room. "We were just discussing tomorrow's cinema plans. Diana has agreed to come."

Nancy slid along the bench with visible reluctance, her smile fixed in place as Jim sat down beside Diana.

"Excellent news. I hear it's quite the picture," Jim said, his eyes holding Diana's for a moment.

"Have you seen it already?" Diana asked, curious about his peculiar choice of words.

His smile suggested mischief. "Let's just say I've heard good things about the performances." He signalled to the barman. "Another round for the ladies, Charlie, and a pint for myself."

"How thoughtful," Nancy murmured, her voice just audible above the pub's din. "You always seem to know exactly what everyone needs, Flight Lieutenant."

Jim raised an eyebrow at her tone but made no comment as Charlie brought their drinks. The wireless behind the bar crackled with static before the BBC announcer's measured tones declared it was time for the nine o'clock news. The pub fell quiet as the announcer described Allied advances in the Ardennes, pushing back the German forces that had mounted Hitler's desperate counteroffensive.

Diana watched Jim's jaw tighten as casualty figures were read out. His eyes met hers, and something passed between them—a shared understanding of war's cost that went beyond what an ordinary officer might feel.

"They say it'll be over by summer," Nancy whispered as the news concluded, her earlier frostiness forgotten in the gravity of the broadcast. "Father heard it from a colonel who stopped at the bookshop."

"Perhaps," Jim said, his tone neutral. "Though Hitler is nothing if not tenacious."

Diana studied him over the rim of her glass. "You sound as if you know him personally."

For a fraction of a second, Jim's composure seemed to slip. Then his easy smile returned. "Merely an observation based on the past five years of his refusal to accept defeat."

"You have so many fascinating observations," Nancy said, her voice honeyed but with an edge that made Ellen glance between them in confusion. "Mother says you've only been stationed here a few weeks, yet you sound as though you've always been here."

Jim's smile didn't falter. "A good officer pays attention to his surroundings, Miss Robbins. It's a matter of training."

Ellen tried valiantly to steer them towards lighter topics as midnight approached. The landlord distributed small glasses of something purporting to be champagne, but which Diana suspected was apple cider with a splash of brandy. No matter—on New Year's Eve 1944, with the war's end in sight, even the medicinal-tasting fizz seemed a luxury.

At five minutes to midnight, Charlie rang the pub's brass bell, calling for silence. "Ladies and gentlemen, we've nearly made it through another year," he announced. "Let's see in 1945 together, shall we?"

Diana stood shoulder to shoulder with Jim as the pub's ancient clock ticked forward to midnight. Nancy had somehow manoeuvred herself to Jim's other side, her blonde hair gleaming in the lamplight. Around them, villagers and service personnel alike raised their glasses in anticipation.

"Any resolutions for the new year, Miss Penn?" Jim asked, his breath warm against her ear.

Diana thought of Ellen's impending disappearance, of the bombs buried in Pickering Park, of the war that would end but leave scars across Europe for generations. "Just one," she replied. "To save those I can and accept that I cannot save everyone."

Jim's eyes darkened with understanding. "A worthy resolution, though a heavy burden to bear alone."

Before she could respond, the clock struck midnight.

The pub erupted in cheers. "Happy New Year!" voices called from every corner as glasses clinked and the wireless burst into an impromptu rendition of "Auld Lang Syne."

"Happy New Year, Diana," Jim said, his use of her Christian name seeming the most natural thing in the world at that moment.

"Happy New Year, Jim," she replied, raising her glass to his.

Before they could clink glasses, Nancy inserted herself between them, her shoulder pressing Jim's arm away from Diana. "Flight Lieutenant! A toast to 1945—may it bring victory and new beginnings." Her voice carried a determined brightness as she raised her glass to his.

Around them, couples exchanged quick kisses—a tradition Diana had observed but never participated in during her first life at this age. She felt a moment's awkwardness as Nancy tilted her face towards Jim, but he simply smiled and clinked his glass against theirs in turn.

"To 1945," he said, his eyes finding Diana's over Nancy's shoulder. "May it bring peace at last."

New Year's Day dawned bitterly cold. Diana pulled open the curtains, only to find her view distorted by the frost covering the bedroom window. Diana dressed carefully for church, selecting her warmest blouse and skirt, and arranging her hair in a style she fondly remembered. Why had she given up styling her hair? It had once been an almost meditative act. Over time, it had dwindled to a quick flick with a brush, a habit shaped by the demands of her job. Efficient. Unemotional. MI6-perfect. But somewhere along the line, she'd become... boring. A shadow of the woman she used to be. How had she let herself settle into that rut?

The morning service passed in a haze of hymns and homilies. Reverend Taylor looked remarkably fresh-faced despite the whispers that he'd been at the Rose and Crown well past midnight. Mr Hayes occupied his usual pew. Diana caught his eye as the congregation stood for the final hymn, and he nodded, a small acknowledgment of what had passed between them.

After church, Nancy cornered Diana in the churchyard, her voice low and urgent. "I'd like a word, if you don't mind."

Diana followed her behind the ancient yew tree, out of earshot from the departing congregation. Nancy's fair cheeks were flushed.

"Flight Lieutenant Crawford has been very kind," Nancy began. "He's shown particular interest in my father's shop and our family. We've had several... conversations."

Diana waited, uncertain where this was leading.

"I'd hate for there to be any misunderstanding between us, Diana," Nancy continued, her blue eyes hard despite her pleasant tone. "But I feel I should mention that my mother has already invited the Flight Lieutenant for Sunday dinner next week."

Diana raised an eyebrow. "That's lovely. I'm sure he'll enjoy your mother's famous roast."

Nancy's smile tightened. "I believe he will. Mother has made it quite clear that she approves of him."

The implication hung in the frosty air between them. Diana felt a flare of irritation. Not at Nancy's transparent attempt to stake a claim, but at the realisation that before, she would have stepped back without question. Yielded the field without even recognising there was a contest.

"How interesting," Diana replied. "Has Jim—Flight Lieutenant Crawford—expressed similar sentiments?"

Nancy's confident expression faltered. "He's a gentleman, Diana. He wouldn't speak so directly. But actions speak louder than words, don't they?"

"Indeed they do," Diana agreed, thinking of the warmth in his eyes when he'd said goodbye after the Christmas lunch. "Thank you, Nancy. It's always good to know where one stands."

Nancy seemed taken aback by Diana's calm response. "Well, then," she said, regaining her composure. "I'm glad we understand each other. I should go. My mother will be wondering where I've got to. Let's not let this get in the way of our outing this afternoon?"

Diana nodded, choosing not to regale Nancy with the fact that Jim had offered to escort her to their group outing to the cinema this afternoon. Instead, she walked silently beside Nancy back towards the gate where Mrs Whitaker waited, deep in conversation with Nancy's mother and the reverend.

. . .

Back at Willow Farm for lunch, Mrs Whitaker fussed over Diana's appearance with maternal concern.

"You'll need your heaviest coat. And a scarf. No sense catching your death just to look pretty for that young man."

"It's a group outing, Mrs Whitaker," Diana protested, her cheeks redder than they needed to be.

At precisely half-past one, Jim's borrowed jeep rattled up the lane. Diana watched from the window as he strode to the door, cap tucked under his arm and his greatcoat buttoned against the cold. She pushed aside the flutter of anticipation in her stomach—ridiculous to feel like a schoolgirl at her age, even if her body appeared much younger.

"Have a lovely time, dear," Mrs Whitaker said, adjusting Diana's coat collar. "And I want to hear every detail of the film, so I can talk about it with Trevor when he gets home." Her voice caught on her son's name, but she pushed on with determined cheerfulness. "Off you go then. Don't keep the man waiting."

The Regal Palace Cinema stood proudly on Market Street, its art déco facade softened by soot and Northumbrian winters, but still graceful beneath the frost-dusted canopy. Twin glass doors flanked a brass ticket booth, and REGAL PALACE glowed faintly above in elegant lettering, the gold leaf bright against the dark green background.

"There you are!" Ellen called, waving from a sheltered spot outside the cinema. She stood with Nancy, whose eyes had widened upon seeing Diana climb out of Jim's jeep. She offered Diana a tight smile. "We were thinking you'd changed your mind."

"The jeep took some persuasion to start," Jim explained, guiding Diana towards the entrance with a light touch at her elbow. "Cold engines and military vehicles are seldom a happy combination."

Nancy stepped forward, smoothly inserting herself between Jim and the ticket booth. "I've reserved our seats," she announced. "Father knows Mr Hargreaves, you see. Best spot in the house—middle row, centre."

"How thoughtful," Jim replied, his tone neutral as he reached for his wallet. "I insist on paying for the tickets, however."

Inside, the cinema's faded grandeur spoke of better days before the war. Plush red seats showed patches of wear, and the gilt trim on the doorways had dulled with age.

The air carried the comforting scents of furniture polish, damp woollen coats, and the faint, lingering sweetness of tobacco and toffees.

They found their reserved seats, with Nancy manoeuvring herself to be seated beside Jim. Ellen glanced quizzically at Diana, who shrugged and settled into the seat beside Nancy. Ellen took the seat next to her. As the lights dimmed, Diana felt a childlike thrill of anticipation. In her previous life, she'd rarely made time for such simple pleasures. They were for other people. Sitting in a provincial cinema on a January afternoon would have seemed like a frivolous waste of time.

The Pathé newsreel flickered to life on the screen, and Diana studied the images of Allied advances and home front heroism. She'd lived through this before, but it all seemed so surreal now. Beside her, Nancy sat rigidly upright, her attention fixed on the screen, though Diana caught her stealing glances at Jim whenever she thought no one was looking.

The newsreel gave way to advertisements, then a Disney cartoon that provoked unexpected laughter from the audience—a welcome relief before the main feature. As the opening credits rolled, Diana settled back in her seat, conscious of Nancy's gloating expression as Jim's arm rested on the shared armrest between them.

Halfway through the film, Diana glanced across to find Jim watching her rather than the screen, his expression unreadable in the dim light. Nancy, engrossed in the film, didn't notice as Jim's hand moved with deliberate slowness along the back of the seat behind her. His fingers brushed against Diana's shoulder, a fleeting touch that sent warmth coursing through her. When she turned her head, his smile was barely visible in the flickering light from the screen, but unmistakable, nonetheless.

They remained that way for the remainder of the film, with Diana acutely aware of Jim's hand occasionally brushing her shoulder whilst Nancy was absorbed by the film. It was childish, perhaps—this clandestine communication behind Nancy's back—but Diana found herself enjoying the small rebellion.

When the film ended and the lights brightened, Jim withdrew his arm, his expression blank as Nancy turned to him with an animated commentary on the film's finer points.

"Well!" Ellen exclaimed, dabbing at her eyes with a handkerchief. "That was splendid! So romantic and philosophical all at once."

"I didn't understand half of it," Nancy admitted with a self-deprecating laugh, her hand resting lightly on Jim's sleeve. "But David Niven was terribly handsome, wasn't he?"

They filed out of the cinema into the waning afternoon light, the winter sun already sinking towards the horizon though it was barely four o'clock.

"Shall we find somewhere warm for tea?" Ellen suggested, hugging herself against the chill. "I'm famished."

"The Grand Hotel serves a decent enough tea," Jim offered. "And it's just around the corner."

The Grand proved to be a generous description for the establishment. But its tea room was warm and inviting, with white linen tablecloths and polished silverware.

They secured a table near the window, shedding their coats and gloves as a waitress approached with menus. Diana ordered tea and a scone, conscious of her limited ration allowance but unwilling to cut short this unexpected afternoon of normality.

"What did you think of the film?" Jim asked, his gaze taking in all three women but lingering on Diana.

"It was... thought-provoking," Diana replied. "Especially the idea that duty might require personal sacrifice."

"Do you believe in that?" Ellen leaned forward, eyes bright with interest. "That some things are worth sacrificing everything for?"

Diana considered her answer, weighing her extraordinary circumstances against her natural scepticism. "I believe our choices matter," she said. "Perhaps more than we realise at the time we make them."

"But some things seem predetermined, don't they?" Ellen persisted. "Like how certain people come into our lives at exactly the right moment?" She glanced between Diana and Jim.

Nancy's teacup clinked against its saucer. "I hardly think a wartime posting can be called 'predetermined,' Ellen. Officers go where they're sent."

Jim's lips quirked in amusement. "Are you suggesting some cosmic force arranged for my engine trouble to strand me at Hayes Farm that day?"

"Stranger things have happened," Ellen declared with confidence.

Yes, they have, Diana thought, remembering the explosion in Pickering Park that had sent her hurtling backward through time. Was that cosmic justice or random chance? And what of Jim Crawford? Was his appearance in this life mere coincidence, or something more deliberate?

He hadn't really been part of her first life. There had been brief encounters in Vienna, she remembered now, where she'd assumed that he was someone who worked the same dark corners she did. They'd crossed paths on more than one occasion, though she'd never been able to place who he worked for. But at the point where she'd begun to lower her guard, after their dinner, he'd disappeared. And she'd never seen him again. Not until he appeared in Cheviot Hills. It was either him, or his doppelganger.

Their tea arrived, along with scones and a small pot of what the waitress proudly announced was "real strawberry jam—not much, mind, but the genuine article." Diana spread a modest amount on her scone, savouring its sweetness as Ellen regaled them with her theories about destiny and true love.

Nancy remained unusually quiet, her gaze flicking between Diana and Jim with increasing suspicion. When Jim offered Diana the last of the precious jam for her second scone, Nancy's teaspoon clattered against her saucer.

"You must find it all rather novel," Nancy said, stirring her tea. "Girls working on farms, I mean. Do you see many doing that back home, Flight Lieutenant?"

Her tone was sweet as sugar, but there was a subtle implication that girls like Ellen and Diana were out of place, and beneath the notice of someone like him.

Jim smiled, not rising to the bait. "I find honest work admirable," he said. "And good company, even more so."

The conversation drifted to safer topics as they finished their tea. By the time they stepped back onto the street, twilight had descended. With the blackout restrictions rendering the town a maze of shadows, Jim offered his right arm to Diana, his left to Ellen. Nancy took hold of Diana's remaining arm, the pressure of her grip making Diana wince.

Nancy's house on Church Lane was their first stop, its substantial Victorian architecture silhouetted against the darkening sky. Nancy hesitated a moment before elegantly climbing from the jeep.

"Thank you for a lovely afternoon, Flight Lieutenant," she said, her voice warm with deliberate emphasis.

"It was my pleasure, Miss Robbins," Jim replied, though Diana noted he remained behind the wheel rather than escorting Nancy to her door.

Nancy leaned forward, her eyes catching Diana's with a cool gleam. "So lovely spending the afternoon with you. Come for tea soon. Mother would love to hear what you've been up to at the farm." The sweetness in her voice didn't quite mask the edge beneath. She turned and walked towards the house, where a single lamp burned in the front window like a watchful eye.

Diana watched her go, trying to remember what had originally fuelled their animosity. The tension over Crawford hadn't existed in her first life. So what had driven the wedge between them then? What had turned Nancy from a potential friend into a lifelong adversary?

Ellen's billet at the Hollisters' farm was their next stop. As they approached the imposing Georgian farmhouse with its symmetrical windows and classical portico, Diana shivered. Was it here, in this house, that something happened to Ellen Wilson? Or did it happen elsewhere?

From what Ellen had shared during their late-night talks at the Twice Brewed, Mr Hollister's wandering hands and Mrs Hollister's cold indifference had made the beautiful old farmhouse a place of quiet dread for Ellen.

"Thank you both for today," Ellen said. "It's been absolute heaven to forget about all this for a few hours."

"Will you be all right?" Diana asked, glancing at the darkened house. "It looks as though no one's home."

Ellen waved away her concern. "The Hollisters are visiting relatives in Newcastle until tomorrow. I've the place to myself tonight, which is a blessed relief. Let me tell you. It's better than a holiday when Hollister's away. That man gives me the absolute creeps, I swear."

"Come back to Willow Farm with me," Diana suggested. "Mrs Whitaker wouldn't mind, as long as I made up the spare bed."

"Don't be silly. I'm fine. Besides, I've plans to reorganise my sketches from last summer's dig," Ellen laughed.

"Professor Winterbourne wants them catalogued for a publication he's preparing." Ellen kissed Diana's cheek, then Jim's. "You two enjoy the rest of your evening!"

Before Diana could protest further, Ellen's silhouette was briefly visible as she pushed open the unlocked door and disappeared inside. Diana stared after her, fighting the urge to follow.

The journey back to Willow Farm passed in companionable silence, the headlamps cutting a narrow path through the darkness, their beams hooded according to the blackout regulations. Diana watched the familiar landscape pass by—stone walls, bare-branched trees, the occasional glimmer of a cottage window through imperfectly drawn curtains.

"Thank you for today," Diana said as Jim slowed the jeep outside Willow Farm's gate. "The cinema, the tea... it was nice to forget about everything for a while."

"I enjoyed it too," Jim replied, cutting the engine. In the sudden silence, his voice seemed more intimate. "Perhaps we could do it again sometime. Without the audience."

Diana smiled despite herself. "Nancy would be devastated to miss our next outing."

"I suspect she'll survive the disappointment." Jim's expression turned more serious. "Would tomorrow afternoon suit? For a walk?"

Diana met his gaze, sensing the weight behind his request. "I'm working at Hayes Farm tomorrow."

Jim nodded, considering. "Perhaps after work? I could meet you at the farm around four, if that's convenient. The days are short, but we'd still have a little daylight for a walk."

"That would work," Diana agreed, calculating the timing. Mr Hayes usually dismissed her by half three, which would give her time to tidy up. "I'll be finished by then."

"Perfect." He hesitated, then added, "I'll have the jeep, so there'll be room for your bike."

Diana nodded, momentarily losing the power of speech, as Jim stepped out of the jeep and came around to open her door. She climbed out, drawing her coat tighter around herself.

"Until tomorrow, then," Jim said softly.

"Until tomorrow," Diana echoed.

For a moment they stood facing each other in the darkness.

Their breath clouding between them. Then Jim leaned forward and pressed a gentle kiss to her cheek—brief, chaste, yet somehow more meaningful than any kiss Diana could remember from her long life.

"Goodnight, Diana," he murmured.

"Goodnight, Jim."

He waited until she reached the gate before returning to the jeep. As Diana walked up the path to Willow Farm's front door, she heard the engine start and the sound of tires on gravel fading into the night.

Inside, Mrs Whitaker was darning socks by the fire, spectacles perched on the end of her nose. She looked up as Diana entered, her expression brightening.

"There you are! Did you enjoy the film?"

Diana hung her coat on the peg by the door, still feeling the phantom warmth of Jim's kiss on her cheek. "Yes, it was rather good," she replied, settling into the chair opposite Mrs Whitaker. "David Niven was quite convincing as an officer whipping his men into shape."

"And how was your Flight Lieutenant?" Mrs Whitaker asked, her tone casual as she continued her darning.

"He's not my Flight Lieutenant," Diana protested, though without much conviction.

Mrs Whitaker raised an eyebrow over her spectacles before setting aside her darning. "Tea? I've saved a bit of cake for you."

As Mrs Whitaker bustled about the kitchen, Diana reflected on the day's events. Nancy's intense hostility had been unexpected. The girl had staked her claim on Jim with a determination that bordered on desperation.

"Penny for your thoughts?" Mrs Whitaker asked, setting a cup of tea and a small slice of fruit cake before Diana.

Diana sipped her tea, considering how much to share. "I was thinking about Nancy Robbins. It's like something has changed between us."

Mrs Whitaker gave a knowing "hmm," as she reclaimed her seat. "That wouldn't have anything to do with a certain officer, would it?"

Diana looked up in surprise. "What makes you say that?"

"Small village, dear. Everyone knows everything." Mrs Whitaker picked up her darning again. "Nancy's had her eye on any eligible young man since she turned seventeen. Her mother encourages it—desperate to see her married well before the good prospects are all claimed or killed."

"I didn't realise," Diana murmured. In her first life, she'd been too wrapped up in her own concerns to notice the dynamics around her.

"The Robbins women have always been ambitious," Mrs Whitaker continued. "Agatha married the only bookseller in the county—a step up from her father's farm. She's determined Nancy will do even better." She glanced up at Diana. "But that young man of yours doesn't strike me as someone easily swayed by just a pretty face."

"He isn't *my* young man,'" Diana insisted, although her cheeks warmed at the phrase.

Mrs Whitaker smiled. "Not yet, perhaps." She set her darning aside once more. "Diana, may I offer some advice? From someone who's seen more of life than you have?"

Diana almost laughed at the irony, but nodded.

"Don't let fear hold you back from happiness," Mrs Whitaker said, her eyes suddenly serious. "This war has taught us how precious life is, and how quickly it can be snatched away. If there's a chance for joy, even a small one, grasp it with both hands." Her gaze drifted to the mantelpiece, where a photograph of her son stood in a silver frame. "Tomorrow is promised to no one."

Diana was realising all too well the truth of those words. She had lived a lifetime watching opportunities for personal happiness slip away while she served Queen and country.

"I'll try to remember that," she replied.

"See that you do." Mrs Whitaker's brisk tone returned as she rose from her chair. "Now, off to bed with you. Early start tomorrow—market day, and Mr Hayes will be expecting you. I'll have the porridge ready by half six."

Diana climbed the narrow staircase to her room, Mrs Whitaker's words echoing in her mind. Through the small window, stars scattered across the winter sky. Somewhere out there, the war continued. Bombs fell, men died, and the world inched towards its reckoning. Yet here she was experiencing a strange kind of peace, before whatever tomorrow might bring.

With her fingers resting on the spot where Jim had kissed her, she dreamed not of bombs or spies or cosmic justice, but of possibilities she'd never allowed herself to experience before.

Chapter Nineteen

January seemed determined to test the patience of even the most hardy of Northumberland residents. Snow piled in drifts along stone walls, turned to treacherous ice on the lanes, and whistled through every crack and crevice of Willow Farm's ancient timbers. The pipes froze twice, requiring Mrs Whitaker to boil kettles of water and Diana to crawl beneath the house with rags soaked in near-boiling water to thaw them.

Yet despite winter's bitter embrace, Diana was happier than she'd ever been before.

"You've got a spring in your step for someone trudging through six inches of snow," Mrs Whitaker observed one morning as Diana prepared for her walk to Hayes Farm. "Anyone would think it was May, not January."

Diana adjusted her scarf, unable to suppress a smile. "The cold makes one more appreciative of warmth," she replied, earning a knowing look from her landlady.

"Indeed, it does. And I suppose that warmth has nothing to do with a certain Flight Lieutenant who's been calling round with remarkable frequency."

Diana felt a blush creep into her cheeks. "He's being neighbourly."

"Is that what they're calling it these days?" Mrs Whitaker chuckled, pressing a small parcel wrapped in waxed paper into Diana's hands. "For your lunch. There's an extra sandwich for your 'neighbourly' visitor, should he appear today."

The walks with Jim had become a fixture of Diana's new existence. Sometimes they strolled through frost-gilded fields, their breath clouding before them as they talked of books and films and music. But never the war. And on bitter days, they'd seek refuge in the Twice Brewed, where Charlie would serve port and lemon for her, and a half of bitter for Jim. Once, when the snow lay deep, Jim had produced a toboggan from somewhere, and they'd spent an hour sledging down the hill behind Hayes Farm like children, their laughter carrying across the crystalline landscape.

It was during one such walk, crossing a stile into Burrell's Meadow, that Jim had first kissed her. Not the chaste peck on the cheek from New Year's night, but a genuine kiss that had left her breathless. His hands had framed her face with surprising gentleness, and time seemed to pause as their lips met.

Diana had experienced two passionate kisses in her first life. One, with a law student friend of a fellow agent at a party in 1947, had been disappointing and awkward. The second, with an MI6 colleague in Istanbul, had been precisely calculated to convince the watching KGB agents of their cover as honeymooning tourists. Her life had never progressed beyond such brief encounters—she'd been too guarded, too focused on her work. Neither had prepared her for the rush of sensation Jim's kiss provoked.

When they'd broken apart, she'd found herself lost for words.

"I've been wanting to do that since the Christmas dance," Jim had confessed, his fingers still touching her face.

"What took you so long?" she'd replied, surprised by her boldness.

Now, trudging through the snow towards Hayes Farm, Diana found herself anticipating their next meeting with a girlish excitement that would have horrified her former MI6 self. She, who had maintained professional detachment through revolutions and coup d'états, was counting the hours until Jim might appear.

The lane curved around Hunter's Wood, and Diana paused, noticing fresh tracks in the snow.

Tracks too large for a fox or badger, and the wrong shape for deer.

Human footprints, partially obscured by the light snowfall of the early morning. They left the lane and disappeared into the trees.

Her intelligence training kicked in. Two sets of prints—one smaller than the other. A man and a woman, moving with apparent purpose into the woods where no path existed. Recent tracks too, given how lightly the new snow had dusted them. Curious. The stories Mr Hawk kept repeating over his frosted pint glass at the Twice Brewed echoed in her mind. The man was adamant he'd both seen and heard smugglers, or Germans, or both, wandering the hills at night. No one believed him, but his story never changed. He'd seen something.

Diana glanced at her watch. She had time enough to satisfy her curiosity and still reach the farm before Mr Hayes would expect her. She followed the footprints, her boots crunching through the snow.

The trail led deeper into the wood, weaving between bare oak and ash trees, their branches clawing at the pewter sky. Then Diana heard voices—a woman's breathless murmur, and a man's lower rumble, followed by what was unmistakably a moan.

She slowed, suddenly regretting her nosiness. Through a screen of hawthorn, Diana saw two figures in a small clearing. One she recognised instantly—Nancy Robbins, her fair hair escaping from beneath a knitted hat, her coat open despite the cold. And a man in an RAF uniform, his hands wandering with familiar intimacy beneath Nancy's skirt.

Diana's cheeks flushed, and she took a step backward, intending to retreat discreetly, when a twig snapped beneath her boot, a sound that seemed deafening in the winter stillness.

Nancy's head whipped around, her eyes widening in horror as she spotted Diana through the trees. "Oh my God!"

The airman broke away, hastily straightening his uniform as Nancy fumbled with her clothes, her face scarlet.

"I'm so sorry," Diana began. "I was just—"

"Spying on me?" Nancy hissed, her embarrassment transforming to fury. "Following me?"

"Not at all," Diana protested. "I saw footprints and thought—"

"I know exactly what you thought," Nancy spat, her blue eyes glittering with humiliation and rage.

"You couldn't stand that Flight Lieutenant Crawford prefers me, could you? You wanted to catch me doing something improper to get back at me," Nancy hissed.

The airman—sandy-haired, with a thin moustache and a face currently displaying acute discomfort—cleared his throat. "Nancy, perhaps we should—"

"Shut up," Nancy snapped without looking at him. She advanced on Diana, trembling with emotion. "Well, congratulations. You've caught me. I suppose you'll be running straight to my mother with this juicy bit of gossip, won't you? Or perhaps Reverend Taylor?"

"I have no intention of telling anyone," Diana said. "What you do is your own business, Nancy. I found you by accident."

Nancy's laugh was brittle. "As if I'd believe that. You've been looking for ways to humiliate me ever since I told you Crawford was coming to our house for Sunday dinner."

"That's not true," Diana began, but Nancy was beyond reason.

"You'll ruin my reputation if word gets out," Nancy continued, voice rising. "Mother will lock me in my room until I'm old and grey. Richard could be transferred, or worse." She stepped closer, jabbing a finger at Diana's chest. "But I promise you this—if you breathe a word of what you saw, I'll make sure everyone knows exactly what sort of girl you are."

The airman—Richard—intervened, laying a hand on Nancy's arm. "That's enough, Nancy. I'm sure she meant no harm." He turned to Diana with an apologetic smile. "Sergeant Richard Thompson, miss. Sorry about the..."

Diana nodded acknowledgment, keeping her expression neutral despite her rising annoyance at Nancy's accusations. "As I said, this is none of my business. I was taking a shortcut to Hayes Farm."

"Through woodland with no path?" Nancy scoffed. "How convenient."

"I'll leave you to your walk," Diana said, ignoring the jibe. "Good day, Sergeant. Nancy."

She turned and retraced her steps to the lane, Nancy's furious gaze burning into her back. Once out of sight, Diana allowed herself a moment's exasperated sigh. Of all the people to encounter in a compromising situation, it had to be Nancy Robbins.

The hypocrisy was breathtaking. Nancy had always presented herself as the epitome of propriety, her attendance at church unfailing, her demeanour with the village elders impeccably respectful. Yet here she was, engaging in precisely the behaviour she condemned in others.

Not that Diana judged her for it. War had compressed lifetimes into months, leaving young women like Nancy desperate for connection before potential suitors flew off, perhaps never to return. But it still rankled.

As she continued on to Hayes Farm, she considered Nancy's threats. Diana would never expose her secret. And she was certain Nancy knew it. Still, she couldn't shake the feeling that the incident would have consequences. Nancy was not one to let perceived slights go unanswered, and her embarrassment would need an outlet.

"You're late," Mr Hayes observed as Diana entered the yard, though his tone lacked any sharpness. Grief had hollowed him, but not hardened him. If anything, Arthur's death seemed to have softened the farmer, as though harsh words no longer had a place in his life.

"Sorry," Diana said, hanging her coat on the peg behind the kitchen door. "The lane was slippery."

Hayes nodded, weary but without reproach. "Aye. Jenny's out with the calf. A little heifer, early drop. Strong enough, thank God, but it'll need watching in this cold."

"I'll join her after I've stoked the range and warmed the kitchen a bit. It's colder in there than it is outside. I'll get some tea brewing too."

During the day Diana's thoughts kept returning to Nancy and their confrontation in the woods. By late afternoon, as she walked back to Willow Farm, she wondered how this might change their personal dynamics. Nancy Robbins had been one of her fiercest critics, spreading whispers about Diana's relationship with Jim. Now, perhaps, she would be too concerned with her own secrets to bother with Diana's?

There was a certain poetic justice to it, Diana supposed, although she took no pleasure in Nancy's distress. The irony was that Diana, who in her first life had lived with such rigid propriety that her MI6 colleagues had nicknamed her "The Nun," was now the subject of scandalous rumours for a few chaste kisses. Meanwhile, proper Nancy Robbins was tumbling with a lowly airman in the woods.

As February approached, and there was still no sign of the dreaded telegram announcing Trevor Whitaker's death, Diana allowed herself to focus on Ellen. She seemed cheerful enough when they met at the Twice Brewed, though Diana noticed shadows beneath her friend's eyes and tension in her shoulders at the mere mention of Hollister's name. Diana had voiced her concerns to Jim, who'd promised to make inquiries about alternative placements where Ellen might be safer from Hollister's unwelcome attention.

Jim himself remained a comforting constant, despite his occasional absences for "war stuff" he couldn't elaborate on. When he returned from these mysterious duties, he would appear at Willow Farm's gate with chocolate or stockings, once even with a bottle of French perfume that had made Mrs Whitaker flush like a schoolgirl.

Diana had settled into a happiness she had never known the first time round. The future remained uncertain. What should she do when the war ended? Return to London as she had before? Or stay in the countryside she had grown to love? She could not remember loving the countryside the first time she'd been here. But for reasons still unknown, she'd retired here, moving into her small Georgian flat on Burn Lane.

If she was being brutally honest, with no one in her life, she'd retired to Cheviot Hills because what better place to die? Although she hadn't foreseen dying so many times.

February 1st dawned, and Diana remembered all too well that Ellen had vanished without a trace during this very month. Rumours had swirled around after her disappearance, with talk of her running off to London, whispers of an inappropriate sweetheart whisking her away, and accusations of thievery. But none of it rang true to Diana. And even back then, she'd felt the shadow of something darker pressing in on them. Now, with the weight of hindsight and a second chance, she couldn't afford to dismiss that feeling. Whether Ellen had run away, or had met a more sinister fate, Diana didn't know. But she was determined that history would not repeat itself.

An opportunity presented itself shortly after, when their days off aligned, and Ellen had suggested a day trip into Newcastle, just them.

"Will you stay in Cheviot Hills?" Diana started, after the conductor had clipped their tickets.

Ellen leaned back, closing her eyes, a long silence stretching between them.

"Ellen?"

The American sighed. "Honestly, Diana, if it weren't for you, I would've hightailed it back to the States months ago. I love this place. I love the countryside, all that history, heck, even the weather. But every night I spend in that house feels like one step closer to going completely batty."

Diana felt her words like a slap across the face. She hadn't realised that it was quite that bad.

"Move in with us," Diana suggested.

Ellen opened her eyes, staring out the window instead of facing Diana.

"It's not that simple."

"It really is," Diana said back. "You tell the Hollisters that you're quitting, and that's that."

"There's a war on remember?"

"You're impossible! Look at me," Diana said, grabbing Ellen's arm. "You have to leave the Hollisters. Everyone can see you're miserable. It's only going to end in tears. Or worse."

"It's too late," Ellen replied.

Diana stared at her friend, trying to interpret her words.

"What do you mean *it's too late*? Too late for what?"

Diana couldn't help herself, as her eyes flicked downwards towards Ellen's lap.

"No, not that, silly!" Ellen laughed. "As much as he's tried, and help me Oh Lord, has he ever tried. He's helping me with my thesis—"

"With his hands?" Diana interrupted.

"Diana!" Ellen whispered, swinging her head around, checking for eavesdroppers. "I need access to his collection of Roman coins, and his reference books. Even with the pause in my studies, I can't fall behind. So I need him. I just have to persevere for a little bit longer. This war will end soon, and I'll never have to see him again."

They both lapsed into silence, watching the landscape roll away behind them.

"He's not a good man," Diana tried again later.

"None of them are," Ellen replied with a smile.

"Except Mr Hayes."

"He's one of the good ones," Ellen agreed.

"Promise me you'll be careful around him. Hollister," Diana said urgently. "I mean it. Promise me."

Ellen turned to look at her, and something flicked across her face. Something too swift for Diana to nail down.

"What do you think I've been doing?" Ellen replied softly.

Chapter Twenty

February brought no relief from winter's grip. If anything, the cold deepened, seeping through stone walls and settling into bones with a persistence that defied even the most robust fires. The village of Cheviot Hills had fallen into the peculiar hush that extreme cold imposes—conversations briefer, visits shorter, everyone moving with purpose between patches of warmth.

Diana was aware of this silence as she entered Blyde's Grocery store, the bell above the door announcing her arrival with jarring brightness. Mrs Blyde, arranging the week's meagre meat ration behind the counter, looked up with her usual friendly smile, then faltered as Nancy Robbins emerged from behind a shelf of tinned goods.

The transformation in Nancy's face was immediate and complete— her pleasant expression hardening into something beyond mere dislike. Her eyes, which had been warm while chatting with Mrs Blyde, went as cold as river stones.

"Good morning," Diana said, determined to maintain civility despite the waves of hostility emanating from her former friend.

Nancy gave a barely perceptible nod before turning back to Mrs Blyde. "I'll collect Mother's order this afternoon, then," she said, artificially bright. "She's not feeling well enough to come out today."

"Nothing serious, I hope?" Mrs Blyde asked.

"Just a headache," Nancy replied. "Though I expect certain company would only make it worse."

The pointed comment hung in the air as Nancy gathered her basket, shunning any contact with Diana as she swept past. The door closed behind her with unnecessary force, rattling the windows.

Mrs Blyde made a sympathetic noise. "Don't take it personally, dear. The Robbins women have always been quick to judge and slow to forgive."

"I've noticed," Diana replied, setting her ration book on the counter. "Just the usual, please. And a tin of golden syrup if, by some miracle, you've got one."

As Mrs Blyde gathered the items, Diana reflected on her deteriorating relationship with Nancy, and others, over the past fortnight. Following her accidental discovery of Nancy and Sergeant Thompson, a chill had descended. She'd expected Nancy's hostility, but hadn't expected it to spread. First to Nancy's mother, who now crossed the street rather than acknowledge Diana or Mrs Whitaker. Then to several women who attended the same sewing circle as Mrs Robbins.

Diana hadn't told a soul about what she'd witnessed in Hunter's Wood, but it scarcely mattered. Nancy believed the worst, and her preemptive campaign had proved effective. Even Reverend Taylor had been distant at last Sunday's service. Whether from genuine disapproval or simply to maintain peace with the formidable Mrs Robbins remained unclear.

"Mrs Robbins was in earlier, asking if I knew anything about your 'situation' with Flight Lieutenant Crawford," Mrs Blyde commented, weighing out butter with practiced precision. "I told her that in times like these, people ought to focus on the war effort rather than their neighbour's private affairs."

Diana felt a rush of gratitude for the shopkeeper's discretion. "That's very kind of you."

"Kindness has nothing to do with it," Mrs Blyde replied. "It's common sense. Besides, my Albert always said that gossips make the best customers for everyone except the grocer—they're too busy talking to shop."

Diana smiled at the homespun wisdom as she paid for her purchases. Outside, the village green lay beneath a fresh dusting of snow, pristine save for Nancy's footprints leading towards the Robbins's ostentatious home. Diana turned in the opposite direction, towards Willow Farm.

Diana quickened her pace, eager to return before the groceries grew any heavier. As she rounded the bend in the lane that led to Willow Farm, she spotted a familiar bicycle propped against the gate—Mr Fleming's, the postman. Her heart stuttered. An unscheduled visit from the postman rarely brought good news.

She found them in the kitchen—Mrs Whitaker seated at the table with Mr Fleming standing by the door, twisting his cap between his hands. Neither seemed to notice Diana's arrival. The telegram lay on the table between them, unopened, its presence as explosive as any bomb

"I could fetch Reverend Taylor," Mr Fleming was saying, his voice gentle in a way Diana had never heard before. "Or perhaps when Miss Penn returns—"

"She's here now," Mrs Whitaker said, looking up at Diana with eyes that had aged a decade in minutes. "No need to trouble the reverend."

Mr Fleming nodded, relief visible in the slackening of his shoulders. "I'll leave you, then. So very sorry, Mrs Whitaker."

He departed silently, his usual cheerful whistle absent. Diana set her shopping basket down and saw him out, before lowering herself into the chair opposite Mrs Whitaker.

"I've been expecting it, you know. Ever since Christmas. A mother feels these things," the older woman said, her voice steady despite the fine tremor in her hands.

Diana reached across the table, covering Mrs Whitaker's fingers with her own. "Do you want me to open it?"

Mrs Whitaker shook her head. Her fingers tightened around Diana's.

Diana felt a profound helplessness in the face of grief she couldn't prevent. In her first life, she'd been too young, too self-absorbed to offer Mrs Whitaker any meaningful comfort. Now, with the wisdom of age but the limitations of her twenty-year-old self, she still found words inadequate.

"You don't have to read it today," she offered. "It will keep."

"What good would waiting do?" Mrs Whitaker asked, not unkindly. With a deep breath, she picked up the envelope and broke the seal, unfolding the single sheet within.

Diana watched as Mrs Whitaker's eyes moved across the sparse lines of text, absorbing the clinical confirmation of a mother's worst fears.

There was no collapse, no wailing. Only a small, broken sound, quickly stifled, and the slow closing of her eyes.

"Near Arnhem. They found his identification tags." She refolded the telegram with methodical precision.

"Would you like some tea?" Diana asked, for lack of anything better to offer.

Mrs Whitaker nodded, her gaze fixed on some middle distance. "That would be nice. And then perhaps you could help me write some letters. People will need to be told."

The rest of the day passed in a strange, suspended state. Diana made tea, prepared a simple lunch neither of them ate, and sat with Mrs Whitaker. Together, they worked through a list of people to notify about Trevor's death. Cousins in Yorkshire. An aunt in Scotland. Trevor's former schoolmaster, who had been so proud when he'd enlisted.

By evening, Mrs Whitaker had retreated into a quiet that went beyond mere silence. She sat in her armchair by the fire, Trevor's photograph in her lap, occasionally running her fingers over the glass as if trying to feel the contours of his face. She declined dinner, accepting only a cup of weak tea before retiring to her bedroom.

Diana heard her moving about upstairs, opening and closing drawers, the floorboards creaking beneath her feet. Shortly before midnight, the sounds ceased, and an even heavier silence settled over Willow Farm.

With Jim called away on another of his mysterious assignments, Diana was left without even the comfort of his brief visits as she took charge of the farm.

The kettle sang on the range, but no one moved to lift it. Reverend Taylor sat on the edge of the armchair, while Mrs Whitaker stood at the window, arms folded, her eyes on the past. Diana hovered near the mantel, her own hands clasped behind her back, feeling the weight of the room settle like dust on her shoulders.

It was the stillness that got to her most—the kind of stillness she remembered too well. Different house, different grieving parent, but the same suffocating hush that fell over everything in the wake of absence.

"I thought perhaps 'Abide With Me,'" Reverend Taylor suggested, glancing between the two women. "It's a comfort to many."

Mrs Whitaker didn't turn around. "He hated that one. Said your organist always played it too slowly. Made it funereal."

There was a pause. Diana stepped forward, "What about 'Be Thou My Vision'? You told me he used to whistle it when he came in from the fields. You said it drove you mad, apart from how good a whistler he was."

At that, Mrs Whitaker blinked and smiled. Her arms dropped to her sides. "Yes. Yes, he did."

The reverend nodded, jotting it down in the small notebook he'd brought. "And a passage? I've a few in mind, but if you had something specific..."

Diana hesitated, and for a brief second, the image of Mr Hayes's son's memorial flickered into view. The same awful finality of planning something for someone who would never come home.

"'Greater love hath no man than this,'" she said softly, "'that a man lay down his life for his friends.'"

Mrs Whitaker turned from the window then, her eyes red but dry. "That'll do."

The reverend nodded again, writing it down. "Trevor's commendation came through this morning," he said, his voice lightening, as though trying to find something to offer comfort. "For bravery, at Arnhem. The citation says he covered the withdrawal, stayed behind under fire. They've awarded him the King's Commendation for Bravery. Posthumous, of course. You must be so proud."

Mrs Whitaker stared at him, her expression unreadable for a long moment. "I'd rather have my son," she said, "than a piece of tin and a letter typed by someone who never met him."

Reverend Taylor dropped his gaze.

The Sunday after the memorial service, Mrs Whitaker had appeared at breakfast still in her robe, and announced that she wouldn't be attending church.

"The god I thought I knew no longer exists for me," she said, her voice resolute. "You go. People will talk if neither of us appears. I'll make my position clear to the reverend later this week."

Diana wanted nothing more than to stay at home, too. Church was a chore, not a core belief. And a chore she'd sloughed off as soon as she'd started working for MI6 after the war. But in a village like Cheviot Hills, absence from church was noted and discussed almost as much as what was worn to it. Without Mrs Whitaker's no-nonsense sensibilities, and Jim's steadying presence, Diana braced herself to face the full brunt of Nancy Robbins's hostility and the accompanying village gossip. She didn't want to go to church, but it was the right thing to do. And that was one thing she was very good at doing.

She dressed carefully in her navy blue suit with the velvet collar. As she pinned her hair into a neat twist, Diana realised she was preparing as she might have for a challenging diplomatic function in her MI6 days— armour against the social barbs to come.

Just as Diana was preparing to leave, Mrs Whitaker appeared at her side, taking Diana's hands in hers. "When you first arrived, you'll forgive me for thinking you were a bit of a cold fish. Always reading in your room, not making any effort to make friends." Here Mrs Whitaker closed her eyes. When she opened them, they were filled with tears. "But I couldn't have made it through this without you. Thank you."

Diana hugged the other woman tightly, barely controlling her own emotions.

The church bells were already ringing as Diana rushed across the village green. February sunshine, weak but welcome, glinted off the stained glass windows of St Michael's. Diana paused at the church gate, suddenly struck by an uncomfortable thought.

Ellen.

In the turmoil of the past days, consumed by Mrs Whitaker's grief, Diana had barely spared a thought for her friend. How long had it been since she'd seen Ellen? Not since their meeting at the Twice Brewed the previous Tuesday, she realised with alarm. Four days without contact.

Diana entered the church, nodding politely to Reverend Taylor as he greeted parishioners at the door. Instead of taking her usual seat, she remained standing at the back, scanning the congregation anxiously. The Hollisters were there, occupying their customary pew near the front, but the space beside Mrs Hollister where Ellen usually sat was empty.

A cold sensation settled in Diana's stomach.

February. Ellen's disappearance.

Distracted by Mrs Whitaker's grief, Diana had taken her eye off the very situation she'd been determined to prevent.

Her gaze swept the pews again—and landed on Jenny, seated several rows behind the Hollisters. When Jenny glanced back, Diana caught her eye and mouthed, 'Where's Ellen?' Jenny gave the slightest shake of her head, uncertainty written all over her face.

The service passed in a blur of familiar rituals that Diana observed without truly participating in. Perhaps Ellen was ill. Or perhaps she'd gone to Newcastle on an errand for the Hollisters. Perhaps...

But Diana knew better. The prickling at the nape of her neck, the tightness in her chest—these were instincts honed through decades of intelligence work, warning her that something was very wrong.

She waited impatiently through Reverend Taylor's benediction, eyes fixed on the Hollisters' pew near the front. But as the final 'Amen' echoed through the church, the press of parishioners surged around her. The couple in the pew beside her gave a pointed cough and shifted expectantly, forcing Diana to step out into the aisle.

By the time she'd disentangled herself, the Hollisters were already out the door, swept along by the flow of the congregation.

Diana followed them outside, where the February sun had retreated behind clouds, casting the churchyard in a grey light that suited her mood. She spotted the Hollisters near the path, engaged in conversation with the Robbins women and Reverend Taylor.

Before she could reach them, a hand tugged gently at her sleeve. Diana turned to find Jenny hovering just behind her, cheeks flushed from the cold or nerves—or both. "I heard something," Jenny said in a low voice. "From Claire George. She says the Hollisters told her mum that Ellen's run off. Disappeared into the night, with some of the family silverware too, apparently. No note. Nothing." She glanced anxiously at the group ahead. "I can't believe it's true. But that's what they're saying."

Diana turned to look at the Hollisters, before marshalling her courage. As she approached, Nancy noticed her first. She whispered something to her mother, who glanced over her shoulder, her face hardening into disapproval. The reaction rippled through the group. Mrs Hollister turned away slightly. Mr Hollister's expression was as vile as his reputation. Even Reverend Taylor looked uncomfortable.

Only a year ago—or rather, sixty years from now—Diana would have retreated from such obvious social rejection. But she was not that woman anymore. She had served King and Queen. She'd faced down KGB agents and navigated the treacherous political waters of a dozen countries. She would not be deterred by small-minded village disapproval.

As she drew near, snatches of their conversation reached her.

"—absolutely disgraceful," Mr Hollister was saying. "Taking advantage of our hospitality, then absconding with family heirlooms. I've already informed the police."

Diana's blood turned to ice. They were speaking of Ellen.

"Mr Hollister," she interrupted, heedless of propriety, "may I speak with you about Ellen?"

The group turned as one, their expressions varying from surprise to disdain. Mrs Robbins made a small huffing sound. Nancy smirked. Mr Hollister regarded Diana with disgust.

"Now hold on there, Miss Penn," he acknowledged with his odd American twang. "This is hardly a conversation for the churchyard, especially coming from someone who was thick as thieves with that girl."

The implication was clear, reinforced by the knowing looks exchanged among the group. Nancy's character assassination had been thorough.

Diana took a measured breath and lifted her chin. "Ellen is my friend. I understand she's missing, and I'd like to know when she was last seen."

"Young women with questionable morals do tend to associate with one another," Mrs Robbins observed to no one in particular.

Diana ignored the barb. "Mr Hollister, I'd appreciate a moment of your time. Privately."

Something flickered in the man's eyes. Diana wasn't sure if it was enjoyment at her discomfort, or a type of cruelty. "Very well, Miss Penn. I will indulge you, despite your... reputation."

He stepped away from the group, moving to a quiet corner of the churchyard where stone angels watched over ancient graves. Diana followed, keenly aware of the hostile gazes tracking her progress.

"Now then," Hollister said once they were out of earshot, his voice clipped with viciousness. "What is it you wish to know?"

"Where's Ellen?" Diana demanded, dispensing with social niceties. "What did you do to her?"

"I don't see how that's any of your business, but if you must know, Miss Wilson appears to have up and disappeared Wednesday night without so much as a word. Along with several valuable items from my study."

"That's absurd," Diana said flatly. "Ellen would never steal. And she wouldn't leave without telling me."

Hollister's smile didn't reach his eyes. "You don't know her as well as you think, Miss Penn. The girl has been restless for months. Poking about where she doesn't belong. We trusted her, and this is how she repays us."

Diana studied his face, noting the faint sheen of sweat despite the bitter cold. Her intelligence training automatically catalogued the signs of deception—the too-steady maintenance of eye contact, the controlled breathing, the slight tension in his shoulders. Something about Hollister's performance felt rehearsed, as if he'd been practising this conversation. Which, Diana realised with a chill, meant he'd been expecting questions about Ellen's disappearance long before she went missing.

"She told me about how you were with her. What does your wife think about why she disappeared?"

Hollister's eyes narrowed. "You ask a lot of questions."

"I find it interesting that you're here, publicly establishing her guilt, before the police have even had a chance to investigate properly," Diana replied, the anger building inside her. "Almost as if you're more concerned with your reputation than finding her."

A muscle twitched in Hollister's jaw. "Be very careful, Miss Penn. Your association with that RAF officer may have given you ideas above your station, but in this village—"

"In this village, young women don't vanish," Diana cut in. "What have you done to her, Mr Hollister? Where is she?"

"I don't like your implications," Hollister said, his voice dropping dangerously low.

"And I don't like your wandering hands," Diana retorted, abandoning caution entirely. "Ellen told me how you were towards her. The 'accidental' touches—"

The slap came with shocking speed, Hollister's open palm connecting with Diana's cheek with enough force to snap her head sideways. The sharp crack echoed across the churchyard, drawing gasps from those near enough to witness.

"You hysterical little fool," Hollister hissed, his facade of civility completely evaporated. "How dare you make such accusations?"

Diana staggered backward, her hand flying to her stinging face, feet tangling in the uneven ground. She attempted to regain her balance, but her heel caught on the stone edging of the path. The world tilted alarmingly as she fell, arms windmilling in a futile attempt to remain upright.

Her back struck something hard and unyielding—one of the churchyard's weathered monuments. Pain exploded at the base of her skull as it collided with the stone. Through rapidly blurring vision, Diana recognised the carved wings of the weeping angel watching over some long-forgotten grave.

She slid to the ground, darkness encroaching at the edges of her sight. Above her, faces swam in and out of focus—Mrs Robbins' shock, Nancy's hand covering her mouth, Reverend Taylor's dismay. Mr Hollister stood frozen, his expression shifting from naked rage to horrified realisation.

From somewhere nearby, she heard a woman's scream, then running footsteps. Jenny's voice called her name. Mr Hayes appeared at the edge of her fading vision, his face contorting with concern.

As darkness closed around her, cold crept through her limbs, a familiar sensation now. Her last thought, as consciousness slipped away entirely, was that perhaps this wasn't the end. Perhaps there would be another chance to set things right.

Diana's heart beat once more, then stilled. And then the world went dark.

Interlude Two
UNIVERSAL LIFE CENTRE

Marta stared at her pyxis, watching the subject carefully fold, mending with precise movements. After months in 1944, the girl was still maintaining the same emotional distance that had defined her first life.

"Still no real progress," Bertellia observed, materialising beside Marta's desk. "Pleasant conversation over tea isn't transformation."

"She's formed friendships—"

"Surface connections. She knows what's coming to the American girl, yet she does nothing decisive." Bertellia's tone was impatient. "The Machine requires genuine change."

Marta watched her subject's reflection in the farmhouse window—composed, controlled, careful. "Perhaps with more time—"

"Time won't solve this. She's maintaining the same rigid patterns." Bertellia's hand moved towards the temporal controls. "She needs to confront the source of her emotional paralysis. Reset her to here."

"That seems harsh—"

"Compassion won't feed The Machine. She's had months to break free from her conditioning. If she can't change voluntarily..." Bertellia's expression was not unkind. "Sometimes we must lose everything to learn what truly matters."

Marta's hand moved protectively over her pyxis. "Very well," she whispered and the pyxis flared white as the timeline shifted once more.

Chapter Twenty-One

Diana Penn opened her eyes.

The first thing she registered was the scent of smoke in the air. Not the comforting smell of wood smoke, but something acrid and harsh. Diana frowned, trying to place it.

A voice called from somewhere down below her. "Diana! You'll be late for your shift if you don't get a move on!"

Surely after what happened yesterday she should be entitled to a sleep in? Or a day off?

Diana pushed herself upright, tensing for the expected pain in her head from the fall. It took a moment before the reality of her situation hit her. She'd been reset again. But this time, something felt different.

For a start, her bed was narrower than it should be. The walls pressed closer and the ceiling hung lower. There were no sloping eaves, and the scratchy sheets lacked the comforting scent of Cheviot Hills.

This wasn't her room at Willow Farm.

"Diana! For heaven's sake, girl! Your porridge is getting cold!"

Not Mrs Whitaker's voice at all, but one Diana recognised. One she hadn't heard in more decades than she cared to count. A voice that had faded from her memory, preserved only in the vaguest impressions of tone and cadence.

Her mother's voice.

Diana's heart stuttered as she fumbled for the bedside lamp. The click of the switch revealed a room she had almost forgotten existed—her childhood bedroom in their terraced house in Bethnal Green. A room Diana hadn't seen since the night of 15th September 1940, now known as the Battle of Britain Day, when a German bomb had reduced it to rubble.

"I can't be here," she whispered, reaching out to touch the faded flower-patterned wallpaper. It felt solid beneath her fingertips, the texture slightly rough. Real.

On the narrow chest of drawers beside the bed sat a silver-framed photograph of her father in his Great War uniform. Impossibly young and solemn. He had died when Diana was seven, leaving behind nothing but this photograph and a small pension that barely kept them afloat. The frame tarnished in spots where her mother's fingers had touched it most.

"Diana Eliza Penn! I won't call you again!"

Diana flinched at the use of her middle name, a sure sign of her mother's dwindling patience. With shaking hands, she pushed aside the blankets and stood. Her legs felt strong, her movements fluid with youth. She glimpsed herself in the mirror above the dresser. Four years younger than she'd been at Willow Farm.

This wasn't a continuation of her timeline in Cheviot Hills with Mrs Whitaker, Mr Hayes, and Ellen. Somehow, she'd been thrown back even further. Back to before everything. Before her mother's death. Before Willow Farm. Before her MI6 career.

A uniform hung from a hook on the back of the door. Not the brown overalls and green jumper of the Women's Land Army, but the dark blue tunic and skirt of the London Auxiliary Ambulance Service. The sight of it yanked a memory from the depths. The weight of the woollen serge on hot summer nights. The collar chafing against her neck, and the constant smell of antiseptic and fear that no amount of washing could erase.

She tried to recall her station assignment. Station... 97? Or was it 79? *By the old parish church*, she thought, but couldn't remember which one. Her regular runs had included Bethnal Green to the London Hospital in Whitechapel, that much she remembered, and something about a route past St Paul's Cathedral. But the specifics slid away like water through cupped hands.

Her fingers trembled as she dressed. Muscle memory guided her through the forgotten ritual of buttoning the stiff uniform, adjusting the belt, pinning her hair into a severe knot that would fit beneath her tin helmet. Each movement felt simultaneously foreign and achingly familiar.

The narrow staircase creaked beneath her weight, each step a countdown to an encounter Diana had never dared imagine possible. At the bottom, the smell of porridge and tea grew stronger, mingling with the faint scent of lavender water that her mother always dabbed behind her ears.

Diana paused in the doorway of the tiny kitchen, her breath catching in her throat.

Her mother stood at the stove, stirring a pot with more force than necessary. Eleanor Penn was a small woman, her once-dark hair now streaked with grey, her shoulders slightly stooped from years of working as a seamstress. She wore her everyday house dress, faded blue cotton worn thin at the elbows, and her sensible black lace-up shoes.

"There you are," Eleanor said, without turning around. "I swear, Diana, you'd sleep through the Second Coming if I let you. And on today of all days, when I promised her next door that you'd drive her sister to the maternity hospital." She glanced over her shoulder, her exasperation clear. "Well? Are you going to stand there catching flies, or are you going to eat your breakfast?"

Diana couldn't move. Couldn't speak. Her mother was alive and whole and as irritable as ever. Not cold and still and buried beneath the wreckage of their home, where Diana had identified her broken body all those years ago.

"Mother," she whispered, the word catching on a sob.

Eleanor turned, a flicker of concern crossing her lined face. "What's the matter with you? You look as though you've seen a ghost."

Diana crossed the kitchen in three strides and flung her arms around her mother, pulling her into an embrace so tight it forced a startled "oof" from the older woman. Eleanor stiffened, clearly uncomfortable with this uncharacteristic display of affection.

"Diana! Whatever is wrong with you?"

But Diana couldn't let go. The solid warmth of her mother, the homely mix of lavender and starch, and the steady beat of a heart she'd thought forever silenced overwhelmed her. A miracle made flesh.

"I'm sorry," Diana murmured into her mother's shoulder. "I'm just... a bad dream."

Eleanor patted her daughter's back, unused to comforting a child who had always been stoic, even as a little girl. "Well, it was only a dream," she said, her voice softening. "No need for all this drama."

Diana released her, stepping back to memorise every detail of her mother's face. The crow's feet at the corners of her eyes. A tiny scar on her chin from a childhood accident. The slight asymmetry of her mouth when she frowned, which was often.

"You look a fright," Eleanor observed, reaching up to tuck a strand of hair behind Diana's ear with uncharacteristic tenderness. "Are you feeling poorly?"

Diana shook her head, unable to trust her voice. She slid into her chair at the table, where a bowl of porridge waited, a precious half teaspoon of sugar sprinkled on top. Her mother's silent concession to affection, sacrificing part of her own sugar ration.

"Eat up," Eleanor instructed, setting a cup of tea beside the bowl. "You'll need your strength. They're saying we might be in for another raid tonight. The warning came over the wireless while you were still asleep."

Diana froze, staring past her mother at the calendar on the wall.

Reality slammed into her like a battering ram. September 15th, 1940 —the night her mother died—was less than two weeks away. The night a German bomb would tear through their house before Eleanor could reach the shelter, killing her instantly and leaving Diana orphaned and adrift.

But not this time. This time, Diana had the advantage of foreknowledge. This time, she could change things.

"Mother," she began, ignoring her porridge, her appetite vanishing, "we should leave London and go up north."

Eleanor looked up from her own breakfast. "Leave London? Whatever for? I have my work here, and you have your obligations. Besides, where would we go? We don't know anyone 'up north'."

"The bombing will get worse. The East End will be hit particularly hard," Diana insisted, leaning forward.

Her mother's expression hardened. "And how would you know that? Been consulting a fortune teller, have you?"

"It's just..." Diana faltered. "The docks are prime targets. And we're only two streets away."

"Every Londoner knows the docks are targets," Eleanor dismissed her. "That doesn't mean we run away at the first air raid siren. Your father didn't abandon his post during the Great War, and I'll not abandon mine now."

Diana bit back her frustration. Her mother had always been as stubborn as a mule, with a sense of duty that bordered on the pathological. It had been a source of constant friction between them. Diana was now remembering Eleanor's rigid expectations.

"It's not abandoning your post to ensure your own safety," Diana argued, surprised by the heat in her voice. "It's sensible."

Eleanor's lips pressed into a thin line. "I'm not going to leave my home because of Hitler and his thugs." She glanced at the clock on the mantel. "You're going to be late. Eat up. I won't have you wasting good food."

Diana recognised the finality in her mother's tone. This wasn't a conversation to be won today. Still, there was time. Not much, but surely enough to shift Eleanor's thinking?

"Fine," she said, standing. "But we should talk about it later."

As Diana retrieved her ambulance driver's cap from the hook by the door, a thought surfaced. They should go to Cheviot Hills. The small Northumbrian village where she was stationed with the Land Army. Where she would meet Mrs Whitaker, who showed her a mother's care in ways Eleanor never had. Where she would encounter Mr Hayes, and later Jim Crawford. A place that had, in her first life, become a refuge after London's destruction. In her subsequent lives, it had been the location for her attempted resetting of things that had gone wrong.

She should convince her mother to evacuate there. To leave London far behind for the safety of the northern countryside. If she could get her mother to Cheviot Hills, they would both be safe. After that... she wasn't sure. But a life with her mother alive would be better than one without her.

"And take your gas mask. Try not to do anything reckless."

At the door, Diana hesitated. Her mother's words weren't warm, but they carried the shape of care. It struck her for the first time that her mother loved her in the only way she knew how—through caution and expectation. Loss had tempered Eleanor Penn. She was a woman who'd learned long ago that softness rarely served. Her strictness had been her armour.

"I will," Diana promised. Then, on impulse, she added, "I love you, Mother."

Eleanor looked up, startled.

They weren't a family that put feelings into words. Emotion was something to be managed, not indulged. Yet the surprise on her mother's face melted into something softer.

"And I you," she replied. "Now go, before I'm forced to listen to her next door complain about your tardiness for the rest of the week."

As Diana stepped onto the street, adjusting her LAAS cap, the reality of her situation hit her with full force. She was in London. The world was at war, and her mother was alive. But so too were the sons of Mrs Whitaker and Mr Hayes. And Ellen Wilson wasn't missing. Nancy Robbins didn't even know Diana existed. But then again, neither did Jim Crawford. She could live with one of those remaining true, but not the other.

What had she done to deserve a chance to save her mother? To change the course of her life once more? Could she use this opportunity to save not just her mother, but the sons of her friends? And Ellen?

The street was barely recognisable from the ordered neighbourhood she remembered. Sandbags were piled high against buildings, windows crisscrossed with sticky tape to prevent shattering. A small mountain of rubble blocked half the road at the end of the street—the remains of the Murray's house, she recalled with sudden clarity. Hit a few nights ago. The acrid smell of dust and burnt timber hung in the air, mingling with the ever-present scent of coal smoke from a hundred hearths.

Diana's ambulance station was half a mile away, she remembered now. Past the bombed-out chemist's shop, then left at the church with the missing steeple. The familiarity was returning in fragments. Jagged pieces of a life she'd packed away decades ago.

The air raid siren began its mournful wail. Diana hurried towards the nearest shelter, her gas mask box bouncing against her hip. Above, the drone of German bombers rumbled like distant thunder. Around her, Londoners moved with purposeful calm towards shelter, their faces set with the peculiar determination that had become the city's hallmark.

Diana quickened her pace. There was no way she was going to let herself die again, not here. Not until she'd persuaded her mother to leave London.

Somehow she needed to get her safely up to Cheviot Hills, and from there... well, she didn't know what she'd do after that. She had four years to fix everything wrong with her life before trying to save Ellen. And she wasn't planning on mucking it up again.

Interlude Three
UNIVERSAL LIFE CENTRE

Marta's fingers traced the edge of her pyxis, the milky white surface rippling like disturbed water. The vast room hummed with quiet activity. Thousands of watchers sat bent over their own cylinders, harvesting the emotions of their charges to feed The Machine.

"You've reset her even further back," came a voice from behind. "Rather audacious of you."

Marta did not turn. She'd known Carrie would notice. After all, Carrie had been monitoring the situation since the beginning. Somehow, she managed to be in many places at the same time.

"Audacious is one word for it," Marta replied, adjusting the temporal focus of her pyxis. "Necessary would be another."

Carrie moved to stand beside Marta's desk, her white garments glowing against the endless expanse of identical workstations. "The standard protocol is to maintain the original reset point. You've deliberately moved her back four years."

Charles appeared at Carrie's elbow, like a reminder. He didn't speak, but simply smiled.

"Yes," Carrie said. "We are allowed, and even encouraged, to find different reset dates now."

As if in confirmation, a small blue bird appeared on Carrie's shoulder. Like Charles, it did not speak, but its presence was enough.

"Four years, three months, and seventeen days." Marta tapped the surface of her pyxis, calling up an image of a narrow London street. Sandbags piled against buildings, windows crisscrossed with tape, smoke rising from the shells of bombed-out homes. "September 1940. The beginning of the Blitz."

"With her mother," Carrie noted, her voice neutral.

"With her mother," Marta agreed. "Before everything."

Carrie sighed, a remarkably human gesture for one who had transcended mortality long since. "Are you certain this was the right choice? The subject was making progress in '44. She'd saved the farmer. She was working towards preventing the American girl's disappearance." She looked at Charles.

Charles closed his eyes, deep in thought. He began to work various equations in the air in front of him.

"Progress?" Marta's fingers stilled on the pyxis. "She died three times in as many weeks. I call that rather inefficient."

"She would have found her way."

"Perhaps." Marta did not sound convinced. "But our subject spent a lifetime mourning her mother's death. It defined her, shaped every decision she made afterwards. The hardness, the isolation, the obsessive focus on duty—all stemming from that single moment."

Carrie leaned closer, studying the images shifting within the pyxis. "So you believe she needs to resolve her relationship with her mother before she can address the other tragedies?"

"She needs to understand where her patterns began." Marta adjusted the temporal focus again, revealing a young woman in a blue uniform flinching as a siren wailed. "Her mother's death fractured something fundamental within her. Without addressing that, she'll continue making the same mistakes."

"You're unusually invested in this one," Carrie observed.

Marta smiled. "I've watched her sacrifice personal happiness for duty time and again. I've seen her pass through life like a ghost, never connecting, never truly living. Even in her reset, she approached each problem with the same rigid determination that defined her first life. As if emotions were a liability rather than a strength."

"And you believe revisiting her time with her mother will change that?" Carrie asked.

"Understanding the source of one's patterns is the first step towards breaking them." Marta's voice softened. "Besides, wouldn't you have wanted a chance to say a proper goodbye to someone you lost suddenly?"

Carrie fell silent, as if her own memories were surfacing. After a moment, she sighed again. "Bertellia won't approve of such sentimentality."

"Her methods are effective, but I sometimes think she lacks compassion," Marta replied.

"Like our subject," Carrie noted with a pointed look.

"Precisely like our subject."

Charles finished whatever complex equations he was working on. "This will work. This will give her the optimal opportunity to succeed."

Marta and Carrie fell silent, contemplating the images within the pyxis. The young woman moved through war-torn London with purpose, navigating rubble-strewn streets and directing frightened civilians to safety. Yet beneath her efficient exterior, both watchers could sense the turmoil. And the desperate need to save her mother from the future she knew was coming.

"She seems different this time," Carrie observed.

"She's learning, evolving," Marta agreed. "Each reset has taught her something new. I think this time she's not merely trying to change events. She's trying to change herself."

"And if she fails again?"

Marta caressed the pyxis. "Then we try again. She deserves the chance. A lifetime of serving her country. Surely that earns her at least one more opportunity?"

Carrie disappeared.

Marta recited the familiar directive, *"Remember we watch, and we don't interfere,"* before leaning closer to her pyxis. "But sometimes, watching isn't enough," she whispered.

The cylinder pulsed in response, as if acknowledging a secret understanding between the watcher and her subject.

Chapter Twenty-Two

Diana's ambulance partner, Gladys, clutched the dashboard as Diana took a corner with practiced efficiency. Gladys was three years Diana's senior, with a delicate touch when tending to the wounded, but an aversion to all things mechanical, including driving.

"Slow down, Penn," Gladys warned. "You'll have us wrapped around a lamppost at this rate."

Diana eased her foot off the accelerator, conscious that her driving skill—honed through decades of intelligence work that hadn't technically happened yet—might seem incongruous with her supposed inexperience.

"Sorry," she muttered. "Just eager to get Mrs Pembroke to hospital."

Their patient, a woman in her third trimester with concerning pains, lay on the stretcher in the back, attended by Sue, another LAAS volunteer. The promised maternity case from "next door" that her mother had mentioned that morning.

"No sense delivering her to hospital if we don't arrive ourselves," Gladys said with reproach. "The London won't thank us for bringing them more work than they've already got if you get us into an accident."

The London Hospital loomed ahead, its imposing Victorian facade marred by sandbags piled high against possible blast damage. Two nurses waited by the entrance, already moving forward as Diana brought the ambulance to a stop.

"Primigravida, thirty-four weeks, complaining of cramps since six this morning," Sue reported as they unloaded the stretcher. "BP ninety over sixty, pulse steady."

Diana watched the efficient transfer, then climbed back into the driver's seat. The passenger door opened, and Gladys slid in beside her, lighting a cigarette with shaking hands.

"Back to the station?" Diana asked, although she already knew the answer.

"Unless you fancy taking tea with the surgeons," Gladys replied dryly.

As they drove, Diana studied the streets of Bethnal Green with fresh eyes. So changed from the modern London she'd left behind, yet painfully familiar in its wartime resilience with its Anderson shelters protruding from tiny back gardens, and Air Raid Precaution wardens patrolling with vigilant expressions.

Yet amid the preparations for nightly bombardment, life continued. Children played hopscotch on pavements, women queued for meagre rations with shopping baskets over their arms, and old men gathered outside the pub that wouldn't open for hours.

"You're quiet today," Gladys observed, exhaling a plume of smoke that curled towards the windscreen. "More so than usual, which I wouldn't have thought possible."

Was that what the others thought of her?

Diana cast a quick glance towards Gladys, who was studiously staring out the other window, her cheeks red.

"I was just thinking," Diana said, still slightly stunned.

"Dangerous pastime, that."

"My mother," Diana began, then hesitated. "I've been trying to convince her to evacuate. Go north."

Gladys snorted. "Good luck with that. My mum says she'd rather face Hitler's bombs than Yorkshire hospitality." She flicked ash out the window. "Though between you and me, I wish she'd take my sister's little ones to the country. They're still having nightmares from the raid last week."

"There's a village," Diana said carefully. "Cheviot Hills, in Northumberland. I've heard it's lovely. Safe."

"Never heard of it. Friend of yours there, is there?"

"Not yet," Diana murmured, too quietly for Gladys to hear.

The ambulance station appeared ahead. A converted parish hall with three other ambulances parked in the yard.

Inside, the station's atmosphere was one of rehearsed calm. A wireless in the corner played music at low volume. A blackboard listed crew assignments and the locations of recent incidents and blocked roads. The smell of cigarettes permeated everything.

Station Officer Briggs, a former bus conductor with a magnificent moustache, looked up from his paperwork as they entered.

"Penn, Johnson," he acknowledged. "Any complications with the Pembroke woman?"

"None, sir," Gladys reported. "Clean handover at the London."

"Good. Tea's fresh."

Diana poured herself a cup from the enamel pot on the side table, stewed to the colour of mahogany and sweet enough to make her teeth ache. She mumbled a quiet *thank you* to the unknown saint who'd somehow added their entire month's sugar ration to the pot.

She settled at the wooden table where two off-duty drivers played a game of gin rummy. Norman, a railway worker deemed unfit for military service due to his poor eyesight, nodded a greeting. Beside him, Violet—a former lady's maid with an incongruously posh accent—barely looked up from her hand.

"Any news about tonight?" Diana asked, wrapping her hands around the warm cup.

Norman shrugged. "The weather is clear. Reckon Jerry won't waste the opportunity."

"My Arthur says they're expecting a big one," Violet contributed. "Something about increased reconnaissance flights yesterday."

Diana nodded, keeping her expression neutral despite the sickening knot of foreknowledge in her stomach. The Blitz would intensify over the coming days and weeks, with East London enduring the Luftwaffe's attention. How many of these people would survive? How many of the streets she'd driven through today would still exist by Christmas?

"Penn," Briggs called from his desk. "Supply run to Whitechapel station at three. Take ambulance four. Johnson's off to Bethnal Green tube with Carstairs."

"Yes, sir," Diana replied, glancing at the clock. Four hours until her shift ended.

The afternoon passed in a blur of routine calls and transfers. Diana fetched medical supplies from the depot, transported an elderly man with a suspected broken hip to the hospital, and waited as other volunteers cleared debris from a partially collapsed terrace house, just in case there were survivors.

Throughout, she maintained the professional distance that had characterised her first time through these events. Only now, she recognised it as a defence mechanism. The emotional walls she would perfect during the rest of her life. She couldn't help mulling over Gladys' words from earlier in the day.

At quarter past six, Diana signed out and headed home, her steps quickening as the light faded. She was determined not to spend another night in a public shelter if she could help it. Better to face her mother's stubborn resistance in the relative privacy of home.

Eleanor Penn was at the kitchen table when Diana entered, darning a pair of stockings by the light of a shaded lamp. The wireless played in the background, a newsreader's clipped tones reporting Allied movements with futile optimism.

"Long day," Eleanor observed without looking up.

"Busy day," Diana replied, hanging her uniform jacket on the hook behind the door. "Have you thought about what I said this morning?"

"About running away to God-knows-where?" Her mother's nimble fingers continued their work. "No, I can't say I have."

Diana sat opposite her, studying the face she'd thought lost forever. Eleanor Penn had never been a beautiful woman. Her features were too sharp and her expressions too severe. But there was a certain dignity in her profile.

"It wouldn't be running away," Diana persisted. "It would be a strategic withdrawal."

That earned her a brief, sardonic glance. "Fancy words."

"Mother, please. You've seen what's happened already, and this is just the beginning."

Eleanor set down her darning. "And what would I do 'up north'? Sit in some stranger's parlour feeling useless while London burns? While people I've known all my life lose everything?"

"You'd be alive," Diana spat back, unable to control her emotions.

Surprise flickered in Eleanor's eyes. "We all die sometime, Diana. The only question is whether we've done our duty before we go."

There it was, Diana thought. The cornerstone of her mother's philosophy, bequeathed to Diana whether she wanted it or not. Duty above all.

"There are other duties," Diana tried, desperate to find the right words. "To yourself. And to me."

Eleanor's expression softened. "My duty to you is to show you how to stand firm when it would be easier to run. Your father—"

"Would want us to be safe," Diana interrupted, despite barely remembering the man.

"Would do his duty, as he always did," Eleanor corrected. "Now, there's rabbit stew for supper. Mrs Collins, from number seventeen, got hold of an actual rabbit and was kind enough to share."

Before Diana could respond, the air-raid siren began its undulating wail. Eleanor sighed, setting aside her darning and reaching for the small bag she kept packed with essentials.

"Just in time for tea, as usual," she said with grim humour. "Grab your gas mask."

Diana hesitated. "Mother, we should go to the tube station. The communal shelter won't be enough if—"

The distant crump of the first bombs cut her off, followed by the ominous drone of approaching German aircraft.

"No time," Eleanor decided, moving towards the door. "The communal shelter will have to do."

"Mother—"

But Eleanor was already halfway down the street, joining the flow of neighbours headed for the communal shelter beneath the old glove warehouse at the end of their road. Diana hurried after her, her heart pounding, praying that the timeline stayed true, That she still had enough time to persuade her mother to leave London.

"Mrs Penn! Diana!" a voice called from behind them. Diana turned to see Mrs Keller, their next-door neighbour, waving frantically. "We're going to the Underground! Come with us!"

Eleanor paused, clearly torn between the closer communal shelter and the safer tube station several streets away. Another explosion sounded, closer still, making the decision for her.

"Very well," she conceded.

They followed the Kellers through narrow streets. Above, the drone of bombers grew louder, punctuated by the sharp crack of anti-aircraft fire. Searchlights swept the night sky, their beams cutting through the darkness in desperate search of targets.

Bethnal Green station's entrance was crowded with people descending the stairs. Diana felt her mother's hand grip her arm as they joined the press of bodies. The stairwell was dim, lit only by blue-shaded bulbs that cast an eerie glow over frightened faces.

"Stay close," her mother said, guiding her through the crowd with the confidence of someone who had navigated far worse situations.

The platform below was transformed. Gone were the usual commuters and empty tracks. Instead, hundreds of East Enders had made the space their nightly residence. Blankets and makeshift bedding covered every inch of the floor. Families huddled together, some attempting to sleep, others sharing mugs of tea from vacuum flasks.

The distinctive smell hit Diana immediately. A peculiar mixture of unwashed bodies, damp wool, the carbolic soap, and the musty scent of the tunnel itself. The curved ceiling amplified every sound: children's whispers became clearly audible conversations, a woman's sob from thirty feet away sounded as though it were right beside them, and the collective breathing of hundreds of people created an eerie backdrop of white noise. The tiled walls sweated with condensation from so many bodies packed into the confined space. Despite the crush, the air remained cool. The subterranean chill rising from the tracks was a constant reminder that they were, quite literally, underground.

The rumble of bombs penetrated even here, causing plaster dust to sift down from the ceiling and children to whimper in fear. A WVS volunteer moved through the crowd, offering tea and reassurance in equal measure.

"First time down here, Mrs Penn?" asked Mrs Keller as they found space against a wall. "It's not so bad once you get used to it. Safer than those Anderson things, that's for certain."

Eleanor looked around, taking in the crowded conditions. "It seems... adequate."

Diana spread her coat on the ground, creating a place for her mother to sit. "It's the safest place in East London tonight," she announced confidently, eliciting a raised eyebrow from her mother.

As if to emphasise her point, a massive explosion sounded above—close enough to shake the station and send a collective gasp through the shelter. Somewhere, Diana knew, the Germans had just erased another London street.

Eleanor sat beside her daughter, spine rigid, dignity intact despite their surroundings. She opened her bag and extracted a small packet wrapped in newspaper. "Here," she said, passing Diana half a sandwich. "No sense facing whatever comes on an empty stomach."

Diana accepted it, throat tight with emotion. This gesture contained more tenderness than any words Eleanor might have said.

They ate in silence as bombs fell and the Underground shelter swelled with more arrivals. Across the platform, a man with a harmonica began playing Vera Lynn's 'We'll Meet Again.' Its hopeful refrain incongruous against the destruction happening above.

"Mother," Diana chanced. "About going north. There's a place I've been told about up north, called Cheviot Hills. They're looking for Land Army Girls. I could do that."

Eleanor sighed. "You're persistent."

"Just... promise you'll think about it? Not forever. Just until the worst is over."

Her mother studied her face in the dim light, seeming to notice something different in her daughter's expression.

"You've changed," Eleanor observed. "Has something happened?"

Diana looked away, afraid her eyes might reveal too much. "War changes everyone."

Another bomb fell nearby, drawing gasps from the sheltering families. Eleanor's hand found Diana's in the darkness, her grip strong.

"I'll think about it," she said at last. "This Cheviot Hills of yours. I promise nothing more."

Diana squeezed her mother's hand, hope flaring in her chest.

"Thank you," she whispered.

As the night progressed and destruction rained from above, Diana watched her mother drift into uneasy sleep, head resting against the tiled wall of Bethnal Green station. This small victory—a promise to consider leaving London—might be enough to alter the path ahead. To save Eleanor Penn from the bomb that had shattered both their lives in Diana's original timeline.

Tomorrow, she would try turning that tentative "perhaps" into a definite "yes." She had to. Because somewhere in Northumberland, the future was waiting—not just for her mother, but for all the lives Diana hoped to save with her impossible second chances. And she was running out of days.

Chapter Twenty-Three

Diana opened her eyes to the familiar creak of the house settling around her, the distant rumble of early morning traffic, and the acrid tang of coal smoke that had perpetually hung over Bethnal Green during the Blitz. For a moment, she lay still, her mind cataloguing the sensations of another morning of war.

How many mornings had she woken like this in her first life? Alone, distant, already armoured against the day ahead before her feet had even touched the floor. The realisation struck her with uncomfortable clarity as she studied the faded flower-patterned wallpaper.

I'm wasting this chance, she thought, pushing herself upright on the narrow bed. Here she was, granted the impossible gift of reliving her youth, and what was she doing with it? Exactly what she'd done the first time by continuing to hold everyone at arm's length.

She recalled two ambulance girls laughing over the tea urn yesterday—Rose and Shirley, she thought their names were. Rose, the copper-haired one, had been doubled over with mirth at something Shirley had said. When had Diana ever laughed like that? When had she ever allowed herself such unguarded moments?

Diana swung her legs over the side of the bed, her feet finding the cold linoleum floor.

If she was reliving her life—and she was still unclear on the cosmic mechanics of how or why—then surely she could challenge the known facts about herself. She didn't have to be the same withdrawn, duty-obsessed woman who'd spent a lifetime avoiding meaningful connections. She could choose differently.

She imagined trying to be someone else. *Could she? Should she try?*

The thought both terrified and exhilarated her as she reached for her uniform, the coarse serge fabric of the ambulance service tunic familiar beneath her fingers. Today, she would try with Rose and the others. Today, she would try being a different person.

Not long after she arrived for her shift, and moments after she'd settled down with the newspaper and a cup of tea, Briggs appeared at her side. "Penn, ambulance three needs checking over. Peterson says the brakes felt spongy on the last run."

Diana nodded, folding the newspaper with careful precision. The day before, and all the days before that, she would have welcomed this distraction from unwanted sociability. Today though, Briggs's reliance on her work ethic was already derailing her planned life do-over. "I'll see to it right away, sir."

As she passed the group of chattering women, Rose Finley—all copper hair and freckles—reached out to touch her arm. "We're going for a drink after shift, Diana. You're welcome to join, you know."

Diana stiffened at the unfamiliar contact. "Another time," she said, panicking at what she should say.

"That's what you said last week," Rose pointed out, her smile fading. "And the week before."

"Enjoy your drinks," Diana replied, moving towards the door, already castigating herself for turning down the invitation. Hadn't her past experience with Ellen taught her anything? Had she already forgotten how to make friends? Was this going to be her lot in life? She shook her head. Useless, that's what she was. Useless.

Outside in the yard, Diana examined ambulance three with methodical care, checking the brake fluid and testing the pedal action. The vehicle needed attention, but not urgently. Still, she spent a full hour making minor adjustments, preferring the company of machines to people.

Machines were predictable. They didn't die unexpectedly or disappear without explanation. They didn't leave you grieving their absence.

When her shift ended, Diana changed out of her uniform with rapid efficiency, avoiding the chatter of the locker room. Doris Carpenter, a quiet girl with glasses who usually respected Diana's desire for solitude, attempted conversation.

"Nasty raid last night," she offered. "My gran's street got hit pretty badly."

"I hope she's all right," Diana said, buttoning her coat.

"She is, thank goodness. But the Millers next door..." Doris trailed off, her eyes dampening. "All three of them gone, just like that."

Diana nodded, unsure what response Doris expected. She remembered tragedy being so commonplace that acknowledging each instance seemed almost redundant. "I'm sorry to hear that," she said at last, the words formal and inadequate.

"We're having a working bee there tomorrow. After shift. To help everyone get back on their feet, as best we can. We'd love an extra pair of hands. And, well, you're so good with electrics and stuff..."

Once again, Diana hesitated. She couldn't do this. This making friends with others. It would only lead to problems down the track.

"I'm afraid I can't," she said, collecting her gas mask box. "My mother expects me home straight away after shift. She's a widow."

Doris's face fell, but she recovered quickly. "Another time, perhaps."

"Perhaps," Diana echoed, doubting whether she could ever accept invitations which had no strings attached. And why had she shared the tidbit about her mother being a widow? That small admission teetered on the cusp of oversharing. A fatal flaw for any intelligence worker. The admission puzzled her.

As she walked home, Diana considered her strategy. Her mother remained stubbornly resistant to evacuation, but Diana wouldn't give up. Eleanor Penn could not—would not—die in the Blitz this time. Diana would save her.

Diana pushed these thoughts aside as she reached their terrace house. Sentiment was a distraction. Duty came first. It always had.

Her mother looked up from her sewing as Diana entered, her eyes sharp with assessment. "You're late," she observed.

"Ambulance needed maintenance," Diana replied, hanging her coat on the peg by the door. "I volunteered to do it."

Her mother nodded, but with her eyebrows raised, and disapproval marring her face.

"There's a war on, Mother," Diana pointed out. "And somehow or other, I appear to be the most adept at keeping the ambulances on the road. So sometimes I can't come home straight away."

Before her mother could respond, the air raid siren began its mournful wail. Eleanor rose with practiced efficiency, collecting their prepared bag of essentials from beside the door.

"Come along," she said, any remaining displeasure vanishing beneath the immediate demands of survival. "The Underground awaits."

As they joined the stream of neighbours heading for the public shelter, Diana wondered what other opportunities she'd overlooked in her first life. What other connections she might have formed had she allowed herself a life outside of service to her country? Connections she might have made if she hadn't been so worried about her duties to her widowed mother?

But such thoughts were dangerous. Connections meant vulnerability. And vulnerability was a weakness she could ill afford. But she was having a hard time persuading herself of that this time, as the bombs fell on London once again.

Chapter Twenty-Four

The ambulance station was quiet when Diana arrived for her early shift. Outside, London still slumbered in the pre-dawn darkness, the brief lull between the all-clear siren and the city's gradual awakening creating an eerie stillness. She hung her coat on the hook by the door, the familiar weight of duty settling across her shoulders as she signed the logbook.

Her eyes darted immediately to the calendar on the station wall—a grimy thing with dates crossed off in red pencil. September 9th. Six days. Six bloody days until the 15th hurtled towards them like a comet on a collision course with everything she held dear.

"You're early, Penn," Station Officer Briggs observed.

"Couldn't sleep," Diana replied.

The station had become almost comforting in its predictability, with the blackboard constantly updated with fresh incidents and blocked routes. The battered blue and white enamel teapot perpetually stewing on the hotplate, with the stench of disinfectant and engine oil and smoke permeating everything else. In the corner, Norman snored quietly, his gangly frame folded awkwardly across two chairs during his rest break.

Diana busied herself checking supplies, counting bandages and arranging instruments. The routine tasks kept her hands occupied, but her mind wandered like a compass needle seeking north.

Always returning back to the calendar, and to the mathematics of mortality. Six days, one hundred and forty-four hours, eight thousand six hundred and forty minutes.

Her movements became increasingly agitated as she sorted through the medical supplies. A roll of gauze fell from her shaking fingers, unraveling across the ambulance floor like a white flag of surrender. When she bent to retrieve it, her hands betrayed her further, fumbling with the simple task of gathering up the now dirty bandage.

Breathe, she commanded herself. *You're no use to anyone if you fall apart.*

Two days had passed since her mother's cautious agreement to consider leaving London. Three days of careful arguments and subtle persuasion over meagre suppers and in the cramped confines of the Underground shelter each night. Eleanor remained resistant, although Diana fancied she could sense her mother's resolve weakening with each near miss and every new pile of rubble that had once been someone's home.

As Diana inventoried the splints, footsteps sounded behind her. Rose Finley, the seventeen-year-old copper-haired ambulance attendant, appeared at the back doors of the vehicle.

"Morning," she said, stifling a yawn. "Want some tea? There's a fresh pot."

Diana blinked, thrown by the offer. After brushing Rose off yesterday, she expected Rose to ignore her going forward, save for work-related necessities. She certainly couldn't remember ever talking to or encouraging Rose the first time round.

"That would be lovely," Diana replied, the words strangely formal on her tongue.

In the makeshift canteen area, a cluster of off-duty drivers and attendants gathered around a wireless, listening to the early morning news with sombre expressions. Diana accepted the cup Rose handed her, noticing how the others seemed to raise their eyebrows at the exchange.

With a start, she realised she'd never interacted with Rose before, unless it was on the job. So what was different now? Diana watched her colleagues with fresh eyes, seeing patterns she'd been blind to before. Gladys murmuring something that made Violet laugh. Norman passing around a newspaper, exchanging comments with each person.

The easy way they leaned towards one another, sharing space and conversation with the unconscious comfort of people accustomed to each other's presence.

Diana stood slightly apart, as she always had. But now, for the first time, she felt the distance as a void rather than a buffer.

"Finley, Penn, ambulance three. Possible casualties on Hanbury Street," Briggs called from the door. "Unexploded ordnance from last night. Fire Brigade's already there."

Diana set down her tea, grateful for the interruption to her uncomfortable realisations. She was back on familiar ground now. Duty came first.

During the tense drive to Hanbury Street, Diana watched Rose check her medical kit for the third time.

"Were you still at school when the war started?" Diana asked, surprising herself with the question as much as she did Rose.

Rose paused in her counting of gauze dressings. She stared at Diana as if she'd started speaking German.

"I—yes," she stammered. "St Margaret's on Cable Street." She hesitated. "You?"

"Dalston Girls' Grammar," Diana replied, navigating around a crater in the road. "Until the evacuations started. I was still young enough to go, but Mother wouldn't even consider it."

Rose nodded, still looking confused by this sudden conversation. "Mine neither. Dad said if we're going to get bombed, might as well be together." A shadow crossed her face. "They got him on his way to work. Never had a chance."

"I'm sorry," Diana said, her words sincere.

"S'alright. Well, it's not, but..." Rose shrugged. "What about your dad?"

"Died of complications from the Great War, when I was seven."

"Gladys said your mum was a widow. Sorry about that."

Diana nodded and opened her mouth to reply, but checked herself. She'd just shared some of the most intimate personal information about her life with a girl who was basically a stranger. She may as well have told Rose about her last bowel movement and about the bizarre situation of reliving her life over and over again. What was happening to her?

The ambulance rounded a corner, bringing Hanbury Street into view.

Their conversation ended at the sight of the cordoned-off area where an ARP warden directed them towards a row of terraced houses. One had partially collapsed, leaving its neighbour dangerously unstable.

For the next three hours, they worked alongside the Fire Brigade and rescue teams. Together they helped extract the family from the damaged building, before transporting the injured to hospital.

By mid-morning, they returned to the station for a scheduled break. The day shift crowded the canteen area, eating the breakfast prepared by Mrs Hadley, the station's unofficial boss.

Diana collected a plate of powdered eggs and toast, then hesitated, looking around the room. Every table seemed full of conversation and camaraderie. She spotted Rose sitting with three other girls around Diana's age, all laughing at something one had said.

For a moment, Diana considered taking her plate to the far corner, as she used to. It would be easier, certainly. Safer. But the memory of her most recent life with Jenny and Ellen, and yes, even Nancy, flashed in her mind. And so, with a deep breath, she approached Rose's table.

"May I join you?" she asked, feeling like a child asking to play.

The conversation wavered. Four pairs of eyes turned towards her with varying degrees of surprise. Rose recovered first.

"'Course," she said, shifting to make room. "Everyone, this is Diana. She's ace in a crisis."

Ace in a crisis. How many times had she been told variations of that in her life?

Diana sat, the weight of the silence settling around her. She groped for something to say, but nothing came.

Shirley, a sturdy girl with dark plaits, nodded in greeting. Doris, slightly older with glasses, regarded Diana with open curiosity.

"We've all been around here for ages," Doris said, a touch wryly. "Strange how we've barely crossed paths?"

Diana's cheeks warmed. "I suppose I've always kept to myself."

"You can say that again," Shirley said with a snort, earning a sharp look from Rose. "What? She does."

"Shirley!" Betty hissed, clearly appalled.

Diana chuckled. "But I'm trying to change that. My mother's the same," she offered. "Always a little apart. I guess I picked it up."

"My mum's the opposite," Betty said. "Knows everything about everyone. Total nightmare."

"Same," said Rose. "Can't get to the end of the street without three detours and a gossip session."

As they talked, the tension inside Diana loosened. The conversation flowed around her, occasionally including her, but never demanding anything from her. Just the simple, mundane exchange of girls who'd seen too much for their years but still found moments to be young.

The conversation moved onto a discussion about what had happened over on Commercial Road the night before, with Rose and Gladys taking turns to fill in the gaps about Rose discovering the missing cat curled up inside an old flour barrel in the back room, covered head to tail in white dust but perfectly unharmed.

"Anyone for more tea?" Doris asked, rising. "I'm parched."

"Please," Diana said. Then, "I could come help?"

Doris looked surprised but pleased. "Two pairs of hands are better than one."

At the tea station, Diana felt Doris's stare. "Are you sure you don't have a twin sister, because last week you wouldn't have given any of us the time of day?"

Diana measured tea into the pot, buying time. How could she explain that she was older than she appeared? Much older. That she'd lived an entire life before being granted this second chance?

"I've never had any friends," Diana offered, peering into the tea leaves, avoiding any eye contact. "And, well, with all that's going on, I think I'm going to need some."

Doris nodded, her expression thoughtful. "My gran says humans shouldn't be on their own. It's not healthy." She poured the boiling water into the teapot.

"Your gran sounds wise."

"She is. Drives Mum barmy with her 'old-fashioned nonsense,' but she's usually right." Doris adjusted her glasses. "Know what she told me when I started here? Said the worst thing about bombs isn't the damage they do to the buildings, but the holes they leave in communities. That's why she won't leave London. She says preserving the connections between people is as important as preserving the structures."

Diana thought of her mother, so determined to stay but out of duty, not because of friends and family. She tried to recall her mother having friends, sharing tea or conversation that wasn't centred on work or obligations. But nothing came to mind. Her mother was an introvert, there was no doubting that, but in the 1940s they probably would have said that she kept to herself. If her mother had been alive in the middle ages, she'd have been right at home emulating St Cuthbert and living the life of a hermit. And hadn't that been what her own life was like before she died the first time? But without the Christian missionary work?

Chapter Twenty-Five

Night had fallen over London, bringing with it the familiar drone of German bombers. Diana sat in the passenger seat of the ambulance as Rose navigated through streets lit only by the occasional flash of anti-aircraft fire. The blackout was absolute; Rose drove with only the thinnest sliver of headlamp visible.

"Opal Place next," Diana said, consulting the clipboard. "Family trapped in a basement. Fire Brigade's already there."

Rose nodded, her copper hair tucked beneath her regulation cap, her face set in professional concentration.

The Germans had been bombing the East End relentlessly all week, but to Diana, tonight's pattern felt wrong. Usually, the bombers came in predictable waves. Tonight, they were more scattered, their approach erratic, as if testing the English air defences for weaknesses.

"Rose," Diana began, unsure how to articulate her concern without revealing impossible knowledge. "I think we should be extra cautious tonight. Something doesn't feel right."

Rose shot her a quick glance. "Been seeing a fortune teller, Penn?"

"Just a feeling," Diana murmured.

They reached Opal Place as the first bombs began falling. Their distant thuds made the ground tremble beneath the ambulance wheels. Three ARP wardens stood outside a partially collapsed terrace house.

Their steel helmets gleaming in the glow of a small fire burning across the street.

"Ambulance service," Diana called as she and Rose approached, medical kits in hand. "Where are they?"

"Basement flat," replied the senior warden, a greying man with a thick moustache. "Mother and two children. Father's trying to reach them through the coal cellar. The Heavy Rescue lads have cleared most of the debris, but we need medical attention standing by. Building's not stable."

Diana followed the warden through a narrow gap in the rubble that the rescue workers had created. The smell hit her. Brick dust, ruptured gas pipes, and the tang of fear. Her torch beam swept across broken timber and chunks of plaster as they descended what remained of the stairs.

In the basement, two Heavy Rescue workers were directing the final clearing operation while a man in shirtsleeves called through a small opening in what had once been a wall.

"Margaret!" the man called. "The ambulance is here. They're ready to help."

A woman's voice, weak but steady, replied from beyond the opening. "We're alright. We're frightened, but we're alright."

The rescue workers stepped back as the family began to emerge. The little girl came first, no more than five years old, her nightdress grey with dust, her body crisscrossed with cuts and abrasions. The mother followed, cradling a toddler against her chest.

Diana and Rose stepped forward with their medical supplies, ready to assess and treat the family's injuries.

As Rose bandaged a vicious gash on the mother's leg, and Diana splinted the little girl's clearly broken wrist, she wondered if this family had survived in her first timeline. Had they escaped the Blitz unscathed? Or had they become three more names in the tally of civilian casualties?

The ground shook as another bomb fell, this one closer, rattling the surrounding windows.

"We have to move," Diana said, urgency sharpening her voice.

Outside, orange flames licked at clouds of smoke, and the silver shapes of barrage balloons floated like spectres against the inferno. The discord of the raid surrounded them—the shriek of falling bombs, the staccato bark of anti-aircraft guns, the distant bells of fire engines racing towards fresh disasters.

"Get in," Diana instructed, hustling the mother and children into the ambulance, with Rose pulling them inside.

Then a whistling sound came from above.

"Everyone down!" she screamed, hurling herself into the back of the ambulance.

The world exploded.

Diana felt herself lifted and thrown. Heat washed over her, followed by a pressure that squeezed the air from her lungs. Something struck her head, and darkness swallowed her.

Pain dragged Diana back to consciousness. She lay still, assessing her situation through closed eyelids as years of training dictated. Trapped. Pinned in what felt like twisted metal. With her right arm wedged against something solid, and an unidentified weight immobilising her legs.

The air tasted of brick dust and smoke. Beneath that, the metallic tang of blood and something else. Death.

She forced her eyes open. Darkness greeted her, save for a faint, flickering orange glow that penetrated through what must be gaps in the wreckage. Slowly, her vision adjusted to show she was in back of the ambulance. Or what remained of it. The vehicle lay crushed beneath tonnes of masonry.

"Rose?" Diana called, her voice emerging as a hoarse whisper. "Rose?"

No response.

Diana extracted her left arm and felt around in the darkness. Her fingers brushed fabric, then something damp and sticky. She moved her hand upward, following the contour of what she now recognised as Rose's uniform, until she reached the girl's neck.

No pulse.

Diana's breathing quickened. She shifted position, ignoring the stab of pain in her ribs. Her movement disturbed Rose's body, causing the head to loll at an impossible angle. Broken neck. Death would have been instantaneous, at least.

"Oh, Rose," Diana whispered.

A vague memory surfaced, but from a different perspective. Diana remembered word coming in that an ambulance had been hit, killing both the driver and the medic, whose name now escaped her. Back then, Rose had just been another name. They'd worked the same shifts occasionally, but Diana had kept everyone at arm's length, including Rose.

They weren't friends, just two people who occupied the same space. Her death was just another wartime statistic.

But whether Diana was with her, whether they were friends or strangers, Rose still died.

"I guess if your time is up, it's up," Diana murmured, the bitter realisation settling into her bones. Perhaps some events were fixed? Immutable despite her presence or actions.

Diana tried to move again, but she was thoroughly pinned. Above her, the precarious mountain of debris groaned. All she could do was wait. It was a comfort knowing that if she died again, she would, hopefully, once again wake up to her mother's voice.

As the hours passed, the sounds of the raid subsided. The distant shouts of rescue workers and the crackle of fire replaced the drone of the bombers. Diana drifted in and out of consciousness, her mind wandering between past and future, between lives lived and lives yet to come.

Rose's body grew cold beside her. She'd overheard Rose and the others talking about films just yesterday, and how Rose had never seen Alfred Hitchcock's *Rebecca*.

Diana thought of Enid Whitaker and Mr Hayes, of Ellen Wilson and Jim Crawford. People she'd cared for in her second chance at 1944. People she hadn't allowed herself to know the first time around. She thought of the pain they would suffer, and she remembered the hollowness in Mrs Whitaker's eyes after Trevor's death, and of Mr Hayes taking his own life. And she thought too of the gaping wound Ellen's disappearance had left in her life. Was this why she had lived so carefully before? Because caring hurt too much?

Never again, she remembered promising herself after her mother's death. Never again would she let someone be close enough to create so much pain when they left. But because of that, Diana had missed out on so much life.

Diana forced her eyes open. Hours must have passed, but something had woken her.

Then she heard it again, a soft whining, muffled by the debris above.

Unmistakably canine. The sound was plaintive, almost human in its distress. Diana held her breath, straining to listen.

"Hello?" she called out.

The whining grew more insistent, then the animal began frantically barking, the sound echoing through the wreckage.

"Good dog," Diana whispered, as though the creature could hear her. "Keep barking. Please keep barking."

The barking grew more frantic, as if the animal was desperately trying to alert someone.

"That's it," she murmured. "Keep making noise. Someone will hear you."

And someone did.

"Got someone!" a man's voice shouted, distant but growing closer.

Chunks of debris shifted above her, allowing thin shafts of grey light to penetrate the darkness. But something was wrong. The light seemed dimmer than it should be, wavering at the edges of her vision like candle flames in a draught.

"Hello? Hello! We're in here!" she called, but her voice emerged as barely a whisper. When had it become so difficult to draw breath?

Thanks, little dog. I'll find you a nice juicy bone when I get out.

Diana tried to shift position, to make herself more visible to her rescuers, but her body wouldn't respond. A strange warmth was spreading through her chest, and she could taste copper on her tongue.

Blood. Her own blood.

The rescue seemed to take an eternity, each piece of rubble removed with agonising care. Diana listened to the methodical work above her, feeling oddly detached from her own body. The pain that had racked her for hours had faded now. All she felt now was a curious lightness.

"Rose," she whispered to the still form beside her, "I'm sorry I didn't try harder to be your friend. I'm sorry I was so bloody stubborn."

Her breathing grew shallower. The voices of her rescuers seemed to echo from a great distance, as though she were hearing them from the bottom of a well. A gap appeared in the rubble above, and the face of a soot-streaked Fire Brigade officer peered through.

"Hold on, love!" he called. "We've nearly got you out!"

But Diana could feel herself slipping away, the edges of consciousness blurring like watercolours in the rain. Her mother's face floated before her.

"I tried, Mother," she whispered, though no sound emerged. "I tried to save you. I'm so sorry."

The last thing Diana heard before the darkness claimed her was the crash of falling masonry as her rescuers broke through. Too late, she thought with something approaching relief.

Her heart beat once more, then stilled.

Chapter Twenty-Six

Diana Penn opened her eyes.

Her first thought was surprise that her head wasn't aching as much as she'd expected. Then she registered smoke in the air. Not the comforting smell of wood smoke, but something acrid and harsh. Diana frowned, trying to place the scent.

A voice called from somewhere below. "Diana! You'll be late for your shift if you don't get a move on!"

Diana pushed herself upright, memories flooding back in a disorienting rush. The ambulance. Rose's broken body beside her. The weight of rubble crushing them both. The long hours waiting for a rescue that came too late. Then darkness.

And now, impossibly, she was back. Back in her childhood bedroom in Bethnal Green, with her mother's voice calling up the narrow stairs.

Diana's hands flew to her face, finding smooth, uninjured skin where there had been blood and grit. She was whole. Alive. Reset once more.

"Diana Eliza Penn! I won't call you again!"

Diana scrambled out of bed, her body responding with the effortless movements of youth. This time, she didn't hesitate. This time, she rushed down the narrow staircase, taking the steps two at a time.

Eleanor Penn stood at the stove, stirring a pot of porridge with more force than necessary. She wore her everyday house dress, faded blue cotton worn thin at the elbows, and her sensible black lace-up shoes.

"There you are," Eleanor said, without turning around. "I swear, Diana, you'd sleep through the Second Coming if I let you. And on today, of all days, when—"

The words died in her throat as Diana flung her arms around her mother's waist, burying her face against Eleanor's shoulder.

"Good gracious!" Eleanor exclaimed, her spoon clattering against the pot. "What on earth has got into you?"

"I love you," Diana murmured, inhaling the familiar scent of lavender water and starch. "I just wanted you to know that."

Eleanor awkwardly patted Diana's hand. "Well, that's... very nice, dear, but your porridge is getting cold, and you're going to be late."

Diana released her mother reluctantly, moving to the table.

"Mother," Diana began, stirring her porridge without eating it, "have you thought about leaving London? Going north?"

Eleanor's expression hardened. "I don't know where this has come from, Diana. My work is here. Your duty is here. I'm not about to abandon my home."

Diana froze. This wasn't going the way she'd hoped.

"I'm not asking you to, but I've heard that the WLA is recruiting in Northumberland. In a place called Cheviot Hills. They're desperate for girls with mechanical experience to work on the farms there. I've got those skills from working on the ambulances here."

"And what would I do in Cheviot Hills?" Eleanor asked, her voice incredulous at Diana's suggestion.

Diana chose her words carefully. "The Ministry of Health is setting up auxiliary hospitals in rural areas. They need seamstresses for uniforms, bedding. Skilled work, Mother. Important work."

"The Ministry?"

"I heard it from Gladys at the station," Diana lied. "Her cousin's already gone. She says it's proper government work, not just evacuation busy-work."

Eleanor appeared to consider it, a crease forming between her brows. "I'll think about it," she said at last. "Mind you, I'm not promising anything. But I'll... look into it."

It was a small victory, but Diana savoured it. This time might be different. This time, she might save her mother.

Diana finished her porridge quickly, then kissed her mother's cheek before retrieving her uniform from the hook by the door. Eleanor touched her own cheek, startled by the gesture.

"Are you feeling quite well?" she asked, peering at Diana.

"Never better," Diana replied honestly. "I'll see you tonight. And remember—Cheviot Hills. Think about it."

The ambulance station buzzed with morning activity when Diana arrived. Station Officer Briggs stood at his desk, assigning the day's routes with military precision. The familiar smell of strong tea and cigarette smoke hung in the air.

"Penn!" Briggs called as she entered. "You're with Finley today. Ambulance three. Supply run to Whitechapel station at ten, then standby for calls."

Diana nodded, her heart quickening at the mention of Rose.

Rose sat alone at a corner table, checking the contents of her medical kit with methodical care, her hair tucked beneath her regulation cap, with a few rebellious copper curls escaping around her temples.

Instead of retreating to the far corner with a newspaper, as she might have done before, Diana approached Rose's table.

"Good morning," she said, setting down her own kit beside Rose's. "Mind if I join you?"

Rose looked up, surprise in her wide green eyes. "'Course not," she replied, though her tone suggested she expected some sort of trick. "Just making sure we're fully stocked. Used the last of the morphine yesterday."

Diana pulled up a chair, noting how Rose tensed at her proximity. "I heard about that," she said conversationally. "Bad business on Commercial Road, wasn't it? You did well, from what Gladys said."

Rose's eyebrows shot up. "You were asking about me?"

"I overheard," Diana clarified. "It sounded like you kept your head in a difficult situation."

"Well, thanks," Rose said, her wariness giving way to cautious pleasure at the compliment. "It was awful, truth be told. Four of them trapped in that shop cellar. The little girl kept asking for her cat." She shook her head, eyes momentarily distant. "Although it was a relief finding the cat, and covered in flour too. The only real bright point. I hate this bloody war."

"So do I," Diana agreed.

Rose studied her curiously. "I don't mean to be rude, but you don't usually talk to..." Rose blushed, clearly uncomfortable voicing her observation.

"Usually I keep to myself," Diana finished for her. "I'm not very good with people."

"That's putting it mildly," Rose said with a startled laugh.

Diana winced. "I'm sorry about that. It's not true at all. I just..." She hesitated, searching for an explanation that would make sense. "I lost someone, and it made me... cautious about getting close to people."

It wasn't entirely a lie. She had lost her mother, even if that loss hadn't yet happened in this timeline.

Rose's expression softened. "I understand that. My dad was killed in the first month. Dock worker." She touched Diana's hand. "But you can't stop living because of it. That's letting them win, isn't it?"

Before Diana could respond, Briggs appeared at their table. "Time to move, ladies. That supply run won't wait."

As they moved towards their ambulance, Diana avoided looking at the calendar. But still, it seemed to mock her from its perch on the wall. A malevolent presence defining her every breath. The 15th would be here before she knew it. She didn't need a calendar to tell her that.

In the ambulance, Diana took the driver's seat, acutely aware of Rose settling beside her. The last time they'd been in an ambulance together, Rose had died. Not this time, Diana vowed. Not if she could help it.

"Where'd you learn to drive?" Rose asked as they navigated through streets already busy with morning activity. "You're better than most of the men I know."

"My uncle taught me," Diana improvised. "Before the war. He had a delivery van for his furniture business."

Rose nodded, seemingly satisfied with this explanation. "Wish my dad had taught me. He always said driving wasn't ladylike." She grinned. "Then again, neither is hauling stretchers through bombed-out buildings, but here we are."

Diana smiled in response. Rose's easy manner was more infectious than she remembered. Had the girl always been this charming? Or had Diana been too wrapped in her own isolation to notice?

"What do you want to do after the war?" Diana asked, genuinely curious. "When all this is over, I mean."

Rose looked surprised, as much by Diana's interest, as well as the question. She was quiet for a moment, her hands still on the medical kit.

"I'd like to be a nurse," she said, a note of longing in her voice. "Proper training and everything. I hope all this experience counts when the time comes."

"You'd be brilliant at it," Diana said sincerely. "You're good with patients. Calm under pressure."

Rose's face brightened at the compliment. "You think so? Most people say I haven't got the temperament for it. Too chatty, they reckon."

"Patients need conversation as much as medicine," Diana replied. "A personal connection can make all the difference. Trust me on that."

They completed the supply run, loading boxes of bandages, splints, and precious bottles of antiseptic into the ambulance. As they were preparing to return to the station, the air raid siren began its mournful wail.

"Christ," Rose muttered, glancing skyward. "Bit early for Jerry today?"

"We should get back," Diana said, a knot of fear forming in her stomach. This was happening too soon. The bombing that had killed them before had been during the evening shift, not the morning.

But perhaps the timeline had shifted? Perhaps her small changes had already altered events, although she doubted that anything she did could alter the Luftwaffe's bombing schedule.

They drove through streets rapidly emptying as Londoners sought shelter. The drone of German aircraft grew louder, and Diana spotted the telltale silver shapes high above—bombers approaching their target.

"There!" Rose pointed to a group of children huddled in a doorway, too far from any proper shelter. "Pull over, quickly!"

Diana stopped the ambulance, and Rose was out the door before the vehicle had fully stopped. "Come on, you lot!" she called to the children. "In you get. We'll find you a shelter."

Five children, none older than ten, piled into the back of the ambulance. The smallest, a girl with dirty blonde plaits, clutched a threadbare teddy bear to her chest.

"Where to?" Diana asked as Rose climbed back in.

"Tube station's closest," Rose decided. "Step on it!"

Diana pressed her foot to the accelerator, heading for Aldgate East station. They were halfway there when the first bombs fell. The ground shook with the impact, and Diana swerved to avoid debris raining down from a stricken building.

"Steady on!" Rose called, clinging to the dashboard. "Bit closer to that one than I'd like!"

Through the rear-view mirror, Diana could see the children huddled together, eyes wide with terror. The little girl with the teddy bear had begun to cry, fat tears tracking through the grime on her cheeks.

They were three streets from the station when Diana heard it—that distinctive whistling sound that had preceded the bomb that killed them before. Instinctively, she slammed on the brakes, wrenching the steering wheel hard to the left, sending the ambulance down a narrow alley.

"What are you—" Rose began, but her words were drowned out by an explosion that rocked the ground behind them. Through the mirror, Diana saw the street they'd just left disappear in a cloud of dust and debris.

"How did you know?" Rose gasped, her face pale beneath her freckles.

"Instinct," Diana replied, her hands steady on the wheel despite the rapid pounding of her heart. "Just... a feeling."

They reached the tube station to find it already packed with sheltering Londoners. Rose organised the evacuation of the children, ensuring each was handed over to the WVS volunteers who would look after them until the all-clear sounded.

"We should get back to the station," Diana suggested once the children were inside. "They'll need every ambulance after this raid."

Rose nodded, following Diana back to the vehicle. As they climbed in, Rose caught Diana's arm.

"That was uncanny," she said, her eyes searching Diana's face. "The way you turned down that alley just before the bomb hit. Almost like you knew."

Diana shrugged, uncomfortable under Rose's scrutiny. "Lucky guess."

"No," Rose shook her head. "That wasn't luck. That was..." She trailed off, seemingly unable to find the right words. "Well, whatever it was, I'm grateful. We'd have been right in the thick of it otherwise."

They drove in silence for several minutes, navigating around fresh craters and emergency vehicles. The raid continued overhead, bombs falling across the East End with devastating effect.

"I've never really talked to you before today," Rose said suddenly. "Not properly. You've always kept your distance."

Diana kept her eyes on the road. "I know. I'm trying to be better about that."

"Why now?"

The question was direct, unexpected. Diana hesitated, unsure how to answer without revealing the impossible truth.

"Life's too short. I've wasted too much time pushing people away," she said.

Rose considered this. "You're an odd one, Diana Penn. But I think I might like you." She paused, then added, "If you give me half a chance."

"I'd like that," Diana replied, surprised to find she meant it.

They were approaching the junction where they'd turn towards the ambulance station when Diana spotted a glint of metal high above. Another bomber, directly overhead.

"Rose," she began, but before she could finish her warning, the world erupted in fire and noise.

The bomb hit the building beside them, sending a cascade of bricks and mortar onto the ambulance. The impact threw Diana sideways, her head striking the window with enough force to crack the glass. Pain exploded through her skull, followed by a warm rush of blood down her temple.

Through a haze of dust and pain, Diana saw Rose slumped against the passenger door, blood streaming from a gash on her forehead. But she was moving, alive.

"Rose," Diana gasped, fighting to stay conscious. "Rose, are you all right?"

"I think so," Rose mumbled, raising a shaking hand to her head. "You?"

Diana tried to respond, but her vision was narrowing to a pinpoint of light. The last thing she heard before darkness claimed her was Rose's voice, growing increasingly frantic.

"Diana! Stay with me, Diana! Don't you dare—"

Then nothing.

After what felt like an eternity, but in reality had been little more than ten minutes, Diana's eyes opened.

The first thing she noticed was Rose's hand gripping hers with fierce intensity.

Their fingers were interlaced so tightly that Diana could feel the other girl's pulse against her palm. The second was the precarious mountain of debris above them, chunks of masonry and twisted metal that groaned ominously with each shift of the wind.

"Thank God," Rose whispered, her voice thick with relief and barely contained tears. "When you went limp like that, I thought you were dead." She squeezed Diana's hand even tighter, as though she could anchor her to consciousness through sheer force of will. "Being stuck down here with a dead body would have been my absolute worst nightmare. I've been talking to you for the past ten minutes, just babbling away, trying to keep myself from going completely barmy."

Diana blinked, her vision clearing enough to make out Rose's face in the dim light filtering through gaps in the wreckage. The girl's copper hair was matted with dust and what looked like dried blood from a cut on her scalp, but her eyes were bright with something that might have been fierce protectiveness.

"I'm not going anywhere," Diana managed, her voice hoarse but steady. Above them, a piece of timber creaked, sending a shower of dust down onto their faces. They both froze, holding their breath until the debris settled again.

Dawn was breaking when Diana heard the barking of a dog. *Why hello, my little canine friend,* she thought, smiling in the dark. The barking was followed by shouts growing nearer. Chunks of debris shifted above her, allowing thin shafts of grey light to penetrate the darkness.

"Hello? Hello! We're in here!" Diana called, her voice stronger now that rescue seemed imminent.

"Got someone!" a man's voice shouted.

The rescue seemed to take an eternity. Each piece of rubble had to be removed carefully, the whole structure liable to collapse at any moment. Diana kept perfectly still, listening to the methodical work of her rescuers, feeling the weight above her gradually lessen.

Finally, a gap appeared, and the face of a soot-streaked Fire Brigade officer peered through.

"How many of you down there?" he asked, his eyes taking in the scene.

"Two," Diana confirmed, glancing at Rose, who was stirring beside her. "We're both alive."

Rose groaned, lifting her head gingerly. "Bloody hell," she muttered, coughing up dust and rubbing her eyes. "Took them long enough! What have they been doing, playing tiddly winks?"

Extracting them from the wreckage was a delicate operation. Diana bit her lip against the pain as circulation returned to her crushed limbs. Rose emerged with a spectacular bruise across her forehead and a cut on her head that had bled impressively but wasn't serious. When they lifted both women free, the morning light seemed supernaturally bright after hours in darkness.

An apocalyptic scene greeted them. The entire street had been levelled. Where terraced houses had stood just hours before, only mountains of brick and splintered timber remained. The ambulance had been crushed beneath the collapsed facade of the building they'd been passing when the bomb hit.

"It's a miracle you survived that," the rescue worker said. But Diana knew better. There were no miracles, only random chance in a universe of chaos.

"Thank goodness that dog led you to us!"

"Mushu? She's a wonder that one. Lost count of how many people she's sniffed out," the rescue worker said, smiling through the grime on his face.

Before Diana could ask more about the dog, the rescue worker had already moved on to his next task. That was one animal that deserved the biggest bone from the butchers.

They wanted to take both women to the hospital, but Diana and Rose refused. They'd only suffered a few bruises, cuts, and what felt like cracked ribs, but nothing that required medical attention. Nothing that wouldn't heal with time and rest.

"I need to go home," Diana insisted. "Mother will be worried."

"Mine too," Rose added, gingerly touching the bandage one of the rescue workers had applied to her head wound. "She'll have kittens if she hears about this before I can tell her myself."

They walked together through streets they scarcely recognised, their uniforms torn and caked with dust, their hair matted with brick dust and dried blood. People stared as they passed, but no one stopped them. London had grown accustomed to such sights.

At the junction where their paths diverged, Rose grabbed Diana's hand. "Thanks," she said. "For staying with me. For not leaving me alone in there."

Diana felt something unfamiliar tighten in her chest. "We look after each other," she replied, surprised by the conviction in her own voice. "That's what we do."

Rose smiled, wincing as the expression pulled at the cut on her cheek. "See you tomorrow, then? Assuming they haven't blown up the station overnight."

"See you tomorrow," Diana agreed.

Her mother stood at the door of their small terraced house, only the whiteness of her knuckles on the doorframe betraying her concern.

"What happened to you?" Eleanor asked, reluctantly stepping aside to let Diana enter.

Diana kissed her mother gently on the cheek before moving past her into the familiar warmth of their kitchen. The normality of life continuing was so far removed from what she'd just endured that it felt absurd—like stepping from a nightmare into a half-remembered dream. The kettle whistled on the hob, the wireless played in the corner, and the smell of toast lingered in the air. As if the world hadn't come crashing down only hours before.

"I was trapped," Diana said, sinking into a chair. "Under a building that collapsed on our ambulance. Rose and I were buried for hours. Then, believe it or not, a dog found us, and alerted the rescuers."

Eleanor's face softened for a fraction of a second before her composure reasserted itself. "Thank goodness for that," she observed, beginning to fill a basin with water from the kettle.

"Yes," Diana said, the word carrying more weight than it should. "We're both alive."

"Then you were fortunate." Eleanor set the basin on the table. "You should wash. I'll make us some tea."

Diana stared at her mother, noting the slight tremor in Eleanor's hands. The older woman's calm facade was just that—a facade. Beneath it, she'd been terrified.

"Mother," Diana said gently. "About leaving London. About going north."

Eleanor's back stiffened, but she didn't turn around. "We've discussed this."

"Rose could have died tonight. I could have died. We nearly did." Diana's voice caught. "What if next time we're not so fortunate?"

Eleanor set down the teapot and faced her daughter. For a moment, her composure seemed to crack, revealing a woman terrified by the horrors surrounding them.

"What would you have me do, Diana? Run away and leave others to face what we're too frightened to endure?"

"I'd have you live," Diana replied. "That's all. Just live."

Eleanor studied her daughter's dust-streaked face for a long moment. Finally, she poured the tea, setting a cup before Diana with trembling hands.

"We'll discuss it later," she said at last. "This evacuation of yours. But not tonight. Tonight, you rest."

Diana threw her arms around her mother, squishing into her soft skin. "Thank you." Her mother hadn't said yes, but at least it wasn't a no anymore. She closed her eyes so that she couldn't see the calendar on the wall, taunting her with the date.

As Diana climbed the narrow stairs to her room, she realised that tonight had changed something fundamental. Not just her mother's growing willingness to consider leaving London, but something in herself. During her time trapped with Rose, she'd felt a real connection with another human being for the first time in any of her lives.

Diana sank onto her narrow bed, still in her filthy uniform, too exhausted to undress. As sleep claimed her, she thought not of the horror of the night, but of Rose's smile and her mother's trembling hands. Perhaps caring for others wasn't the weakness she'd always believed it to be. Perhaps it was the very thing that made living worthwhile.

Chapter Twenty-Seven

"Diana! You'll be late for your shift if you don't get a move on!"

Diana opened her eyes. Every muscle ached, a symphony of bruises and stiffness serving as a vivid reminder of the previous night's ordeal. She shifted, wincing as her ribs protested the movement.

The accident. The ambulance crushed beneath tonnes of rubble. Rose's hand gripping hers in the darkness, both of them alive against all odds, thanks to a dog she never got to meet.

Her mother's voice carried up the stairs with its usual brisk efficiency, but Diana detected an underlying note of concern. Eleanor had seen her come home, battered and dust-covered, and for once had allowed her emotions to show.

Diana eased herself out of bed, each movement deliberate and careful. Her left shoulder bore a spectacular bruise where debris had struck her, and her ribs ached with every breath. But she was alive. And they were both alive.

She dressed slowly in her uniform, wondering what changes she'd face today, and if she'd be allowed to live out the whole day.

"There you are," Eleanor said as Diana entered the kitchen, her sharp eyes cataloguing her daughter's careful movements. "How are you feeling?"

"Sore," Diana admitted, settling gingerly into her chair. "But grateful."

Eleanor nodded, placing a bowl of porridge before her with unusual gentleness. "When I think of what could have happened..." She trailed off, shaking her head.

"Well, I'm still here. And that's worth celebrating," Diana replied. "Life is precious. I'm trying to remember that."

Her mother studied her with the sharp gaze that had always seen more than Diana was comfortable revealing. "This sudden appreciation for life wouldn't have anything to do with that Cheviot Hills business, would it?"

Diana paused while measuring tea leaves. "Yes, partly."

Eleanor sighed. "I spoke to Mrs Hadley this morning when she was passing. She confirmed that they're looking for seamstresses for those auxiliary hospitals up north. I'm not promising anything, mind. But she's written away for more information for me."

Diana's heart leapt. "That's wonderful, Mother. What changed your mind?" Diana asked.

Eleanor was quiet for a long moment. "Seeing you come home last night," she said. "Covered in dust and blood, barely able to walk straight. Realising how close I came to losing you." Her voice caught. "I may believe in duty, Diana, but I'm not ready to sacrifice my only child to it."

Diana couldn't stop grinning.

"Don't get ahead of yourself," Eleanor cautioned, waving her finger in Diana's face. "There's plenty to consider before making such a decision. My work here, your duties at the ambulance station. But after what happened..."

"They need ambulance drivers everywhere," Diana pointed out. "Especially in rural areas where the distances are greater."

Eleanor gave her daughter a shrewd look. "You've given this quite a bit of thought."

"I have," Diana admitted. "I think it could be good for both of us. A fresh start. We should go this weekend."

"This weekend? Impossible. Maybe at the end of the month, at the earliest," she said, jabbing her finger at the accursed wall calendar. "Now eat your porridge before it gets cold."

Subdued, Diana picked at her breakfast, scared that she'd just derailed all her earlier progress. She couldn't let her mother die on the 15th. She just couldn't.

"I love you, Mother," Diana tried. "I don't think I say that enough."

Eleanor's hand patted hers as she reached for Diana's empty bowl. "You are in an odd mood," her voice gentler than usual. "I love you too, my girl. Now off with you, or you'll be late. And tonight we'll talk more of going north. And I'll corner Mrs Hadley later today and quiz her for more details on the seamstress jobs."

At the station, Diana found the mood subdued, despite the previous day's successes. Word of her and Rose's close call had spread, and her colleagues regarded her with a mixture of respect and concern.

"Penn," Station Officer Briggs greeted her as she signed in. "How are you feeling? You could take sick leave if you need it."

"I'm fine, sir," Diana replied, though her careful movements suggested otherwise. "Ready for duty."

Briggs nodded. "Good show. You and Finley showed real courage yesterday. The sort of thing that keeps this operation running."

Diana found Rose in the supply room, checking bandage rolls with her usual methodical care, her copper hair tucked neatly beneath her cap.

"Morning," Diana greeted her, noting how Rose's face brightened at her appearance.

"Diana! Thank goodness you're here. I was worried you might not be up for work today." Rose set down her clipboard and studied Diana's face. "You look like you've been through a wringer."

"So do you," Diana admitted. "But I'm here. We both are."

Rose's expression grew serious. "About yesterday. When I thought you'd died..." She shook her head. "I don't think I've ever been so frightened in my life."

"But we looked after each other," Diana replied. "That's what matters."

"Yes," Rose agreed, her smile returning. "We did, didn't we? Proper partnership, that was."

As they prepared their ambulance for the day's duties, Diana noticed the curious glances from their colleagues. Her newfound closeness with Rose had not gone unnoticed.

"To start with, they were wondering if a German spy had replaced you," Rose observed as they checked the vehicle's supplies.

"But Doris has upgraded her theory. Now she thinks a much friendlier alien has replaced you," she said, laughing.

Diana winced. "An alien? I'd rather be a German spy. Have I really been that bad?"

"The old Diana Penn never voluntarily spoke to anyone before noon, or after," Rose commented dryly.

Diana laughed, the sound genuine and unguarded. "What do you think?"

"I think yesterday changed you," Rose said thoughtfully. "There's nothing like nearly dying together to put things in perspective. You'll laugh when I tell you that one of Doris's original theories was that you're royalty, forced to slum it with us commoners for the duration."

Before Diana could respond, Briggs called from the doorway. "Penn, Finley! Supply run to Whitechapel, then standby for calls."

Rose stared at her, her freckled face serious despite her teasing words. "But I think that in reality, it's just because you're scared of getting too close to people. And of losing them."

Diana stilled, caught off guard by the young woman's perception. "That's... remarkably insightful."

"I notice things." Rose shrugged. "Goes with the job, doesn't it? Observing people, seeing what they need?"

"Penn, Finley! That supply run won't complete itself!" Briggs yelled.

In the ambulance, Diana took a different route than usual, still cautious about the areas where previous raids had left unstable buildings.

"Shortcut?" Rose asked as Diana turned down a narrow lane between warehouses.

"Avoiding the damage on Commercial Road."

They completed the supply run efficiently, loading boxes of bandages and medical supplies into the back of the ambulance. As they prepared to return to the station, the air raid siren began its mournful wail.

"So early," Rose muttered, glancing skyward. "Jerry must be getting desperate."

Diana's pulse quickened. This was where it had gone wrong before. "Come on, let's get to the Underground."

They secured the ambulance as best they could and made their way to the tube station entrance.

Already a stream of Londoners was flowing down the stairs, gas masks in boxes dangling from shoulders, small bags clutched in nervous hands.

They sat in silence as the raid continued above. Around them, families huddled together, children dozed against parents' shoulders, and elderly couples held hands with the comfortable familiarity of decades together.

After what seemed like hours, the all-clear siren sounded. The collective relief was palpable as people began gathering their belongings and making their way back to the surface.

Diana and Rose emerged into a transformed landscape. The street outside the station was barely recognisable. Buildings that had stood intact just hours before were now smoking ruins. Rescue workers were already digging through rubble, searching for survivors.

"Bloody hell," Rose breathed, taking in the destruction. "If we'd tried to drive through that..."

Diana nodded grimly. "Come on. We need to check if the ambulance survived."

To Diana's relief, they found the ambulance undamaged, protected by the solid brick warehouse on one side and a fortuitous pile of sandbags on the other. A few windows had shattered from the concussive force of nearby bombs, but the vehicle was otherwise intact.

"Right," Diana said, sliding behind the wheel. "Let's get these supplies to the station, then come back to help with the rescue efforts."

The station was in organised chaos. Two ambulances had been hit during the raid, with their crews miraculously saved from any serious injury. Briggs was directing operations from his desk, his usual military precision unaffected by the surrounding mayhem.

"Penn! Finley!" he barked as they entered. "Thank God. There's a collapsed shelter on Poplar High Street. Multiple casualties."

Diana and Rose worked without pause, transporting injured civilians to hospitals, assisting in rescues, and delivering urgent medical supplies where needed. The sun set and rose again before they returned to the station, exhausted beyond words.

During one luxuriously blessed break at the station, Diana stared at the station calendar again, willing the dates to rearrange themselves, to grant her more time. The red X marks through the previous days looked like tiny wounds in the white paper.

"You've been staring at that thing for at least five minutes," Rose observed, settling beside her with a cup of tea. "Expecting it to suddenly sprout wings and fly away?"

Diana's laugh came out sharp and brittle. "Something like that."

"A hot date coming up? Or a bad anniversary?"

The worst sort of anniversary, Diana thought. But she couldn't explain that without sounding completely mad, so she simply nodded and turned away from the calendar that had become her personal instrument of torture.

"Get some rest," Briggs ordered later, as they logged their final journey of the shift. "Eight hours, then back on duty."

Diana sank onto a chair in the day room, every muscle aching with fatigue. Rose collapsed beside her, her hair escaping its cap in wild tendrils, her uniform stained with blood and grime.

"We did good today," Rose murmured, eyes already drifting closed. "Saved lives."

"We did," Diana agreed, her own exhaustion threatening to overwhelm her.

"And you saved mine," Rose added sleepily. "Don't think I'll forget that."

Diana started to protest, but Rose was already asleep, her head drooping against Diana's shoulder. Carefully, so as not to wake her, Diana shifted to make them both more comfortable.

Across the room, Doris caught Diana's eye and smiled approvingly. Shirley gave her a discreet thumbs-up. Even Norman, the perpetually grumpy mechanic, nodded in acknowledgment. Diana felt something unfamiliar in her chest. A sense of belonging. Something she'd denied herself for so long, believing it made her vulnerable. A vulnerable spy was a risk.

Rose shifted against her shoulder, and Diana found herself gently adjusting her position again so the sleeping girl would be more comfortable. The simple gesture surprised her. When had caring for someone else become instinctive rather than calculated?

As exhaustion finally claimed her, Diana's last conscious thought was of her mother's voice that morning, proud and worried in equal measure. Tomorrow would bring new calls, new emergencies, new chances to make the connections she'd spent a lifetime avoiding.

Eight hours later, Diana and Rose were back in their ambulance, responding to another call. The day was cloudless, the sky a mockery of blue serenity after the previous day's destruction.

"Careful here," Diana warned as they approached a junction where rubble narrowed the road to a single lane. "The buildings on the right aren't stable."

Rose peered at the precarious structures. "How do you know? They look all right to me."

Diana hesitated, then decided on a partial truth. "See how the front wall is leaning? And those cracks along the foundation? Classic signs of structural instability."

"Blimey," Rose said, impressed. "Where'd you learn that?"

"I read a lot," Diana replied, which wasn't a lie. She had read extensively during her lifetime, especially as after she retired, there wasn't a lot else for her to do.

Diana returned her attention to the road ahead. They were approaching the area where she'd died in her second attempt. Despite the clear skies, she felt a prickle of unease at the base of her skull.

"Let's take the long way round," she suggested, turning down a side street before Rose could protest.

"You and your shortcuts," Rose remarked good-naturedly. "At this rate, we'll know every back alley in London by Christmas."

"Better that than—" Diana began, but the sudden wail of the air raid siren cut short her words.

"Not again," Rose groaned. "Middle of the bloody day, too."

Diana's hands tightened on the steering wheel.

"There's a public shelter two streets over. Behind the school."

Diana accelerated, the ambulance lurching forward with new urgency. Above them, the drone of aircraft engines grew louder, but the clear sky made it impossible to spot the incoming bombers.

"There it is." Rose pointed to a concrete bunker set in an embankment beside a school playground. Already, people were hurrying inside, mothers dragging protesting children, shopkeepers abandoning their premises.

Diana parked the ambulance as close to the shelter as possible and they joined the flow of civilians seeking safety. The concrete walls were reassuringly thick, the ceiling reinforced with steel beams.

"We should be safe here," Diana said, more to herself than to Rose.

They found space against a wall, surrounded by frightened Londoners. A woman with two small children huddled beside them, the youngest whimpering.

"Shh, Harry," the mother soothed. "It will be over soon."

Rose smiled at the children, her expression deliberately cheerful. "I spy with my little eye, something beginning with... D."

The older child, a girl of about six, looked around the dimly lit shelter. "Door?" she ventured.

"Good guess, but no." Rose laughed.

"Darkness?" the girl tried again.

"Nope. Give up?"

The child nodded.

"Dog!" Rose pointed to a small terrier peeking out from beneath an elderly man's coat across the shelter.

The girl giggled, momentarily distracted from her fear. Even the younger child stopped whimpering to look for the dog.

"Your turn," Rose prompted the girl.

The bombs began falling, each impact sending tremors through the shelter. The children's game faltered as the explosions grew closer, their faces pale with renewed fear.

"I spy with my little eye," Diana said, surprising herself as much as Rose, "something beginning with B."

The girl looked at her doubtfully. "Bombs?"

"No." Diana smiled. "Bracelet." She pointed to the colourful string of beads on the child's wrist. "Did you make it yourself?"

The distraction worked. Soon the children were showing Diana their treasures—the girl's bracelet, the boy's toy soldier, a shiny brass button the mother had found on the street and kept as a lucky charm.

Rose caught Diana's eye over the children's heads, her expression approving. "You're good with kids," she mouthed silently.

Diana shrugged, though she felt pleased by the observation. In truth, she'd had little experience with children. Her MI6 career hadn't exactly lent itself to family life.

The raid seemed interminable, but eventually the all-clear sounded and people began preparing to emerge into whatever remained of their neighbourhood.

"That wasn't so bad, was it?" Rose said to the children as they prepared to leave. "You were very brave."

The little girl looked up at Diana. "Will you play I Spy again next time?"

Diana hesitated, then nodded. "If we're sheltered together again, yes."

"Promise?"

"I promise," Diana replied, surprised to find she meant it. For the first time in decades, she was making commitments to the future, to connections with other people.

Outside, the destruction was less severe than Diana had feared. Their ambulance stood undamaged, though a lamppost had fallen across the road nearby.

"Well, that's a stroke of luck," Rose remarked as they cleared the obstruction. "Sometimes these raids feel like they're aiming for ambulances specifically."

Diana suppressed a shudder. "Let's get going. There will be casualties that need transport."

As they drove towards the areas most affected by the bombing, Rose glanced at Diana. "You really are different today. Yesterday too. It's like... I don't know, like you've had some kind of revelation."

Diana kept her eyes on the road. "Perhaps I have."

"Care to share?"

"It's complicated," Diana admitted. "But let's just say I'm trying to... live more."

Rose considered this. "Well, I like this new Diana Penn. She's much more fun than the old one."

Diana smiled despite herself. "The old one had her reasons for keeping people at a distance."

"And the new one?"

"The new one is starting to think those reasons might have been flawed."

Chapter Twenty-Eight

Diana stood at the narrow kitchen window, watching Mrs. Collins from number seventeen take in her washing despite the ash that blew through the streets like snow. The woman's determination to stick to her daily routine struck Diana as bordering on the insane.

She heard the front door open and close. Her mother was home.

"You're going to be late for your shift," Eleanor observed, already pulling off her coat and stowing her purse on the dresser. Her shift at the garment factory was over for another day.

Diana turned from the window, her stomach churning with more than just the weak tea and toast she'd forced down earlier. Today was the day. In her first life, her mother had died tonight while Diana had been on duty. She wouldn't let that happen again.

"Mother," Diana began, setting down her cup. "I've called in sick today."

Eleanor's eyebrows rose. "Sick? You look perfectly well to me."

"I'm not ill," Diana said, forcing herself to meet her mother's judgmental stare. "I just... I don't want to leave you tonight. Not with the raids getting worse."

Eleanor's mouth tightened into a thin line. "Diana Eliza Penn, the ambulance service needs you. People depend on you. And you're shirking your duty because of what? Nerves?"

"People depend on you too," Diana said weakly.

"That is precisely the sort of thinking that loses wars," Eleanor snapped. "When everyone starts believing their personal fears matter more than their obligations. I raised you better than this."

If only you knew how many duties I've performed, Diana thought. *How many lives I've saved, how many secrets I've kept... how many times I've put service before everything— including you.*

"Sometimes," Diana said quietly, "duty means staying with the people you love."

Something in her tone must have convinced Eleanor, because she hesitated, then tipped her head to the side and nodded. "Now that you mention it, you do look a tad on the pale side."

Diana laughed. "Cup of tea?"

"Go on then. Put the kettle on. I'll get the cups and saucers. I can't have you dropping my wedding chinaware in your invalided state!"

Diana couldn't remember having such a light-hearted conversation with her mother before. It was unfamiliar territory, but she was glad to be in it.

But as the evening wore on and they readied for bed, her anxiety returned. She'd stayed home, and so far the siren hadn't sounded. *Perhaps the timeline has changed for the Germans too,* she thought.

It didn't last.

They were both fast asleep when the sirens woke them. Pulling on their overcoats and grabbing their gas masks and small overnight bags, they hurried through the darkened streets towards the Bethnal Green station. Though the entrance was already crowded with shelter-seekers, it was oddly quiet, as if silence itself might keep them safe from the Luftwaffe roaring overhead.

The platform was filling fast. Families claimed spaces along the curved tunnel walls, laying out blankets, unpacking bread, tins, and flasks as they prepared for another long night below ground.

Eleanor and Diana found a spot near the wall. Down here, the rhythms of war resumed: children played between the rails; friends whispered news and gossip. In the dim light, people did their best to feel human.

"It's not so uncomfortable," Eleanor murmured, settling onto the blanket beside Diana. "Could do with some dusting, though."

The bombing started around two o'clock. The distant thrum of aircraft filtered down through earth and concrete. With each impact above, fresh dust fell from the ceiling.

"You see?" Diana whispered. "We're safe here. Deep enough to weather anything Jerry can throw at us."

Then Diana felt a shift in the air. A tremor. Barely perceptible, but wrong. And she wasn't the only one who felt it.

Voices faltered. A child whimpered. The crowd leaned into the silence.

Then the lights flickered. Dimmed. Went out.

Which meant no one saw the first crack appear overhead.

But they heard it.

"Diana—" Eleanor's voice was cut off by the roar of collapsing stone.

The tunnel gave way, and London fell down upon them.

Diana felt her mother's hand grasp hers in the dark.

"I love you," Diana whispered, unsure if Eleanor could hear her over the sound of their world ending.

"And I love you," came the answer.

They died together, with Diana's head resting on Eleanor's shoulder, their fingers still laced.

Chapter Twenty-Nine

Diana Penn opened her eyes.

No pain. No difficulty breathing. No crushing pressure of rubble pinning her and her mother beneath collapsed buildings. Just the familiar chill of her childhood bedroom.

Her hands flew to her face, finding smooth, uninjured skin where there should have been cuts and grime. The acrid smell of smoke and brick dust that had filled her lungs was gone, replaced by the ordinary scents of home.

From somewhere below came Eleanor Penn's voice, sharp with impatience.

"Diana! Your porridge will get cold if you don't come down soon!"

She was back.

"Diana!" Her mother's voice carried more bite now. "I won't call you again!"

"Coming, Mother!" Diana called back, hastily pulling on her uniform.

The narrow staircase creaked beneath her feet as she hurried down to the kitchen. Eleanor Penn stood at the gas cooker, stirring a pot of porridge with more force than strictly necessary. She too wore a uniform of sorts—a faded blue cotton number with deep pockets and sensible black lace-up shoes.

"There you are," Eleanor said, without turning round. "I swear, Diana, you'd sleep through the Second Coming if I let you."

The familiar litany of complaints and responsibilities washed over Diana like a tide. She crossed the small kitchen in three strides and wrapped her arms around her mother's waist, burying her face against Eleanor's shoulder.

"What on earth has got into you?" Eleanor exclaimed, the wooden spoon clattering against the pot.

"I love you," Diana murmured, inhaling the comforting scent of lavender water and starch. "I just wanted you to know that."

Eleanor patted Diana's hand awkwardly. "Well, that's nice, but your porridge is getting cold, and you're going to be late."

Diana released her mother reluctantly and moved to the breakfast table. But as before, she had no appetite.

"Mother," Diana began, stirring her porridge without eating it. "Have you thought at all about leaving London? Going north?"

Eleanor's expression hardened. "North? What on earth for? My work is here. So is yours."

"You don't understand, the bombing is only going to get worse," Diana insisted, her voice rising.

How could she explain knowing, with terrible certainty, that on the 15th of September, death would knock on their door? That she'd lived an entire lifetime having identified her mother's broken body in the rubble.

"And what would we do up north?" Eleanor asked, her disdain for the idea completely apparent.

"The WLA is recruiting in Northumberland. A place called Cheviot Hills. They're desperate for girls with mechanical training to work on the farms there. I could apply."

Eleanor's glance towards the mantel clock ended the conversation. "Enough of that now. You promised to help with the shopping today before your shift. I need you to queue early if we're to get anything decent."

Diana nodded. She'd have to try persuading her mother later. They *had* to leave London.

She kissed her mother's cheek before retrieving her gas mask from its hook by the door. Eleanor touched her own cheek, as if startled by the unexpected gesture.

"Are you feeling well?" she asked, peering at Diana.

"I love you, and I'm worried about you," Diana replied honestly. "I'll see you later. Please think about Cheviot Hills."

The world was on fire, yet here she was, armed with only a small buff-coloured ration book, which determined what they could and couldn't buy. It was its own war, the queuing for meat and butter, the precious tins of golden syrup that appeared sporadically, and the hope that fresh eggs might be available. She'd forgotten how cut-throat the queues were. It was almost worse than smuggling a defector through Check Point Charlie into Berlin. And that had been challenging.

The whole time she stood in line, all she could think of was how to save her mother. How to persuade her to leave London before the 15th. One argument her mother had thrown back at her was that Diana's request was akin to asking the King of England to forsake his subjects. Her mother pointed out that he'd stayed. His wife and daughters too. And if that was good enough for King George, then that was good enough for her mother. There was no way she could argue that logic. She needed another angle.

These thoughts bounced around Diana's head whilst she queued, during the entire walk home with the groceries she managed to secure, and then throughout her journey to the station.

The ambulance station buzzed with morning activity when Diana arrived. Briggs stood at his desk, assigning the daily taskings, and the familiar smell of strong tea and cigarette smoke hung in the air, mixing with the ever-present odours of antiseptic and engine oil.

"Penn!" Briggs called as she entered. "You're with Johnson today. Supply run to Whitechapel, then standby for calls."

Diana nodded, signing in before running her eye over the incident blackboard—their operational lifeline. It displayed the day's routes and blocked roads, and was updated constantly as fresh incidents occurred.

As Diana checked supplies in ambulance three, Rose Finley appeared at the back doors. The copper-haired attendant smiled with the same bright warmth from each of Diana's earlier lives. That at least was a constant.

"Morning," Rose said, stifling a yawn. "Ready for another day of London's finest hospitality?"

"Ready as I'll ever be," Diana replied.

Chapter Thirty

The days passed with the relentless inevitability of an approaching execution. Diana clung to her mother with an intensity that bordered on the pathological, volunteering for every household task that might keep them together a few minutes longer.

"You're hovering, Diana," Eleanor observed on the third day, not looking up from her mending. "It's most unlike you."

Diana perched on the edge of the sofa, watching her mother's capable fingers work the needle through a torn seam. "I thought you might like the company."

"Company, yes. A nursemaid, no." Eleanor's tone held a note of irritation. "You've barely left my side. Don't you have friends to see? Places to go?"

Only eight more days, Diana thought, her stomach churning. Eight days before the whistling descent, the flash of white light, the terrible silence that would follow.

"Mother, about Cheviot Hills—"

"No." The word came sharp as a blade. Eleanor's needle paused mid-stitch. "I've told you my answer. I won't discuss it further."

But Diana couldn't stop herself. The approaching date drove her like a fever, compelling her to try again and again despite the futility.

She attempted logic first, presenting carefully researched arguments about agricultural work contributing to the war effort. When that failed, she resorted to emotion, allowing tears to fall as she begged her mother to reconsider.

Eleanor remained unmoved. "Tears won't change my mind, Diana. I'm not leaving London, and that's final."

On the fifth day, Diana tried a different approach. "What if I went first? Found us a place and then sent for you later?"

"Absolutely not." Eleanor's voice turned flinty. "I won't have you gallivanting off to the countryside whilst London burns. Your duty is here."

Duty. Always duty. The word that had shaped both their lives, that would ultimately destroy one of them.

Diana became someone she didn't recognise—desperate, pleading, almost unhinged. But Eleanor would not be moved.

Through every shift at the ambulance station, Diana found herself counting backwards obsessively. Eight days. Seven days. Six. Each sunrise bringing her closer to the date that had haunted a lifetime of her dreams. The date on the kitchen calendar taunted her with its proximity.

Sleep had become impossible. Diana lay awake each night, listening for her mother's breathing in the next room. She'd tried staying awake on purpose, reasoning that if she didn't sleep, somehow the days wouldn't pass. A child's logic, but desperation had no rules.

On the fourth day, she'd attempted bribery, offering to give Eleanor her entire sugar ration for the month if she'd just consider a brief holiday in the countryside. Eleanor had looked at her as though she'd taken leave of her senses.

"I don't know what's brought on this sudden terror of London," Eleanor said one day, her voice gentler than her words. "But running away isn't the answer. We face what comes, Diana. That's what decent people do."

Decent people. That phrase would kill her mother.

Two days before the 15th, Diana made one final, desperate attempt. She fell to her knees beside her mother's chair, grasping Eleanor's hands.

"Please," she whispered, no longer caring how deranged she might sound. "I'm begging you. Something terrible is going to happen. I can feel it. We have to leave London. We have to."

Eleanor's expression softened. She cupped Diana's face in her work-worn hands, studying her daughter's hollow-eyed desperation.

"My dear Diana," she said gently. "Terrible things happen every day. That's the nature of war. But we can't live our lives in fear of what might come."

But I *know what's coming,* Diana wanted to scream. *I know exactly when and how and where you're going to die, and I can't save you because you won't let me.* Instead of screaming, she pressed her face against her mother's knees and wept for all the years that were about to be stolen from them both.

Chapter Thirty-One

The end of Diana's next shift brought a bone-deep weariness that no amount of youth could ease. Twelve hours of transporting the wounded, comforting the dying, and clearing rubble had left her uniform stained with blood and soot. Her hands, raw from hauling stretchers, trembled as she signed out.

Tomorrow night a German bomb would zero in on their house, and her mother would die. And she still hadn't persuaded her mother to leave London. Tonight was her last chance. Her only chance. She'd drag her kicking and screaming from their flat if she had to.

She had to.

"You look done in," Briggs observed as she returned her logbook. "Take tomorrow morning off. Report back at noon on the 16th."

"Tomorrow's the 15th, sir," Diana said, her exhausted mind trying to process the dates.

Briggs checked his own logbook, then looked at her with concern. "No, Penn. Tomorrow is the 16th. Today's the 15th. When did you last get a proper night's sleep?"

The blood drained from Diana's face as a terrible realisation crashed over her. Tonight. It was tonight. Her mother was going to die tonight, and Diana was here, miles away. How could she have got it so wrong?

She bolted from the station without another word, her exhaustion forgotten as she ran through the darkening streets filled with the now-familiar scent of burning timbers, brick dust, and something worse—the sweet, sickening odour of death.

Diana had almost reached the junction for home when the air raid siren began its banshee wail. Around her, people streamed from their homes and pedestrians quickened their pace, heading for shelters with the weary resignation of people too acquainted with danger to be afraid.

Diana plunged through the stream of Londoners heading towards the nearest Underground. Her only thoughts were of her mother. She checked her wristwatch. By now Eleanor would have heard the sirens and would, hopefully, be making her way to the nearest shelter with her knitting and a thermos of tea, to wait it out with her characteristic stoicism. Diana picked up her pace, panic fuelling her speed.

The bombing, when it began in earnest, seemed more intense than usual. Each impact sent tremors through the streets. Diana cowered in a doorway, counting the seconds between explosions, trying to gauge how close they were falling. Taking her chances between explosions to stumble her way closer to her home. To her mother. She had time. Surely she had enough time?

Smoke filled the air, and the orange glow of fires lit the night sky in every direction.

Diana pressed on through the chaos, trying to navigate streets she'd known since childhood but which were now alien in the smoky darkness. Familiar landmarks had vanished. The corner shop where she'd bought sweets as a child was nothing but rubble, the bright red postbox that had marked the halfway point home lay twisted on its side. She turned down what she thought was Clematis Street, only to find herself facing a crater where the road should have been. Doubling back, she tried another route, the anxiety threatening to smother her.

A glow caught her eye—an orange-red haze too bright and too near. Diana's steps faltered as she rounded the corner, her breath catching in her throat.

Where a neat row of terraced houses should have stood, a wall of flame roared into the sky. The central houses had already collapsed into heaps of burning rubble, and the fire was spreading rapidly to those still standing.

Fire wardens directed feeble streams of water towards the inferno, their efforts pitifully inadequate against the conflagration.

Her mother's house—their home—was at the centre of the blaze.

"No," Diana whispered, the word barely audible even to herself. "No, no, no."

She broke into a run, frantically scanning the crowd of survivors and rescue workers gathered in the street. Faces illuminated by the glow of flames, some soot-streaked, others blank with shock—but none of them her mother's.

"Mum!" she called out, pushing through the clusters of displaced residents. "Eleanor! Has anyone seen Eleanor Penn?"

She grabbed the arm of a woman she recognised from the corner shop. "Have you seen my mother? Did you see her in the Underground?"

Mrs Davis shook her head, her eyes wide with shock. "I didn't see her, love. But then, it was so crowded…"

Diana spun around, accosting anyone who might have information. "Eleanor Penn, from number twenty-one? Grey hair, about this tall? Did anyone see her?"

Head shakes, apologetic murmurs, but no answers. The growing knot of dread in Diana's stomach tightened with each negative response.

"Mum!" she screamed, lunging towards the burning building. "MUM!"

Strong arms caught her from behind, restraining her as she struggled to break free.

"You can't go in there, lass," a man's voice said in her ear, his grip unyielding. "Building's about to go."

"My mother might be in there!" Diana fought against his hold, her training forgotten in the rush of blind panic. "Let me go! I have to find her!"

"You can't help her now," the fire warden said, his voice gentle despite his firm grip. "I'm sorry."

As if to punctuate his words, the remaining portion of the roof caved in with a thunderous crash, sending a fountain of sparks and cinders spiralling into the night sky. The heat blasted against Diana's face, searing her lungs with each gasping breath.

Diana's struggles weakened as the reality of what she was seeing penetrated her desperation.

Around her, the street had become a tableau of human misery. Neighbours stood in knotted clusters. A woman cradled a sobbing child against her chest, tears cutting clean trails through the soot on her cheeks. An elderly man sat on a kitchen chair someone had dragged from a nearby house, staring at the inferno with vacant eyes.

The warden's grip on Diana loosened as her legs gave way. She sank to her knees on the cold pavement, her gaze fixed on the burning ruins of her childhood home. Cinders and ash drifted down like black snow, settling on her uniform, tangling in her hair.

She had failed. Again.

"Eleanor," whispered a voice nearby. "Oh, poor Eleanor."

Diana turned to see Mrs Collins from number seventeen, her grey hair in curlers, a man's overcoat thrown over her housedress.

Mrs Collins knelt beside her, heedless of the grime on the pavement. "It came out of nowhere. The sirens had only just sounded. The next..." She gestured helplessly at the burning rubble.

"Was she..." Diana couldn't finish the question, but Mrs Collins understood.

"She was inside, dear. I'd just been speaking with her a few minutes before the siren. She borrowed a bit of darning wool." Mrs Collins's voice cracked.

The sob that tore from Diana's throat didn't sound human. It was the raw, keening sound of an animal in unbearable pain.

All her careful planning, all her attempts to change fate—useless. In her first life, her mother had died when the bomb struck their house. In this reset, despite Diana's warnings and persuasion, her mother had died in exactly the same way.

The fire warden still stood behind her, his hands now resting lightly on her shoulders, holding her upright as her body threatened to collapse.

"Perhaps she made it to the garden?" Diana said, grasping at the thinnest thread of hope. "Perhaps she changed her mind and is in the Anderson shelter—"

"She didn't, love," Mrs Collins said, her eyes filling with fresh tears. "She was inside. I saw her closing the front curtains on my way to the shelter, just before..." She couldn't continue.

Diana stared at the flames, willing them to reveal some miracle.

Some sign that her mother had escaped. But the fire told only one story, and it ended in ash and ruin.

Diana's mind replayed every moment of the day. She'd kissed her mother goodbye that morning. Told her she loved her. Had seen the surprise and pleasure in Eleanor's eyes at the unexpected affection. It was so little, and somehow everything.

"She was that proud of you," Mrs Collins said suddenly, breaking into Diana's thoughts. "Always telling everyone about her daughter, the ambulance driver. 'Doing vital war work,' she'd say. 'Saving lives while the rest of us just try to keep body and soul together.'"

A fresh wave of grief crashed over Diana. Of course that's what her mother would focus on. Work. Duty. The same values she'd instilled in Diana from childhood. The same rigid adherence to responsibility that had shaped Diana's entire life. Both this one and the first.

Mrs Collins squeezed Diana's hand. "You can stay with us tonight, love. Happy to have you. It'll be a squeeze, but we'll manage."

Diana was unable to think beyond the present moment. Where would she go? What did it matter? She'd failed in the one task that had given this reset purpose.

Tonight remained the worst night of her life. Of all her lives. This was the night that had shattered her world the first time around, now repeating itself with cruel precision despite all her foreknowledge, all her careful attempts to change course.

Somehow, she ended up in Mrs Collins' front room, a cup of tea pressed into her hands, and a scratchy blanket draped around her shoulders. Diana sat on the sofa, surrounded by neighbours whose kindness felt like sandpaper against her raw grief.

Hours passed, or perhaps minutes. Time lost meaning as Diana stared at nothing, the cup of tea growing cold in her hands. Around her, neighbours made plans for alternative accommodation and emergency childcare for the newly made orphans.

That was her. An orphan. She might not still be a child, but she was an orphan again, nonetheless.

"Diana! Diana Penn!"

The voice cut through Diana's fog of misery. She looked up to see Rose Finley pushing her way into the front room, her copper hair escaping its regulation cap, her uniform as filthy as Diana's own.

"I've been looking everywhere for you," Rose said, dropping to her knees in front of Diana. "Someone at the station said your street got hit. I came as soon as I could." Her eyes searched Diana's face. "Your mother?"

Diana couldn't speak. She shook her head, and that was enough.

"Oh, Diana." Rose's face crumpled. Without hesitation, she sat beside Diana and pulled her into a fierce embrace. "I'm so sorry. So terribly sorry."

It was this genuine compassion that broke Diana. The sobs came in waves, tearing through her chest with physical pain. She wept against Rose's shoulder, decades of grief pouring out of her.

Rose held her through it all, one hand smoothing Diana's hair, the other steady around her shoulders. She didn't offer empty platitudes or useless reassurances.

"I tried to save her. I tried so hard."

Rose pulled back, her eyes searching Diana's face. "What do you mean?"

Diana realised her mistake too late. How could she explain that she'd lived this moment before? That she'd spent three attempts trying to prevent exactly this outcome?

"I knew London wasn't safe," she amended. "I'd been trying to convince her to leave. She was so close to finally agreeing, and now..."

"It's not your fault," Rose said. "None of this is your fault. Blame that madman in Germany."

But it was her fault, wasn't it? Diana had known the bomb would fall. She'd known the exact date her mother would die. And despite that, she had failed to prevent it. Some events, it seemed, were fixed points.

"What will you do now?" Rose asked, still holding Diana's hand in a warm, steadying grip.

What would she do? What purpose remained now that her primary mission to save her mother had failed?

"I don't know," she admitted. "I haven't thought that far ahead. There's nothing left for me here," Diana said, before taking a deep breath. "But I can still honour my mother by continuing to help with the war effort. It's just that I don't think I can stay here and work. Sorry. It would be too hard. We were talking about going up to Northumberland..."

"Then you should go," Rose announced, squeezing Diana's hand. "Stay here tonight, but come to us tomorrow," Rose offered.

"And then we can work out what to do with you. I'll come by in the morning to collect you, and I'll let Briggs know what's happened here," Rose continued.

Diana nodded, too exhausted to refuse. As Rose left, Mrs Collins appeared.

"The rescue workers asked me to give you this," she said, pressing something into Diana's hand. "They... they found it with your mother. Thought the family should have it."

Diana looked down to see her mother's locket—a simple silver oval on a thin chain that Eleanor had worn every day for as long as Diana could remember. Inside would be a tiny photograph of Diana's father in his uniform and her mother in an elegant high-necked wedding gown, and a lock of Diana's baby hair.

"Thank you," Diana whispered, her eyes wide. She closed her fingers around the small treasure.

"Let me put it around your neck," Mrs Collins offered, before fastening the delicate chain around Diana's neck.

That night, Diana fell asleep with her hand curled around her mother's locket at her throat. Hanging on to her humanity for dear life.

True to her word, Rose was there when Diana awoke.

Outside, dawn had broken over a wounded London. The air still tasted of smoke and dust, the first pale rays of sunlight giving the scene a horrific beauty.

"I need to go back," Diana said quietly. "To my house. Just once."

Rose nodded without question, understanding written across her freckled face.

They picked their way through streets littered with debris, past the remnants of what had once been Diana's neighbourhood. When they reached the site where her home had stood, Diana stopped, surveying the rubble with a strange detachment.

"There," she said, pointing to a glint of white porcelain amongst the broken bricks. Somehow, impossibly, one of her mother's teacups sat intact amidst the rubble, its delicate pattern unmarked by the devastation around it.

Diana retrieved it carefully, cradling the rescued teacup.

In her first life, she'd rescued this same cup herself. But the necklace around her neck was new, a treasure she'd never had before.

"Ready?" Rose asked gently.

Diana nodded, clutching the salvaged memories of her mother. There was nothing else here for her now. Only ahead, to Cheviot Hills, to the others she might yet save.

As they walked, Diana whispered a silent promise to the mother she had lost twice now: I will make this life count. I will not waste this second chance.

Chapter Thirty-Two

The days following Eleanor Penn's death passed in a grey haze for Diana. Rose's family had taken her in without question—a kindness that pierced through her numbness when she least expected it. Their flat in Stepney was cramped at the best of times; with Diana occupying the sofa in their tiny sitting room, it became claustrophobic. Yet no one complained.

How different this was from her first life, when she'd endured a few awkward days with Mrs Collins before retreating to a women's hostel—one of those establishments for "respectable single ladies" where silence was enforced and human contact discouraged. Back then, Diana had actually welcomed the isolation, finding comfort in the rigid rules and her own company. The thought of returning to such deliberate loneliness now felt unbearable.

"You're welcome as long as you need, love," Mrs Finley had assured her, pressing a cup of weak tea into Diana's hands on that first morning. Her soft West Country accent reminded Diana of one of her MI6 colleagues—whom she might or might not meet in this life.

Rose had given up her morning shift to accompany Diana to what remained of their house. The Fire Brigade had deemed it unsafe to enter, but Diana insisted on seeing what she could salvage.

"There's nothing," the ARP warden told her, not unkindly.

"Direct hit, I'm afraid. The basement might be intact, but the structural engineers won't allow access for weeks," he clarified.

Diana stood before the blackened ruins, her hand gripping her mother's locket at her neck.

"Was there anything specific you were hoping to find?" Rose asked, her arm linked through Diana's in silent support.

Diana thought of her mother's modest possessions—the kitsch honeypot with the porcelain bee on top, her unfinished knitting, the framed pen and ink sketch of Salisbury Cathedral her mother had bought from the artist whilst there on her honeymoon, the small collection of books, the photograph of Diana's father in its polished frame. All gone now. Reduced to ash and rubble.

"No," she replied, though this wasn't true. She had hoped for a sign that her mother had somehow survived, despite Mrs Collins's certainty. Despite the devastation before her. "There's nothing left."

The memorial service took place three days later at St Matthias's Church.

As Diana once again sat in the front pew, her mother's death pressed against her with physical weight. The church wasn't even half-full. Possibly due to Eleanor's private nature, and definitely because of the grim regularity of such services in wartime London. The minister spoke of Eleanor's dedication to duty, her skill with needle and thread, her dignity.

"Eleanor Penn served her community through her work and her example," he intoned, his voice echoing in the vaulted space. "Though she has left us too soon, her legacy lives on in her daughter and in the countless lives she touched through her service."

Diana stared at the memorial wreath positioned where her mother's coffin might have been. Its chrysanthemums—autumn flowers for an autumn death—the only physical tribute to Eleanor Penn. What legacy had Eleanor left? Dedication to duty, yes. Service above self, certainly. But also a rigid adherence to protocol that had, perhaps, prevented her from forming the human connections that might have made her life richer.

A legacy Diana had embraced all too thoroughly.

After the service, a handful of mourners gathered in the church hall for weak tea and sandwiches prepared by the Women's Institute.

Diana accepted condolences from neighbours and her mother's colleagues from the garment factory where she'd worked, each conversation a blur of platitudes and awkward sympathy.

"Your mother was ever so proud of you," Mrs Collins repeated, patting Diana's hand. "Always talking about her brave girl driving ambulances."

Rose remained at her side throughout, a silent sentinel diverting well-meaning but exhausting expressions of sympathy when Diana's energy flagged. When the last mourner departed, Diana sank onto a wooden folding chair, bone-weary.

"Let's get you home," Rose said. "There's cottage pie for supper."

Home. The word seemed to mock her. Diana had no home now. Not in this time, or in any time. She was adrift, a temporal vagrant cut loose from all moorings.

That night, lying on the Finleys' lumpy sofa beneath a scratchy woollen blanket, Diana confronted the question that had been haunting her since the air raid: Why?

Why was she granted this impossible second—no, fifth, or was it a sixth—chance at life if not to save those closest to her? What cosmic purpose was served by allowing her to rescue strangers like Rose while her own mother remained fixed in her tragic fate?

Diana had altered some events. She had saved Mr Hayes from suicide, had made connections with Rose that never existed before. Yet Eleanor Penn had died on the same night, in exactly the same way, despite Diana's warnings and persuasions.

Some destinies, it seemed, could not be changed.

If that were true, what did it mean for her other objectives? Could she save Mrs Whitaker's son? Mr Hayes's Arthur? Ellen Wilson? The questions circled like carrion birds.

The days that followed established a grim routine. Diana returned to her ambulance duties, finding cold comfort in the familiar work of transporting the injured and recovering the dead. Each shift blurred into the next, punctuated only by air raids and brief respites at the Finleys' cramped flat.

Rose watched her with growing concern. "You're not sleeping," she observed one evening as Diana picked at Mrs Finley's potato and leek soup. "And you've barely eaten a proper meal in days."

Diana shrugged. "I'm managing."

"That's not the same as living," Rose countered, her freckled face serious beneath her copper curls. "Your mum wouldn't want you to just... exist. Neither do I."

The words struck Diana with unexpected force. Wasn't that what she had done throughout her first life? Existed rather than lived? Performed her duty protecting the world around her?

"I'm trying," Diana said, the admission costing her more than she'd expected. "It's just... difficult."

Rose squeezed her hand. "No one said it would be easy. But you don't have to do it alone."

The following morning, Diana attempted to connect with her work colleagues. She joined Doris and Shirley for tea during their break, listening to their chatter about film stars and local gossip. She helped Norman repair the wireless when it crackled and failed during the morning broadcast. She even complimented Station Officer Briggs on his moustache, earning a startled blink and gruff thanks.

Small steps. Tiny openings in the walls she had built around herself for protection.

Yet it was tempting, so tempting, to retreat into her old patterns. To focus solely on duty and protocol, shutting out the messy, painful business of human attachment. Hadn't her attempt at saving her mother proven the futility of caring too deeply?

Two weeks after Eleanor's funeral, Diana found herself with a rare day off. The Finleys' flat felt suffocating, despite Mrs Finley's kindness and Rose's attempts at distraction.

"I think I'll go for a walk," Diana announced after breakfast, needing space to breathe, to think.

The air was sharp with the coming winter as Diana wandered through streets she had known since childhood. Many were unrecognisable now, transformed by bombing into jagged landscapes of rubble and half-collapsed buildings. Through gaps where houses had once stood, she caught glimpses of the Thames, its dark water reflecting a sky heavy with clouds.

Her feet carried her without conscious direction until she found herself standing before a recruitment poster plastered to the wall of the post office. A young woman in dungarees smiled beneath bold lettering screaming: "THE WOMEN'S LAND ARMY NEEDS YOU!"

A powerful sense of déjà vu washed over her. She had stood in this exact spot in her first life, had seen this exact poster. She even remembered impulsively entering the recruitment office, driven by grief and a desperate need to escape London's daily reminders of her mother's absence.

Before she registered her decision, Diana pushed open the door of the recruitment office. The interior was unchanged from her memory—a scarred wooden counter, walls plastered with posters extolling the virtues of country living, a harried-looking WAAF officer shuffling papers.

"Interested in the Land Army, are you?" the officer asked, glancing up as Diana approached. "We've positions all over the country. Plenty of need now that the harvest is in and winter work's begun."

Diana nodded, the script familiar from her first time through this scene. "I'd like to apply."

"Any preferences for location? We're short in the East Anglia region."

Had she named a preferred location the first time around? She couldn't remember. Had the recruitment officer suggested East Anglia then? Knowing how compliant she'd been in her original life, she would have accepted a posting to East Anglia.

"Northumberland," Diana said without hesitation. "Cheviot Hills, if possible."

The WAAF officer raised an eyebrow. "Particular reason? Got family there?"

Diana thought of Mrs Whitaker, and Mr Hayes, and Ellen. And Jim. The second time around Jim. She had never known him the first time.

"Yes," she said.

As the officer rummaged through a filing cabinet, the office door opened, admitting a blast of cold air and a tall man in an RAF uniform. Diana glanced up, then froze, her heart stuttering in her chest.

For a fraction of a second, she glimpsed a familiar profile—the strong jaw, the straight nose, the way he carried himself with casual grace. Then he turned, and Diana saw only a stranger with a superficial resemblance to Flight Lieutenant James Crawford.

Not Jim. She was seeing ghosts where none existed, projecting her memories onto random strangers.

"Here we are," the WAAF officer said, drawing Diana's attention back to the counter. "We have openings in the Cheviot Hills area. Several farms need replacement workers before winter sets in." She pushed a form across the counter. "Fill this out, and we'll arrange transport. You will be there by next week."

Diana completed the application with mechanical efficiency, her mind racing ahead to Cheviot Hills. She knew she could make a difference there. Not on any large cosmic scale, but there were lives she could save.

As for Mrs Whitaker's Trevor and Mr Hayes's Arthur... perhaps she could write to them. Anonymous warnings, phrased to avoid suspicion but specific enough to alter their fates. It was worth trying, at least. What did she have to lose? And after all, coded messages were her forte.

"All set," the officer said, stamping Diana's application. "Report to King's Cross Station on Monday, 0800 hours. Your uniform and equipment will be issued upon arrival at Hexham before you're transported to your assigned farm." She peered at Diana over her glasses. "You're certain about this? The work is hard, and the conditions are primitive compared to London."

Mrs Whitaker's kitchen sprang to mind, warm and fragrant with baking bread. And memories of the crisp Northumberland air, so different from London's smoky pall. And of the potential friendships awaiting her. Sure, she'd be leaving Rose, but England's postal service was still the best in the world, despite Hitler's attempts to destroy their country. She could write to her every day if she liked.

"I'm certain," she replied.

The weekend passed in a flurry of preparation. After supper on Sunday, Rose presented Diana with a small wrapped package and red-rimmed eyes.

"A going-away present," she said, her voice thick with emotion. "Nothing fancy, just... something to remember us by."

Inside was a small address book bound in soft leather, its pages organised alphabetically with a birthday calendar section at the back. Diana opened it to find Rose had already filled in her own details—the Stepney address written in careful script, and in the birthday section, she'd entered her birthday under April 15th.

"It's got quotations from Shakespeare's plays for each day," Rose explained, her voice breaking. "You always seemed the literary type. Look at mine."

Diana turned to April 15th and found Rose's birthday marked with a short quote in elegant italic print: "The fault, dear Brutus, is not in our stars, but in ourselves."

"It's from Julius Caesar," Rose added. "Seemed fitting, somehow. We make our own destinies, don't we?"

Diana's throat tightened. "Thank you. It's perfect."

"I wish I could come with you," Rose continued, her voice breaking. "But Mum needs me here, and the ambulance service... well, they can't spare anyone right now."

They embraced, clinging to each other as if physical contact could bridge the distance that would soon separate them.

"Write to me," Rose whispered. "Promise you'll write."

"I promise," Diana replied, meaning it.

Monday morning dawned grey and drizzly as Diana made her way to King's Cross, a small suitcase containing her few remaining possessions in her hand. To her surprise, she found Rose and several colleagues from the ambulance station waiting on the platform, their faces solemn in the weak morning light.

"Couldn't let you leave without a proper send-off," Rose announced, though her eyes were suspiciously bright. "Briggs gave us an hour."

Doris pressed a small packet of sandwiches into Diana's hands. "For the journey," she explained.

Even Shirley had come, carrying a thermos of tea. "It won't be the same without you," she said. "Never thought I'd hear myself saying that about you!"

Diana laughed.

The station was crowded with soldiers on leave, evacuees being relocated, and harried officials trying to maintain order amid the chaos. Diana's train—an ancient, coal-powered monster belching steam into the vaulted ceiling—waited at Platform 5, already half full of passengers heading north.

As the final boarding call echoed through the station, Rose caught Diana's arm. "This isn't goodbye forever," she said. "When the war's over, we'll see each other again."

"I hope so," Diana replied, her voice barely audible above the station noise.

"And look after yourself up there. Trust those instincts of yours." Rose's voice wavered. "You've got a gift for keeping people safe."

Diana boarded the train, finding a window seat in a compartment occupied by a young mother with two small children and an elderly man with an impressive white beard. As the train prepared to depart, she looked out to see her colleagues still gathered on the platform, Rose at their centre, waving with determined cheerfulness despite the tears streaming down her face.

As the train pulled away from the station, Diana watched London recede through the rain-streaked window, her friends becoming smaller figures until they disappeared. She had left this city once before, fleeing from her mother's death without processing her grief. This time felt different—she was still fleeing, but with purpose rather than panic, carrying her mother's memory with her rather than trying to escape it.

The journey north unfolded in a rhythm of stops and starts, the landscape transforming from London's bomb-scarred sprawl to green fields and scattered villages. Diana sat in silence, her mother's locket around her neck, the leather notebook unopened in her lap.

She woke with a start as the train rattled across the High Level Bridge into Newcastle, the vast expanse of the Tyne stretching below. In her first life, she had barely registered the city. She'd been too wrapped up in her grief to notice her surroundings. Now, despite her numbness, she pressed her face to the window, absorbing details as if storing them for her mother, who would never see them herself.

Newcastle Central Station rose around them, its magnificent curved glass roof still intact despite the bombing. The sight of such enduring beauty amid wartime destruction brought unexpected tears to Diana's eyes—the first she had shed since learning of her mother's death.

She had an hour before her connecting train to Hexham. Diana ventured out of the station into the city beyond, moving like a sleepwalker through streets lined with grey stone buildings, many bearing the scars of recent bombing. Gaps in the street showed where direct hits had occurred, but the overall impression was one of stubborn resilience. Shops remained open, their windows crisscrossed with tape. Women queued outside a butcher's, ration books in hand.

A group of shipyard workers marched past her, their caps pulled low against the drizzle, their faces set with the same determined expression Diana had seen on Londoners.

She stopped at a small café near the station, enticed by a sign promising "Hot Tea – No Waiting." The warm interior, foggy with steam from the massive urn behind the counter, meant every table was occupied, but an elderly woman at a corner table beckoned her over with a warmth that made Diana's chest ache.

"Divven't stand there catchin' yer death," she called. "Plenty room here, hinny."

After a fortifyingly strong cuppa, Diana returned to the station, thinking of what she'd left behind. Rose would be back at the ambulance station now, partnered with someone new, carrying on the vital work of saving lives in a city under siege. The thought brought both comfort and guilt—comfort that the work would continue, guilt that she was abandoning her post. The worst of it was that Diana had no idea if Rose survived the war at all. And that made her heart ache more than she could have imagined.

The train to Hexham was smaller, older, and emptier than the express from London. As it pulled away from Newcastle, following the Tyne westward, Diana thought of what lay ahead. It seemed easier now, with Eleanor's locket warm against her skin. She reopened Rose's gift, planning to read the Shakespeare quotations, only to find that all the girls from the station had also entered their addresses and birthdays. She'd gone from having no friends to a book full of them.

Chapter Thirty-Three

The train from Newcastle wheezed to a halt at Hexham station with the weary sigh of an overworked engine. Diana gathered her modest belongings—a gifted suitcase from Rose's aunt and the scuffed box containing her gas mask—and stepped onto the platform. The November air bit at her cheeks with a sharpness that London's smoky atmosphere had never possessed.

The station had the quiet dignity of a place long used to comings and goings. Low, soot-streaked stone buildings huddled beneath a canopy of iron girders and glass, its panes smudged with coal dust. Faded enamel signs advertising Cadbury Cocoa now shared space with government posters asking 'Is Your Journey Really Necessary?' and reminding the locals that 'Walls Have Ears'. The sandbags stacked around the stationmaster's office were a grim reminder of the world beyond the tracks.

Beneath the shelter, a cast-iron bench bore the deep-polished shine of countless waiting passengers, while a nearby trolley stood loaded with crates of eggs and sacks of flour bound for military depots or country grocers. A porter in a worn greatcoat wheeled another cart towards the goods yard, his breath puffing in clouds.

A small cluster of young women had already formed near the station building, their city clothes marking them as fellow Land Army recruits.

Diana recognised the type—shop girls from Manchester, factory workers from Birmingham, a few who might have been teachers or secretaries before the war swept them into agricultural service. They chattered amongst themselves, clutching official papers and peering about with the wide-eyed uncertainty of displaced urbanites.

"Land Army volunteers?" A brisk voice cut through their murmurs. A woman in her fifties approached, clipboard in hand, her WLA uniform immaculate despite the early hour. "I'm Mrs Patterson, regional coordinator. If you'd form a queue, I'll assign your billets and transport."

Diana joined the line, her heart beating with a mixture of anticipation and dread. She knew what lay ahead, or rather, she thought she did. Mrs Whitaker's kitchen, the clay soil at Mr Hayes's farm clinging to her boots regardless of the weather. The cottage pies at the Twice Brewed. Her mouth salivated at the thought. Then there was Jenny and even Nancy. To them, she would be a complete stranger. A grieving Londoner fleeing the Blitz, nothing more. Ellen came later. She remembered that.

"Diana Penn," she said when her turn came, handing over her papers.

Mrs Patterson consulted her list. "Ah yes, Penn. You're assigned to Willow Farm, Mrs Enid Whitaker. She's been expecting you. Transport's waiting outside." Mrs Patterson pointed towards the station yard. "Mr Telford will take you and Miss Morrison to your billets. Mind, you're ready for work tomorrow morning. Our farmers don't make allowances for city softness."

Miss Morrison proved to be a pale, nervous girl from Coventry who looked as though a strong wind might blow her away. She clutched her suitcase with white knuckles and jumped at every sound as they loaded their belongings into the back of Mr Telford's ancient lorry.

The lorry reeked of old oil, damp canvas, and something like spilled milk curdled in the sun. As it growled along the narrow country lane, the stink of fuel and machinery clashed with the clean scent of wet leaves and cold earth. Hedgerows blurred past in a rush of green and brown, birds scattering ahead, startled by the alien noise.

Diana cleared her throat, and forced herself to make polite conversation, which still didn't come easy to her. She realised that she'd found it easier conversing with Communist double agents than it was making small talk with strangers her own age. "First time in the country?" she finally managed, her voice cracking as the lorry lumbered onwards.

"Yes," Miss Morrison whispered. "I've never been further than Birmingham before. They said I had to choose something when I volunteered, and this seemed safer than the factories."

Diana gave no response other than a grunt of acknowledgment. The trip, and the grief, had depleted whatever social reserves she thought she had.

If their driver had an opinion on their conversation, he gave no sign. Broad-faced and with a nose that looked like it had once lost more than one fight, Mr Telford guided his lorry through narrow lanes lined with dry stone walls. The landscape unfolded before them. Bare trees etched stark patterns against the pewter sky, with sheep huddling in fields gone dormant for winter.

Diana drank it in. She'd forgotten how vast the sky could be without buildings to frame it. In her memories, this journey had been a blur of grief and disorientation. Now, even in her numbness, she could appreciate the austere beauty of a landscape preparing for winter's embrace.

"That'll be Morrison's billet," Mr Telford said, pointing to a substantial stone farmhouse set back from the road. "Thomas Hawk's place. They'll work you hard, lass, but they're fair."

Miss Morrison's face went even paler as they turned into the yard, where a formidable-looking woman in a brown apron waited by the kitchen door.

Diana squeezed the girl's hand. A gesture the old her would never have done.

"You'll be fine," she said. "You're stronger than you think."

Where did that platitude come from?

Miss Morrison nodded once before gathering her courage and climbing down from the cab. Diana watched her walk towards her new life, shoulders squared with determined bravery, and felt an unexpected surge of maternal pride. When had she begun caring about the welfare of virtual strangers?

"Next stop, Willow Farm," Mr Telford announced, putting the lorry back into gear. "Mrs Whitaker's been looking forward to having help again. Last girl went home after harvest. She couldn't take the isolation."

The lorry turned down a familiar lane, and Diana's breath caught. There it was—Willow Farm. The stone cottage with its slate roof, the small wooden sign hanging from a post, the garden gate freshly painted.

Smoke curled from the chimney, and golden light spilled from the kitchen window, creating a picture of such domestic tranquillity that Diana's eyes filled with tears.

Home. The word echoed in her mind with startling force. Not her mother's terraced house in Bethnal Green, nor any of the cramped flats she'd occupied during her MI6 career, but this heaven on earth. Willow Farm.

"Here we are then," Mr Telford said, pulling to a stop beside the gate.

The kitchen door opened, and Diana's heart nearly stopped as Enid Whitaker stepped into the yard. Stout and practical, with greying hair escaping its pins and kind eyes. Wearing a floral house dress protected by an apron, her capable, gentle hands, which had served Diana untold cups of tea, were dusted with flour.

"There you are!" Mrs Whitaker called, hurrying to the gate with a smile that could have melted the frost. "I was worried the train had been delayed again. These wartime schedules are dreadful, aren't they?"

Diana climbed down from the lorry, and for a moment, she stared at the woman who had become her second mother. Mrs Whitaker was younger than Diana remembered, and not yet touched by the grief that would age her when Trevor's death was confirmed. Her face was rounder, her eyes bright with the resilience of someone who believed her son would come home, and that the war would be over within the year.

"Diana Penn," she managed, her voice hoarse with suppressed emotion.

"Welcome to Willow Farm, Diana," Mrs Whitaker said with a smile, taking Diana's free hand in both of hers. Her touch was warm, dry, and comforting. "I hope you'll be happy here. It's not much compared to London, I'm sure, but we'll do our best to make you comfortable."

You already have, Diana wanted to say. *You made me a home when I'd lost everything, and you taught me what kindness looked like when I didn't even know it existed.*

Instead, she nodded and followed Mrs Whitaker to the farmhouse, leaving Mr Telford to unload her belongings with a cheerful "Right then, I'll leave you ladies to get acquainted."

Walking into the kitchen was like watching a rerun of your favourite movie. It was as Diana's memory had preserved it, with the scrubbed pine table, the range with its perpetual kettle, the wireless on the shelf.

Several well-thumbed cookbooks and a framed photograph of Trevor in his uniform filled the rest of the shelf.

"Sit yourself down," Mrs Whitaker instructed, already bustling towards the range. "You must be famished after that journey? There's a shepherd's pie keeping warm, and I've just popped a batch of scones into the oven."

Diana sank into the chair that would become "hers" over the coming months and watched Mrs Whitaker move about her kitchen. The older woman hummed under her breath as she prepared a plate of food that made Diana's mouth water.

"I know it must seem strange," Mrs Whitaker continued, setting the plate before Diana along with a cup of tea, "leaving everything familiar behind. But country life has its compensations. Fresh air, good honest work, and peace and quiet when the day's done."

Diana remembered the nights she'd lain in the small upstairs bedroom listening to owls call across the fields. After London's constant noise—the drone of aircraft, the crash of bombs, the wail of sirens—the countryside's silence had been profound enough to keep her awake for hours.

"Tell me about yourself," Mrs Whitaker prompted, settling into the chair opposite with her own cup of tea. "Have you any experience with farm work? Animals?"

Diana took a bite of the pie, rich with lamb and vegetables from the farm's own garden, and tried to remember what she'd told Mrs Whitaker the first time round. Not that it mattered. If she was being honest with herself, and it embarrassed her now, she'd barely spoken to the woman after her arrival back then. She'd hidden herself away in her room, emerging only for meals, or for work. They'd essentially lived separate lives, albeit under the same roof.

"None at all," Diana admitted. "I worked as an ambulance driver in London until..." She paused, touching her mother's locket through her jumper. "Until I lost my mother in the Blitz. I needed to get away."

Mrs Whitaker's expression softened with sympathy. "Oh, my dear. How dreadful for you. And no other family?"

"No one." The words emerged like a stone dropped into still water.

"Well," Mrs Whitaker said, "you've family here now, such as we are. It's just myself most of the time—my son's away fighting." Here she gestured towards the photo on the mantel.

"But you'll be working with Mr Hayes at his farm, and there are other land girls in the area, so you won't be lonely," Mrs Whitaker said.

Diana's stomach clenched with sudden anxiety. The other girls—Jenny Jenkins with her rope-splicing skills and easy flirtation, and Nancy, and Ellen Wilson with her American confidence and archaeological sketches. Had she imagined that they'd had a friendship in that first life? One that went south? Or had it not ever been a friendship, and they were nothing more than acquaintances whose relationship had come to a natural end? Had she been holding onto the hatred of a person who had been nothing more to her than another face in church? And if so, what did that say about her as a person?

The thought terrified her more than any bomb or collapsing building ever had. What if she retreated into her old patterns of isolation? What if she spent this precious time repeating the same cold distance that had characterised her first time through?

"Are you quite all right, dear?" Mrs Whitaker's voice seemed to come from very far away. "You've gone rather pale."

Diana blinked. "I'm sorry, I was just... it's been difficult since Mother died. I don't want to be a burden to anyone."

The admission surprised her with its honesty.

"Oh, my dear girl. Grief makes us all feel isolated, doesn't it? But you mustn't worry about being a burden. The other Land Army girls I've met are lovely. Full of life and laughter. Just what you need, I'd say. Would you like to see your room? And after that, fresh scones for both of us, I think. I've got plenty of jam left from last season. One silver lining to being on my own."

Diana nodded, following her hostess up the narrow staircase she remembered so well. The small bedroom under the eaves remained the same. The iron bedstead with its faded quilt, the washstand with its chipped basin, the window that looked out over fields stretching towards the distant hills.

"It's not much," Mrs Whitaker said apologetically, "but it's clean and warm. Well, reasonably warm," she amended with a self-deprecating smile. "These old houses never quite seal properly."

"It's perfect," Diana said, meaning it.

Mrs Whitaker beamed at her enthusiasm. "I'm so glad. Now, you rest a bit and unpack, then pop back downstairs when you're ready."

"Tomorrow, I'll take you to meet Mr Hayes. He's expecting you at eight o'clock sharp. A good man, if a bit gruff on the surface. Lost his wife some years back, and his Arthur is away fighting too. It's a shame Arthur and Trevor couldn't have stayed together. Best of friends, those boys." She smiled, but her mind was thousands of kilometres away.

After Mrs Whitaker left, Diana sat on the edge of the narrow bed, staring out the window. Everything felt different. She was different. The grieving woman who'd first climbed these stairs had been broken by loss and armoured against any further pain by emotional isolation. This Diana carried decades of experience in her young body, and was learning the value of the kindness being offered to her.

She unpacked her few belongings, placing the Spode teacup on the small shelf beside the window, where morning light would catch its delicate pattern. Everything else she had wasn't even hers. How different this was from her first life, when she'd arrived at Hayes Farm with nothing but a Red Cross emergency parcel—a grim collection of charity donations that smelled of mothballs and other people's lives. The clothes she put away in the drawers now consisted of a far nicer collection that Rose and the other girls had hastily assembled after the bombing. A jumper that had belonged to Doris, a wool skirt from Shirley, two blouses that Mrs Finley had contributed from her own wardrobe. Rose herself had donated a warm cardigan in soft green wool, its pockets still carrying the faint scent of the lavender sachets Mrs Finley tucked into all her drawers. There were undergarments purchased with a collection taken up at the station— practical cotton vests and knickers that bore no resemblance to Diana's destroyed belongings but would serve their purpose. Even her nightgown was a donated flannel affair that Gladys had declared "decent, if not glamorous."

The kindness of these donations struck Diana anew as she folded each item with care. These women—most of whom she'd never spoken to in her first life—had given freely from their own meagre wardrobes. In wartime Britain, where clothing coupons were precious and new garments a luxury, they'd clothed her without thought of recompense.

Diana fingered the sleeve of Rose's cardigan, remembering how the younger woman had pressed it into her hands. "It'll suit you better than me anyway," Rose had insisted.

Diana suspected the girl had treasured the cardigan for the way its colour brought out her eyes. "Besides, you'll need something warm for those northern winters."

The address book she left on her pillow, planning to write to Rose that very evening.

Over a plate of still warm scones with jam, Mrs Whitaker kept up a gentle stream of conversation, touching on local gossip, observations about the weather, stories about the various WLA girls stationed in the area.

Diana smiled, relaxing despite herself. She realised now that this was what she'd missed in her old life—the simple pleasure of sharing a meal and conversation with someone who wanted nothing from her in return. She still hadn't mastered the art of small talk, but Mrs Whitaker was doing enough for both of them. And the difference with this life was that Diana was present, instead of hiding in her room.

"Now, let me tell you what to expect tomorrow," Mrs Whitaker said as they were clearing away the dishes. "Mr Hayes will start you with the basics. Feeding the animals, collecting eggs, perhaps some light maintenance work. That sort of thing," Mrs Whitaker said, vigorously drying a plate with her tea towel. "But if you've got any special skills, make sure to tell him. He's not one of those dinosaurs who thinks a woman's place is in the kitchen. He's one of the more enlightened men in Cheviot Hills. And they are few and far between, you mark my words. One can but hope that this war will knock some sense into the rest of them. Some more than others."

Chapter Thirty-Four

The cockerel's crow pierced the pre-dawn darkness, rousing Diana from the deepest sleep she'd enjoyed in weeks. For a moment, she lay still beneath Mrs Whitaker's heavy woollen blankets, listening to the sounds of the countryside awakening. An owl hooted somewhere in the distance, and she could hear the gentle lowing of cattle stirring in nearby fields.

No air raid sirens. No bombs. No screams cutting through the night.

Diana sat up, her body responding with the easiness of youth despite the previous day's travel. Frost had etched delicate patterns across her bedroom window, and her breath misted in the cold air. The small room felt like a sanctuary after the cramped quarters she'd shared with the Finleys.

A gentle tap at her door interrupted her thoughts.

"Diana, dear?" Mrs Whitaker's voice carried through the thin wood. "I've porridge on the range and tea brewing. Best not keep Mr Hayes waiting on your first day."

"I'll be right down," Diana called back, already reaching for the clothes she'd laid out the night before.

She dressed in the brown corduroy breeches and a green woollen jumper that comprised her Land Army uniform, the fabric rough but serviceable against her skin.

The boots were stiff and new, donated by the Women's Land Army along with her regulation slouch hat and armband. Everything smelt of mothballs and institutional efficiency.

Downstairs, Mrs Whitaker bustled about her kitchen with practised ease, her greying hair already pinned into a neat bun despite the early hour. The range radiated blessed warmth, and the smell of porridge and bacon made Diana's mouth water.

"Sleep well?" Mrs Whitaker asked, spooning porridge into a bowl and adding a precious knob of butter. "I worried the quiet might keep you awake. City folk often find country nights too still."

Diana accepted the bowl, remembering how the silence had indeed disturbed her during her first stay at Willow Farm. This time, however, exhaustion had claimed her the moment her head touched the pillow.

"Like a baby," she replied, taking her first spoonful. The porridge was creamy and substantial, flavoured with a hint of honey that spoke of Mrs Whitaker's connection to local beekeepers. "This is wonderful."

"It's nothing fancy, but it's fresh." Mrs Whitaker poured tea from a brown earthenware pot, the liquid dark and fragrant. "You'll need your strength today. Mr Hayes will put you through your paces, I expect."

Diana nodded, though she knew exactly what to expect from her first day at Hayes Farm. She could picture it all: the dairy with its six stalls and temperamental cows—though none would prove as challenging as Bertha, who'd been a challenger from the moment she'd arrived. The morning routine of feeding and milking that would become as familiar as breathing.

The challenge would be appearing suitably novice whilst avoiding the mistakes that had killed her in previous iterations.

"Tell me more about the other land girls," Diana said, stirring her tea.

Mrs Whitaker's face brightened. "Oh yes, lovely girls. There's Jenny Jenkins—she's working at Hayes Farm, too, so you'll meet her today. Bit scatty, that one, but sweet as anything." She paused, considering. "Then there's the new girl up at the Hollisters. An American. Ellen something... Wilson, I think. I haven't met her yet. Their last girl wasn't at all suited to the work."

Diana's pulse quickened at the mention of Ellen. "How did an American end up here?"

"She was studying archaeology at university and refused to go home when Chamberlain declared war, stayed to finish her degree."

"Until her course got shut down. Poor lass. Now she's doing her bit for the war effort." Mrs Whitaker whistled. "It takes courage to stay in a foreign country during a war."

Or foolishness, Diana thought, considering Ellen's mysterious disappearance.

"There's also Nancy Robbins," Mrs Whitaker continued, "not strictly part of the WLA. She lives in town and helps her mother with the Women's Institute and such. You'll meet her at church on Sunday, no doubt."

Diana nodded, filing away the information. After leaving Cheviot Hills, she'd avoided going to church like the plague. Oddly, she found the prospect of returning to St Michael's and listening to Reverend Taylor's sermons comforting. It certainly wouldn't kill her to go to church. As long as she steered clear of any confrontations with Mr Hollister in the churchyard...

After breakfast, Mrs Whitaker walked with her down the lane towards Hayes Farm, pointing out landmarks and sharing village gossip with the enthusiasm of someone starved for fresh conversation.

"That's the old mill," she said, indicating a stone building beside a narrow stream. "Been abandoned since before the war. The children like to play there, though I'm not sure it's safe." She adjusted her headscarf against the morning chill. "And there's the church spire through those trees. St Michael's. Beautiful Norman architecture. Some of the stones came from the Wall."

"The wall?"

"Hadrian's Wall. When it's fine, we'll walk a part of it. It's not too far."

The walk took fifteen minutes, winding through countryside that glowed despite the overcast sky. Bare trees created intricate lacework against the grey clouds, and frost sparkled on the grass verges like scattered diamonds.

Hayes Farm appeared around a bend in the lane, its collection of stone buildings arranged around a muddy yard. Smoke rose from the chimney, and Diana could hear the restless movement of livestock awaiting their morning feed.

"There's Mr Hayes," Mrs Whitaker observed, nodding towards a stocky figure emerging from the largest barn. "And that'll be Jenny with him."

Diana's breath caught as she recognised the slight figure beside the farmer—Jenny Jenkins, her animated gestures visible even at this distance.

"Mr Hayes," Mrs Whitaker called as they approached. "Here's your new land girl."

Frederick Hayes turned towards them and smiled.

"Mrs Whitaker," he acknowledged with a tip of his cap. "Miss Penn, is it?"

"Diana," she replied, extending her hand. His grip was firm and callused.

"Well then, Diana, let's see what you're made of. Jenny here will show you the ropes."

Jenny stepped forward with a grin that lit up the entire farmyard. She was smaller than Diana, barely reaching Diana's shoulder, with eyes that sparkled with mischief.

"Welcome to Hayes Farm," she said, her accent carrying traces of the coast. "Hope you don't mind getting your hands dirty, because that's about all we do here." She laughed.

Diana smiled. "I don't mind hard work," she replied.

"Good, because there's plenty of it," Mr Hayes said, already moving towards the barn. "Right then, let's start with the basics. Morning milking waits for no one."

Mrs Whitaker departed and Diana followed Jenny into the dairy. Diana paused on the threshold to breathe in the perpetual smell of hay and warm milk.

"Now," Jenny said, collecting two milking stools, "the trick with milking is to stay calm. Cows can sense nervousness, and they don't much like it." She demonstrated the proper positioning, her small hands moving with practised efficiency.

Diana watched, pretending to absorb information she'd already mastered. When Jenny handed her a stool and bucket, she approached the nearest cow with deliberately clumsy movements.

"That's Rosalind," Jenny said helpfully. "She's as gentle as a lamb. Perfect for beginners."

Diana positioned herself beside the familiar cow, letting her hands remember the rhythm whilst keeping her expression uncertain. The warm stream of milk hitting the bucket created a soothing percussion, and she relaxed into the routine.

"Blimey, you're a natural," Jenny observed after a few minutes. "Are you sure you've never done this before?"

"Beginner's luck," Diana quipped. "My mother always said I had steady hands."

The morning progressed with surprising ease. Diana appeared suitably incompetent whilst avoiding any genuine disasters, asking the right questions and making small mistakes. Jenny turned out to be an enthusiastic teacher, chattering constantly about everything from proper cow handling to village gossip.

"See that one there?" Jenny nodded towards a large Ayrshire with distinctive markings. "That's Lotte. She hates it if your hands are cold. And she will let you know. Kicks up merry hell! Leave her to me until you've got your feet under yourself."

Diana shuddered, remembering Bertha's lethal hooves. "Lotte doesn't like cold hands, right! I'll keep my distance then."

"Wise choice. Though between you and me, the poor thing's probably just fed up with the whole business. She's probably only got another year or so in her."

After the milking came feeding—hauling heavy buckets of grain and armfuls of hay to the various animals scattered across the farm. Diana's muscles might have remembered the work from her first life, but she still paced herself. It wasn't easy to forget how, as she'd aged, even twisting the wrong way could pull a muscle.

At midday, they broke for lunch at the farmhouse kitchen. Mr Hayes joined them, washing his hands at the deep stone sink before settling at the scrubbed wooden table. Thick vegetable soup, crusty bread, and sharp cheese that tasted of the local pastures.

"You'll do," Mr Hayes pronounced after observing Diana's morning performance. "Got common sense, which is rarer than you might think among city folk."

Jenny beamed as though personally responsible for Diana's success. "A quick learner, this one. Must be the teacher."

The afternoon brought different tasks. The mending of a fence, cleaning out chicken coops, and preparing feed for the following day. Diana threw herself into the work with an enthusiasm that surprised even her. And as they worked, Jenny kept up a steady stream of conversation.

"I was working in Whitby," she explained as they repaired the fence.

"Ladies' fashions. Dull as dishwater, but it paid the bills. My dad always said I should've gone to sea like him, but they don't take girls on fishing boats." She grinned. "Although I bet I could've handled it better than half the lads he worked with."

"Where is he now?" Diana asked, though she remembered Jenny mentioning her father's death during their previous encounters.

Jenny's expression darkened briefly. "Convoy duty. North Atlantic. Ship went down with all hands just before Christmas." She shook her head, forcing the brightness back into her voice. "But enough of that. What about you? What brings you to Cheviot Hills?"

Diana hesitated, then decided on sharing most of the truth. "My father died when I was little. Lost my mother in the Blitz. I couldn't stay after that."

Jenny's face softened with sympathy. "Oh, I'm so sorry. That's awful." She reached across the fence post to squeeze Diana's hand. "We'll look after you."

The simple gesture of comfort nearly undid Diana completely. Was this what friendship gave you?

"Thank you," she managed.

By late afternoon, Diana's muscles ached from the unaccustomed work, and her cheeks burned from the cold air. As they finished the day's tasks, Jenny stretched and yawned.

"Right then, that's us done for today. Fancy coming to the Twice Brewed with us Friday night?" Jenny asked. "There's always a good crowd then, and the other Land Army girls will be there, so you can meet them all properly."

In her first life, Diana had declined, claiming fatigue. The thought of socialising with strangers was as appealing as a cup of cold vomit. Besides, any downtime from work was for rest, not wasting time socialising with a group of girls she had nothing in common with. But she wasn't going to make that mistake again. This time she found herself nodding in agreement.

"I'd like that," Diana said.

Jenny's face lit up. "Brilliant! Everyone is dying to meet you. A new girl in town is always exciting."

Waving goodbye, Diana continued towards Willow Farm, her step lighter than it had been in literal decades.

Mrs Whitaker was waiting with supper ready to be served when Diana arrived, eager to hear about her first day. Diana didn't disappoint her, sharing her observations about her new life and her coworker.

After supper, Diana sat at the kitchen table, composing her first letter to Rose. This was going to be her first ever letter written to a friend, and she was at a complete loss as to how to start, or even what to say.

How did one begin such correspondence? Her only experience with letter writing had been official communications—reports to superiors, carefully coded messages to contacts, the sort of clinical prose that conveyed information without revealing anything of the writer's inner self.

Diana chewed the end of the pencil, a habit her mother had always scolded her for, and tried to imagine what Rose would want to hear. Did friends write about the weather? About their daily activities? About their feelings?

The concept of sharing feelings in writing felt as foreign as speaking Mandarin. In her MI6 career, emotions had been carefully compartmentalised, filed away in mental boxes where they couldn't interfere with operational efficiency. Personal correspondence had been limited to the occasional formal note of condolence, or congratulations on a colleague's wedding. Sometimes, it was tempting to muddle the two up...

She started several times, each attempt more stilted than the last.

Dear Rose, I hope this letter finds you well...

No, too formal. She started again.

Dearest Rose, Thank you for all your kindness...

That sounded like a thank-you note to an elderly aunt. After crossing that out, she sighed.

Mrs Whitaker looked up from her knitting, spectacles perched on the end of her nose. "Struggling with something?"

Diana felt heat rise in her cheeks. "I'm trying to write to my friend in London. The girl who helped me after my mother died. But I don't know how to begin. I've never written a personal letter before."

"Never?" Mrs Whitaker's eyes widened.

Diana shook her head, suddenly embarrassed by the admission. "There wasn't anyone to write to."

"The trick," Mrs Whitaker explained, "is to imagine you're speaking to them directly. What would you say if they were sitting right here in this kitchen?"

Diana considered this, picturing Rose's bright face across the homely table. What would she say? That she missed her terribly? That she was grateful beyond words for the friendship Rose had offered?

"I'd tell her about the farm," Diana said slowly. "About Jenny, and how kind you've been. How peaceful it is here. And I'd tell her..." She paused, the words catching in her throat. "I'd tell her how grateful I am that she didn't let me disappear into my own grief."

Mrs Whitaker smiled. "That's much better than any formal correspondence. Friends want to hear about your life, your thoughts, your feelings. They want to know you're well and happy."

"But what if I say something wrong? What if I sound foolish?"

"Foolish?" Mrs Whitaker laughed softly. "True friends love us despite our foolishness, not because we're perfect."

Mrs Whitaker winced as she laid aside her knitting and stood up, her hand pressing against the small of her back.

"Are you okay?" Diana asked.

"I've been hunched over a bit too long tonight," Mrs Whitaker admitted, rotating her shoulders gingerly. "That's a tricky pattern I'm working on, and this weather doesn't help."

"Would you like me to pop into the chemist tomorrow?" Diana offered. "And pick up something for the pain?"

Mrs Whitaker's face brightened. "Would you? Kevin O'Hara is the chemist. Ask for his special liniment—he makes it himself. Calls it 'Gladiator Oil' of all things." She chuckled. "Daft name, but it's the only thing that takes the ache away properly."

The following week established a rhythm that was both new and familiar. Early rising, breakfast with Mrs Whitaker, the walk to Hayes Farm, farm chores with Jenny, lunch with Mr Hayes.

On the Friday evening after work, Diana found herself walking towards the stone-walled Twice Brewed Inn with a flutter of anticipation in her stomach. The darkness was absolute, blackout regulations ensuring not even the thinnest sliver of light escaped the stone building.

Stepping through the outer door into a narrow vestibule hung with thick black fabric, Diana pushed through the inner curtain into sudden warmth and golden light.

The Twice Brewed had been transformed by the blackout into something more intimate than it likely was in peacetime. Table lamps with deep shades cast pools of light onto scrubbed wooden surfaces, whilst the fireplace painted dancing shadows on the low-beamed ceiling.

The air was thick with pipe smoke and the lingering aroma of mutton and root vegetables. Perhaps two dozen or so patrons occupied the space—farmers, Home Guard members, a small cohort of ramblers, and couples sharing quiet conversations in the amber glow.

Jenny waved from a corner table, where two other young women sat with her.

As Diana approached the table, she saw Nancy Robbins for the first time in this life. Diana had to suppress any feelings she may have had because, so far, the poor girl had done nothing wrong. It wouldn't be fair for Diana to judge her for something which may, or may not, happen in the future.

Beside her sat Ellen Wilson, and the American girl was exactly as she remembered—dark hair in elegant waves, intelligent brown eyes, and an aura of sophisticated confidence that seemed out of place in the Twice Brewed. She wore a burgundy dress that probably cost more than most people's monthly wages, and her smile revealed the sort of perfect teeth that spoke of American prosperity.

"Everyone, this is Diana," Jenny announced as Diana reached their table. "The new girl I've been telling you about."

"Diana Penn," she introduced herself, offering her hand first to Nancy, then to Ellen.

Nancy's handshake was firm and direct. "Nancy Robbins. Pleased to meet you. Jenny says you're from London? I can't tell you how much I miss going down to London."

Ellen's grip was confident, her accent unmistakably American. "Ellen Wilson. How are you finding country life?"

"Different from London," Diana replied carefully, settling into the remaining chair. "But peaceful. I needed peace."

The conversation flowed easily once Diana relaxed into it. Nancy proved to be well-informed about local affairs, sharing gossip about various villagers with a sharp wit that made Diana laugh despite her misgivings about the future Nancy. Ellen entertained them with stories of her adjustment to British customs.

"You Brits sure do love your lines!" Ellen was saying, her American accent crisp. "Back home, if someone made us stand around like this without griping, we'd probably start a riot. But here? You all act like it's some kind of civic duty."

Nancy giggled. "Wait until you've been here long enough for rationing to really bite. Then you'll understand why we queue so beautifully. It's survival, not politeness."

"Speaking of rationing," Jenny interjected, "did you hear about Mrs Morley's black market butter scandal? Apparently, she's been trading eggs for extra dairy rations with that farmer near Wooler."

"Mrs Morley?" Diana asked, intrigued by the local drama. It sounded more complex than the plot lines of *Coronation Street*.

"Pillar of the Women's Institute, lectures everyone about patriotic duty. Meanwhile she's been hoarding butter like it's gold bullion," Nancy explained with relish.

Shaking her head, Jenny turned to Ellen and asked, "How's your billet now?"

"The Hollisters are... accommodating. Mrs Hollister is quite proper, very concerned with standards. Mr Hollister is..." she paused, choosing her words carefully, "...an interesting character."

Jenny made a face. "Bit of an odd duck, if you ask me. Always staring when he thinks no one's looking."

"Oh, he's harmless enough," Ellen replied quickly, although her smile didn't quite reach her eyes. "Just his American manner, I suppose."

Diana filed away the interaction, noting the tension beneath Ellen's casual words. In her first life, she'd missed these early warning signs. But after what had happened in the churchyard between her and Mr Hollister, she didn't trust him as far as she could throw him.

"Did you ever find out what happened to the girl who was there before you?" Nancy asked with the casual cruelty of youth. "The one who left so suddenly?"

Ellen shrugged. "Family emergency, apparently. I arrived a week after she departed, so I never met her. Mrs Hollister seemed quite put out by the whole affair. She didn't even leave a forwarding address. Just packed up and vanished overnight, from what Mrs Hollister told me."

Jenny leaned in, lowering her voice with relish.

"Left her uniform behind, too. Boots still by the bed. Gave the daily a fright when she came in."

"The Women's Land Army supervisor was livid," Nancy added. "She's friends with my mother, so I heard all about it. She looked a bit like you though, Ellen. You could almost have been sisters."

Diana listened carefully, filing away this new information. How odd that the Hollisters had already lost one billet. It might be nothing, but given Ellen's disappearance in her past lives, it might be important.

"We should make this a regular thing," Ellen suggested as they tucked into the steaming hot pies. "Friday nights at the Twice Brewed. Our own little society."

"I thought it was a usual thing?" Jenny announced, leading to much mirth from the others.

"The Cheviot Hills Ladies' Appreciation Society," Nancy declared with mock seriousness. "Dedicated to the consumption of cottage pies, and the thorough discussion of local scandal."

Diana found herself laughing, truly laughing. The sound surprised her with its genuine joy.

"I'd like that," Diana added, meaning it completely.

As they parted ways outside the inn, Jenny linked her arm through Diana's for the walk back towards their respective billets.

"Told you they were lovely," she said with satisfaction. "Ellen's a bit posh, but she's got a good heart. And Nancy knows everything that happens in this village before it happens, care of her mother mostly."

Diana nodded, thinking of the friendships she'd begun to forge. The first time around, she'd attended perhaps three social gatherings during her entire stay at Cheviot Hills, always as an observer, never as a participant. That had started to change when she'd been given a second, and third (or was it fourth?) chance. But this time, she was determined to be present for every moment.

"Thank you," she said to Jenny as they reached the junction where their paths diverged. "For including me, I mean. I haven't had friends in… well, in a long time."

Jenny squeezed her arm. "What are friends for? Besides, you're one of us now. We look after our own in Cheviot Hills."

As Diana walked the final stretch to Willow Farm, she reflected on how much had changed in just one week.

The work at Hayes Farm was becoming second nature. Her relationship with Mrs Whitaker was deepening beyond mere landlady and tenant, and she'd begun to build the friendships that had eluded her in her previous life.

More importantly, she was changing.

But it wouldn't be all smooth sailing. She just had to stay alive long enough to navigate her newfound friends through the challenges ahead. And that scared her more than anything.

Chapter Thirty-Five

Diana settled into the rhythm of farm life with surprising ease, although she constantly marvelled at how different it felt this time around.

On her first day off, Diana found herself walking along the banks of the slow-moving Cheviot Burn until she reached a sheltered spot out of the wind, where she settled down against the trunk of a tree. With her eyes closed, a long-forgotten memory of Belgium surfaced. One of those peculiar solo holidays she'd taken during the sixties, when her cover required familiarity with Western Europe's tourist routes. She'd paid the dreaded single supplement without a murmur, joining a coach tour filled with retired couples and enthusiastic widows armed with guidebooks and sensible walking shoes.

The tour guide, a gaunt-looking Belgian fellow with an encyclopaedic knowledge of local history, had stood beside the Meuse River near Dinant, gesturing towards the modern concrete bridge that spanned the dark water. "This bridge," he'd announced in accented English, "was blown up during the war. The retreating Germans destroyed it in 1944, along with so many others. We rebuilt it stronger. We Belgians are practical people."

Diana had stood amongst the cluster of tourists, her camera hanging around her neck, watching the water flow beneath the replacement bridge.

The guide had gone on to talk about the unstable riverbank, and the engineering work done after the war to strengthen it.

A widow from Bournemouth standing beside her had struck up a conversation. "My Herbert always said bridges were meant to bring people together, not keep them apart," the woman had said, adjusting her headscarf against the wind. "God bless his soul."

Diana had agreed politely whilst drinking in the woman's mannerisms and her particularly English way of stating the obvious. Filing the information away in case it became useful at some point in the future.

She'd found those solo trips brilliant for picking up little quirks she could use later in her role. She always played the slightly introverted English spinster with her camera and her interest in local history. The perfect camouflage for someone who needed to travel widely.

Diana opened her eyes, the memory fading as the present reasserted itself. The sound of the Cheviot Burn and the chill Northern air brought her firmly back to England.

The morning routine at the farm had become as familiar as breathing. The clatter of the milk pails against the dairy walls, the warm breath of cattle creating clouds in the frigid air. Even Lotte, the Ayrshire with the aversion to cold hands, had grudgingly accepted Diana's presence.

"You're getting the hang of this," Jenny observed one bitter morning as they worked side by side in the dairy, her breath misting with every word. "Remember when you first arrived? I thought you might faint dead away at the sight of a cow's udder."

Diana laughed, the sound genuine. "Was I really that obvious?"

"Like a deer caught in headlamps," Jenny grinned. "But look at you now. Proper farm lass, you are."

The compliment warmed Diana more than she would have thought.

And it wasn't long before Mr Hayes trusted her with more complex work—helping to repair a damaged roof on one of the outbuildings. Diana's knowledge of basic construction, gleaned from decades of MI6 fieldwork, served her well, though she was careful to appear appropriately uncertain when required. Her performance would have impressed any theatre critic.

"You've got good instincts," Mr Hayes observed as they secured the last of the replacement slates. "Most city folk wouldn't know a hammer from a handsaw."

"We all had to pitch in at the ambulance station," Diana improvised. "I just picked it up a little easier than the others."

Mrs Whitaker had noticed the change, too. "You're blooming," she declared one evening as they sat by the fire, Diana writing another letter to Rose whilst Mrs Whitaker worked on her endless knitting. "When you first arrived, you looked like a ghost. All pale and distant. Now there's colour in your cheeks and life in your eyes."

Diana paused in her letter-writing, considering this observation. She felt different. The rigid control that had defined her first life had softened. She laughed at Jenny's jokes, shared her own anecdotes during their lunch breaks, even humming along to the wireless whilst helping Mrs Whitaker with the washing up.

The following day, Diana was mucking out the chicken coop when she heard the rumble of Mr Hayes's lorry returning from the village. The engine coughed twice before falling silent, followed by the slam of the driver's door and heavy footsteps across the yard.

"That bloody fool," Mr Hayes muttered, loud enough for Diana to hear as he passed the coop. "Playing with ordnance as if it's a child's toy."

Diana looked up from her work. "Everything all right, Mr Hayes?"

He paused, shaking his head. "Just been to the Home Guard meeting. Since old Ruddle went into hospital for his hernia, Aldridge has put himself in charge of the training munitions. He's treating the whole business like it's a Guy Fawkes party." Mr Hayes removed his cap and ran a hand through his hair. "Mark my words, that man'll blow us all to kingdom come if he's not careful."

"Surely there are proper procedures for that sort of thing?" Diana ventured.

"Aye, there are. But following procedures requires effort, doesn't it? And effort's never been Aldridge's strong suit." He shouldered his bag with obvious disgust. "I've seen what happens when men get careless with explosives. Too many good lads were lost in the last war to incompetence."

With that, he stomped back to the farmhouse.

The weekly gatherings at the Twice Brewed became the highlight of Diana's social calendar.

Each Friday evening, she would walk the familiar path to the inn, anticipation building with each step. The Twice Brewed was a sanctuary where the four young women escaped their wartime responsibilities. A glass or two of Charlie's port and lemon, alongside a slice of the most perfect pie, also helped immeasurably.

Ellen had proven to be a fascinating companion, her American perspective offering fresh insights into British life that Diana had never questioned. During one memorable evening, Ellen had regaled them with her attempts to understand the intricacies of the class system.

"At home, if you've got money, you're somebody," Ellen explained, gesturing with her half pint of ale. "Here, you can have all the money in the world, but if your grandfather sold fish on a street corner, you'll never be quite respectable. It's bewildering."

Nancy had choked on her drink. "You should hear Mother on the subject of 'new money'. She can trace the social failings of half the county back at least four generations."

Jenny leaned forward. "And what about old money with no money? Like the Ashfords up at the Hall? They've got a title as old as the Battle of Hastings, but they're so skint they can't afford to heat more than one room at a time."

"Ah," Nancy nodded, "that's where breeding comes in. Better to freeze nobly than warm yourself vulgarly. That's what Mother would say. And she's adamant that I marry *up*. How am I meant to meet someone suitable in Cheviot Hills? This is why I need this damn war to be over, otherwise I'm going to end up on the shelf."

These conversations delighted Diana. They were unlike anything she'd experienced before. In her previous life, her social interactions had all been an act. Coldly professional. But here? Here she was part of a community. She didn't need to put on airs or graces, or hide who she was and what she thought.

She remembered Cologne in 1963, sitting in a smoky café near the cathedral, nursing a bitter coffee whilst waiting for her contact. Heinrich had been one of her most reliable assets—a railway clerk with access to East German transportation schedules. For three years, they'd met fortnightly, always in different locations, always maintaining the careful dance of handler and source.

Heinrich had spoken of his daughter's wedding, his voice thick with pride as he described the ceremony. Diana had listened with professional interest, filing away personal details that might prove useful for leverage if needed. When he'd pulled out a worn photograph of his daughter in her wedding dress, Diana had admired it with calculated warmth, saying precisely what was required to maintain their working relationship.

She'd never once asked about Heinrich's own feelings, never wondered if he missed his daughter who'd moved to Hamburg, never considered that his willingness to betray his government might stem from loneliness rather than ideology. To Diana, he'd been Asset Cologne-7, not a father grieving his empty nest.

She'd cultivated dozens of such relationships across West Germany, priding herself on her professionalism and her ability to maintain distance whilst extracting maximum intelligence. She'd been bloody good at her job.

But here, laughing at Jenny's stories about the chemist's romantic misadventures, Diana understood what she'd missed. Heinrich hadn't been just a source—he'd been a human being seeking connection, offering trust, perhaps even friendship. And she'd treated him like a resource rather than as a person.

The work at Hayes Farm had evolved beyond basic animal husbandry. Mr Hayes, recognising Diana's unexpected aptitude for mechanical problems, had begun assigning her more complex tasks. When the ancient tractor developed a persistent starting problem, Diana found herself elbow-deep in its engine.

"How'd you know to check the fuel line?" Mr Hayes asked, admiration in his voice as the engine roared to life.

Diana wiped her greasy hands on an old rag, thinking quickly. "My uncle had a delivery lorry. Used to help him with repairs during school holidays. Plus working as an ambulance driver. They needed every hand they could use."

The lie came easily, but it served its purpose, explaining away skills that would otherwise seem inexplicable in a young woman from London.

The photograph of Arthur Hayes on the cluttered farmhouse mantelpiece haunted her during their lunch breaks, his young face frozen in time, smiling with the confidence of youth the world over.

During one particularly reflective moment, she'd asked Mr Hayes about his son and how often they wrote to each other.

"Oh, he's always been a good correspondent," Mr Hayes replied, his face brightening. "Writes every week, tells me about his mates, the places they've been. Well, as much as he can. Last letter, he mentioned they'd be moving on. Couldn't say where, of course, but he seemed in good spirits."

Diana's stomach clenched with the knowledge of what was coming.

She began drafting a dozen different letters to Arthur in her mind. Letters with warnings which might prevent his death without revealing her impossible knowledge. But each attempt foundered on practical impossibilities. How could she warn him without sounding like a madwoman? And what if her intervention somehow made things worse?

Finally, she approached Mr Hayes one afternoon as they finished mending a gate post. "Would it be terribly forward of me to write to Arthur?" she asked carefully. "It's just... after losing my mother, I can imagine how much letters from home can mean. And I thought he might enjoy hearing about life on the farm from a fresh perspective?"

Mr Hayes's face transformed with such genuine pleasure that Diana felt a stab of guilt for her ulterior motives. "He'd be delighted, I'm sure. He's always asking about the farm, and the animals, and what's happening in the village. And there's only so much an old codger like me can tell about the goings on in town."

That evening, Diana sat at Mrs Whitaker's kitchen table, crafting her first letter to a dead man. She wrote about the personalities of the various cows, Jenny's latest mishaps with the rope splicing, about her impressions of the Twice Brewed—the perfection of the pies. But she also tried weaving in carefully constructed stories about her imaginary travels before the war, in an attempt to warn the lad about the dangers he would face as the war progressed.

I remember visiting Belgium once, she wrote, *particularly the area near the Meuse River. Beautiful countryside, but terribly treacherous in winter. The locals warned me about the riverbanks—how deceptively unstable they could be, especially after heavy rain or snow.*

One fellow told me his grandfather had lost three friends in a single incident when a bank gave way.

She posted the letter with trembling hands, knowing Arthur would receive it at least a year before he would be fighting in Belgium. Her second letter followed a fortnight later, filled with more pastoral observations and another geographical anecdote—this time about the dangers of advancing too quickly through unfamiliar terrain without proper reconnaissance, which she'd couched in terms of coming face-to-face with a wolf in Italy, somewhere near Monte Cassino, and how it had frightened the life out of her. She'd been with a hiking guide, who'd castigated himself for not fully checking out the area around their campsite. She hoped that the young man she'd never met would be filing away the information. She didn't care if he thought she was loopy. She just needed him to be more cognisant of his surroundings. Diana wished more than anything that she'd had access to his war records, to see if they contained further details of his death. But alas, it'd be quite a few years until all those were digitised and accessible from her laptop.

Mr Hayes began looking forward to hearing about her letters as much as Arthur seemed to enjoy reading them. "He mentioned your last letter," he told Diana proudly. "Said it made him feel like he was back home. And that you've got a gift for writing, how you make the farm come alive on the page."

With each letter, Diana grew bolder, embedding more specific warnings within her travelogue stories. She wrote about a bridge collapse she'd once witnessed. One which had stood since Roman times, but which had become weakened due to erosion, and she followed this up with advice about the importance of checking structural integrity before crossing any old bridge. All fictional stories, but each tale was crafted to seem like innocent reminiscence whilst containing potentially life-saving information.

The irony wasn't lost on her. She was using every skill she'd learned as an intelligence operative to try to save a young soldier's life, rather than to gather secrets or eliminate threats. For once, her training served life instead of death.

Chapter Thirty-Six

The months that followed unfolded with a rhythm Diana had never known existed—the gentle, purposeful flow of rural life that seemed almost untouched by the war raging across Europe. By January 1943, Mrs Whitaker had settled into treating Diana less like a grieving evacuee and more like the daughter she'd never had. Their morning routine became sacred—porridge sweetened with honey from a local beekeeper and tea strong enough to wake the dead. Diana found herself contributing stories of her own, carefully edited tales of London life that made Mrs Whitaker laugh whilst folding her endless pile of knitting.

Diana was helping Mrs Whitaker knead dough for the day's bread when an almighty boom echoed across the valley, rattling the kitchen windows and sending the chickens into a frenzy.

Both women froze, their flour-dusted hands suspended mid-work, eyes meeting in shared alarm. Mrs Whitaker glanced at the wall calendar, counting under her breath before she rolled her eyes.

"Damn Aldridge and his boys playing with dynamite," she said, brushing the flour from her hands. "Their foolish live training exercises. Hardly training exercises. More like living out a real Boys' Own adventure if you ask me. Busy trying to recapture their lost youth whilst the rest of us get on with the real work of winning this war."

Diana's work at Hayes Farm had evolved beyond basic animal husbandry into something approaching mastery. Diana could milk the entire herd single-handedly now, her hands moving in the steady rhythm Jenny had taught her, though she still gave Bertha a respectful wide berth. Mr Hayes now trusted her with the more complex machinery—the temperamental threshing equipment, the ancient tractor that required a particular combination of swearing and mechanical sympathy to coax into life.

"You've got the touch," he'd told her one afternoon as she successfully started the stubborn beast on the third attempt. His face creased into something approaching a smile. "Takes some folk years to understand machines like this. You've done it in months."

The Friday evening meals at the Twice Brewed were the cornerstone of Diana's social existence in a way that astonished her. She, who had spent decades avoiding unnecessary human contact, now looked forward to these gatherings, and the famous Twice Brewed cottage pies, with an anticipation that bordered on giddiness. The four of them—Diana, Jenny, Nancy, and Ellen—had claimed a corner table as their territory, establishing what Ellen grandly termed "The Cheviot Hills Society for the Appreciation of Life Beyond Farm Animals."

Jenny regaled them with increasingly elaborate tales of her romantic adventures. There had been Flight Sergeant Morrison from the local RAF base, who'd wooed her with a tin of peaches and offers to show her his Spitfire. The romance had lasted precisely three weeks before Jenny discovered he'd made identical offers to half the girls in Northumberland.

"The peaches were lovely, though," she'd concluded philosophically. "And he did have a Spitfire. Can't fault a man for truth in advertising."

Nancy had blossomed from the slightly sharp-tongued girl Diana remembered into someone with genuine wit and surprising depth. Her observations about village life were delivered with surgical precision that made them all gasp with laughter.

"I know I'm not one of you Land Army girls," Nancy announced one evening, "but being the Land Army coordinator has gone to Mrs Patterson's head."

"She thinks she needs to know every detail about every WLA girl's business. I swear she can hear a whisper from three villages away. Yesterday she knew about Sarah Fletcher's engagement before Sarah knew about it herself."

Ellen had become Diana's favourite, though she'd never admit such a thing to the others. The American girl possessed an infectious enthusiasm for British eccentricities that made Diana see her own country through fresh eyes. Ellen collected peculiar English customs like a lepidopterist collected butterflies, preserving them in letters home that she sometimes read aloud for their entertainment.

"I wrote to my sister about Morris dancing," Ellen had confided one evening, her eyes bright with mischief. "She's convinced I've lost my mind. Grown men in bells and ribbons, hopping about with handkerchiefs? She thinks it's some sort of British fever dream."

The RAF base provided a steady supply of young men for village social events, transforming what might have been rather sedate affairs into something approaching gaiety. Diana danced with pilots whose names she forgot by morning, sharing stories over halves of bitter with navigators who spoke of exotic places with the casual familiarity of men who'd seen too much sky. It didn't pay to become too close to any of them, though. Their lives were as fleeting as hers.

The monthly visits to the Regal Palace Cinema became expeditions of almost military planning. They'd meet outside Robbins's bookshop at precisely half-past six, Nancy armed with information about which films were showing and Ellen clutching a paper bag of humbugs she'd procured from her mysterious American contacts. The cinema itself was an art déco gem, with gleaming brass fittings and red plush seats worn soft by countless Saturday night audiences.

Diana had never realised how much she'd missed the simple pleasure of losing herself in flickering images on a silver screen. They'd seen *Mrs Miniver* three times, weeping openly during Greer Garson's performance. *The Ghost Train* had them all holding hands and walking home in terrified silence, checking over their shoulders for any ghostly apparitions. And the lighter fare—Bob Hope comedies that made Jenny snort with laughter, and the musicals that had Ellen humming for days afterwards—felt like small acts of rebellion against the war's grim insistence on sacrifice and duty.

The Regal's proprietor, Mr Hargreaves, often rewarded their weekly devotion to the cinema with a free bag of pear drops denied to the other patrons. Sometimes they'd arrive to find half the personnel from the local bases in attendance, transforming the sedate cinema into more of a social club with the fug of cigarettes filling the air amidst whispered conversations and stolen kisses.

Even the weekly church service had evolved from a reluctant duty, and an effort to fit in, to something approaching pleasure, largely because Reverend Taylor had developed the knack of keeping his sermons both brief and thoughtful.

The seasonal celebrations had taken on significance she'd never bothered with before. Harvest festival had meant helping Mrs Whitaker arrange vegetables into artistic displays whilst sampling her experimental elderberry wine. Guy Fawkes Night had found them all crowded around a bonfire behind the Twice Brewed, singing songs that grew increasingly bawdy as the evening progressed. Christmas had been a revelation of warmth and generosity that left Diana feeling simultaneously grateful and guilty for the happiness she'd discovered in the midst of a war.

Diana had ceased to think of herself as a Londoner temporarily resident in Cheviot Hills. Cheviot Hills was now her home. She still corresponded regularly with Rose, whose letters arrived weekly with news of London's gradual recovery and increasingly pointed questions about whether Diana had found herself a nice farmer yet. Diana's responses had grown progressively more detailed. She was documenting a world she'd never loved before. But she held off talking about any one man in particular. Mainly because there was only one man she'd ever been interested in. And he hadn't yet appeared. The one worry which gnawed away at her was that he wouldn't. That she'd changed so many things that the likelihood of Jim Crawford turning up was almost negligible.

The war, whilst never forgotten, was more background noise in their small corner of Northumberland. They knitted socks for soldiers, collected scrap metal with patriotic determination, and observed blackout regulations. But the battles raged in distant lands, and their greatest martial excitement came from the practice flights that roared overhead, and the semi-regular training exercises with PC Aldridge and the Cheviot Hills Home Guard.

Diana had learned to recognise the different aircraft by sound alone—the throaty roar of Wellingtons heading out on training missions, the higher whine of Spitfires performing aerobatic displays that made her heart race with vicarious joy.

It was during one of their regular Friday gatherings in the late autumn of 1943 that Diana noticed something amiss with Ellen. The American girl had arrived later than usual, apologising with her characteristic bright smile, but Diana's trained eye—still sharp despite months of rural contentment—caught the careful way Ellen positioned her left arm.

"Sorry I'm late," Ellen announced, sliding into her usual seat at the Twice Brewed with a spectacular bruise on her wrist, partially concealed by the long sleeves of her jumper but visible when she reached for her drink.

"Good Lord, Ellen, what happened to your arm?" Nancy asked, the first to comment, although all of them had gasped when they'd seen it.

Ellen glanced down, as if noticing the bruise for the first time. "Oh, that? Clumsy accident in the dairy. Caught it on the milking stall when one of the cows shifted unexpectedly."

Jenny frowned, her practical experience with livestock making her naturally sceptical. "That must have been some push. That bruise looks dreadful. Are you sure it's not broken?"

"Animals are stronger than they appear," Ellen replied quickly, pulling her sleeve down to cover the bruising.

The conversation moved on to lighter topics—plans for Christmas celebrations, speculation about whether the war might end in the coming year, Jenny's latest romantic entanglement with a Home Guard member from the next village. But Diana kept returning to Ellen's injury. There was something in Ellen's behaviour which was off. She was giving them a performance instead of her usual spontaneous self.

As they prepared to leave at evening's end, Diana lingered outside the inn until Ellen emerged, falling into step beside her for the walk towards the Hollisters' farm.

"Lovely evening," Diana ventured, testing the waters.

"Mmm," Ellen agreed, though her usual vivacity seemed dimmed. "Jenny was in fine form tonight. That story about the chemist's romantic tribulations had me in stitches."

They walked in silence for several minutes, before Diana couldn't hold her tongue any longer.

"You know you can talk to any of us if you're having difficulties? I mean, if there's anything troubling you?" she said carefully,

"Difficulties? I can't imagine what you mean? Everything's perfectly fine."

Diana heard the brittleness beneath Ellen's words, the same forced cheerfulness she'd perfected herself during her first life.

"Sometimes," Diana said gently, "people find themselves in situations that aren't their fault. Situations where they feel trapped or… compromised. If that ever happened to you, you wouldn't have to face it alone."

They'd reached the junction where Ellen would turn towards the Hollisters' farm. She stopped walking entirely, turning to face Diana in the moonlight. For a moment, she looked frightened before seemingly shrugging off Diana's concerns.

"I don't know what you're suggesting," she said, her voice cracking ever so slightly.

"I'm not suggesting anything," Diana replied. "I'm simply saying that if you ever need help, I'm here."

Ellen stood at the crossroads for a moment, as the wind rustled through the bare hedgerows, carrying with it the scent of wood smoke from distant cottages.

"Thank you," she said finally. "That's very kind of you to say."

They hugged, and Diana watched Ellen walk away, noting the slight hunch to the other girl's shoulders. There was something going on, and tomorrow, she decided, she would begin making careful inquiries about the Hollisters. If this was the precursor to Ellen disappearing, then she'd do everything in her damn power to nip it in the bud. Ellen Wilson would not disappear on her watch. Not this time.

The weeks slipped past in a flurry of Christmas preparations. Mrs Whitaker had been hoarding ingredients for weeks, trading favours and carefully marshalling her rations to create something approaching a traditional Christmas dinner.

Diana found herself pressed into service, helping to make mince pies with pastry so thin it was barely there, the filling stretched with grated apple and carrot to make the precious dried fruit go further.

"Before the war, I'd have used a pound of suet for pastry like this," Mrs Whitaker lamented as they rolled the dough with a milk bottle pressed into service as a rolling pin. "Now I'm grateful for the two ounces I've saved."

Sunday's church service carried an atmosphere of anticipation. Christmas was only days away, but the war's shadow was long. Too many pews boasted noticeable gaps, their usual occupants serving overseas or lost entirely.

Diana spotted the Hollisters near the front of the church, Mr Hollister's tall frame unmistakable even from behind. Ellen sat beside Mrs Hollister, her posture perfect, her attention apparently focused on the service. At no point during the service did any of the Hollisters' party acknowledge each other or look anywhere other than towards the pulpit. The epitome of devotion to God. Or trouble in paradise? Diana knew where she'd place her bets.

After the service, Diana made a point of greeting various parishioners, gradually working her way towards the Hollisters. As she approached, she caught fragments of Mr Hollister's conversation with Mr Weatherby from the drapers.

"...quite remarkable finds, actually," Mr Hollister was saying, his American accent lending an air of authority to his words. "Third century, by all accounts. Found them whilst clearing drainage ditches near the old Roman road. Ellen's been invaluable in helping me catalogue them properly—her archaeological training from Cambridge, you know. Sharp eye for detail, that girl. Very... thorough in her approach."

Diana's skin crawled at the tone of his voice—a proprietary satisfaction that seemed to have little to do with Roman antiquities.

Mr Weatherby nodded enthusiastically. "The Romans certainly left their mark on these parts, didn't they?"

"Oh indeed," Mr Hollister continued, his voice dropping slightly. "We've been spending considerable time together examining the finds. You have to be so exact with coins, and Ellen is quite the research assistant."

Diana's jaw tightened. She'd encountered enough predatory men during her intelligence career to recognise the type—charming, authoritative, and entirely too comfortable with power over other people.

She watched Mr Hollister tip his hat to Mr Weatherby, before offering his arm to his wife and leaving the aisle of the church, completely ignoring both Mrs Whitaker and herself. An icy shiver made its way down Diana's spine as the man walked past, his eyes straight ahead, his heels clicking on the memorial stones embedded into the church's floor.

Later that night, whilst helping Mrs Whitaker with the supper dishes, Diana asked, "What do you know about the Hollisters?"

Mrs Whitaker's hands stilled in the washing-up water. "They're well-established in the area. Mr Hollister inherited the farm from his English wife's family, though he's American born. They've no children of their own." She paused, seeming to choose her words carefully. "Why?"

"I overheard him talking about some Roman coins he'd dug up," Diana said, testing the waters. "He said Ellen's been helping him catalogue them. Seemed quite... enthusiastic about her assistance. I worry about Ellen being a bit isolated out there."

Mrs Whitaker resumed her washing with slightly more vigour than necessary. "Mmm. I wouldn't want to speak ill of anyone, particularly without proof. But I've heard whispers about Mr Hollister. Nothing specific, you understand, just... whispers."

The unsaid whispers hung between them like smoke from the fire.

"What sort of whispers?"

Mrs Whitaker glanced towards the windows, as if checking that no one might overhear. "The kind that suggests he's a man who takes liberties." She dried her hands on her apron. "Of course, such things are often exaggerated. Village gossip has a way of growing in the telling. There was the odd story about the girl who came before Ellen, but I'm not sure I believed them. That wife of his wouldn't let anything happen under her roof. She's wound up tighter than a ten-bob watch."

Diana nodded. The pieces of a troubling picture were assembling themselves, despite Mrs Whitaker's assertions that nothing was amiss. Diana didn't know if Ellen would still disappear in this new timeline. If history would repeat itself. So all she could do was keep her eyes peeled for any trouble. She didn't know what would happen if she outright warned Ellen, but it was definitely an option.

Chapter Thirty-Seven

Another Christmas passed as the war marched on into 1944.

But just after the New Year's celebrations had ended, Trevor Whitaker arrived home.

Mrs Whitaker flew into the farmyard, her usual composed demeanour abandoned entirely as she enveloped a stranger in a full-length woollen coat in an embrace that seemed to last an eternity.

"My boy," she kept repeating, her voice thick with tears. "My boy."

Trevor barely resembled the framed photo on the mantelpiece. His once boyish face now bore the lean angles of a man who'd seen too much. But his smile remained unchanged—the same warm grin that had apparently charmed the village girls before the war swept him away.

Within days, that smile had found a new target. Jenny Jenkins. Trevor had visited Hayes Farm to pass on a packet of letters from Arthur and promptly fell in love. And to Diana, it appeared to be mutual, noticing Jenny blushing scarlet whenever Trevor appeared, her usual confident chatter dissolving into tongue-tied stammers. Trevor, for his part, seemed to find excuses to visit Hayes Farm whenever Jenny happened to be working, despite there being plenty to occupy his time at Willow Farm.

"Look at them," Mr Hayes murmured to Diana one afternoon, watching as Trevor helped Jenny repair a section of fence. "Like a pair of lovesick puppies," he added with a rare chuckle.

Diana said nothing. In her original timeline, Trevor Whitaker had died near Arnhem. Another name etched into stone. Another young life consumed by the war's bottomless hunger. To see him here, alive and laughing, as Jenny feigned ignorance about how to hold a hammer, felt like watching a ghost given borrowed time.

"Perhaps they shouldn't get too... attached? With the war still on, and Trevor having to return to his unit..." Diana began.

"Life goes on, doesn't it? Besides, Jenny'll keep that boy on his toes."

Diana watched as Jenny laughed at something Trevor whispered. His hand lingered over hers as he guided her grip on the fence wire. Young love in wartime bloomed with desperate urgency—like spring flowers racing to open before winter closed in again.

When Trevor announced his engagement to Jenny the day before his leave ended, Mrs Whitaker wept with joy. The wedding would wait until his next leave, or more likely until the war ended, whichever came first. Jenny wore her happiness like armour, glowing with the sort of radiant certainty that made Diana's heart ache.

"Isn't it wonderful?" Jenny confided in Diana as they walked home from Hayes Farm that evening. "I never thought... I mean, I always hoped, but I never dared believe it! Love at first sight."

Diana squeezed her friend's hand, forcing a smile. "I'm very happy for you both."

And she was, despite the fear that gnawed at her. Perhaps whatever strange forces were governing her journey through time would allow Trevor to live longer than his original fate. Perhaps they would let him survive the war. It wasn't too much to ask, was it?

The next day, the platform at Cheviot Hills station gleamed with morning frost, each wooden plank edged in silver. Trevor stood beside his kit bag, the maroon beret of the Parachute Regiment marking him as something different from the boy who'd first left Cheviot Hills. His greatcoat hung on his lean frame, boots polished to mirror brightness despite the muddy lane from Willow Farm.

Mrs Whitaker fussed with his collar one last time, her fingers trembling as much from emotion as from the cold. "You mind yourself," she whispered. "No heroics."

Jenny hung off his arm, silently. Her usual chatter had deserted her, leaving only the bright shine of unshed tears.

"I'll write every week," Trevor promised, his voice steady despite the slight tremor in his hands. "To both of you. And I'll be back before you know it."

"You'd better be," Jenny managed, her words barely audible above the train's impatient huffing. "I'll be waiting."

The guard's whistle cut through the morning air like a blade. Final call.

Trevor kissed his mother, then Jenny, stepping back before either of them could lose their resolve. He swung his kit bag onto his shoulder and climbed aboard the waiting carriage. As the train lurched into motion with a groan of metal and steam, he appeared at the window, hand raised in farewell.

Diana watched her friend's face crumple for just a moment before she forced her chin up, waving back with determined brightness.

The train disappeared around the bend, leaving only wisps of steam and the gradually fading rhythm of wheels on rails. The platform felt too large, too empty.

Diana slipped her arm through Jenny's. "He'll come back," she said, hoping her voice carried more conviction than she felt.

What she hadn't told Jenny, and what she'd made Trevor promise not to tell his betrothed, was that she'd cornered the young man in the woodshed the day before.

"I need to speak with you about something important," Diana had said, closing the door behind them, sealing in the smell of creosote and sawdust.

Trevor had looked up from the wood he'd been loading into the basket for the kitchen, eyebrows raised. "Sounds serious."

Diana had rehearsed this conversation a dozen times, but the words still felt clumsy on her tongue. How did one warn someone about their death without sounding completely mad?

"Arthur mentioned in his letters that you were the cautious one of the two of you," she began carefully. "Good at avoiding trouble."

"Funny thing is that Arthur says that you're the one who's cautious," Trevor replied.

"What did he say about me?"

"Enough. That your letters always seemed to include stories about your travels, which just happened to be where his unit was going to be deployed next. Almost like you knew." Trevor's eyes sharpened as he studied her face. "How'd you know?"

"I didn't," Diana said, which was both true and completely false. "I just... I worry. About people I care about getting hurt."

Trevor leaned against the stone wall, waiting.

"There's going to be a big operation," Diana continued, her mouth dry. "Sometime in September, probably. Something involving airborne troops." She took a breath. "I think you'll be part of it."

"How could you possibly know? All the way up here?"

"I know how this sounds," she pressed on. "But if it happens—when it happens—promise me you'll be extra careful. Don't trust anything that looks too easy. Don't assume the intelligence is accurate. And if you're in Holland, near Arnhem..." She faltered, not knowing how to finish.

Trevor was quiet for a long moment, his expression unreadable. "Arthur said you had the sight," he said finally. "Said sometimes when you talked about places, it was like you'd been there yourself."

Diana said nothing.

"Arthur trusts you," Trevor continued. "That's good enough for me." He straightened, his voice taking on the formal tone of a soldier receiving orders. "If we're still in this mess in September, I'll remember what you've said."

"Promise me," Diana insisted. "Promise me you won't take unnecessary risks. That you'll question everything, even orders from superior officers, if something feels wrong."

Trevor's eyes widened at that last bit. But he nodded. "I promise."

Diana had wanted to say more, to give him specific warnings about drop zones and the chaotic German withdrawal, about the failure of communications and the tragedy of Operation Market Garden.

"Just... be the cautious one Arthur says you are," she'd finished lamely. "I don't know what your mother would do without you. She loves you beyond words. And Jenny needs you too."

Now, watching the train disappear with Trevor aboard, Diana wondered if her vague warnings would be enough.

In her original timeline, thousands of paratroopers had died at Arnhem—a bridge too far, as someone would later call it. Trevor Whitaker had been one of them.

Perhaps Trevor would remember her words when it mattered most and choose caution over valour.

She hoped it would be enough.

Chapter Thirty-Eight

Diana was mending a section of fence wire when she heard the a voice calling across the farmyard.

"I say, could someone point me towards Cheviot Hills village?"

She looked up to see a tall figure in RAF flying overalls standing by the gate, his cap tucked under his arm. Even at this distance, something about him made her pulse quicken.

"Lost, are you?" Jenny called out, abandoning her work with the chickens to approach the stranger. "Happens to the best of us round here. Nothing's signposted properly anymore."

Diana set down her tools and followed. As she drew closer, the airman turned towards her, and their eyes met across the muddy farmyard.

"Flight Lieutenant James Crawford," he introduced himself, though his gaze lingered on Diana's face. "But my friends call me Jim. I had some engine trouble, which forced me down about two miles back. I'm afraid I've rather lost my bearings."

"Diana Penn," she replied, extending her hand without the hesitation that had once characterised her interactions with strangers. "The village is just over the next rise," she continued, surprised by how steady her voice sounded. "You can't miss the church spire."

"Very kind of you, Miss Penn." Jim's eyes held hers a moment longer than propriety demanded. "Perhaps I'll see you again?"

"Perhaps," Diana replied, though she already knew with absolute certainty that he would.

As he walked away, Jenny appeared at her elbow with a knowing grin. "Handsome devil, wasn't he? And the way he was looking at you—like he'd just found whatever he'd been searching for." She started humming the wedding march, a mischievous smile plastered across her face.

Diana watched Jim's retreating figure, her heart hammering against her ribs. This time, she wouldn't waste precious moments keeping her distance. Life was too short.

The days following Jim's arrival passed in a blur of anticipation. Unlike in her previous timelines, Diana threw herself into the preparations for the Christmas dance with genuine enthusiasm. She helped Jenny practise her steps in the Hayes Farm kitchen during their lunch breaks, laughed at Nancy's increasingly elaborate theories about which RAF officers might attend, and found herself looking forward to the village's biggest social event of the year. She'd even persuaded Mrs Whitaker to throw caution to the wind and come with her.

Jim made good on his promise to see her again, turning up at Hayes Farm with a sheepish smile and a bar of real chocolate—glossy-wrapped and unmistakably off-ration.

"A thank you," he said, holding it out. "For the directions."

Diana accepted it, eyebrows raised. "Black market?"

"Absolutely not," he replied with a wink.

Diana laughed, the sound surprising even herself. In a world where sweetness was rare and time rarer still, it felt like the beginning of something worth savouring.

"You're glowing," Mrs Whitaker observed that evening as Diana returned from her shift at Hayes Farm. "Is there a particular reason?"

It was true. Diana felt more alive than she had in any of her lives—past or future. Not just because of Jim's smile or the stolen sweetness of the black market chocolate, but because, for the first time in years, she felt hope for the future. Real, solid hope, and undeniably hers.

The morning of the Christmas dance, Mrs Whitaker appeared in the kitchen doorway with something draped over her arm, a hint of shyness in her voice.

"I've been working on this," she said, shaking out the garment. "Thought you might like to wear it tonight."

Diana's breath caught. It was a dress—not new, but beautifully transformed. The deep forest green satin had been expertly altered, the skirt full and swinging, the bodice fitted with a sweetheart neckline and delicate cap sleeves.

"It's my old wedding dress," Mrs Whitaker explained, colour rising in her cheeks. "Well, it was white originally, but there's not much call for white satin these days. I dyed it and took it in. Thought the colour would suit you."

Diana reached out to touch the dress with reverent fingers. The hours of work that must have gone into transforming an outdated wedding gown into this fashionable creation made her throat tighten with emotion.

"It's beautiful," she managed. "But I can't possibly—"

"Nonsense," Mrs Whitaker said firmly. "What good is it doing hanging in my wardrobe? Besides, someone should dance in it." Her eyes grew distant for a moment. "I had such a lovely time in that dress, once upon a time. It deserves to see joy again."

"Thank you," Diana whispered—inadequate words for such a gift.

"Now, see that you enjoy yourself," Mrs Whitaker replied, her eyes sparkling with affection.

"Only if you promise to do the same," Diana laughed. "I'm sure there are a dozen men itching for a dance with you."

Mrs Whitaker blushed. "Get away with you now. A dozen! Oh my goodness, you're a fine one to talk. I'll promise to enjoy myself if you promise to save a dance for that young Flight Lieutenant I've heard whispers about."

At that, Mrs Whitaker winked, and it was Diana's turn to blush.

Inside, the village hall blazed with warmth and light. Paper chains and sprigs of holly had transformed the utilitarian space into something magical, whilst the RAF band performed their own magic with their instruments on stage.

Diana smoothed the forest green satin of Mrs Whitaker's altered wedding dress.

The sweetheart neckline and cap sleeves made her feel elegant in a way she'd never experienced before, and the full skirt swirled satisfyingly with each step.

"You look stunning," Ellen declared as the four friends met in the hall. "That colour is perfect on you."

"Doesn't she just," Nancy agreed. "I'm sure all the officers will be queuing up for a dance."

Jenny bounced on her toes with excitement. "This is going to be such fun! I can hardly contain myself."

"You're a betrothed woman, remember?" Ellen admonished laughing.

The hall was already crowded with villagers and servicemen, the air thick with anticipation and the lingering scent of Mrs Patterson's famous Christmas punch. Diana's eyes sought out Jim among the sea of RAF blue, finding him near the refreshments in conversation with several other uniformed officers.

As if sensing her gaze, he looked up. His face broke into a smile as he excused himself from his companions and made his way through the crowd towards her.

"Miss Penn," he said, offering a slight bow. "You look radiant."

"Thank you, Flight Lieutenant," she replied. "You clean up rather well yourself."

The band struck up a waltz, and Jim extended his hand. "Would you do me the honour?"

Diana allowed him to lead her onto the dance floor. His hand at her waist was warm and sure, and she marvelled at how perfectly they moved together, as if they'd been dancing together for years.

From the corner of her eye, Diana caught sight of Nancy standing at the edge of the dance floor watching them. But Diana was too absorbed in the moment to give it much thought. The warmth of Jim's hand, the way he looked at her as if she were the only person in the room, the only thoughts running through her head.

They danced three times in succession, breaking apart only when propriety demanded it. During a brief interlude, Diana found herself at the punch bowl with her friends.

"My goodness, Diana," Nancy said with forced brightness, "you've certainly made an impression on Flight Lieutenant Crawford. He's barely taken his eyes off you all evening."

"Has he?" Diana asked, genuinely surprised by the observation. "I hadn't noticed."

Nancy's laugh had a brittle edge. "Oh, I think everyone's noticed. Including my mother."

Ellen squeezed Diana's arm. "Pay no attention to Nancy. She's just miffed because the Flight Lieutenant hasn't asked her to dance yet."

"I am not miffed," Nancy protested, but the colour in her cheeks suggested otherwise. "Besides, Mother has invited him to Sunday supper, so we'll have more than enough time to get properly acquainted."

The evening flew by in a whirl of music and laughter. Diana danced with other officers, but always found her way back to Jim. At one point during the evening, Diana spotted Ellen being led onto the dance floor by Mr Hollister, his tall American frame towering over her petite figure. From across the hall, Diana could see the rigid set of Ellen's shoulders. Her usual smile had been replaced by a polite mask that didn't reach her eyes. And when Hollister's hand shifted lower on her back than propriety demanded, Diana felt a surge of anger. Before she could act, the dance ended. She watched Ellen escape to the refreshment table, leaving Hollister with a satisfied smirk on his face that made Diana's skin crawl.

When the band announced the final waltz, Jim was already leading her onto the dance floor, and the issue of Ellen and Hollister evaporated.

"This has been the most wonderful evening," she said as they swayed to the gentle melody.

"It doesn't have to end yet," Jim replied. "May I walk you home?"

Mrs Whitaker had already left, safe in the company of Mr Hayes and his ancient truck, so Diana was free to accept Jim's offer without hesitation.

"I'd like that very much," Diana replied.

They collected their coats and slipped outside. Stars scattered across the clear sky, and their breath misted in the cold air.

"Beautiful night," Jim observed, offering her his arm.

"Perfect," Diana agreed, surprised by how natural it felt to walk beside him.

They strolled in comfortable silence until they reached the gate of Willow Farm. Diana turned to face him, suddenly nervous.

"Thank you for a lovely evening," she said.

"Thank you for the pleasure of your company," he replied, stepping closer. "Diana, I hope—"

She didn't let him finish. Rising on her toes, she pressed her lips to his in a kiss that was soft and sweet and full of promise. When they broke apart, Jim's eyes were wide with surprise.

"I've been wanting to do that all evening," Diana confessed, amazed by her own boldness.

Jim's smile could have lit up the entire village. "Then I'm very glad you did."

He kissed her again, longer this time.

"Goodnight, Diana," he whispered against her hair.

"Goodnight, Jim."

She watched him walk away until he disappeared into the darkness, then touched her fingers to her lips. Could there be anything better than the perfect first kiss?

Chapter Thirty-Nine

Christmas morning dawned crisp and clear over Willow Farm, and Diana woke to the sound of Mrs Whitaker humming "Silent Night" as she bustled about downstairs, preparing for their festive gathering.

The farmhouse kitchen had been transformed for the occasion. Mrs Whitaker's mother's wedding china graced the table, alongside the best crystal glasses that hadn't seen daylight since before the war. A sprig of holly, carefully picked from the hedgerow, sat in the centre, its red berries gleaming like jewels against the white linen tablecloth.

"Right then," Mrs Whitaker announced as Diana appeared in the doorway, still smoothing her hair. "Ellen's already here helping with the vegetables, and the lads will be along shortly. Christmas waits for no one."

Ellen looked up from the sink where she was peeling turnips, her face bright with genuine happiness. "Merry Christmas, Diana! Isn't this lovely? Much better than sitting alone at the Hollisters. They're with family in Newcastle. Not that I'm complaining. This is far more pleasant."

The kitchen filled with warmth and chatter as the others arrived. Jenny appeared first. "Mince pies!" she announced cheerfully, waving a covered basket.

"Mother managed to get her hands on some proper currants. I can't stay long, mind—the whole family's gathering at ours later, and Mother will have my head if I'm not back to help."

Mr Hayes appeared moments later, stamping his boots on the doormat and carrying a bottle wrapped in brown paper. "A little something I've been saving," he said with uncharacteristic cheerfulness. "Elderberry wine. Thought today might be the right occasion."

Jim Crawford arrived last, slightly out of breath and grinning broadly. "Sorry I'm late! Problems with that damn jeep again."

Jenny stayed just long enough to down a glass of wine and scoff one of her own mince pies, her laughter brightening the kitchen. When she finally gathered her coat and kissed Mrs Whitaker's cheek goodbye, Diana noticed how tightly Mrs Whitaker hugged her back.

"Give my love to your mother," Mrs Whitaker said.

"I will," Jenny promised, her voice catching slightly. "And Trevor will be back before we know it. He has to be. He promised."

After Jenny's departure, the remaining group moved into the dining room. The feast that emerged from the kitchen was modest by peacetime standards but felt positively luxurious in wartime. A plump chicken sat at the centre of the table, surrounded by roasted turnips and parsnips from the kitchen garden. There were Brussels sprouts that had survived the frost, sweet and tender, and potatoes roasted in precious beef dripping. Jenny's remaining mince pies sat alongside a Christmas pudding that had been made with grated carrots to eke out the dried fruit.

Mr Hayes took his place at the head of the table with obvious pleasure, raising his glass of elderberry wine. "To absent friends," he said solemnly, his voice carrying the weight of all those who couldn't be with them, "and to those gathered here today."

"To absent friends," they echoed, each thinking of their own losses and separations, the momentary shadow touching their faces before warmth returned.

As they ate, conversation flowed as freely as the wine. Ellen described Christmas traditions from her hometown in Massachusetts, making them all laugh with her tale of her grandfather's annual battle with the Christmas tree lights. Mr Hayes shared memories of Christmases past at the farm, and stories of the mayhem Arthur had got up to with Trevor in their youth.

When the meal was finished and the washing up done, they gathered around the small pile of gifts that had appeared on the kitchen dresser. Diana felt her heart squeeze as she watched the careful exchange of small treasures.

She distributed her lavender sachets—small muslin bags filled with lavender she'd dried from Mrs Whitaker's garden, and tied with ribbon. "For your drawers," she explained, feeling suddenly shy. "To keep the moths away and make everything smell nice."

"Oh, Diana," Mrs Whitaker breathed, holding the sachet to her nose. "This takes me back to my mother's linen cupboard. She always had lavender sachets."

Jim had a bar of Cadbury chocolate for everyone. Received by all with genuine reverence. Ellen had knitted mittens for everyone, which matched the scarves Mrs Whitaker had knitted for them all.

Diana had to laugh at the subterfuge the two of them must have undertaken to make this happen.

But it was Mr Hayes who provided the most touching surprise. From a cloth bag, he produced small wooden figures—delicately carved swallows. One had its wings spread wide in flight, another perched as if listening, a third caught mid-dive towards invisible prey.

"Made them during the long evenings," he said gruffly, his weathered hands gentle as he distributed them to the women. "Seemed fitting somehow. Swallows always come back, don't they? Give us hope that winter won't last forever."

Ellen's eyes filled with tears as she cradled her swallow, its tiny head tilted enquiringly. "Mr Hayes, Fred, this is the most beautiful thing anyone's ever given me."

As afternoon faded into evening, they lingered around the table, reluctant to let the magic end. The wireless played softly in the background, the carols from King's College transporting them beyond the farm kitchen to a world where bells still rang and choirs still sang.

"This is what Christmas should be," Ellen said softly, her American accent making the words sound almost like a prayer. "Not grand or fancy, just... this. People caring for each other."

Diana nodded, her throat tight with emotion. In her first life, Arthur Hayes had died and his father had... no, she didn't want to think about what happened to Mr Hayes.

She'd spent a good part of her week slightly on edge that Mr Fleming would arrive with the dreaded telegram in hand. And it really wasn't until now that she was satisfied that somehow Arthur's fate had taken a different path. Hopefully Trevor's too.

As the evening wound down and Jim drove the others home, Diana helped Mrs Whitaker with the last of the dishes. The older woman paused in her work, resting a wet hand on Diana's arm.

"Thank you, dear," she said quietly. "For being here. For making this feel like a real Christmas."

Diana squeezed her hand, unable to trust her voice. Outside, snow had begun to fall in soft, fat flakes. Tomorrow would bring a return to routine, but tonight, Diana allowed herself to believe that some things were truly worth fighting for.

Chapter Forty

Diana adjusted the strap of the canvas satchel Mrs Whitaker had lent her for their expedition. Inside were sandwiches complete with precious slices of ham saved from the weekend joint, spread with Mrs Whitaker's own piccalilli, along with a thermos of tea and three apples from the farm's ancient orchard.

"I wish spring would hurry up and arrive. I'm positively over winter now," Ellen exclaimed, stamping through the thin layer of frost on the edges of the path. Her hair had escaped its pins during the walk, creating a cloud of waves around her face. "At home, spring arrives like a baby taking its first steps. Here, it's like the earth has decided to hold us all hostage."

Nancy settled herself on a moss-covered stone wall to retie her shoelace. "Wait until the bluebells come out in Hunter's Wood next month. Absolutely breathtaking. The whole floor looks like someone's spilled an ocean of sapphires across the ground."

"How have you not already taken me there?" Ellen asked.

"You have to be worthy!" Nancy said. "Some people think they're automatically entitled to special treatment, but the rest of us know better."

Diana caught the edge in Nancy's voice but said nothing, focusing instead on adjusting her own laces. She studied Nancy's face as the other girl retied her shoes. In her previous timeline, Hunter's Wood had been where she'd accidentally discovered Nancy kissing an RAF sergeant.

Had that encounter already happened this time around? Was Nancy a better actress than Diana had given her credit for?

As Diana waited for Nancy to fix her laces, she looked across the valley. Today's destination was Hexham, where Ellen hoped to find books at the second-hand shop. Nancy wanted to visit the abbey, and Diana simply craved the novelty of somewhere that didn't smell of cows. They'd left Jenny daydreaming at home, the young girl refusing to spend a penny on anything that wasn't wedding related.

The walk had taken them past dry stone walls so old their origins were lost to memory. They crossed streams where primroses nodded from mossy banks and climbed stiles worn smooth by generations of walkers.

"I love these expeditions," Nancy said, producing a small pair of field glasses from her coat pocket. "Mother thinks I'm becoming quite rustic, but honestly, I'd rather spend a day walking through the countryside than sitting inside pretending to enjoy the vicar's wife's conversation about her prize dahlias. And they're much better than sitting about waiting for invitations that never materialise."

Oblivious to Nancy's tone, Ellen flopped down beside her on the wall. "Back home, Mother would have a fit if she knew I was walking fifteen miles for pleasure. She thinks anything more strenuous than a gentle stroll around the garden is utterly improper for a lady."

Diana joined them on the wall, grateful for the rest. The physical demands of farm work had strengthened her considerably, but a day's hiking still left her muscles singing with fatigue. "What does she think you've been doing the whole war then?"

"Oh, she's convinced I'm having this wonderfully romantic adventure," Ellen grinned. "She probably pictures me being swept off my feet by some dashing British officer with plans to marry in a quaint little village church before the war ends. If she only knew that in reality, it involves considerably more muck and fewer silk stockings."

Nancy snorted. "There have been more than enough dashing officers sniffing around the village lately. Not that they're particularly discriminating about their company, it seems. Wouldn't you agree, Diana?"

Diana felt heat rise in her cheeks. Nancy was clearly referring to Jim. She didn't know how to answer her, so kept her lips pressed shut. *If you can't say a kind word...*

They resumed walking, the conversation flowing as easily as the streams they crossed. The morning grew slightly warmer, and Diana braved shedding her cardigan, tying it around her waist with a freedom that would have scandalised her mother. Eleanor Penn would have considered such casual dress completely inappropriate for a young lady, even in wartime.

The thought of her mother brought the familiar pang of loss, but it was gentler now. Diana touched the locket at her throat and felt a sense of peace rather than the sharp anguish that had once accompanied any memory of her mother.

Hexham rose before them as they crested the final hill, its abbey tower dominating the skyline with the sort of medieval grandeur that made Diana catch her breath in wonder. The market town spread below them, its grey stone buildings clustering around streets that had witnessed Saxon kings and Norman lords, Border reivers and Jacobite rebels.

"Every time I see it, I can't quite believe it's real," Ellen murmured. "Back home, we consider anything from the 1700s practically prehistoric. This place was already old when the Mayflower sailed."

They descended into the town proper, their boots echoing on the cobblestones. The Saturday market was in full swing, stalls displaying what produce the war allowed—root vegetables stored through winter, early spring greens, precious eggs, and the occasional luxury of fresh fish from the coast. Alongside the food, local women offered their handiwork: thick woollen mittens knitted from unravelled jumpers and small wooden toys carved by men invalided out of service.

The second-hand bookshop proved to be a treasure trove housed in a building so narrow it seemed to lean against its neighbours for support. Inside, towers of books reached towards a ceiling blackened by decades of coal smoke, their spines creating a kaleidoscope of faded colours. The proprietor, a cadaverous man with wire-rimmed spectacles, greeted them with the enthusiasm of someone starving for customers who appreciated literature.

Ellen immediately gravitated towards a section devoted to archaeology and ancient history, exclaiming with delight as she discovered a volume on Roman Britain that she'd been seeking for months. Nancy found herself absorbed in a collection of poetry by someone Diana had never heard of, whilst Diana herself was drawn to a shelf of detective novels.

"Dorothy Sayers," she murmured, running her finger along the spine of *Murder Must Advertise.*

"An excellent choice," the proprietor observed, appearing beside her with the silent movement of someone long accustomed to navigating cramped spaces. "Though if you enjoy mysteries, you might consider this as well." He handed her a slim volume with a green cloth cover. "Agatha Christie's latest. *The Body in the Library.* Barely used."

Diana's breath caught. She recognized the title immediately. It was the same one she'd borrowed from Mr Hayes's study in her previous life, the novel she'd lent to Ellen before she'd disappeared. The coincidence sent a chill down her spine, as if the universe were offering her a message she wasn't quite ready to decode.

"Thank you," she managed, "But I already have that one. I'll take the Dorothy Sayers book," she said, handing over some coins with a slightly shaky hand before joining her friends outside.

The inside of the abbey proved to be every bit as magnificent as the outside. They wandered through the ancient stones whilst Ellen provided an impromptu lecture on Norman architecture, pointing out details that transformed the building from merely old to actively alive with history.

"The real treasure," Ellen said, her eyes bright with enthusiasm, "is below, in the crypt. It's one of the oldest Christian sites in Northumberland." She gestured towards a narrow stone stairway.

Giggling and holding hands, Ellen and Nancy went down into the crypt, followed closely by Diana. The narrow passage opened into a small vaulted chamber. The rough-hewn walls bore the marks of Saxon masons. Fragments of Roman inscriptions were clearly visible where stones from Hadrian's Wall had been repurposed.

"Imagine," Ellen whispered, running her fingers along a carved panel, "this chamber has witnessed more history than any of us could dream of."

Diana had no answer for that. If only they knew what she had experienced. What she was experiencing.

The journey home took longer than expected, each girl lost in her own thoughts as if they'd run out of conversation. Their earlier chatter had given way to a comfortable silence, broken only by the crunch of their boots on the road and the distant bleating of sheep. By the time they reached the junction where their paths diverged, the sun had begun its descent towards the horizon.

"Thank you for today," Ellen said, adjusting her satchel. "It's been lovely having sane people to talk to."

"Same time next week?" Nancy asked, straightening her hat, her earlier coolness seemingly forgotten in the face of Ellen's genuine warmth.

"Absolutely," Ellen replied, then added quietly, "I'm grateful for any excuse to be away from Oregon House during the day." She glanced towards the imposing Georgian facade visible through the trees. "Mr Hollister seems to find so many reasons to seek me out when I'm alone."

Diana and Nancy exchanged knowing looks. None of them spoke of it directly. It was as if they had an unspoken understanding that such things were better left unsaid—but they both nodded their silent acknowledgment of what Ellen hadn't quite put into words.

Diana waved goodbye to her friends and continued alone down the lane to Willow Farm. The cottage came into view around the final bend, its darkened windows betraying no hint of the life within. But the thin seam of light escaping beneath the kitchen door and the scent of cooking drifting on the evening air spoke of Mrs Whitaker preparing the evening meal. But as Diana approached the gate, she stopped short, her breath catching.

A figure sat on the doorstep. A young man in a khaki uniform with a canvas kit bag at his feet, a pair of crutches by his side, smoking a cigarette with the careful economy of someone who'd learned to make luxuries last. He looked up as her footsteps crunched on the path, and Diana stared into a face she knew from a photograph at Hayes Farm.

Arthur Hayes had come home.

He was smaller than his photograph had suggested, though still tall and lean in the way of young men who'd grown up doing physical work. With military-short brown hair, his face bore the sort of tan that spoke of foreign sunshine rather than Northumbrian weather. When he smiled, Diana could see his father's stubborn chin and steady eyes.

"You must be Diana," he said, rising to his feet, his hand outstretched. "I'm Arthur. Arthur Hayes. You've been writing to me."

Diana's throat tightened. In her previous timeline, Arthur had been killed near the Meuse River, with the telegram confirming his death arriving on Christmas Eve 1944.

That telegram had never arrived this time, and so Christmas had passed in a blessed state of happiness for them all. Seeing Arthur here, alive, felt like a miracle she'd dared to hope for but never quite believed possible.

"It's a pleasure," she managed, shaking his hand. "You got my letters, then."

"Every one of them," Arthur said, his smile slipping slightly. "And I wanted to thank you. It sounds odd to say it aloud, but you saved my life."

"I did?"

"That story you told about the bridge collapsing in Italy saved the lives of my entire unit."

Diana's blood ran cold. "How?"

"We had to cross this old stone bridge during an advance. Looked as solid as the day it was built, but your story kept nagging at me. Made me insist we send a scout party across first." Arthur's voice grew quiet. "Good thing too. They'd wired the whole bridge with explosives. Would have taken out all of us if we'd all crossed together."

It worked. It actually worked. Happy tears sprang to her eyes—an unusual thing for Diana.

"I'm just glad you were careful," she said, staring at Arthur. "I never thought..."

Arthur stared back at her. "Mother would have called it divine intervention. The old man will say that it was luck. But I know it was all you."

Chapter Forty-One

Diana matched her pace to Arthur's careful gait. His wooden crutches clicked against the cobblestones, a sound that had become as familiar as breathing over the past fortnight since his return from the continent.

Arthur had been invalided home with a leg wound that had shattered his left shin, leaving him with a pronounced limp that the doctors assured him would improve with time. Diana thought he carried himself remarkably well for someone who'd narrowly escaped death—first from the bridge explosion, and later from the German artillery shell that had finally sent him home.

"You didn't want to make me walk any further?" Arthur asked, resting against the stone wall of the town hall. His face was pale, but his eyes twinkled with the same warmth as his father's.

"We could have walked to Hexham, they're showing the same film, but I was being easy on you," Diana joked, fully aware that joking was as new to her as friendship was.

Arthur laughed. "After weeks in a field hospital, being able to walk into town is better than paradise." He shifted his weight, testing his injured leg.

Diana felt a flutter of guilt at his gratitude.

In her original timeline, Arthur Hayes had been dead for months by now, his father driven to suicide by grief on Christmas morning. The knowledge that her intervention had saved both father and son should have filled her with satisfaction. But she still couldn't let go of the worry about Ellen. And Trevor.

They resumed walking towards the cinema, Arthur's crutches finding sure purchase on the uneven stones.

"What's this film supposed to be about, then?" Arthur asked as they approached the twin glass doors.

"*The Way Ahead* with David Niven," Diana replied. "It's about training new recruits for the army. Though I suspect you'll find it rather tame after your experiences."

"A bit of Hollywood nonsense might be just what the doctor ordered," Arthur replied.

They had nearly reached the entrance when Diana spotted them inside the cinema's small foyer. Ellen Wilson stood at the brass ticket counter, her distinctive auburn hair pinned in the neat victory roll she favoured for special occasions. But it wasn't Ellen's presence that made Diana's step falter—it was the man beside her.

Sergeant Richard Thompson, the man she last saw in the woods with Nancy, stood close enough to Ellen that their shoulders touched, his hand resting possessively on the small of her back as he leaned forward to speak with the ticket clerk. As Diana watched through the glass doors, Ellen turned to say something to Thompson, and he responded by brushing a strand of hair from her face.

What was she doing with Thompson?

"Do you know them?" Arthur asked, following her gaze.

Diana's throat went dry. "Yes, that's my friend Ellen. I don't really know the man she's with though."

"Shall we go in and say hello? I'd rather like to meet her properly. You wrote about her so often."

"I don't think—" Diana began, but Arthur was already reaching for the door handle, his face bright with the prospect of social interaction after weeks of convalescence.

"Come on," he urged. "It'll be nice to put faces to the names from your stories."

Diana could see that Ellen and Thompson were completely absorbed in each other's company. After receiving their tickets, Thompson's hand lingered at Ellen's waist as he guided her towards the auditorium entrance, his fingers splayed possessively across the fabric of her coat.

"Actually," Diana said quickly, catching Arthur's sleeve, "they look rather... occupied. Perhaps we shouldn't disturb them."

Arthur followed her gaze more carefully this time, his expression shifting as he took in the scene before them. "Ah," he said. "I see what you mean. How long have they been stepping out?"

"I didn't know that they were stepping out."

Just then, Ellen glanced towards the window, and their eyes met through the glass. Ellen said something to Thompson, who turned to look in their direction.

"Too late to pretend we haven't seen them now," Arthur murmured.

Diana wanted nothing more than to flee, but Ellen began moving towards the entrance, with Thompson following close behind.

"Diana! What a lovely surprise," Ellen said, her face breaking into a bright smile. "I didn't expect to see you here today."

"Nor I you," Diana replied carefully. "Ellen, may I present Arthur Hayes? Mr Hayes's son. Arthur, this is my friend Ellen Wilson."

Arthur shifted his weight to one crutch and extended his hand. "Miss Wilson, Diana's written about you extensively. All good things, I assure you."

Ellen's smile widened as she shook his hand. "How wonderful to meet you at last! Diana told us you'd returned home safely. We were all so relieved."

"Thanks in large part to Diana's letters," Arthur said warmly. "She may well have saved my life."

Thompson cleared his throat, and Ellen started, as though she'd forgotten his presence entirely.

"Oh, forgive me," she laughed. "This is my friend, Sergeant Thompson. Richard, may I present my friend Diana Penn, and Arthur Hayes? Surely you two have met before?"

Thompson stepped forward. "Pleasure to finally meet you, Miss Penn. Ellen has told me quite a lot about her adventures with you in Cheviot Hills."

"Has she indeed?" Diana replied, her tone carefully neutral.

"Richard and I share an interest in archaeology. He studied classics at Manchester before the war."

"How fascinating," Arthur said politely. "Which period particularly interests you, Sergeant?"

As Thompson launched into a detailed discussion of Roman Britain, Diana watched Ellen. Her eyes never seemed to leave Thompson. The girl seemed completely smitten with the sergeant.

Their conversation continued for several more minutes, touching on everything from archaeological excavation techniques to the relative merits of various RAF bases together with some good-natured taunts about army versus the air force heroics.

Finally, Ellen glanced at her watch. "Goodness, we should go to our seats. The film is starting soon."

"Of course," Arthur said. "We don't want to keep you from your afternoon."

"Perhaps we'll see you afterwards?" Ellen asked, directing the question to both Diana and Arthur.

"Maybe," Diana replied, "depends on how long the invalid lasts on his feet."

As Ellen and Thompson disappeared into the cinema, Arthur turned to Diana with raised eyebrows.

"The good sergeant seems rather smitten with your friend Ellen. And unless I'm mistaken, the feeling is mutual."

They settled into seats near the back of the cinema, the flickering light from the screen casting strange shadows on the surrounding faces. Diana found it impossible to concentrate on David Niven's performance, her attention repeatedly drawn to the couple several rows ahead.

During the film's quieter moments, she could see Thompson leaning close to Ellen, whispering comments that made her laugh softly. His hand had returned to the back of her seat, their faces close enough to suggest an intimacy that went beyond casual friendship.

When the credits rolled and the lights came up, Ellen and Thompson were the first to leave, with Diana and Arthur following more slowly, Arthur's crutches requiring careful navigation of the crowded aisles.

Outside, the late afternoon sun was sinking towards the horizon, casting the market square in shades of gold and amber. Ellen and Thompson were nowhere to be seen.

"Fancy a cup of tea before we head home?" Arthur suggested. "I recall there being a decent enough café just round the corner?"

Diana nodded absently, her mind still on Ellen and her new friend. As they made their way across the square, Arthur glanced at her with concern.

"You're worried about something. Would you care to share?"

Diana paused beside the war memorial, a grey stone obelisk already listing the names of too many young men, with more to be added. "Arthur, what do you know about relationships between local girls and servicemen? The... complications that can arise?"

Arthur leaned heavily on his crutches, considering the question. "I've seen it often enough during my service. Men away from home, forming attachments elsewhere when they have obligations back home... it rarely ends well." He studied Diana's face. "This Sergeant Thompson—you suspect he's not being entirely honest with your friend?"

"I'm worried that Ellen might not be the only girl he's stringing along. I have an odd feeling that there's someone else..."

"In my experience," he said finally, "the truth has a way of coming out, regardless. The question is whether it emerges gently or explosively."

Sitting in a pair of wooden chairs beside the cafés steamed windows, Diana reflected on Arthur's words. She had spent so much effort trying to manipulate events, to prevent disasters before they occurred, that she'd forgotten the simpler virtues of friendship and loyalty.

But even as she resolved to be a better friend to Ellen, she worried about what the afternoon's encounter might mean. Could Thompson's romance with Ellen somehow lead to her disappearance? And what of Nancy? Could her jealousy create the kind of situation that might explain Ellen's fate?

"Penny for your thoughts?" Arthur offered as they waited for Fred to pick them up in his lorry.

"I'm just thinking about how quickly things can change," Diana replied. "This morning, everything seemed settled, predictable. Now..."

"It's rather like the war in that respect," Arthur finished. "Long periods of routine punctuated by moments of chaos."

Chapter Forty-Two

Diana woke with a sense of foreboding. Sunday morning. Which meant St Michael's. Meaning that she'd be seeing both Ellen and Nancy in the same place, at the same time, which filled her with dread.

Nancy had been treating her like a pariah since their outing to Hexham, and had actively seemed to be avoiding Diana at every opportunity. Even Jim had noticed Nancy's absence on their regular group outings to the cinema.

She couldn't believe she had to deal with that on top of worrying about whether Ellen would still disappear in this timeline. She'd tried persuading herself that it wasn't going to happen again, not after all the changes she'd made. After all the warnings she'd given Ellen. Wasn't having Arthur Hayes toiling away in the barn beside her at Hayes Farm enough evidence that she had the power to change the future?

Already dressed for church, Mrs Whitaker hummed softly as she prepared breakfast. "Beautiful morning for church, isn't it?" she said cheerfully when Diana appeared in the kitchen. "Cold as charity, but lovely and bright."

Diana couldn't shake the feeling of impending disaster. Her morning porridge could have been cardboard, for all she could taste. The hot tea, as bitter as arsenic.

Diana pushed both away, her stomach churning. She envied Mrs Whitaker, who knew nothing of Diana's dilemma, and instead sat behind her morning newspaper devouring the news.

St Michael's rose before them, its Norman tower built from honey-coloured sandstone blocks salvaged from Hadrian's Wall. Diana paused at the lychgate with a small shudder at the sight of the weathered headstones scattered across the churchyard.

She scanned the familiar faces, noting who was present and who was absent. She'd spied Nancy, who'd quickly turned her head, and sat resolutely facing the pulpit, refusing to meet Diana's eye. The Hollisters sat in their usual pew near the front, Mr Hollister's American accent carrying clearly as he spoke with the other parishioners. Mrs Hollister maintained her typical expression of refined disapproval.

But it was Ellen's absence from her usual spot that made Diana's heart stop.

"Where's Ellen?" Mrs Whitaker whispered, following Diana's gaze. "She's never missed a Sunday service."

Jenny Jenkins materialised at their side, her face pale.

"Did you hear?" Jenny whispered urgently. "Ellen's disappeared. Vanished in the night, she did. Mrs Hollister found her room empty this morning, and most of her belongings gone."

No. It couldn't be true. It just couldn't be.

Mrs Whitaker gasped. "Disappeared? Where?"

"Nobody knows," Jenny continued, her voice dropping even lower. "And that's not the worst of it. Mr Hollister's saying she's taken valuables from the house."

As the service progressed, Reverend Taylor's words barely registered. Diana's eyes kept drifting to the space where Ellen should have been sitting. When the service ended, she was one of the first to leave, intent on seeking out her friend. But as she made her way towards the church gate, she overheard a conversation that made her blood run cold.

"...quite remarkable finds, actually," Mr Hollister was saying to PC Aldridge.

Diana knew Aldridge well from her Land Army duties, and from his often spurious visits to the farm. She'd long ago decided that the man was as useful as a scarecrow in a winter fog.

"Early third century Roman coins. Very valuable to collectors," Mr Hollister finished saying, as if he actually knew the difference between early and late third century coins. That was Ellen's area of expertise. Not his.

"Are they the only items missing?" PC Aldridge asked, producing a well-worn notebook.

What?

"Those and a silver letter opener that belonged to my wife's family, among other sundry items. The timing is hardly coincidental. She's a thief. Pure and simple."

Diana approached slowly, her heart sinking with each word.

"Mr Hollister," she interrupted. "I'm sure there's been some mistake. Ellen would never—"

"Miss Penn," PC Aldridge interrupted, "I understand you're friends with Miss Wilson?"

"Why? What's that got to do with Ellen being missing?"

Hollister's smile leaked across his face, like oil on water. "I'm afraid the evidence suggests that your friend is a thief."

Before Diana could think up a response, Nancy's voice cut through the air.

"Sorry to interrupt," Nancy said, approaching the group with her mother and Mrs Campbell in tow. "But I feel I must share something that might be relevant to the situation."

Diana froze.

"Ellen confided in me about her plans, swore me to secrecy," Nancy continued, her voice carrying across the churchyard. "She said she'd grown quite discontented with her circumstances here. The Hollisters, her work, even her friendships. She mentioned feeling that she deserved more than her wages for all her expertise."

"That's not true—" Diana protested, but Nancy wasn't finished.

"She mentioned Mr Hollister's coins," Nancy continued, conspiracy dripping from her voice. "She felt they belonged in a museum rather than a private collection. When I suggested she discuss her concerns with Mr Hollister, she became quite agitated." Nancy shrugged theatrically.

Ellen's character assassination was swift. Several parishioners had drifted closer, drawn by the drama, and Diana could see the way public opinion was shifting with each of Nancy's carefully chosen words.

"Ellen would never steal anything," Diana tried again, but no one seemed willing to listen to a friend of the alleged thief.

"Wouldn't she?" Mrs Robbins chimed in with obvious relish. "We know nothing about the girl's family. She is American, after all."

Diana didn't want to point out the obvious, that Mr Hollister himself was American. In any case, it already felt futile. Diana wanted to scream, to shake these people, to make them see that they were destroying an innocent woman's reputation based on lies and prejudice.

Aldridge made careful notes while the character assassination continued around him. "Miss Wilson's disappearance will have to be reported, and the theft charges will require investigation," PC Aldridge said finally.

"She hasn't stolen anything," Diana insisted, but even she could see the hopelessness of the situation.

"PC Aldridge may say that these girls come and go as they please," Mrs Patterson interjected, pushing through the crowd. "But I know my girls. Ellen Wilson wouldn't simply abandon her post. And I'd wager my life that she's not a thief."

Mr Hollister turned to Mrs Patterson with a condescending smile. "With respect, Mrs Patterson, you're far too soft with these girls. They need a firmer hand, not mollycoddling. Miss Wilson clearly took advantage of your trusting nature."

Mrs Patterson's face flushed. "I've been coordinating Land Army placements for the entire war. I know the difference between a reliable worker and a troublemaker."

"Do you indeed?" Hollister's tone was patronising. "Then perhaps you can explain why your 'reliable worker' absconded with my family heirlooms?"

Neither Mrs Patterson nor Diana had an answer for that. But Diana was certain that Ellen Wilson was no thief.

Watching Hollister's satisfied smirk as he rejoined his wife, Diana felt her intelligence instincts screaming that this man hadn't just driven Ellen away—he'd done something far worse, and the missing items were a convenient cover for a much darker crime.

As the crowd dispersed, Diana stood alone in the churchyard, staring at the weathered tombstones. The wind picked up, sending leaves skittering across the ancient stones like scattered accusation letters. Behind her, she could hear Nancy's voice, bright with false concern, as she discussed poor Ellen's "obvious instability" with anyone willing to listen.

But Diana had not survived forty years in intelligence work by giving up at the first setback. If Ellen Wilson was to be saved—from scandal, from false accusation, or from whatever darker fate might have befallen her— Diana would need to employ every skill she had learned in the shadows of the Cold War.

The game, as Sherlock once said, was afoot.

Chapter Forty-Three

In the days following Ellen's disappearance, life carried on with the relentless demands of agriculture, war or no war. Cows needed milking, fields required tending, and the Ministry's production quotas waited for no one's personal tragedies. Yet the absence of Ellen hung over Diana like an oppressive London fog.

One bright note had been Mrs Patterson's refusal to assign any other Land Army girl to the Hollisters. And despite all the cajoling from Mr Hollister, the woman had remained resolute, much to the delight of all the other girls.

A telegram from Jim had arrived three days after Ellen vanished—a brief, maddeningly vague message: "Called to London unexpectedly. Will be in touch when able. J." No explanation, no indication of when he might return. Just the stark formality of official communication.

Diana had no way of contacting him, no forwarding address or telephone number. All she could do was wait and try to be patient. The timing felt cruel. Just when she'd allowed herself to hope for something beyond duty, both Ellen and Jim had been swept away.

She threw herself into her work. The physical labour provided a welcome distraction from the constant churning of her thoughts, though she found herself scanning every lane and footpath with the trained eye of someone searching for clues.

"PC Aldridge seems decent enough," Arthur said one afternoon as they shared tea in the Hayes farmhouse kitchen.

Diana shook her head. "He's out of his depth with this sort of investigation. Missing persons cases require resources he simply doesn't have. And he's lazy. Even your father agrees with me." She raised her eyebrows meaningfully. "He always takes the easiest path, not necessarily the right one. Or the legal one."

Arthur stirred his tea, his convalescent pallor making him appear older than his years. "What about the War Office? Surely they'll send someone?"

"Eventually, perhaps. But they're hardly going to prioritise a case involving a missing girl." Diana's expression darkened. "Particularly when the local busybodies already have her convicted of theft."

The gossip machine had indeed worked with devastating efficiency. Nancy had emerged as its chief engineer, spreading her carefully crafted narrative of Ellen's supposed discontent with the skill of a professional propagandist. Within days, the story had taken on a life of its own, with each retelling adding additional details that painted Ellen in an increasingly unfavourable light.

Mrs Whitaker had tried to maintain a charitable perspective, but even her natural kindness was being eroded by the constant stream of speculation and accusation.

"I just can't understand it," she said one evening as they listened to the wireless after tea. "Ellen always seemed such a sensible girl. And honest. You could see it in her eyes."

Diana had no answer, and so let the music from the wireless fill the lull in their conversation. The BBC was playing something soothing and patriotic, which was perfectly accompanied by Mrs Whitaker's knitting needles clicking away in their familiar rhythm. The warmth of the kitchen, the comfort of hot tea, and the worry over Ellen's whereabouts triggered an unexpected memory.

Istanbul, 1956. The Tarihi Gedikpaşa Hamami.

Diana closed her eyes, and for a moment she was back in Istanbul. The ancient Turkish bath had been her sanctuary during those tense weeks of the Suez crisis, when every coffee house conversation might conceal enemy ears and every diplomatic smile might mask deadly intent.

Diana had discovered the bathhouse quite by accident whilst following a suspected Soviet contact through the labyrinthine bazaar.

Her Turkish had been rudimentary at best—enough to order tea, ask for directions, and conduct the most basic of conversations. But in the bathhouse, language was irrelevant. The bath attendants communicated through gentle gestures and knowing smiles.

There was nothing comparable in England. Nothing that could replicate the profound solace of lying on those heated marble slabs, feeling centuries of tension dissolve as steam rose around her. The domed ceiling, pierced with star-shaped openings that allowed shafts of light to penetrate the humid atmosphere, was more beautiful than any cathedral she'd ever entered.

But it was the silence that Diana treasured most. Oh, there had been conversation—soft murmurs in Turkish, occasional laughter echoing off the domed ceilings—but no one had expected anything from her. Her halting Turkish and obvious foreignness had created a blessed barrier. She was just another woman seeking cleansing. The bath attendant had required no conversation to understand exactly what Diana needed.

For those precious hours each week, Diana Penn, the intelligence operative, didn't exist. She was only a woman momentarily free from the weight of the world.

"Diana?" Mrs Whitaker's voice cut through the memory. "You're very quiet. Are you okay?"

Diana opened her eyes, blinking in the warm light of the farmhouse kitchen.

"Just wool-gathering," Diana said, taking another sip of her tea. "The warmth reminded me of... somewhere else."

Mrs Whitaker's needles paused mid-stitch. "Somewhere nice, I hope?"

"Yes," Diana replied softly. "Somewhere very peaceful."

But even as she said it, Diana realised that the peace she'd found in Istanbul had been the peace of solitude. With the gift of hindsight, surely the baths would have been an even better experience with a friend?

"I do hope your friend is somewhere nice, too. If she is innocent. To be wrongly accused would be terrible."

Diana held her tongue, although she burned to defend her missing friend. To throw Nancy under the proverbial bus. Nancy and her relationship with Thompson.

Then there was her concern for Jenny, who seemed to be particularly affected by Ellen's disappearance. Her naturally cheerful disposition had been replaced by a melancholy that no amount of encouragement seemed able to lift.

"It's the not knowing. Is she safe? Is she hurt? Did she really..." Jenny confided to Diana the next morning, her voice trailing off.

"Ellen didn't steal anything," Diana said firmly. "Whatever's happened to her, she's not a thief."

Jenny's eyes brightened. "You believe that?"

"I'm certain of it."

But certainty, Diana was learning, was a luxury in short supply. Ellen's belongings had indeed disappeared from her room at Oregon House, but there was no evidence of where she might have gone. It was as though Ellen Wilson had simply vanished into the night. Just as she'd begun to accept the frustrating lack of progress in Ellen's case, an entirely different tragedy struck Willow Farm. One that had nothing to do with Ellen's disappearance.

Diana was helping Mrs Whitaker with the weekly washing when the postman arrived. Arriving quietly, Fleming appeared in the doorway, a single telegram held to his chest.

Oh.

There was only one reason for a telegram, and Diana had hoped, prayed, that this wouldn't have happened this time round.

Mrs Whitaker wiped her shaking hands on her apron before taking the telegram from Fleming's gloved hand. As she read the brief, official words, her face crumpled as any hope she might have had finally died.

"My boy," Mrs Whitaker whispered, clutching the paper to her chest. "My poor boy. And poor, poor Jenny."

Diana moved to comfort her, but Mrs Whitaker shrank in on herself, becoming suddenly fragile in a way that could never be reversed.

Three days later, Mr Hayes transported them all to St Michael's Church for the memorial service.

Jenny wept openly throughout the service, her sobs echoing in the ancient stone walls.

Diana thought of all the other Trevor Whitakers—the other young men whose lives had been cut short by bullets and bombs, whose mothers would spend the rest of their days in the shadows of what they had once been.

Mrs Whitaker stared at the space where her son's coffin should have been, her lips moving in silent words that only a mother's heart could speak, her hand resting on Jenny's knee. A shared grief.

After the service, as the mourners dispersed into the grey February afternoon, Diana noticed a familiar figure in the back of the church. Jim.

"Miss Penn," he said, removing his cap as he reached her. "Mrs Whitaker. Please accept my condolences on your loss."

Mrs Whitaker managed a small smile. "That's very kind of you, Flight Lieutenant. Trevor would have appreciated the sentiment."

"He was a good soldier."

"Did you know him?" Diana asked, studying Jim's face.

"Not personally, no. But friends in the Parachute Regiment spoke highly of him." Jim paused, glancing around the churchyard with the sort of casual surveillance that Diana recognised from her own training. "I wonder if I might borrow Miss Penn, just for a moment?"

Reverend Taylor was already shepherding Mrs Whitaker away, leaving Diana alone with Jim among the weathered tombstones.

"Walk with me?" he suggested, offering his arm.

They moved through the churchyard, past graves that marked the history of Cheviot Hills' residents. Jim waited until they were well away from the dispersing congregation before speaking.

"I'm not entirely what I seem, Miss Penn. Although I suspect you've already guessed that."

Diana's pulse quickened. "Haven't we all got our secrets, Flight Lieutenant?"

"Some more than others." He stopped beside an ancient headstone, its inscription worn smooth by time and weather. "Tell me, what do you know about the current situation in Europe? Beyond what you read in the newspapers, I mean."

The question was so unexpected that Diana almost stumbled. "I beg your pardon?"

"You're an intelligent woman. You understand that wars are won and lost by more than just soldiers and bullets."

Diana chose her words carefully. "I understand that information is often more valuable than ammunition."

Jim's smile was approving. "Precisely. And whilst I'm a proud RAF man, I'm also in the business of gathering that information. For His Majesty's Government."

The admission hung between them like a challenge. Diana felt a thrill of recognition—the sense of meeting a fellow professional in a world of amateurs.

"Intelligence work," she said. It wasn't a question.

"Of a sort. Though my particular remit involves recruitment rather than field operations." Jim's eyes never left her face as he spoke. "We're always looking for individuals with the right combination of intelligence, discretion, and devotion to duty."

"And you think I possess these qualities?"

"I think you possess a great deal more than you let on, Miss Penn. The question is whether you'd be interested in putting those qualities to better use than milking cows and mucking out stables."

Diana felt the ground shifting beneath her feet. This was how it had begun in her original timeline, although not through Jim. Now she wondered if he'd somehow had a hand in it. She remembered responding to a flier Mrs Patterson had handed her after the war - something vague about 'administrative work requiring discretion and attention to detail.' Only after months of filing reports and transcribing interviews with displaced persons had she realised she was processing intelligence from German informants and former Nazi officials. By the time she understood what she'd become, she was already part of the machine and sent away for formal training.

"What sort of work?" she asked, although she already knew the answer.

"The sort that requires individuals who can blend in anywhere, who can observe without being observed, who can be trusted with secrets that could affect the future. Not only your future, but the whole nation." Jim's voice carried the weight of absolute conviction. "Work that would take you far from Cheviot Hills, if that's what you choose."

"And if I'm not interested?"

"Then you continue milking cows. You'll probably marry a nice boy from town, and together you'll raise a family, and live happily ever after."

Jim's smile was neither warm nor cold. A far cry from his usual demeanour. He was all about business today. "But I suspect you're not the type of woman who's content to leave important matters in other people's hands," he continued, one eyebrow raised, a hint of warmth finally making its way to his eyes.

Before Diana could respond, Jim tipped his hat, and began walking towards the church hall, stepping through the doorway to join the wake. As always, the best way to face grief was with tea and cake.

Diana remained among the graves, running through the implications of what had just occurred. A part of her had hoped that in this new life, she and Jim might... but no, there was no point in such fantasies. She was learning there were limits to what she could change, and perhaps some patterns were too fundamental to alter. She'd already forgotten how much of herself that she'd changed in the lives that she'd lived. The last thing she wanted was to join the mourners in the hall, but to absent herself would invite gossip that Mrs Whitaker didn't deserve. Not today. So, marshalling her composure with the same discipline that would one day serve her in far more dangerous circumstances, she made her way into the hall.

Chapter Forty-Four

The evening air carried the first tentative promise of spring as Diana, Jenny, and Arthur made their way along the lane towards the Twice Brewed. April had brought with it longer days and the kind of hesitant warmth that made the brutal winter seem bearable at last. The hedgerows showed the faintest hint of green, and a few brave daffodils had pushed through the earth in the village's gardens.

Arthur managed the walk well enough, although Diana noticed him leaning more heavily on his walking stick as they approached the inn. His leg would probably never fully heal, but his determination to help search for Ellen had been unwavering.

"Right then," Diana said to Jenny, pushing open the heavy oak door of the Twice Brewed. "You and Arthur get a table, and I'll get the drinks."

The weekly routine of searching for any sign of Ellen, followed by a late supper and a pint at the Twice Brewed, was wearing thin. Two months had passed since Ellen's disappearance, and their evening searches had yielded nothing. Nothing but sympathetic shakes of the head and the same repeated assurances that no one had seen hide nor hair of the American girl since the February night when she'd vanished.

Along with the Hollisters' silverware, some would mutter under their breaths.

The Twice Brewed's interior welcomed them with its familiar embrace of tobacco smoke, watered ale, and the lingering aroma of whatever had been cobbled together from the week's rations. The blackout curtains remained firmly in place. The war wasn't over yet, although whispers suggested it soon would be.

"Evening, girls. Arthur." Charlie appeared from behind the bar, wiping his hands on his apron. "The usual, is it?"

"Please," Diana replied. "Three pints of mild, and we'll have whatever's on offer for supper."

Charlie's face brightened. "You're in luck. Managed to get my hands on some proper kidney from the Davies' farm, enough to stretch into pies with plenty of potato and swede. The pastry's made with that new margarine allocation, but I've added a touch of dripping to give it flavour."

As Charlie bustled away to sort their order, she climbed onto a barstool to rest her legs, and was immediately drawn in by the conversation beside her.

PC Aldridge was holding court with a rapt audience. "Brilliant idea, really," he was saying, gesturing with his pint. "Council wanted that eyesore of a bandstand demolished anyway. The damn woodworm had made it a death trap. So I volunteered the lads for demolition practice."

"So you used the leftover training ordnance?" asked the bespectacled Ed Fries from The Clocksmith's Bench.

Charlie appeared with her drinks, and Diana clambered down from the stool, gathered up the glasses, and carefully stepped over Ed's beloved bulldog, snoring on the floor.

Diana joined her friends at their customary table near the window, already moving on from the conversation she'd just overheard.

With the drinks delivered, Diana sipped her mild ale, grimacing slightly at the thin, bitter taste, and turned her attention to the more pressing concern at hand as she fell into the conversation flowing between Arthur and Jenny. "She didn't go of her own accord. I don't think she planned to disappear at all."

They were words which had been repeated ad nauseam by one or the other of them over the past weeks. The conversation was as familiar as the taste of the famous Twice Brewed pies.

Arthur took a long draw of his own drink. "You still think something happened to her?"

"Ellen Wilson was many things, but she wasn't a thief," Diana said firmly. "And she wasn't the sort to abandon her friends. The Ellen I knew would have said goodbye."

Charlie appeared with their food, setting down three plates before them. "There's turnips and carrots from our own garden, and some tinned tomatoes. Should fill you up well enough."

They ate in companionable silence for several minutes, savouring the food that, whilst far from luxurious, clearly made the most of the limited resources. The pastry was dense but not unpleasant, and the filling had a rich, earthy flavour enhanced by herbs from the inn's kitchen garden.

"These are so good," Jenny said, cutting into her pie before adding wistfully, "Trevor loved them, I think more than his mother's own cooking." She paused to take a sip of her ale. "I still say we should speak to Thompson again. He was sweet on Ellen. You and Arthur saw that with your own eyes. If anyone might know where she's gone..."

Diana nodded, though she harboured private doubts whether Sergeant Thompson had anything to do with Ellen's disappearance. There was only one suspect in her mind. And the others knew that.

As if summoned by their conversation, the door opened to admit Nancy, her hair carefully pinned. Diana's stomach tightened. Their relationship had never recovered from Nancy's accusations regarding Ellen's supposed theft.

Nancy's eyes swept the room before settling on their table. For a moment, it seemed Nancy might simply ignore them, but instead she approached them with a tight smile on her face.

"Nancy." Diana's voice was carefully neutral. "Good evening."

"Is it?" Nancy's smile was sharp as a blade. "I suppose that depends on whether you're planning to spend another evening bothering decent folk with your questions about that American girl."

Jenny's face flushed with anger. "Ellen was our friend. We're worried about her."

"Ellen Wilson was a thief," Nancy replied coldly. "And you're wasting your time looking for her. She's long gone. Good riddance, I say."

"She was your friend as much as she was ours," Diana countered.

The Twice Brewed's door opened, and Diana's attention was caught by the arrival of Sergeant Thompson. The man paused in the doorway, as if he was looking for someone.

He seemed to find that someone when he clocked Nancy. He smiled, but his smile faded quickly when he also noticed Diana and Arthur. His cheeks flushed and he moved towards them with what Diana thought was obvious reluctance.

"Sergeant," Arthur acknowledged with military courtesy.

"Hayes. Ladies." Thompson's response was clipped as his eyes skated over Diana's face without quite meeting her gaze. Was this simply the embarrassment of a man caught in an affair? Or was there something more sinister in his discomfort?

"Nancy, shall we?" Thompson said, offering his arm to the woman standing beside their table.

Nancy didn't even bother with any niceties before she trailed after Thompson to a table at the far end of the room.

"Well," Jenny said quietly, "that was illuminating."

Diana nodded. "That's one way of putting it."

"Does her mother know?" Arthur asked.

Diana frowned. "Why would that matter?"

"He's hardly what Mrs Robbins has planned for her only daughter, I can assure you," Arthur replied. "I doubt that the woman would settle for anyone less than a son of a peer of the realm. A lowly sergeant will not be walking her daughter down the aisle."

"Does Nancy know that?" Diana wondered aloud.

"It won't be going anywhere once the war ends, mark my words," Arthur said. "Another round?" he suggested, clearly trying to change the subject.

"I'll get them," Jenny offered, rising from her seat. "You rest that leg."

The evening stretched on, filled with the comfortable rhythm of conversation and friendship.

As they gathered their things to leave, Nancy appeared at their table once more, Thompson hovering awkwardly behind her.

"I just wanted to say how sorry I am that you've had no luck with your little investigation." Nancy's tone was mock-sympathetic. "Perhaps it's time to accept that some mysteries aren't meant to be solved."

"Perhaps," Diana replied evenly. "Or perhaps some people are simply better at keeping secrets than others."

Nancy's smile faltered for just a moment, and Diana caught a flicker of something. Either fear or guilt.

"Some secrets are worth keeping," Nancy said quietly. "Especially when revealing them would only cause pain to innocent people."

With that cryptic warning, she turned and walked away, Thompson trailing behind her like a well-trained spaniel.

"Nancy knows something," Jenny said with conviction. "She definitely knows something about Ellen."

Diana nodded. "The question is what?"

Chapter Forty-Five

The church bells of St Michael's began their triumphant peal shortly after three o'clock on Tuesday afternoon, 8th May 1945, their bronze voices carrying across the Cheviot Hills. Diana was spreading muck across the potato field when the sound reached her. She'd never heard the bells before. They'd been silenced since 1940, used only for invasion warnings. But now they were ringing freely.

She dropped her fork. The bells weren't invasion warnings; they were celebration bells. It must be official. The war was over.

"Mr Hayes!" she called, running towards the farmhouse. "The bells! Do you hear them? Churchill must have finally announced it—the war is over!"

Mr Hayes appeared in the kitchen doorway, his face wreathed in a huge smile. "Aye, victory at last. We knew it was coming after yesterday's announcement, but to hear it from Churchill himself."

"He was on the wireless?"

"He said it plain—the German war's finished, and we've won. Said we should celebrate, but remember there's still work to do with Japan."

"Victory in Europe," Diana whispered. "It's really finished."

Arthur joined them outside, where the sounds of celebration were building.

Distant shouts from the village, the honking of motor car horns, and underneath it all, those glorious bells ringing. "We should go into the village," he said. "This is history, and I, for one, wouldn't want to miss it."

"Come on," Diana agreed, her own voice thick with emotion. "Let's go. All of us."

The three of them climbed into the lorry, their laughter and the honking of the horn creating what would become an everlasting memory. Diana brushed the mud from her Land Army uniform as best she could. It seemed important to look presentable for victory, even if she'd been mucking out fields only an hour before.

The village had already been transformed overnight in preparation for the official announcement. The Union Jack hung from every window, hastily sewn from scraps of fabric in patriotic colours. Someone had dragged the piano out from the church hall into the square and was already thumping out "Rule, Britannia" whilst a growing crowd sang along with voices hoarse from joy and disbelief.

Mrs Whitaker was already in the square when they arrived, having abandoned her kitchen to join the celebration. She spotted Diana immediately and hurried over, flour still dusting her apron despite her hasty attempt to brush it clean.

"Diana, my dear! Arthur! Fred! Isn't it wonderful?" She wiped tears from her eyes with the back of her hand. "I was just putting bread in the oven when those bells started. They gave me such a fright at first, and then I remembered..." Her voice caught.

Diana enveloped her in a hug, tears streaming down her face, before a blonde whirlwind joined their embrace.

"Jenny!"

"It's wonderful, isn't it? Although I keep thinking of Trevor..."

"He'd want you to celebrate," Arthur said gently, having followed Diana through the crowd. "He'd want all of us to celebrate. This is what we were fighting for. This moment."

The celebration continued throughout the day. Tables appeared in the square as if by magic, laden with food that seemed impossible after years of rationing. It looked like every household had contributed their hoarded treasures. Tinned fruit, precious eggs, even a joint of beef that made Diana's mouth water. Children who had never known peacetime ran wild between the adults, drunk on the infectious joy.

Nancy Robbins stood with her mother near the post office, and when their eyes met across the square, Nancy turned away. The coolness between them had calcified over the weeks since Ellen's disappearance. Nancy's accusations and Diana's knowledge of her affair with Sergeant Thompson made an unbridgeable chasm.

Diana thought of Ellen, as she did every day. She hoped that somewhere out there, Ellen was celebrating too. The official investigation seemed to have petered out and Diana's own enquiries had proved equally fruitless. Half of her hoped Ellen had run away to greener pastures, but the more practical side of her suspected foul play. With the Hollisters at the centre of it.

As evening approached, the town square filled with light. Everyone's blackout curtains were already ripped from the windows. Someone had strung lights between the trees, a proper dance band materialised from somewhere, and couples began to move across the improvised dance floor in the market square.

As Diana took a breather from dancing, she settled beside Arthur and his walking stick. His dancing days were over for now.

"You know," Arthur said, "Jenny's been wondering if you'll be staying on in Cheviot Hills after the Land Army programme ends."

Diana looked towards Jenny, who was dancing with Mr Hayes, both of them laughing at something. "What did you tell her?"

"That it wasn't my place to say. But..." Arthur's grip tightened slightly on her hand. "I hope you'll stay. Both of us do. You've become part of this place, Diana. Part of our family."

Diana felt her throat constrict. Family. "The war is over, Arthur. Things will change now."

"Some things, yes. But not everything has to change." His eyes met hers seriously. "Think about it?"

Diana nodded, acutely aware that today marked the end of something as much as a beginning.

The war was over, but what came next? Her Land Army work would continue for now, but everyone knew it was winding down. Many of the girls were already talking about returning home, reuniting with sweethearts, and taking up the threads of lives interrupted by six years of conflict.

Diana sat at the window table in the Border Café, nursing a cup of tea whilst waiting for Jenny to finish her errands. Through the glass, she could see a commotion near the edge of Pickering Park. PC Aldridge stood with three or four of his Home Guard cronies, all of them mud-streaked and dishevelled, leaning on their spades like exhausted gravediggers.

From her vantage point inside, Diana saw Aldridge wiping his face with a handkerchief, whilst the others appeared to be sharing what looked like a hip flask, all looking rather pleased with themselves.

Diana shook her head. Trust Aldridge to have his men digging trenches or some other pointless exercise when the war was already over. The man's capacity for foolishness seemed to know no bounds.

"There you are!" Jenny said, bustling through the café door with her shopping basket. "Sorry to keep you waiting. The queue at Blyde's was endless—everyone wanting to celebrate with something special, hoping that rationing might have already eased up. No such luck there though."

"No trouble," Diana replied, gesturing towards the window. "What's Aldridge been up to? They look like they've been digging up the park."

Jenny peered outside, then laughed. "Oh, that'll be the bandstand cleanup. Dad mentioned it last night, although he didn't put his hand up to help. Aldridge volunteered his lads to clear up the mess they'd left after they demolished the old thing."

Later that week, over the breakfast dishes, Mrs Whitaker cleared her throat. "What will you do?" she asked.

"Pardon?"

"Now that it's over. What will you do? Will you stay, or..."

How to answer?

"I've already had a job offer. In London."

"London? With who?"

"A government agency that helps reconnect displaced families. It was in a flier Mrs Patterson gave me. But I don't want to leave you alone," Diana said, worry filling her voice.

Mrs Whitaker followed her gaze out the window. "I won't be alone. Last night, Arthur Hayes asked about the cottage at the end of the lane. The one that's been empty since old Mrs Chitty died. I don't think Jenny will be alone much longer either..."

"Jenny and Arthur Hayes?" *How had she missed that?* "You think they'll marry?"

"I think they've found comfort in each other's grief, and sometimes that's the best foundation for lasting happiness. Arthur's a good man, and Jenny needs someone steady. They understand loss in a way that will bind them together." Mrs Whitaker wiped her hands on her apron. "Don't get me wrong," she said, turning towards Diana. "You have become the daughter I never had. And if you go, I will miss you almost as much as I miss my boy. You should go and live your life. But remember, there will always be a place here for you to come home to."

Mrs Whitaker paused to wipe her eyes. "Look at me, blubbering like a baby. Off you go to the post office now, if you want those letters on the train today. I'll be fine. Just... just don't you forget about me."

Diana was walking past the town hall when she heard familiar voices through the open window. PC Aldridge was addressing what sounded like a small group. "Thank you for returning all outstanding weapons and ordnance to the designated collection points," Aldridge's voice carried clearly, and was followed by a chorus of laughs.

"We've certainly done that."

"How do they know if everything has been returned?" someone asked. "It's not like we were ever asked to do a stocktake."

"Exactly," Aldridge had replied. "It's all sorted now, anyway. So not our problem anymore."

Diana shook her head, and carried on towards the post office, her latest letters to Rose and Gladys in her hand.

And it wouldn't be until much later that this conversation would come back to haunt her.

The wedding took place on a sunny September morning. Jenny looked radiant in a dress of cream silk, her hair crowned with late roses from Mrs Whitaker's garden. Arthur stood tall and proud beside her, his walking stick abandoned for the ceremony.

Diana served as Jenny's maid of honour, wearing her beloved green Christmas dress and a borrowed hat. As she watched Arthur slide a simple gold band onto Jenny's finger, she thought of Jim and her life in London.

Of her second chance at life. She didn't know who to thank for this opportunity, but she knew she'd be forever in their debt.

"Do you, Arthur, take Jennifer Jenkins to be your lawfully wedded wife?" Reverend Taylor intoned.

"I do," Arthur replied, his voice strong and certain.

Diana smiled through her tears, knowing that some endings were really beginnings, and that love could bloom even in the aftermath of loss. Ellen would have adored this wedding. She would have cried happy tears and thrown rice with abandon, before dancing long into the night.

Chapter Forty-Six

When her train pulled away from Cheviot Hills on a grey December morning, carrying Diana towards her future in London, Mrs Whitaker, Mr Hayes, Arthur, and Jenny stood on the platform, waving until her carriage disappeared around the bend.

The countryside rolled past the window. Behind her, Jenny and Arthur were settling into married life, Mrs Whitaker was adapting to her new role as surrogate mother-in-law, and Nancy Robbins was probably spreading fresh gossip about Diana's abrupt departure. That was one fractured relationship that time hadn't changed.

The train picked up speed, carrying her towards her destiny. In her reflection in the window, Diana saw not the broken woman who'd first arrived in Cheviot Hills, but someone stronger, who'd discovered that love was worth the sacrifice.

Diana stepped off the train at King's Cross, her modest suitcase in hand, when she heard a familiar voice calling her name above the station's din.

"Diana! Diana Penn!"

She turned to see Rose Finley pushing through the crowd.

"Rose!" Diana set down her case as Rose enveloped her in a fierce hug.

"I can't believe you're finally here!" Rose exclaimed, stepping back with a beaming smile. "How was the journey?"

"Long but uneventful," Diana replied. "How's nursing school?"

"Better than I expected," Rose grinned. "Although the hours are murderous. And I'd rather have Briggs bossing me around than Matron! But never mind that now." She linked her arm through Diana's, and scooped up Diana's case. "Mum's got the spare room ready, and she's been cooking all week in your honour."

"That's very kind of her," Diana said warmly.

"And you start your new position on Monday?" Rose asked as they made their way through the crowds.

"Yes, though I've been warned I'll likely be sent away at short notice quite often, which is why they've offered me accommodation with some of the other girls."

Rose squeezed her arm. "Well, we'll just have to make the most of the times you're here. Come on, let's get you home and have a proper catch up!"

The following Monday, Diana stood before the imposing facade of Ashford Manor, the Georgian stately home that served as one of the Service's most discreet training facilities. The manor was half-hidden by a screen of ancient oaks and tucked at the end of a long gravel driveway that deterred casual visitors. A brass plaque beside the oak front door proclaimed it the "Institute for Historical Research," though the only history being studied inside was how to make it.

From her bedroom window on the second floor, Diana watched a group of trainees practice silent movement across the manicured lawn. Their instructor gestured sharply as one recruit's footfall crunched too loudly on the frost-stiffened grass. Diana remembered this exercise from her first life—the humiliation of being singled out repeatedly, the way the other trainees had kept their distance from the cold, unapproachable woman who seemed to radiate "do not touch."

This time felt different already.

"Bit nerve-racking, isn't it?" came a voice behind her.

Diana turned to find her roommate, Patricia Henley, a cheerful young woman from Cornwall whose cover story involved studying medieval manuscripts. In Diana's first timeline, she'd barely exchanged ten words with Patricia beyond polite pleasantries.

"Rather," Diana agreed, then surprised herself by adding, "Though I imagine we'll muddle through somehow."

Patricia grinned. "That's the spirit. Fancy a cup of tea? I've smuggled in some proper biscuits from home."

In her previous life, Diana would have declined with some polite excuse. This time, she nodded. "Sounds lovely. And at least you're already excelling at smuggling!" which caused them both to giggle uncontrollably. Giggling was definitely a newfound skill for Diana.

The training itself proved both familiar and revelatory. Diana's previous experience served her well during the physical components—silent movement, lock-picking, basic firearms handling. She knew exactly which instructors to watch carefully and which exercises would trip up her fellow trainees. But it was the interpersonal dynamics that surprised her most.

Where once she'd been the isolated figure eating alone in the dining hall, Diana now found herself part of conversations, included in evening discussions about tradecraft techniques. Her willingness to share observations—carefully edited—made her seem insightful rather than merely competent.

"You've got good instincts, Penn," observed Major Blackwood during a surveillance exercise in the nearby village of Farnham. "Most recruits take weeks to develop that kind of situational awareness."

The weeks passed in a blur of code work, weapons training, and elaborate role-playing exercises. Diana excelled, but not in the solitary way she once had. She formed study partnerships, shared techniques with struggling classmates, and even found herself mediating a heated argument between two recruits over the proper method for establishing dead drops.

It was during her fourth week that the post from Cheviot Hills arrived via a circuitous route through the Service's London office. Jenny's careful handwriting on the envelope lifted Diana's heart, with the contents proving to be both amusing and tragic.

Dearest Diana,

I hope your work is progressing well, although I still think you should have stayed put. Arthur sends his regards and says to tell you he's finally mastered Mrs Whitaker's shortbread recipe, though he'll deny it if you ask him directly.

Nancy has caused quite the scandal! It seems her parents' prohibition on seeing Sergeant Thompson has only made him more determined. Her mother spotted him lurking about the village, and last Tuesday Charlie caught them embracing outside the Twice Brewed. He's not even from around here—Cornwall, I think. So I can't decide if it's terribly romantic or completely improper.

Mrs Whitaker mutters about "young people these days" but I caught her smiling when she thought no one was looking. Between you and me, I think she rather admires Nancy's spirit, even if she'd never admit it.

Arthur and I are well, though he still frets about you going off to London all alone. I've assured him you can look after yourself, but you know how protective he can be. We miss you terribly and hope you'll visit soon. I still can't imagine you as a secretary.

All our love, Jenny

Diana smiled as she folded the letter. In her first life, she'd lost touch with everyone from Cheviot Hills almost immediately. There had been no point. They weren't her friends. Even when she'd retired there, apart from the occasional polite interaction in the supermarket, she'd kept to herself. But now these connections were lifelines, anchoring her to the person she'd become rather than the one she'd been.

She couldn't help but feel for Nancy after her parents had vetoed any relationship with Sergeant Thompson. Regardless of her feelings for Nancy, she believed people should be free to love whomever they chose. Part of her wondered now if this was why Nancy had become more bitter than a lemon.

That evening, she sat at the small writing desk in her room and began her reply to Jenny:

Dearest Jenny,

Your letter was exactly what I needed after a challenging week! I'd much rather be mending the tractor. Please tell Arthur that I'm eating properly and getting enough sleep, and so far I haven't been threatened by any temperamental typewriters. There are no cows with murderous intentions here, thankfully!

I'm not entirely surprised about Nancy. It's hard for me to say, but I hope her parents give in. Perhaps Nancy would be a nicer person if she could be with her sergeant?

Give my love to Mrs Whitaker, although I will write to her when I have a minute to spare.

A month later, they were told that their training cohort would graduate early, fast-tracked into active service due to increasing tensions in Eastern Europe. As Diana packed her belongings, Patricia knocked on the door frame.

"I don't suppose we'll see much of each other after this," she said, a note of genuine regret in her voice. "Different, you know, departments, or countries, and all that."

"Perhaps not," Diana agreed, knowing full well that even if she asked Patricia where she'd been assigned, the other woman wouldn't tell her. Spycraft 101. "But I'm sure our paths will cross again." Diana opened her address book, the one Rose had gifted her. "And we can always write to each other when we have a chance. I'll give you my friend Rose's address for now. So, what address should I write down for you?"

Chapter Forty-Seven

The year between graduating from her course and starting her new life passed in a careful blur of constructed normality. Diana had established herself in a cramped bedsit in Bloomsbury, complete with a convincing employment history at Whitehall's Ministry of Information—a department sufficiently bureaucratic and tedious that few people enquired too deeply about her work there. A ministry which was later absorbed into the Home Office, but still sufficiently non-descript that none of her friends ever questioned her too deeply.

Diana and Rose had fallen into an easy pattern of meeting when their schedules allowed. Rose had tried introducing her to her cousin Michael over tea, a pleasant enough man who worked in banking. But as he spoke about his plans for the future, all Diana could think of was Jim's laughter, and she'd made her excuses. Apologising to Rose later, she'd said, "He's a nice enough man, but not the one for me."

Diana's cover story was straightforward: case worker for displaced persons, tracking down missing family members and processing reunification paperwork. Worthy enough work that people respected it, yet depressing enough that they rarely asked for details about her frequent trips to "interview refugees" across Europe. In reality, these trips were her preliminary training sessions.

Weekends spent learning surveillance techniques, wireless operation, and the delicate art of extracting information from unwitting sources.

But her most important trip had been her first return to Cheviot Hills since leaving at the end of 1945.

Jim had offered to pick her up and drop her at the station on a crisp April morning. Their all-too-rare embrace beside the car, one of their few unguarded moments together, was annoyingly interrupted by an impatient taxi driver tooting behind them. Diana reluctantly waved him off and found her seat on the train north, travelling to visit Mrs Whitaker for Easter. The countryside rolled past her window, the familiar stations flashing by—York, Darlington, Newcastle, Hexham, and finally the quaint Cheviot Hills station. Diana found herself fidgeting with her mother's necklace, as the train pulled into the station.

Mrs Whitaker met her at the station with more hugs than she'd had since leaving Cheviot Hills, fussing over her appearance and declaring her far too thin. Willow Farm appeared unchanged, although Mrs Whitaker herself seemed frailer, the loss of Trevor having left its mark.

But it was what Diana didn't find that troubled her most. When she'd asked if there'd been any news of Ellen's whereabouts, Mrs Whitaker had shaken her head.

"Not a word since she vanished," Mrs Whitaker had said, her voice dropping to the conspiratorial tone reserved for village mysteries. "Not that the Hollisters seem remotely concerned. I've not heard anyone mention the poor girl since you left."

Diana had nodded, her heart heavy with her failure to prevent Ellen's disappearance.

After the Good Friday service at St Michael's, Diana had literally bumped into Nancy in the churchyard, prompting a terrifying flashback to when Mr Hollister had pushed her and she'd cracked her head open.

"Watch yourself," came the sharp response.

As she went to apologise, Nancy had flashed her an openly hostile look. Any pretence of Christian charity was gone.

"Poor Nancy's had rather a difficult time of it. Terrified of being left on the shelf, I suspect," Mrs Whitaker observed later as they walked home from church, her voice carefully neutral. "That sergeant of hers moved on to a posting in Germany last autumn—married a colonel's daughter within three months, from what I hear."

"Left Nancy rather high and dry, though there were whispers for a while that... well, perhaps it was for the best that nothing came of it." Mrs Whitaker's diplomatic pause spoke volumes. "Her parents have been keeping her on an even tighter leash since then. Some people respond to disappointment by becoming kinder. Others..." She glanced back towards the church where Nancy could be seen speaking in sharp, animated tones to her mother.

But the sweetest surprise was catching up with Jenny for morning tea on the Saturday. Jenny greeted her at the gate of Hayes Farm, her hand resting protectively over a noticeable bump beneath her coat.

"Diana!" Jenny had cried, embracing her warmly. "Oh, how wonderful to have you here. You look so sophisticated. Quite the London lady now."

"And you look radiant," Diana had replied, her eyes drawn to the gentle curve of Jenny's figure. "Are you? You never told me! Why didn't you tell me in your letters?"

"We wanted to surprise you. It was Arthur's idea. You don't know how many times I nearly blurted it all out. I'm terrible at keeping secrets."

Diana laughed. "When are you due?"

"August," Jenny had beamed, her happiness infectious. "Arthur's over the moon, though he's terrified he'll drop the baby the moment it arrives. Come inside. We've got so much to talk about."

Jenny had outdone herself with the morning tea spread, despite the recent unpopular extension of the rationing system.

Sitting across from Jenny at the table, Diana noticed a gold bracelet encircling Jenny's wrist—oak leaves and acorns engraved into the band. She recognised it instantly.

"That's a beautiful bracelet," Diana said, reaching across the table.

Jenny's face lit up even more. "Isn't it lovely? Fred gave it to me for Christmas. He said it had been his wife's, and that she'd always intended it for Arthur's bride someday." She twisted it gently on her wrist, the gold catching the light. "I treasure it, knowing it connects me to the family history, to Elizabeth. Arthur says she would have adored having a grandchild to spoil."

Diana managed a smile, though her heart ached with the bittersweet irony. In a previous life, that bracelet had been her Christmas gift from Mr Hayes—Fred—given in the aftermath of losing Arthur.

Now, in this timeline where Arthur lived, it had found its rightful place on Jenny's wrist, where it truly belonged.

"It suits you perfectly," Diana said, and meant it entirely.

Diana had spent the rest of her week-long visit taking long walks through Cheviot Hills, ostensibly to "restore her constitution after months of London air." But in truth, she found herself scanning the banks of the Cheviot Burn, the meadows, the hidden places where someone might have... what? Hidden Ellen's body? Left a sign? She couldn't say what she was looking for, only that she couldn't stop herself from looking.

The Cheviot Burn ran clear and cold, still swollen with spring melt from the hills. Diana followed its course for miles, past the familiar landmarks of her Land Army days. There was the old stone bridge where she and Jim had shared a second kiss, the meadow where she and Jenny had gathered blackberries, eating more than they'd put in their baskets, the sheltered spot where she and Ellen had shared a picnic on a long ago day off, laughing until their sides ached at Ellen's impression of Mrs Hollister's morning ritual with her cold cream. She couldn't look at a jar of Pond's without recalling that moment, and wondering what had happened to Ellen. More than once she'd finished her walk outside the stone walls of the Twice Brewed, the familiar scent of cooked meat and fermenting hops beckoning her inside. She'd forgotten just how good Charlie's cottage pies were. And as she tucked into a second serving, she knew her abundant appetite would make Mrs Whitaker happy.

On her final evening, she'd walked further than usual, following a tributary that wound through stands of birch and rowan. The dusk light filtered through the new leaves, dappling the path with shifting shadows. It was there, caught on a branch overhanging the water, that she'd found it —a single hair ribbon, faded blue silk that reminded her of Ellen.

Diana had stared at it for a long time. It could have belonged to anyone, but something about its placement, the way it fluttered in the evening breeze like a signal, made her certain it was Ellen's.

She'd folded it carefully into her handkerchief, though she couldn't say why. But it seemed important.

Her journey back to London was subdued, the ribbon heavy in her handbag. She'd returned to her bedsit determined to excel in her training.

Determined to become the kind of agent who could prevent such disappearances, who could uncover the truth behind such mysteries.

After her Easter break in Cheviot Hills, Diana had been summoned back to Ashford Manor, for reasons unsaid.

Now she stood in the grounds of the secluded home observing the next intake of mostly Cambridge and Oxford graduates practising their clumsy attempts at stealth. Most of them were crashing through the undergrowth like carthorses.

The déjà vu was overwhelming. She'd stood in this exact spot in her first life, watching different trainees make the same mistakes. Even the instructor's corrections were word for word, to what she remembered.

Diana hadn't wrestled with the decision to return to intelligence work, despite knowing full well the sacrifices it would demand. She could have chosen any number of other paths—teaching, nursing, or working in one of the new government departments that were expanding after the war. But nothing else would have given her the same sense of satisfaction as serving something greater than herself.

Despite the loneliness of her first life, her work had provided an anchor, a reason to exist. When she'd successfully unravelled a Communist cell in Prague, or prevented a diplomatic disaster in Berlin, she'd felt such fierce pride. And perhaps, with the wisdom of experience and her newfound ability to form genuine connections, she might even excel at it this time whilst keeping hold of her humanity.

"Miss Penn." The voice behind her belonged to Colonel Hawley, her training supervisor. "How do you find our newest recruits?"

Diana turned. "They're eager," she replied diplomatically. "Although enthusiasm doesn't always translate to competence."

Hawley's mouth twitched in what might have been amusement. "Quite. I hear your analytical work has been making quite an impression in Whitehall. That assessment of the Belgian network failures, particularly your insights into communication weaknesses."

Diana inclined her head, suppressing a smile. If only he knew that her insights came from having lived through the consequences of those exact failures decades in the future. In her first life, the same analysis had taken her six weeks and had been far less comprehensive.

Hawley glanced around. "I shouldn't be telling you this, but there's talk of a Vienna posting coming up. The sort of thing you'd be perfect for."

He straightened. "Of course, that's not my decision anymore. You'll be hearing from the appropriate channels soon enough, I expect."

Diana accepted the information with careful neutrality. She'd been posted to Vienna in her first life as well, although as a junior operative with limited responsibilities. This time, she'd at least know the terrain, the contacts, the pitfalls that had trapped other operatives. What would that do for her career? Her life?

"When might that be decided?" she asked, fiddling with her mother's necklace, a nervous tell she didn't know she had.

"Soon, I'd imagine. You've acquitted yourself remarkably since qualifying, Miss Penn." Hawley paused, studying her face. "The powers that be have taken notice."

After Hawley departed, Diana lingered in the gardens, watching this intake fumble through their exercises. She remembered being that nervous, eager to please, making the same elementary mistakes she now observed. Her advantage was staggering. Where other recruits struggled with lock-picking, Diana's memories from her first life guided her fingers without thinking. When they fumbled with wireless transmissions, she could tap out Morse code in her sleep.

The challenge had been concealing her expertise. Too much competence too quickly would raise uncomfortable questions. She'd deliberately made small errors, feigned uncertainty about techniques she could perform flawlessly, and asked naïve questions about procedures she could have improved upon. The performance was exhausting, but necessary.

More difficult had been watching instructors teach outdated methods she knew would prove fatal in the field. When one of the instructors had demonstrated a particular type of dead drop that the Russians would crack within six months, Diana had bitten her tongue until it bled. When they'd taught radio procedures that would be child's play for enemy code-breakers, she forced herself to nod and take notes like an attentive student.

The Vienna posting came through three weeks later, in June 1947, just as Hawley had predicted. Diana found herself cataloguing bomb damage to baroque churches, among other more secretive activities. The sort of work you wouldn't want splashed across the pages of *The Times*, or even the *News of the World*. It was methodical work, requiring patience and precision—qualities Diana possessed in abundance.

This time she wielded them with the confidence of someone who'd already walked these streets in the shadows.

The years that followed established a pattern that would define both her career and her relationship with Jim. They moved through the intelligence world like planets in elliptical orbits. Sometimes drawing close enough to touch, other times separated by continents and classified assignments that couldn't be discussed even between lovers.

Prague was memorable due to a stolen evening in a cellar restaurant that served goulash and asked no questions. Then again in Berlin, when their paths crossed at a diplomatic reception. Jim's hand brushed hers as they reached for the same canapé, and later, in a shadowed alcove of the embassy garden, they shared champagne kisses.

Then in Istanbul in '56, during the Suez crisis, they'd shared a hotel corridor for three nights, and for those brief, stolen hours, they pretended they were simply James and Diana—not operatives with secrets that could topple governments.

"We could resign," Jim said afterwards, his fingers tracing patterns on her bare shoulder. "Find a cottage somewhere. Raise chickens."

Diana laughed. "You'd be bored within a fortnight, and I'd probably analyse the chickens' behaviour patterns until they stopped laying."

But there was truth beneath the jest. They were shaped by their work in ways that made ordinariness impossible.

The 1960s saw Diana's finest operational years. The Café Landtmann in Vienna became her sanctuary, where she coordinated networks of assets across the divided city whilst appearing to be simply another well-heeled Englishwoman taking her afternoon coffee. Jim, now a senior figure in Whitehall, would occasionally appear at diplomatic functions she attended, their eyes meeting across crowded reception rooms. And when they managed to steal time together, conversation was unnecessary.

"I've been thinking," Jim said once, "about what we're doing. Whether it's fair to either of us."

"Are you suggesting we should stop?"

"We deserve more than stolen moments and coded telephone calls."

Diana's heart ached with wanting what he offered. And she knew he felt the same. But loving someone and building a life with them were two entirely different propositions.

"You know I want that," she said. "But wanting and having..." She trailed off, unable to finish the thought.

Their timing had always been impossibly wrong. When Diana was posted to Prague, Jim was recalled to London. When he was assessing the situation in Cyprus, she was deep undercover in Budapest. They were like ships passing in the night, their courses set by others, their brief encounters all the more precious for their rarity.

The reality came into sharp focus when Jim was assigned to the embassy in West Berlin in 1969. Within eighteen months, word filtered back through the intelligence grapevine that he'd married—a translator named Greta, someone who could share his world without the constant shadows and secrets. The marriage lasted barely two years, ending as quietly as it had begun, but Diana understood. Jim had tried to find with someone else what circumstances wouldn't allow them to build together.

As the years progressed, they saw less and less of each other, until a chance encounter in Cairo in '73, where they managed dinner at a restaurant overlooking the Nile.

"I sometimes wonder," Diana said, watching feluccas drift past in the twilight, "what we might have been in another life."

Jim reached across the table and took her hand. "In another life, we'd have met at the Christmas dance, married far too quickly, with Nancy as your bridesmaid, and then spent our evenings arguing about the crossword instead of whether our covers were blown."

"Nancy as my bridesmaid! Heaven forbid."

Jim laughed. "But just imagine living another life where we could be together?"

Diana had imagined. Deep down she knew that too much time had passed for that to happen now. But it was enough that she had become someone who could love deeply. And with that thought, she leant across the table and kissed the only man she'd ever loved.

The telephone call came on a grey February morning in 1982. Diana was reviewing intelligence reports when a colleague rang with the news.

Heart attack. Sudden and massive. Jim had collapsed in his office whilst preparing briefing papers for the Falklands crisis. He'd barely made it into his sixties.

The funeral was held at St Margaret's, Westminster, the small church tucked beside the Abbey, the parish church of the House of Commons.

Diana sat three rows back, wearing a black coat that Jim had once complimented. Jenny and Arthur had made the long trek down from Cheviot Hills to be with her, despite them not having seen Jim since the war. Diana didn't know if she could have faced the funeral without their support. It wasn't lost on her that in her first life she had neither needed, nor had she been needed. And now, she couldn't imagine being without her friends.

Theirs wasn't a conventional love story. She supposed it could have been, if either of them had pushed the issue. But it had been theirs, and it had been enough. And in a world where so much was uncertain, perhaps "enough" was actually everything.

That evening, Diana opened Rose's now ancient and well-tattered address book. Beneath Jim's name and contact details, she added a single line in her careful script: "1921-1982."

Chapter Forty-Eight

The bell above the door of the Old Curiosity Shop chimed softly as Diana Penn stepped inside, the familiar musty scent of old furniture and forgotten treasures enveloping her like a comfortable embrace. London's crisp December air followed her in, stirring dust motes in the weak afternoon light that filtered through grimy windows.

She'd taken the train down to London from Cheviot Hills that morning, ostensibly to collect some papers from her former solicitor and settle a few final matters. As a woman in her eighties, she really should be tidying up any loose ends rather than leaving them for others to sort through. But truthfully, she'd needed the time away from Cheviot Hills, away from the well-meaning neighbours who insisted on checking on her welfare with the persistence of anxious relatives.

The shop was a cavern of accumulated memories—Victorian furniture arranged in impossible configurations, oil paintings stacked against walls like fallen dominoes, and glass display cases filled with jewellery, china, and curiosities that had outlived their original owners. Diana picked her way carefully between the narrow aisles, her walking stick tapping against the uneven floorboards, breathing in the peculiar mixture of beeswax polish, old leather, and that indefinable scent of time itself.

It was whilst examining a bizarre wooden mask that she spotted it.

On a small mahogany table between a tarnished silver photograph frame and a collection of vintage hat pins, sat a complete Spode tea service. The familiar blue and white pattern stopped her dead—hand-painted bluebells dancing around each piece, their delicate petals edged with gold that caught the weak London light like captured memories.

Diana's breath caught in her throat. It was identical to her mother's set, the one lost in the Blitz all those decades ago. The same bluebells, the same gilt edging that would catch the morning light.

"Lovely, isn't it?" came a cheerful voice.

Diana looked up to find a young woman with hair twisted into a messy bun, her name tag reading *Nicole Pilcher* in neat block letters. Somewhere in her early twenties, she had the sort of fresh-faced enthusiasm that suggested she'd be the kind of girl who'd cross oceans just for the sheer experience of it.

"Been trying to find a home for that set for months," Nicole continued, approaching with the careful movements of someone accustomed to navigating between fragile antiques. "Shame, really—someone clearly treasured it. Look at the condition. Not a chip or crack anywhere."

Diana's fingers hovered above the teapot's handle, not quite daring to touch. She could almost hear her mother's voice, reminding her to be very careful when doing the washing up.

"It's exactly like my mother's, but most of it was lost in the war," Diana said. She shivered a little as she remembered the terrible night of her mother's death, and of Mrs Collins placing the single surviving cup from her mother's set into her hands at the funeral. "I never thought to replace it. Too busy, I suppose."

"And now?" Nicole asked.

Diana thought of her ancient address book, full of the names of friends, some new, some old. They deserved better than supermarket china and instant coffee. In fact, this coming Tuesday was her regular morning tea with Jenny Hayes. Widowed now almost seven years, they'd remained the best of friends despite Diana's frequent unexplained absences. After Diana's retirement to Cheviot Hills, picking up the long strands of their friendship had been as natural as breathing.

"Now I find I've rather more friends than I know what to do with," Diana said, surprised by the admission. "And they deserve better than cartoon cat mugs and whatever's cheapest at the shops."

She lifted the teapot carefully, testing its weight.

"Yes, I'll take the set, please," Diana said firmly.

Nicole beamed and began wrapping each piece in tissue paper. "Six tea cups, saucers and plates, a milk jug, a sugar bowl, and the teapot. It's rare to get this set still with the teapot intact."

"Usually the spout is damaged or the lid lost?" Diana finished, repeating her mother's constant worry about that very fragility.

"Exactly!" Nicole secured the wrapped teapot in a sturdy box. "Someone's looked after this set. Probably only ever used it for special occasions. It would be so perfect for high tea."

Diana smiled as an old memory rose. The 1974 Women's Institute baking competition—the year Mrs Friedrich's apple strudel had caused such a stir by winning first prize. Nancy Robbins had been so scandalised that a German recipe could triumph over traditional British puddings, despite Mrs Friedrich having lived in Cheviot Hills her entire life. Nancy had tried to have the decision overturned, and Diana had found herself defending Mrs Friedrich to all and sundry, pointing out that excellent pastry knew no nationality.

Diana had now learnt that every occasion with friends was special. That the china shouldn't wait for perfect moments, or the perfect pastry, because perfect moments were made, not found.

"There we are," Nicole announced. "I hope it brings you as much joy as it clearly brought its previous owner."

Diana lifted the boxes, feeling the substantial weight of possibility within. "I rather think it will."

Chapter Forty-Nine

The morning mist hung low over Cheviot Hills as Diana Penn walked down the path behind Willow Farm, her collie Sage padding along beside her. At eighty-six, she'd slowed down, the uneven ground more of an enemy than anything she'd faced in the Cold War.

She'd inherited Willow Farm from Mrs Whitaker's estate in the 1970s, along with a letter that had made her weep for the first time since 1945. "To Diana, who brought light back into this old house when we needed it most. May you find the peace here that you've given others." The irony wasn't lost on her that she'd returned to the place where her second chance had begun. Where she'd finally found friendship and happiness.

The farmhouse looked much as it had during the forties, though Diana had added central heating and a proper telephone line. She'd kept Mrs Whitaker's Royal Doulton china, displaying it in the same oak sideboard where it had weathered the war, joined now with the Spode tea set she'd bought in London. Sometimes, when the light fell just right through the dining room windows, she could almost hear the echoes of Christmas dinners.

Sage paused at a rabbit hole, tail wagging with optimistic determination.

"Come along, old girl," Diana called, although at thirteen, Sage was considerably younger than her human companion. The dog trotted over, tongue lolling with unbridled joy.

They crested the hill that overlooked the village, and Diana paused as she always did at this particular spot. From here, she could see the children's playground that had been built where the old Victorian bandstand once stood.

Then a memory struck her with the force of a physical blow.

When the old bandstand had been condemned due to woodworm infestation, Aldridge had volunteered his Home Guard unit for the demolition work, boasting to the council that it would serve as an excellent training exercise for his lads. "Two birds with one stone," he'd declared proudly.

The pieces fell into place with devastating clarity.

Aldridge's voice: "Thank you for returning all outstanding weapons and ordnance." The chorus of laughs. "Not our problem anymore."

Mrs Whitaker's disgust at Aldridge's training exercises and Mr Hayes's warning that Aldridge would probably blow them all to kingdom come.

The Secretary of State for War's directive: "All weapons must be properly accounted for."

Against this, Aldridge's incessant grumbling about paperwork at their Saturday training sessions echoed in her memory.

Diana's hand flew to her mouth. Rather than follow proper procedures, Aldridge, as lazy as a fox in a henhouse, had buried the lot rather than admitting he hadn't followed the regulations.

And thanks to Aldridge's incompetence, those devices had been sitting beneath the village for decades, just waiting for someone to dig them up.

She'd known. Deep down, she'd always known.

The new playground in Pickering Park. She'd only just read about it in the *Cheviot Hills Gazette.* The council had finally found the funds for a new playground, building it exactly where the old bandstand had once stood. Replacing the current playground, which had become a decaying safety hazard. A playground which had unwittingly been built atop live ordnance many, many years ago.

Diana fumbled for her mobile phone, her arthritic fingers struggling with the tiny buttons. She had to warn them.

The construction crew would be arriving soon to begin the final phase of installation, and somewhere beneath their feet lay devices that PC Aldridge's incompetence had allowed to remain buried for sixty years.

"Police," she gasped when the call connected. "There are unexploded bombs beneath Pickering Park. You must evacuate the area immediately."

A pause. "I'm sorry, madam, could you repeat that?"

"Unexploded ordnance," Diana said more slowly, trying to keep the irritation from her voice. "Devices from the war, buried beneath the playground in Pickering Park."

"Right." The operator's tone had shifted to the carefully patient voice used for elderly callers reporting suspicious activity. "And how exactly do you know about these... devices?"

Diana's jaw clenched. "That's not important. What matters is—"

"Madam, I need to ask—have you actually seen these bombs yourself?"

"No, but I know they're there." Even from her spot on the hilltop, Diana could hear the lorry's engine now, growing closer. "Listen to me carefully. There are workmen about to start digging. If they hit those devices—"

"Mrs...?"

"Miss Penn. Diana Penn."

"Miss Penn, I understand you're concerned, but we can't evacuate a public area based on... well, based on a feeling. Do you have any evidence of these alleged explosives?"

Diana watched in horror as workers in hi-vis jackets began unloading equipment at the park's edge. "For God's sake, I spent forty years with MI6! I know what I'm talking about!"

Another pause, longer this time. "MI6? Right. Well, Miss Penn, I'll... I'll make a note of your concerns and pass them along to the appropriate—"

Diana snapped, her professional composure finally cracking. "Those men are about to die because you think I'm some batty old woman seeing things?" She stabbed the call end button.

She had to reach them herself. Diana called for Sage and began picking her way down the hillside path, her arthritic knees protesting with each jarring step. The uneven ground that had never troubled her in youth was now more treacherous than MI6's Kim Philby.

"Bloody hell," she gasped, grabbing at the nearest bush for support.

Gorse thorns bit through her skin, but she pressed on, driven by the sound of machinery in the distance.

Halfway down, her left ankle turned on a rabbit hole hidden by long grass. Pain shot up her leg, and she stumbled, only Sage's solid presence beside her preventing a complete fall. The collie whined anxiously, sensing her distress.

"I'm all right, girl," Diana lied through gritted teeth, forcing herself upright. Her breath came in harsh puffs, her heart hammering against her ribs with the sort of rhythm that her doctor had warned her about. But below in the park, she could see the excavator positioning itself over the exact spot where Aldridge had buried his "harmless" training devices.

By the time she reached the park's edge, the excavator was already on the edge of the old bandstand site, its bucket poised to begin digging. Diana stumbled across the grass, waving her arms frantically.

"Stop!" she wheezed, her voice barely carrying over the engine noise. "Don't dig there!"

The operator, a young man in a hard hat, looked down at her with obvious confusion. An elderly woman in a torn coat, accompanied by a border collie, hardly presented an authoritative figure.

"You need to stop," Diana gasped, clutching at the machine's tracks for support. "There are bombs. Buried right where you're about to dig."

The operator rolled his eyes and exchanged a look with his colleague. "Right, love. And I suppose you've seen UFOs too?"

"I'm not making this up. I'm telling you that there are unexploded devices from the war under there," Diana panted, pointing at the churned earth beneath the bucket. "And they've been there since 1945. If you hit them with that machine..." She didn't finish the sentence.

The foreman hurried over, his expression skeptical. "Look, love, I appreciate your concern, but we've had the site surveyed. There's nothing down there."

"The survey was wrong," Diana said firmly, her training finally overriding her physical distress. "I have it on good authority that they buried live ordnance here after the war. After they pulled down the old bandstand. I was here when it happened. But I didn't realise it, not until now. Oh my God, you have to believe me."

Something in her tone made the foreman hesitate.

"Well," he said slowly, "I suppose it wouldn't hurt to hold off for a bit. Check the plans again, eh?"

Diana caught her breath, leaning heavily against the digger. Sage pressed close to her side, sensing her exhaustion. One of the younger workers offered to drive her home, no doubt prompted by the foreman. On a normal day, Diana would have waved him off. But this time, she and Sage accepted the offer.

Almost as soon as they reached Willow Farm, the young lad's mobile rang. The contractors, it seemed, were now refusing to continue work until the site was thoroughly investigated. Seemed that they'd done some surface shovel work, before encountering something which clearly shouldn't have been there. "Better safe than sorry," the foreman had told the council. And now the bomb disposal unit was being called in from Newcastle.

PC Aldridge's failure had created a sixty-year time bomb, but Diana's intervention had finally defused it. The circle was complete.

As darkness gathered outside the windows, Diana felt a lightness in her chest, as though some invisible burden was finally lifting. Her mouth tightened as her breathing grew shallower. Sage whimpered softly, and Diana reached down to stroke the dog's soft fur one last time.

"Good girl," she whispered. "Mrs O'Hara from the village will take care of you."

Diana Penn closed her eyes and thought back over this last life. She'd been given the rarest of gifts. A chance to redo her life. A chance to choose connection over isolation, love over duty, humanity over protocol. She had an address book full of friends and photos of them on her mantelpiece. She'd done her duty to her country to the best of her ability, but hadn't forsaken herself. Well, mostly. She and Jim had remained close through the decades, but it had never quite worked out—different assignments, different timing. Perhaps some things were meant to remain unfinished. She'd done her best.

The teacup slipped from her fingers and shattered on the kitchen tiles. The sound echoed through the farmhouse like a final bell. But Diana didn't hear it.

Interlude Four

UNIVERSAL LIFE CENTRE

Diana Penn opened her eyes.

The ceiling above her was blindingly white, stretching endlessly in all directions without seam or shadow. No plaster imperfections, no water stains, no familiar cracks that might anchor her to any place she'd ever known. The whiteness was absolute.

She sat up slowly, her movements fluid and painless in a way they hadn't been since arthritis had claimed her joints decades ago. The ache in her lower back, her constant companion for the past fifteen years, was simply gone.

"Welcome," came a voice beside her.

Diana turned to find a woman standing perhaps ten feet away, though the strange geometry of this white space made distance difficult to judge. Elegant in an otherworldly way, with her silver hair swept back in a chignon that would have done credit to any Mayfair salon.

"My name is Marta," she said, smiling with genuine warmth. "Hello, old friend."

Diana took inventory of herself with methodical precision. Her body felt wrong, somehow. Not injured or ill, but displaced. Like wearing a favourite coat that had been altered whilst you weren't looking.

"Where am I?" she asked, although part of her already suspected the answer.

"The Universal Life Centre," Marta replied, moving closer. "The White Room, specifically. It's where souls come when their earthly journeys reach certain... transition points."

Diana looked around the endless white expanse. No walls, no doors, no furniture save for the bench she found herself seated on.

"I died," Diana said. It wasn't a question.

"You finished your time on Earth," Marta replied, settling onto the bench with fluid grace. "And now you're here. The question, Diana Penn, is what comes next."

"What do you mean?"

"How many people have you loved?"

Diana thought of her mother, buried in the Blitz. Of Rose. Mrs Whitaker, and Trevor, and Arthur Hayes and Jenny. Even Nancy, to a degree. And Ellen, who despite all her foreknowledge, she'd failed to save. She'd carried the weight of that failure her whole life.

"I couldn't save Ellen," Diana said quietly. "Even knowing what was going to happen, I couldn't prevent it."

"No," Marta agreed. "You couldn't. But that wasn't really the point, was it?"

Diana frowned. "I'm not following."

"In your first life, how many true friendships did you have?"

The question hit Diana with unexpected force. She thought of her carefully anonymous existence and the deliberate distance she'd maintained from everyone around her.

"Not many," she admitted.

"And in your most recent cycle? The one that just ended?"

Diana considered this. Mrs Whitaker's maternal fussing, and Rose's cheerful chatter and unwavering friendship until cancer had stolen her away. She been enveloped by the easy camaraderie amongst the Land Army girls. Memories of Jim Crawford's gentle courtship still made her heart quicken. And the raw grief over Trevor Whitaker's death had never left her. She held dear the love and protectiveness she felt towards Ellen, and her satisfaction at helping Arthur Hayes, and his father, survive the war.

"I was loved," she said slowly.

"Precisely." Marta's smile was radiant. "You learned to love. That was your lesson, not preventing Ellen's disappearance."

Diana felt tears prick at the corners of her eyes. "But Ellen—"

"Ellen Wilson's journey is her own," Marta said gently. "Your job was never to save her. Your job was to save yourself."

The white space pulsed gently around them, responding to some cosmic rhythm Diana couldn't quite grasp. She thought of all the things she'd left undone, all the words unspoken.

"What happens now?" she asked.

Marta stood, smoothing down her ethereal white dress. "There are some people waiting to see you."

As if summoned by Marta's words, three figures materialised from the white expanse, their forms gradually solidifying like photographs developing in a darkroom. Diana's breath caught in her throat as she recognised them.

Her mother came first, vibrant and whole, her dark hair pinned in the victory rolls she'd favoured, wearing the blue dress with tiny white flowers that had been her favourite. Behind her walked Rose Finley, that familiar mischievous glint in her eyes, her arm linked through Jim Crawford's.

"My darling girl," Eleanor said, "I've been waiting such a long time to tell you how proud I am of everything you've done." She reached out, her touch real and solid as she cupped Diana's face in her hands.

Then Rose stepped forward with her characteristic boldness, pulling Diana into a fierce embrace that echoed of lavender soap and London smog. "Took you long enough," she said with mock severity, although her eyes sparkled. "Twenty years I waited for you to visit my grave, and when you finally did, all you brought was a wilted bunch of daffodils from the petrol station." She pulled back, grinning. "Though I suppose saving my life more than makes up for your poor flower selection."

Jim came last. "We probably just needed another lifetime to make it work, Penn. I might not have been able to call you my wife, but at least it was an honour to call you my friend."

Review

Dear Reader,

Thank you for reading The Deadly Life of Diana Penn, and for giving this international collaboration a chance! What a joy it has been creating the town of Cheviot Hills, and continuing the wold of Middle Falls.

Coming next is *The Helpful Life of Gris Morley*.

If you enjoyed Diana's story amidst the rolling Northumberland hills, could you please leave a review or a rating on your preferred digital platform?

Reviews are essential to authors.

Thank you

Kirsten McKenzie and Shawn Inmon

Author's Note - Kirsten McKenzie

Back in February 2025, Shawn and I both happened to be on a Zoom call with Podium Audio, our audiobook publishers. After that brilliant call, I wanted to ask Shawn for some advice regarding my own audiobooks, so I sent him a very polite Facebook message. Bear in mind that apart from being in some of the same author Facebook groups, I didn't know him at all! The next thing I knew, Shawn was asking if I'd be interested in writing in his world. My eldest daughter was the only one home with me and when I asked her advice, her reply was, "Duh, yes, of course!"

I'd just published *Ithaca Found*, book three in my Ithaca time travel trilogy, and was casting about for another project. Right before Shawn approached me, I'd read an article online about WWII bombs being found under a playground in Wooler, Northumberland. Ordnance discovered with fuses and detonator bursters still intact! So when Shawn asked me to pitch a story idea, Diana Penn's story emerged fully formed.

This proved to be the fastest book I've ever written, beaten only by my rather frenzied vampire thriller I wrote whilst recovering from major surgery last year—those anaesthetic drugs do peculiar things to one's mind! I think Diana Penn flowed so easily because Shawn guided me patiently throughout the process, particularly through the Universal Life Centre sections, which were rather like kryptonite to me.

When you write in someone else's world, sometimes you must defer to what exists in their imagination, because it's impossible to fully grasp the intricacies of their world-building. This is why in my early drafts, I didn't include any direct references to Mushu or Moondog—thinking that they were simply too special for me to attempt. Until I somehow subconsciously wrote in a barking dog when Diana and Rose were trapped in the ambulance. Divine intervention? And before I knew it, Mushu had wrangled her way into the book! I also appropriated the uncle of Michael Hollister. It seemed reasonable to imagine that if Michael's father was dreadful, perhaps, by extension, Michael's uncle might be too. I hope you feel I've done the Hollister name justice.

Whilst writing Diana Penn, I spent my evenings reading Shawn's backlist. I've now made it through twenty Middle Falls books and I'm still going—I've adored every single one. There have been tears, rereads of one particular book (I wonder if you could guess which?), and I've developed a sincere literary crush on Shawn's books, rather akin to my devotion to Mr King—my first adult literary love. My childhood literary love was, and always will be, Enid Blyton.

I often go through phases of reading an author's entire backlist after stumbling across a book, usually one I've found in a Little Free Library or through a friend's recommendation, or from meeting an author at a literary festival. But there are only a handful of authors whose books I purchase without even reading the blurbs: Stephen King, Richard Osman, Mark Gillespie, Andrene Low, Elizabeth Oakey, and now Shawn Inmon. That, dear reader, is a wonderfully eclectic list!

My first time travel book was published in 2015, written after my little brother told me I "never finish anything." So I had a point to prove. Two time travel trilogies and four standalone supernatural thrillers later, I think I've rather proved my point. But without that kick up the backside, you wouldn't be reading about Diana Penn. I'm incredibly proud of book eleven, and I hope you've enjoyed it as much as I did writing it.

I'm tremendously grateful to Shawn for the opportunity to write in his world, albeit on the other side of the Atlantic Ocean, and in British English rather than American English. Please be kind and don't mistake the extra 'u's', and the 's's' instead of 'z's' for grammatical errors!

Next up you'll be reading about *The Helpful Life of Gris Morley*, a Cheviot Hills resident who gives and gives and gives, until he has nothing left of himself.

Thank you once again for taking a chance on this collaboration.

With warmest regards,

Kirsten McKenzie

Author's Note – Shawn Inmon

Ten years ago, I thought of a story. A man, haunted by a teenage tragedy, dies after an unfulfilling life, only to awaken as a fifteen-year-old with all memories intact.

I liked the story idea because it promised the possibility of redemption. Second Chances. Who among us doesn't need that?

It was just that, though – a single story. I never dreamed that it would grow into what it has become—twenty-three volumes and counting, and the most important works in my career.

I've grown to love the small town of Middle Falls and how the residents there react to their impossible do-overs.

I always wondered, though—what would this same redemptive opportunity look like if it arrived somewhere other than my favorite small town in Oregon?

What, for instance, if this happened in the UK? Or South America? Or Africa? How would that impact the story?

I knew immediately that I couldn't write that story. Part of what makes Middle Falls special is that, in almost all instances, I lived through the times and places I write about. I was born in 1960, came of age in the seventies, and lived through the eighties, all in small towns on the West Coast of the USA. I could write confidently about what that life was like because I had lived it.

I knew I couldn't bring that same sense of verisimilitude to another location.

So I began looking for a time travel author who lived far away from me that might be interested in writing in my world.

It wasn't an easy search. In fact, it went on for eight years before I had the pleasure of finding Kirsten waiting for me in my inbox one day.

I had high standards. It couldn't just be a time travel author. It had to be someone whose books I have read and enjoyed. The Middle Falls universe really is my baby and it wasn't easy to trust to someone else.

Then, like a miracle, Kirsten did indeed show up in my inbox. I had read her *15 Postcards* and really enjoyed it. I knew she not only could write, she was a better writer than I am in many ways. It always makes sense to work with someone who forces you to raise your game.

I offered, Kirsten accepted, and now you've read the result of this partnership in your hands.

Kirsten wrote 99% of the book. All of the elegant descriptions and colorful scene-setting is much more her bailiwick than it is mine, and I really love what she did with this story. My only real job was to make sure that the story fit inside the Middle Falls universe. It was easy and rewarding work.

Thank you for giving this story a chance. It means a lot to me.

Shawn Inmon
August 2025
Tumwater WA

Cast of Characters

Arthur Hayes - Frederick Hayes's son.
Bertellia - Watcher at the Universal Life Centre.
Betty - Diana's colleague at the London ambulance station.
Billy Thomas - Cheviot Hills village lad who later becomes the local MP.
Carrie - Watcher at the Universal Life Centre.
Charles Waters - Watcher at the Universal Life Centre.
Charlie - Barman at the Twice Brewed pub.
Claire George - Cheviot Hills resident.
Diana Penn - Retired MI6 agent.
Doris - Ambulance driver colleague of Diana's in London.
Ed Fries - Owner of The Clocksmith's Bench in Cheviot Hills.
Eleanor Penn - Diana's mother, a seamstress.
Ellen Wilson - American archaeology student turned Land Army girl.
Enid Whitaker (Mrs Whitaker) - Diana's kindly landlady at Willow Farm.
Fleming - The village postman.
Frederick Hayes - Farmer who employs Diana at Hayes Farm as a Land Army girl. Father of Arthur Hayes.
Gladys - Diana's ambulance colleague in London.
Jenny Jenkins - Land Army girl who works at Hayes Farm.

Jim Crawford - RAF Flight Lieutenant.
Kathy Morrison - Land Army girl who works at the Hawks' farm.
Margaret - Land Army girl from beyond Cheviot Hills village.
Marta - Watcher at the Universal Life Centre.
Mr Hollister - American landowner and employer of Ellen Wilson.
Mrs Blyde - Cheviot Hills shopkeeper.
Mrs Campbell - Chairwoman of the Women's Voluntary Service.
Mrs Finley - Rose's mother.
Mrs Hollister - Mr Hollister's English wife.
Mrs Morley - Women's Institute member.
Mrs Patterson - Land Army coordinator.
Mrs Robbins - Nancy's Robbins mother.
Nancy Robbins - Village girl involved with the Women's Institute.
Nicole Pilcher - Shop assistant at the Old Curiosity Shop in London.
Norman - Railway worker at the ambulance station.
PC Aldridge - Local constable and Home Guard leader.
Reverend Taylor - Village vicar at St Michael's Church.
Richard Thompson - RAF sergeant.
Rose Finley - Diana's colleague at the London ambulance service.
Shirley - Ambulance colleague.
Station Officer Briggs - Former bus conductor who runs the London ambulance station.
Susan - Land Army girl.
Trevor Whitaker - Mrs Whitaker's son.
Violet - Ambulance driver.